DEATH AT THE LYCHGATE

AN AMY ROWLINGS MYSTERY (BOOK 2)

T.A. BELSHAW

SBB

First published in 2022 by SpellBound Books

For my son, Daniel. A better father than I could ever hope to be.

PREAMBLE

The parish church of Saint John the Evangelist sits proudly at the centre of the Kentish town of Spinton. Constructed in the twelfth century, the blue-grey church, built from local ragstone, boasts a Norman tower that stood unaltered for centuries, surviving minor earthquakes, violent storms, civil war and mining. Then, in the eighteen-fifties, a Victorian Alderman, aptly named, Mason Meddle, raised the funds to add a clock, a spire and a low, red brick extension (thankfully hidden from view behind the main structure) that was used for Sunday School, Temperance Society gatherings, and until the Town Hall was built some seventy years later, Parish Council meetings.

The surrounding graveyard is split by two paths. The first, the main walkway to the church, is a ragstone-paved avenue that leads from the church's main gates directly to the vestibule. The second, a winding path made mostly from broken slate and gravel, is accessed from the lychgate, a timber built, gabled structure that has been the dead parishioners' gateway to the afterlife for centuries.

The lychgate, or corpse gate, was used to shelter the body of the deceased until the funeral service could take place. In years gone by the corpse could rest there for up to two days, accompanied by friends or relatives who would sit on the hard plank seats built into the structure, sometimes as an act of vigil, but often as a presence to ward off the body snatchers that preyed on the poor of the district.

CHAPTER ONE

THE EARLY MORNING MIST THAT CRAWLED ACROSS THE LAND FROM THE Kent coast, covered the tombstones like a thin grey cloak as a pale, almost water-colour March sun began to rise from behind the church tower.

In the town, men slept off the excesses of their Saturday night drinking while their wives bathed a new black eye or cut lip before starting to prepare breakfast for the family. Children would be scrubbed and dressed in their Sunday best clothes before being packed off to be lectured about their heathen ways at Sunday School. Although most of the working-class adults shunned the church, having far more important things to do on a Sunday morning, it was thought that the weekly disciplined routine was good for the children, though there was the added benefit of getting them out of their hair for an hour.

At nine o'clock precisely, Mrs Rosegarden climbed off her bicycle and wheeled it across the pavement to the church gates. Finding them still locked, she frowned, looked at her wrist-watch, then checked the time again by the church clock.

'Villiers,' she snorted into the misty air. The aging, but surprisingly sprightly woman turned her bike around and rode across the pavement to the west side of the church where the lychgate entrance was situated.

The brittle haired, bespectacled Sunday School teacher was a woman to be feared, even by the toughest of the ragamuffins that attended her scripture lessons. Quick to anger and swift to punish she patrolled the room like a prison guard. Armed with a bible in one hand and a leather strap in the other, she stalked the three, wooden benches quoting from both testaments, threatening dire consequences, both in the present and in the afterlife for anyone who closed their ears to the word of God.

'Drunk again, Villiers,' she hissed as she dismounted by the lychgate. She leaned her bike against the high, stone wall and lifted the catch that secured the rough, wooden pole gates. Pulling them open, she looked through the gabled, porch-like structure to the mist covered tombstones beyond.

Sighing, she retrieved her bicycle and wheeled it over the grey-slab paving towards the gravel path that led to the church.

As she strode under the roof of the lychgate she glanced to her right-hand side where the figure of a grey haired, bespectacled man was slumped on the vigil seat. On the floor beneath the seat, a bible reference had been written in yellow chalk. Romans 13.13-14.

The man's eyes were open, staring at nothing, his shoulders were hunched and his neck was twisted at what must have been a very uncomfortable angle. His lips were parted and his teeth were bared in a skeleton-like grin.

'Reverend Villiers!' Mrs Rosegarden exclaimed. Leaning her bike against the vigil seat on the opposite side of the lychgate, she reached out and grabbed the vicar by the shoulder. When he didn't respond she shook him. When that failed to rouse him, she squatted down, grabbed the lapels of his grey jacket and shook him again.

As the vicar's head slumped forward, the Sunday School teacher stood and turned in one movement. Forgetting her bicycle, she hurtled into the main road shouting at the top of her voice. 'Help... someone help.... It's the Reverend Villiers. He's dead.'

CHAPTER TWO

AMY ROWLINGS BRUSHED A STRAY WHISP OF FLAXEN HAIR OUT OF HER eyes and pulled her knitted woollen hat a little further down over her ears. Although it was late March, spring wasn't showing any sort of eagerness to arrive and the chill easterly breeze that had swept in from the coast announced that winter was only bidding a reluctant farewell.

She looked up the hill towards the ancient Norman church and again pushed away the strands of hair that whipped across her face. At least the fog had lifted, that was a bonus. The Kent mist tended to cling to you, it got under your turned up collar and seeped into your hair, leaving it feeling damp and uncomfortable.

Amy had just turned twenty-one, and worked at the local clothing factory, nicknamed the Mill, as a machinist. She was an attractive girl with a good figure and there was no shortage of admirers among the male population of Spinton. She also possessed a razor-sharp mind and could pick out the murderer in a movie long before the on-screen detective had worked out a motive. She was a collector of American 78 records and devoured the novels of her beloved Agatha Christie. Only two months previously she had assisted Detective Sergeant Bodkin, who had been new to the area, in solving a complicated murder case, the victim of which was the son of the owner of the Mill.

She adjusted her thick, raised collar then turned and smiled towards her parents who were walking arm in arm a few paces behind. Her mother smiled back and raised her hand to hold her wool blend bucket hat in place.

Mr Rowlings turned his face into the wind and raised his brown trilby to two women who were striding purposely past them, eager to get into the warmth of the church.

'Mrs Flannery, Mrs Witcombe.'

Looking back towards the church he craned his neck to peer over the heads of the young family walking just in front.

'There's quite a gathering at the lychgate. Do we have a celebrity visitor today?' He looked puzzled. 'I'm sure I'd have heard if we had.' Mr Rowlings was a close friend of the vicar and helped him write the weekly Sunday sermons.

Amy took a couple of paces to the side and looked towards the lychgate. A large crowd of people had gathered. Something had their attention, that was certain, as none of them were moving away.

'Oh, I hope someone hasn't fallen ill,' she said, more to herself than to her parents.

Mr Rowlings pointed towards the main road where an ambulance was just pulling up.

'It must be quite serious if they've sent for an ambulance,' he said.

Amy increased her pace and was soon on the edge of the

crowd. She bobbed up and down to see if she could get a better view but the people in front were doing the same thing. After moving along the line and still unable to get a better vantage point, she tapped a man on the shoulder and asked him what the fuss was all about.

'Someone's dead, love,' he replied. 'The police are here.'

'Oh, my goodness.' Amy held her hand to her mouth. She turned to look for her parents and found them standing patiently on the edge of the crowd.

'Someone's dead,' she hissed.

Mrs Rowling's face fell. The deeply religious Mr Rowlings began to whisper a prayer.

'Wait here, Mum,' Amy said hurriedly, 'I'm going to try to get around the side to see what's happening.'

'Don't get too close, Amy,' her mother warned. 'Whoever it is might be contagious. There was a case of smallpox in the town only last month.'

Amy hurried around the left-hand side of the crowd until she made it to the church railings but to her annoyance, she found the mass of people was just as dense. She stood on her tiptoes but still couldn't see above the swarm of heads, shoulders and hats that blocked her view. She was still some ten yards away from the lychgate itself.

Frustrated and desperate to know what had happened, Amy made a swift decision and turning away from the crowd, she made her way along the railings until she came to a couple of red brick outbuildings that were used by the church groundkeepers to store their tools. Between the two buildings was a wrought iron side gate. Amy lifted the latch and pushed hard. The gate opened with a loud squeal. She stopped for a moment in case the sound had carried across the churchyard, then, after waiting a few more seconds, she slipped through and made her way along the narrow gravel path, that partitioned the cemetery.

To her left was a mound of wet earth that sat beside a freshly dug grave. It had rained heavily on the Friday and the gravediggers had covered the newly excavated grave with green tarpaulin to stop it being flooded with water. A shovel had been left behind, sticking out of the mound of what looked more like clay than soil. A second shovel, snapped off part way along the handle, lay on the side of the mound as a testament to the weight of the wet earth. Amy didn't envy them the job they'd have when they returned to fill in the grave after the funeral.

Stepping off the path, Amy meandered through the old graves taking care to tread in the narrow, wet grassy areas between the gravestones. In front, two large stone crypts blocked her view of the lychgate. She crept up behind the one built by the Belvedere family during the eighteenth century and crouching low, made her way along the smooth stone wall to the ornate Roman-style pillar that formed the front left-hand corner of the mausoleum.

Taking a deep breath, a still crouching Amy looked around the pillar towards the lychgate. She could see the backs of three helmeted policemen as they guarded the entrance to the churchyard. Within the lychgate itself, two men wearing grey raincoats and black hats watched as a third man she recognised as Doctor Mortensen, examined a hunched figure sitting on the lychgate bench. To her horror, she realised that the subject of the doctor's attention was her father's friend, the vicar of the parish, the Reverend Villiers.

Amy's hand shot to her mouth to cover the cry of dismay that was forming. Then, as she stuck her head out further to get a better view of the proceedings, one of the figures looked in her direction. Amy snapped her head back but she knew it was too late. She had been spotted.

Still crouching behind the mausoleum wall, Amy slid carefully backwards. She had just reached the rear edge of the structure when she heard a familiar voice.

'I might have known it was you.'

Amy closed her eyes and screwed up her face, then slowly straightened up.

'Hello, Bodkin, how are you?'

The policeman was tall, with broad shoulders, his grey raincoat flapped open revealing a creased white shirt which had begun to fray around the collar. He took off his black fedora and despite the chill in the air, ran the back of his hand across his brow to wipe away the beads of sweat that had formed there. He was a handsome man in a rugged sort of way, the weekend stubble highlighting his strong cheekbones. His brown eyes narrowed slightly as he looked at her.

'Never mind the pleasantries, Amy, this is a murder scene. You can't be seen hanging around here.'

'MURDER! The vicar?' Amy's mouth gaped open. 'I didn't know, Bodkin, honestly. I was at the back of the crowd, I just wanted to know what was happening.'

Bodkin sighed and flashed a quick, but genuine smile as he replaced his hat.

'I know. But you can't be here, Amy. Chief Inspector Laws is on his way and you know what he thinks about you.'

She grimaced. Bodkin's boss had a very low opinion of her. He saw her as an interfering busy body despite the help she had given the police in a previous murder case.

'Laws?'

'Laws,' Bodkin repeated. 'And he'll be here imminently, so I suggest you—'

His voice faltered as the yell of his superior officer echoed across the churchyard.

'Bodkin!'

'Go, quickly.' Bodkin turned around and used his body as a shield as Amy scurried back across the churchyard towards the little side gate. By the time she reached it, the detective had disappeared from view.

CHAPTER THREE

As Amy re-joined her parents on the hill outside the lychgate, she heard the booming voice of Detective Constable Stanley instructing the officers guarding the entrance to push the crowd back and give access to the stretcher-bearing ambulance men who had been unable to force their way through the horde of onlookers. The crowd seemed to have almost doubled in size in the few minutes that Amy had been absent. The church would have been delighted with such a congregation on any other Sunday morning. Sadly, more than half the throng were only there to witness the scene and they would be about their business within minutes of the body being removed.

Amy put her hand on her father's arm and gave him a sad smile.

'Have you heard who it is?'

'There's a rumour buzzing through the crowd, Amy, but I'm truly hoping that's all it is.'

'It's not a rumour, Dad. Reverend Villiers is dead and...' she looked around to see if she could be overheard, '...he's been murdered.'

'Murdered... how? Why would anyone do that?' Mr Rowling's face was a mask of horror.

'I have no idea, Dad,' Amy replied. 'I don't have any details. I saw Bodkin in the graveyard, so I know it's true.' She reached out to give her father a hug. 'I'm so sorry, Dad, I know how much you thought of him.'

Amy's father accepted the hug for a few seconds, then stepped away from his daughter. Taking off his hat, he closed his eyes and offered up a quick prayer for the deceased.

'He was a good man. He had his faults just like we all do, but he was a good man.' He blinked away a tear and looked at his wife who was wiping her own tears away. 'Who on earth would want to do such a thing?'

Amy shook her head.

'I honestly don't know, Dad. Perhaps it was an attempted robbery?'

'I can't see that somehow, Amy. The man wouldn't have had anything on him that was worth stealing except his silver crucifix and where would a thief get rid of that around here?'

Amy shrugged. 'I've got no idea why anyone would want to harm the vicar either, Dad.' She leaned towards him. 'But I'll try to get some more information out of Bodkin later on.'

'Don't get involved, Amy,' her mother warned. 'You don't want to get on the wrong side of the police again.'

'Bodkin's not the police, Mum... well, he is, but he's a friend too. He might want to talk to us all anyway.'

'Why would he want to talk to us?' Mrs Rowlings looked puzzled.

'Because Dad is... was a close friend of his. They're bound to want to ask him whether he knows of anyone he might have argued with, owed money to, upset in some way or other.'

'Oh dear.' Mrs Rowlings looked towards her husband. 'I do hope you don't have to go to the police station to be questioned, people may get the wrong idea. They might think we were involved.'

Mr Rowlings patted her arm.

'I'm sure people won't think anything of the sort, dear.' He looked up as the crowd began to part and the two ambulancemen, who were shaking their heads and muttering between themselves, carried their still empty stretcher back towards the waiting ambulance. A few minutes later, six more uniformed officers arrived and began to break up the crowd of onlookers.

As the crowd dispersed, Amy moved slowly through the thinning throng towards the lychgate. As she approached, she spotted Bodkin with his boss as Laws barked out orders to the three uniformed officers guarding the gate. He was a stout man in his fifties with pure white hair sticking out in clumps from beneath his peaked cap. He wore a dark blue uniform that strained to encase his portly frame.

'No one gets in until the forensic pathologist has examined the body and has had a chance to look over the scene,' he snapped, glaring at Detective Constable Stanley. 'And that includes stretcher bearers.'

Amy froze as his gaze rested on her.

'Miss Rowlings,' he said, emphasising her surname. 'I don't know what you are hanging around for, but let me assure you of this, there is nothing here that will be of interest to you, we will NOT require your assistance at this particular moment or at any time in the future. Do I make myself clear?'

'Chief Inspector—'

'Acting Superintendent Laws,' he corrected with a sniff.

'But...'

'No buts, no ifs, no maybes, Miss Rowlings. So, unless you have any information that might be relevant to this case, I'd like you to move on. I have a job to do and I don't want you meddling or obstructing this investigation. You have been warned.'

'But...'

'BUT WHAT?'

'Has the church service been cancelled? That's why I'm here.'

'How the hell should I... Bodkin?' Laws glowered at his sergeant.

'I'll check, sir.' Bodkin rolled his eyes at Amy and stepped smartly away heading towards the main entrance to the church where many of the regular worshipers were now accumulated. Amy turned away from Laws and stood with her parents until the detective returned.

Bodkin smiled at Amy and nodded to her parents as he hurried back down the hill.

'This morning's service has been cancelled but Evensong will go ahead. They're sending another vicar from Rochester, a man named Daley, are you familiar with him?'

'We are indeed, laddie. But he won't be coming from Rochester. He's already in Spinton. He's been here for a few weeks now. He's looking after his sick mother, she lives here.'

Mr Rowlings accent switched immediately from his usual North Kent, to a thick Scottish brogue as it always did when he was speaking to someone he wanted to impress. He was only one sixteenth Scottish but he wore that ancestry like a badge of honour. Rowlings was an engineer who worked for a company based in Gillingham.

Bodkin bit his cheek in an effort to stop himself grinning. He was used to Mr Rowlings' little eccentricities.

'I'm sure he'll do a sterling job,' he said, when he had recovered his poise.

'Harrumph!' It was obvious that Mr Rowlings didn't share that view.

'He's not to your taste then?' Bodkin asked.

'Taste doesn't really come into it, Sergeant Bodkin, he's a man of the cloth after all. But he'll be full of himself, that's for certain. He's had his eye on this parish for many a year.'

Bodkin nodded.

'I see. You were close to Reverend Villiers, weren't you?'

'I was indeed, laddie. We were good friends.'

'Jimmy used to help him with his Sunday sermons,' Mrs Rowlings put in.

'I used to write them in their entirety,' Mr Rowlings corrected. 'Harold would just provide the theme.'

'Would I be correct in assuming the Reverend Daley won't seek such help?' Bodkin asked.

'You would, laddie. The man is far too convinced of his own abilities to ask for anyone else's assistance.'

'I'm sorry about that. But, well, perhaps he won't be the bishop's choice for the parish. You never know, you might get someone new parachuted in.'

'We might, but I doubt it. As I said, Reverend Daley has coveted Spinton for many a year. It's not just the famous old church that attracts him. He was born here. He tried to get Harold... No, I won't go into that here, not with him lying dead only a few feet away.'

Bodkin sucked on his bottom lip, then rubbed his jaw with the palm of his hand.

'Perhaps we could talk about this a little later?'

Mr Rowlings nodded.

'If there's anything I can do to help, rest assured I'll do it.'

Bodkin turned back to Amy.

'Are we still on for the Old Bull later? I'm so sorry about last night. I really missed our evening at the pictures. Blooming work seems to get in the way of any sort of social life these days.'

Amy nodded.

'All right, the Old Bull it is, seeing as you have apologised for your absence. You missed a good film. It was a romantic comedy, You Can't Take It With You with James Stewart and Jean Arthur. You'd have liked it.' Amy brushed away a stray strand of hair. 'I thought I'd been stood up until Constable Ferris popped out of the police station to tell us you'd been called to Gillingham to solve some crime or other.'

'I'm sorry I missed it. I'll be there on time next week.'

Amy smiled softly.

'I do understand, Bodkin. I was only teasing. Alice and I had a really good time.' She hesitated before she spoke again. 'I'd better get Mum and Dad home; this has been an awful shock for them.'

Bodkin nodded slowly.

'I can fully understand that. It's a shock to all of us, even those who don't frequent the church.' He held out his hand to Mr Rowlings, who shook it firmly. 'If we could have a bit of a chat this evening, I'm sure it would be most helpful.' Bodkin smiled at Mrs Rowlings and lifted his hat. 'About six-ish?'

'I'll make some sandwiches,' Mrs Rowlings said, almost to herself.

Amy waved her fingers towards Bodkin and mouthed, 'See you later,' but as she turned away, the detective suddenly spoke again.

'Oh, there was one thing you might be able to help me with before you go, seeing as you're the bible expert and all.'

Rowlings turned his eyes back to Bodkin.

'Yes?'

'We found a bible reference written in chalk on the floor beneath the lychgate bench. Romans 13.13-14. Could you help me with the actual quotation? I'm not a particularly religious man as you are aware.'

Rowlings fished into the pocket of his overcoat and brought out a pocket bible. Opening it expertly at the New Testament section, he flicked through a few pages until he found what he was looking for.

'The epistle to the Romans is the sixth book in the New Testament,' he said. 'It was written by Saint Paul himself. Now, where are... ah yes, here it is.' Rowlings put his finger on a line on the page, then leaned towards the book narrowing his eyes as he read. 'Verse 13... Let us walk honestly, as in the day; not in rioting and drunkenness, not in chambering and wantonness, not in strife and envying.' He looked up at Bodkin, then returned to the quotation. 'Verse 14... But put ye on the Lord Jesus Christ, and make not provision for the flesh, to fulfil the lusts thereof.'

'Blimey! That's quite an accusation,' Bodkin said rubbing his chin thoughtfully. He looked at Amy as he spoke his thoughts aloud. 'What has our vicar been up to?'

CHAPTER FOUR

After lunch, Amy held the collar of her coat tight to her neck and ducked her head into the biting wind as she hurried down Long Lane to Mollison Farm. The farm was owned and run by her best friend, Alice.

Alice was still only nineteen but had already given birth to a daughter, Martha, the previous year. The father of the child, Frank, was no longer around and Alice was happy to bring the child up alone, much to the horror of some of the locals. Amy and Alice had been best friends since they first met at infants' school.

She found her friend in the yard at the back of the farm-house, tossing handfuls of corn to a flock of clucking, scratching, chickens.

'Doesn't that encourage rats?' Amy asked as she opened the five barred gate to let herself into the yard.

'This lot won't leave any lying around,' Alice replied. 'There are lots of rats about, but Jemima keeps their number down.'

As if she had been summoned, a large grey, feral looking

cat, crept out of the barn and sauntered across the farmyard towards Alice.

'Talk of the devil,' Alice said with a laugh. 'There's nothing here for you, Jemima, go find a rat or two if you're hungry. You won't be fed until six, you know the rules.'

'I always find it odd when you call her Jemima,' Amy said, walking towards the back door steps. 'Everyone else calls her Slasher, it suits her temperament so much better.'

Alice tipped the corn bowl upside down and tapped the base to release any kernels that had stuck to the bottom and followed Amy up the back steps towards the kitchen.

'She'll always be Jemima to me. You wouldn't have questioned her name if you'd seen her the day my dad carried her out of the barn. Her mother was a stray and had vanished, she was a tiny little thing. She was lucky to survive really. Dad was going to kill her and feed her to the pigs. Not that they'd have got much of a meal out of her.'

Amy pushed open the big oak door and stepped into the warm, welcoming kitchen. It was a large room with a huge timber fireplace at one end and a big Belfast sink on the side wall that overlooked the yard. There were comfortable armchairs on either side of the blazing fire and in the centre of the room was a long, wide, solid oak table that had been scrubbed and oiled so much over the years it had developed a yellowish tinge. Martha had been born on that table; Alice being unwilling to give birth to her in the bed that her mother had almost died in when bringing her into the world.

'Hello, lovely.'

Miriam, nominally Alice's housekeeper, lived on the farm. In reality she was Alice's right arm and she couldn't have run the busy farm without her. Miriam was the daughter of one of Mollison Farm's long dead workers, she had come to live with

Alice when the last of her children left home. She was an attractive woman with thick, jet-black hair that didn't sport a single grey strand despite her being in her late forties. Miriam was in an on-off relationship with a local builder. She lifted the kettle and turned on the tap as Alice followed Amy through the door.

'Tea?'

'Oh, go on then, you talked me into it,' said Amy with a smile. She took off her heavy coat, hung it on a hook on the back of the door, then pulled a heavy rail-back chair from under the table and sat down. 'I suppose you've heard the news by now?'

Alice put the empty bowl into the sink and rinsed it before placing it on a draining rack at the side.

'We heard at lunchtime. I got a telephone call from Ada Parsons. I've never heard her so animated. I've no idea why she called me. It's not like we're best friends or anything.'

'Ada likes the sound of her own voice, just like her daughter, Big Nose Beryl, neither of them could keep a secret if their life depended on it.' Amy said with a sigh. 'How long has Ada had a telephone anyway? It seems everyone's getting connected except my family.'

Alice sat down next to Amy and patted her hand.

'You'd only use it to talk to me.'

Amy sighed again. 'That's what Dad says.'

Alice laughed. 'He's not wrong though. You even call me from the telephone kiosk at the end of the lane. It's almost as quick to walk here as it is to walk there from your house.'

'Oh, shush.' Amy reached out and took a steaming mug of tea from Miriam. She blew into the blue striped mug then took a short sip. 'Ah, now, that's hit the spot. Thank you, Miriam.'

Miriam handed a mug to Alice then sat down herself.

'Why is your father so against having a telephone installed? Is it because of his religion or something?'

Amy snorted, spilling drops of tea down the side of her mug.

'No, nothing like that. We could actually have one installed for free, and it wouldn't cost us anything to use. Dad's firm would cover all the expenses. He won't have it though. He says he'd aways be at their beck and call every time there was a problem at the factory.'

'He's right though,' Alice said.

'Oh, I know, it's just that... well, it would be so... convenient, wouldn't it? I mean, could you make do without your phone now?'

'I only really use it for business and to talk to you of course. I get more calls from you than any of the wholesalers I deal with.'

Amy narrowed her eyes as she looked at her best friend.

'I only ever call when there's something important to discuss.'

Miriam choked on her tea but catching Amy's eye, said nothing.

'So,' Alice said after a brief pause. 'What exactly happed to our spiritual leader?'

'Someone's done him in,' Amy replied.

'I'm aware of that. Don't you have any more of the sordid details?'

'Not yet. They found him all scrunched up on one of the lychgate benches. There was a bible reference written in chalk underneath the bench. I nipped into the graveyard to have a better look but Bodkin caught me and chucked me out.'

Alice cocked her head to one side as she looked at Amy.

'Really? You mean he didn't invite you over to have a look at the corpse?'

'Stop teasing. I only wanted to see what was going on.'

Alice and Miriam exchanged glances.

'Nothing new there then,' Alice said, raising her mug to her lips to hide the smile that had formed.

Amy gave her another narrow-eyed look.

'So, you don't want me to report back when Bodkin comes around this evening to give us all the grisly details then?'

'I didn't say that, did I?' Alice replied. 'Of course, we want to know. We want every tiny, seemingly irrelevant detail.'

Amy finished her tea and placed her mug carefully on the table.

'He's coming for tea at six. Mum's doing cake and sandwiches. I'll grill him then. You know Bodkin, he can't resist my feminine wiles. He'll soon spill the beans.'

'I thought you were having cake and sandwiches,' said Alice with a querying look.

'I don't think you deserve to be told anything after that dreadful joke,' Amy replied with a frown.

'You mentioned a bible reference,' said Miriam. 'Do you know what it was?'

'It was just chapter and verse numbers. Romans 13.13-14.'

'And do you know what it refers to?'

'Dad had his bible with him as always so he looked it up. It's a warning from Saint Paul about the sins of drunkenness and debauchery.'

'Well, the murderer obviously knew him,' Alice said. 'Oops, sorry, Amy, you know I'm not... wasn't a big fan of our vicar.'

'He had his personal demons, I'll grant you.'

'He was a blooming hypocrite, Amy. All that preaching about the devil's brew and all the time he was dancing around the churchyard at midnight wearing just his underpants and waving a bottle of wine in the air whilst cursing both the living and the dead.'

'He was caught once... all right, possibly more than once,' Amy replied. 'Look, I'm not defending him, I know he had a drink problem, I'm just not sure why someone would want to bump him off for it.'

'It does seem odd. There has to be more to it than that,' said Alice thoughtfully.

Amy got to her feet and pulled on her coat.

'I'm sure we'll find out soon enough. Oh, Bodkin and I are going to the Old Bull for a drink about seven if you'd like to join us.'

Miriam shook her head and picked up her knitting. Alice got to her feet and put the empty mugs in the sink.

'Not for me either. I'm up at the crack of dawn, unlike some.'

'I'm up at six myself,' Amy replied. 'I have to work too.'

'I still won't bother. I think I'll leave you two lovebirds to it,' Alice said, looking away from her best friend. 'I hate playing gooseberry.'

'LOVEBIRDS! Gooseberry? I... what? ... there's nothing going on between us, he's older than me, he's scruffy, he's virtually a heathen, he's... he's... BODKIN!'

'Methinks thou dost protest too much,' said Alice with a wink.

'I... He's BODKIN!' Amy repeated, turning away to hide her blushing face. 'I'm going home now.'

'Give me a call if you find anything out,' called Alice as Amy closed the kitchen door behind her.

CHAPTER FIVE

Amy and her mother had just finished laying the table when Bodkin knocked on the door.

Amy fussed with her hair in the hall mirror for a few moments before opening the door and stepping aside to allow him to enter.

'Perfect timing,' she said. 'It's ham sandwiches and a slice of Mum's famous jam sponge for tea.' She took his mac and hung it on the coat rack before pointing to the open living room door. 'You know the way.'

Amy followed the detective into the back room and waited as he greeted her parents. The voices of the Ovaltiney club children singing their famous show closing song, came from an ornate radio cabinet in the corner.

'We always listen in to the Ovaltineys,' said Mr Rowlings. 'It's sort of a family tradition.'

Bodkin grinned. 'I listen in when I can too.'

'Do sit down, Mr Bodkin,' Mrs Rowlings held out her hand towards the table. 'I've saved a place for you next to Amy.' She looked across at her daughter and smiled. 'She never stops talking about you, you know. Bodkin says this and Bodkin says that, you'd think—'

'Mum!'

Bodkin sat down and turned his face away from the horrified Amy.

'It's nice to know someone other than my boss mentions my name now and again,' he said.

Mr Rowlings took his place on the other side of the table as his wife placed a dainty, china tea pot on a mat in the centre. When Amy and her mother were seated, he bowed his head and said grace.

'For what we are about to receive, may the Lord make us truly thankful.'

'Amen,' muttered Amy and her mother. Bodkin remained silent, his eyes looking down at the flower-patterned plate that had been placed before him.

'Would you mind if we left our... erm, discussion until we've eaten, laddie?' asked Mr Rowlings. 'I'm sure our appetites would be ruined and all of this wonderful food would go to waste, otherwise.'

'There's absolutely no rush,' replied Bodkin, taking two triangle cut sandwiches from the plate offered to him by Amy.

Throughout the meal, they discussed trivial matters concerning the local area. Amy pricked up her ears when Bodkin announced that the new police apartments had finally been completed.

'Whereabouts is it, Mr Bodkin?' asked Mrs Rowlings. 'Would it be that new development on Farley Lane just across the road from the police station? I've been keeping my eye on that as I pass by on the bus. It seems to have gone up in no time.'

'That's the one,' Bodkin replied. 'All mod cons inside.'

Mrs Rowlings clapped her hands.

'Good, it's high time they did something about that part of town, it's been an embarrassing eyesore for years.'

'It was more of an alley than a lane,' put in Amy. 'We live on a lane and it's about four times as wide as Farley.'

Bodkin pursed his lips. 'Well, it's no longer a lane, so it won't be embarrassed by the comparison to Long Lane any more, it's being renamed Constabulary Way. The actual block of flats is to be called, Bluecoat House.'

'Oh my goodness. Couldn't they be a little more imaginative?' asked Amy.

'Acting Superintendent Laws is the man responsible for naming the place. He doesn't have an imagination.'

Amy laughed.

'He doesn't have much of a personality either.'

'Now, now, Amy,' her father chastised her. 'I'm sure the man has both.'

'Have you met him?' Amy asked incredulously.

At six-thirty, as the BBC Dance Orchestra began to play some of the popular songs of the day, Mrs Rowlings cut into the sponge cake that Bodkin had been eyeing since he had first taken his seat, and using a cake slice, slipped a large portion onto his plate.

'Freshly made this very afternoon,' she said proudly.

After eating the cake and drinking yet more tea the Rowlings got up from the table and settled into two fireside chairs. Mr Rowlings reached across and turned off the radio as Amy and Bodkin sat on the two-seater sofa facing them.

'Right, Detective Sergeant Bodkin,' Mr Rowlings said in his broad Scottish brogue. 'Let's get on with it. What do you want to know?'

Bodkin stroked his stubble-covered chin thoughtfully. 'How long have you known the Reverend Villiers?'

'Twenty-one years, ten weeks and three days,' replied Mr Rowlings.

'That's very precise.'

'We met him when we were arranging Amy's christening. He did it at short notice for us. She was only a few weeks old and was quite ill with the flu, we weren't sure if she would make it.'

'Ah, I see. Did you get on from the start?' Bodkin asked.

'Oh, yes. We had a good long chat about the bible, didn't we, love?' Rowlings looked across towards his wife.

Mrs Rowlings nodded. 'Oh yes, it seemed like hours.'

Amy stifled a giggle. She knew what her father was like when the subject of the bible came up.

'Anyway,' Mr Rowlings shot Amy a quick look, 'he appeared to be impressed with the extent of my knowledge. I told him I used to write for the church periodical. He asked me if I could write sermons because he hated writing them. I said I'd give it a go and it started from there.'

'How many have you written for him now?'

'Oh my goodness, that's a question.' Mr Rowlings frowned as he did a quick calculation. 'Well over a thousand if you count the extra ones at Easter and Christmas. I also wrote some speeches for him and the content for some talks he gave to aspiring clergymen at the university.' He pointed to an ancient typewriter that sat on the end of a walnut sideboard. 'I wrote them all on that old contraption.' He thought for a moment, then addressed Bodkin again. 'I, er, I wouldn't mind having them back, as a sort of keepsake. They're no use to Harold now. Do you think that might be possible?'

Bodkin nodded. 'I don't think that would be a problem, Mr Rowlings.'

'I'll pick them up for you in the week,' Amy volunteered.

Bodkin waited a few seconds, then turned the conversation back to the Reverend Villiers.

'He was well thought of then... the reverend?'

'Back then he was. His image has been tarnished somewhat of late.' Mr Rowlings looked down at his hands.

'The drink?'

'Precisely, it's become a lot worse over the last five years or so. He always had a fondness for it and he didn't like himself for his weakness, hence the number of times he asked me to mention the demon drink in the sermons. I think he was hoping some of it might sink in, as it were.'

'Did his... erm, how shall we put it, late night graveyard performances, occur on a regular basis?'

Mr Rowlings looked uncomfortable.

'I can't really answer that as I haven't been there when he's performed. I have heard the gossip though. A lot of people have seen him when they've been passing on their way home from the pub at night.'

Bodkin nodded. 'Indeed, some of those reports made it to the police station.' He wriggled about on the sofa and altered his position, leaning forward slightly. 'Do you know of anyone who might wish him harm?'

'No, laddie. All right, he put some people's backs up. He was called a hypocrite on occasion, but never to his face.'

Bodkin nodded slowly.

'It's hard to imagine someone doing that to him merely because he liked a few glasses of wine. Did he drink all the time? Was he an alcoholic?'

Rowlings shook his head. 'No, not all the time. He

never touched a drop in the day. He only used to drink in the late evenings, after Evensong and after all the committee or parish meetings were over and done with. He did used to have a glass of wine at social events, wakes, weddings, that sort of thing and at times if there was a celebration of a birthday at one of the meetings. He kept some cheap stuff in the cupboard for those events. He wouldn't waste his precious stock of Entre Deux Mers on anyone else.'

'So, he was particular about his wines?'

'Wine, singular. He used to pick up a case every week from a dealer in Rochester when he visited the bishop for their weekly meetings. He kept a cheap bottle or two in the cupboard in his study. He had some reasonable port in there too, but he seldom touched it.'

As if the mention of strong drink had set off a timer in his brain, Mr Rowlings got to his feet and crossed the room to a side table on which sat a half-full bottle of scotch and four glasses.

'Can I tempt you, laddie?'

Bodkin shook his head. 'Not for me thank you, I'm a beer man through and through.'

'You don't know what you're missing. Do you mind if I partake of a wee dram?'

'Don't hold back on my account,' the detective replied.

When Rowlings was settled again, Bodkin returned to the subject of Villiers.

'So, as far as you are aware, he had no enemies. Did he have money worries?'

Rowlings sipped his scotch and shook his head.

'None that I am aware of. He could afford his precious wine and that's all he was concerned about. It's quite an expense, buying a case of good quality French wine every week, so I honestly doubt he had any monetary problems.'

'He wasn't a gambler then?'

'Good heavens no. He had me write many a sermon about the evils of gambling.'

'And, what about his personal life. Could he have upset someone close to him. Was he in a relationship with anyone?'

Rowlings shot a quick look at his wife, then concentrated his attention on his whisky.

'Not that I'm aware of.'

'Are you certain? I mean, I'm not suggesting anything untoward, but he is a single man, he must have certain needs.'

'We never discussed his personal life.'

'Were there any rumours going around about him? Again, I'm not making any allegations as to his sexual preferences but he must have had some emotional needs, we all do.'

'If you mean, was he a homosexual, the answer is no. He was close to a woman back in the day, they were to be married I believe, but she died of Spanish flu in nineteen-nineteen. I think maybe he still carried her memory in his heart.'

Bodkin rubbed his chin.

'That's twenty years. A long time for a man with a normal libido.'

Rowlings shrugged. 'I'm a one-woman man myself, Sergeant Bodkin.' He reached out and took his wife's hand.

'I'm sure you are,' replied Bodkin with a smile. 'But, what about his housekeeper, Mrs Gatting, is it? She's a very attractive woman I'm told. Has she been with him long?'

'Please don't besmirch Mrs Gatting's reputation, Sergeant. She's a clean-living, God-fearing woman.'

'I'm not besmirching her character, Mr Rowlings, it's just that a relationship can develop when a man and a women share a dwelling. There were only the two of them living in the vicarage I take it?'

Rowlings nodded. 'I understand what you're saying, of course I'm aware that things like that happen, but in this case you'd be wrong. Caroline is a very respectable woman. She's a widow, despite her young age. Her husband died in a railway accident more than ten years ago, unfortunately; they had no children.'

'How old is she? Mid-thirties?'

'Around that age. Does that matter?'

Bodkin shrugged. 'Not especially, but she may be thinking that life is passing her by and if she doesn't find someone soon, she may never find anyone.'

Amy snorted.

'That's a typical male attitude, Bodkin. Do you think women get so desperate that they'll jump into bed with anyone when they reach a certain age?'

'AMY!' Mrs Rowling's mouth opened wide.

'I'm sorry, Mum, but we don't live in Jane Austen's time. Women aren't just interested in eligible bachelors; we have other interests now. We have aspirations above that of finding a suitable husband. Women are beginning to realise they weren't just put on this earth to be brood mares.'

'That is correct and it is to be welcomed, but things aren't always the better for it,' said Mr Rowlings seriously. He gave Amy one of his looks.

Bodkin held up his hands and looked from Amy to her father.

'Look, I'm sorry, I didn't mean to start an argument about the place of women in society, and I really wasn't accusing Mrs Gatting of doing anything immoral. It's just that, well, these things have to be looked into and sadly it's my job to ask questions like that.'

Rowlings nodded slowly and sipped at his drink.

'I understand, Mr Bodkin, it can't be very nice for you either.'

'It goes with the territory, Mr Rowlings. I'll have to interview her soon. Tomorrow evening perhaps. We should have the doctor's interim report on the vict... Reverend Villiers by then. The post mortem is taking place tomorrow afternoon, but it will be the end of the week at the earliest before we get any toxicology results. We'll have a better idea of what happened to him by tomorrow evening.'

'Toxicology?'

'There are always blood and organ tests taken at a post mortem. Sometimes they're important, but most times they aren't.' Bodkin looked at the wall clock, then at Amy. He rubbed his hands together and stood up. 'Seven o'clock. The Old Bull will be opening its doors. Shall we go and say hello to Stan?'

As Amy walked out into the hall to get her coat, Mr Rowlings got to his feet and offered a hand to the detective.

'Good luck with your investigation, laddie. I hope you find the dastardly man who did this.'

'It's not always a man, Mr Rowlings,' Bodkin replied.

CHAPTER SIX

The back room at the Old Bull was warm and welcoming. The snug was never particularly busy on a Sunday as it was generally the room where the ladies gathered and most of the regular Saturday night drinkers were at home, ironing overalls or checking the state of their children's clothes as they got things ready for Monday morning.

Amy sat in the corner on a heavy oak bench seat that had once been a pew in Saint John the Evangelist's church, and smiled at one or two familiar faces who were either childless or had, like her, prepared their own work clothes earlier in the day.

A couple of minutes later, Bodkin joined her and placed a port and lemon and a pint of amber bitter on the table. After sitting down opposite her on an oval backed chair, he picked up his pint and held it aloft.

'Cheers.'

Amy picked up her drink and clinked his glass with hers.

'Bottoms up,' she replied.

Bodkin took a deep slurp, then put his glass back on the table and wiped his mouth with the back of his hand. Amy sipped at hers, then held it to her chest as if protecting it.

'So, what aren't you telling me, Bodkin?'

'I'm sorry?'

Amy sighed.

'About the case, I know you're holding something back, I also know that you're too much of a gentleman to discuss a victim's injuries in front of his closest friends.'

'Amy, look, I can't... Not after last time.'

'Oh yes you can, Bodkin, I virtually solved that case. The police would have still been chasing shadows if I hadn't worked it all out for you.'

Bodkin grunted. 'I'd have got there eventually.'

Amy put her glass down, then leaned across and patted his arm.

'You might have, Bodkin, but that oaf of a superior officer of yours couldn't spot a vital clue if came wrapped in a package labelled, here's a vital clue.'

Bodkin smiled.

'I couldn't possibly comment.'

'So, what aren't you telling me?'

'Amy, I can't, if Laws got to hear, you'd be in the deepest of deep do dos, and I'd be out of a job.'

'Who's going to tell him?'

'Amy—'

'Oh for pity's sake, man. You know I can help. No one knew the Reverend Villiers as well as my family did. I already know more about him than most people will ever know. You're starting out from scratch, hence asking Dad all those basic questions.'

Bodkin took another sip of his beer.

'I'm not the only one holding back information, am I?'

Amy looked away, then studied her hands.

'No, you're probably not. I noticed how evasive Dad was when you asked certain questions.' She suddenly grabbed hold of Bodkin's sleeve and looked into his face earnestly. 'But I might be able to help with that too. I'm a Daddy's girl, he'd do anything for me. I think I can work on him; it will have to be done carefully though. He doesn't like to discuss smutty things like sexual relations with his innocent little daughter.'

'Laws will have my guts for garters.'

Amy smiled sweetly. *Almost there, one more little push.*

'Does Laws ever use the services of anyone outside of the force in an investigation?'

'Yes, we have several outside sources including criminal informants, or snouts as they're known in the trade. We also use the press to help us out now and then. It's amazing what a reporter will tell you if he thinks there's a scoop in there for him.'

'Private investigators, do you use their services too?'

'We do. There's a list of the ones we trust to dig into things we either don't have the time or the resources for. Why do you ask?'

'Oh, nothing. I just wondered.'

Amy emptied her glass and got to her feet.

'My round,' she said.

Bodkin grinned.

'Do you really think you can bribe a police officer into divulging the important details of a case?'

Amy winked at him. 'I know I can.'

By the time she had returned from the bar, Amy had decided to try a different tack.

'Is this an unusual case? I mean, you don't see vicars bumped off every day, do you?'

'It's not a common occurrence I have to admit. I've only worked on one similar case in the past, but that turned out to be mistaken identity, the killer thought he was someone else. I was in uniform then.'

Amy tipped her head to one side and studied the detective.

'No, I can't see you in a silly hat and a tight blue tunic, Bodkin. Whenever I think of you, you're wearing a creased shirt, and crumpled trousers.'

Bodkin laughed.

'That might change when I move into my new police flat, I'll hopefully have enough space to use an ironing board properly. My digs are so cramped there isn't room to swing a mouse, let alone a cat.'

'I haven't seen you in a nicely laundered shirt since you left your room at Alice's farm, and you only wore a nice, crisp one then because Miriam used to iron it for you.' Amy lifted her drink. 'When, erm, when do you move in anyway?'

'Midweek. I've been to see the one they're offering me. It's a first-floor apartment. I have my own kitchen but I have to share a bathroom with whoever else is on the same floor. There's only one other flat on that level so it won't be too bad. I have to share a phone too, it's on the ground floor.'

'You'll be at their beck and call then, Bodkin. You're only a stone's throw from the police station and they have you on the end of a phone line too. I think you might be missing many a Saturday night at the pictures.'

'The phone is downstairs. I can always make out I'm not in if someone else answers it and comes up to pass on a message.'

'Good idea, Bodkin. Learn from the criminals, be devious.'

Bodkin grinned again as Amy looked at him earnestly.

'Am I allowed to visit? I mean, you don't have to be chaperoned when you have a visitor to your apartment do you?'

Bodkin shook his head.

'No, nothing like that. You'd always be welcome to drop in. I'm not sure what your mum and dad would make of it though.'

Amy put her finger to her lips.

'I won't tell them if you don't.'

Bodkin held up a thumb. 'It's a deal.'

Amy suddenly tossed her head. 'Don't go thinking there's more to it than a quick cup of tea either, Bodkin, because there isn't.'

'Perish the thought,' he replied.

Amy patted the back of his hand. 'Good boy. Now, about the Reverend Villiers. Can you at least tell me how you think he was killed? I mean, it will be common knowledge by tomorrow. No one gossips like those secretaries at the police station and most of the policemen are as bad.'

Bodkin sighed. 'I wondered when you'd get back to that.'

'Well, wonder no more, Mr Policeman. Come on, out with it.'

'All right. Anything to stop the nagging.'

The detective was silent for a few moments, then he picked up his beer and looked into it as though he'd spotted a face in the froth.

'We suspect that he was poisoned, at least Doctor Mortensen does. He could tell by the way the body muscles were all cramped up, the snarl on his face, the way his fingers were curled up.'

'Does he think it was it cyanide? I read an Agatha Christie short story where someone was killed with that. Was there a smell of almonds? That's always a big clue.'

'No, there was no almond smell. We've got our own ideas on what it was, but we have to wait on the toxicology until we know for sure.'

'Strychnine then... YES! That makes sense. It sends the body into violent spams. Agatha used that poison in her first book, The Mysterious Case at Styles.'

Bodkin shook his head. 'You really are quite remarkable.'

Amy grinned. 'I know, have you only just realised?'

Bodkin swished his beer around in his glass. 'I think it's strychnine, but Laws isn't convinced. Besides, there's the fact that he had a fair bit of caked blood on the back of his head.'

Amy stared at the wall opposite as she gathered her thoughts.

'Blood... hmm... He may have done that when he was thrashing about... but, that doesn't explain how he managed to get across to the seat. No... someone put him there, then scrawled the bible quote, that's for certain.'

Bodkin watched her face closely as she frowned, then closed one eye as she concentrated.

'Wine bottle!' she announced suddenly.

'Pardon? Which wine bottle are we talking about?'

'The one he was drinking from, silly. Honestly, Bodkin I sometimes wonder how you ever managed to become a detective.'

'That,' said Bodkin thoughtfully, 'is a very good point.'

'What is? My remark about your sleuthing skills or the question about the wine bottle?'

'The wine bottle,' Bodkin mused. 'We haven't found it, but he almost certainly would have had it with him. We have a witness who states that they saw him at just after nine o'clock, waving it in the air as he staggered about, cursing the dead, but in reality, they wouldn't bet their lives on it having happened on that particular day.' He leaned across and patted her hand. 'Well done, Amy. Well done.'

'See, you can't solve this without me,' she said, waving her empty glass at him. 'Your round, Bodkin.'

CHAPTER SEVEN

The blustery wind that had plagued the town over the weekend had eased slightly by the time Amy made her way past the telephone box opposite the Old Bull. Carole, her best friend at work, was waiting for her outside the pub. Amy walked behind the double decker bus that was offloading Mill workers and nodded to one or two of them as they alighted. The vicar's death seemed to be the only topic of conversation on their lips.

'Hi, Amy,' Carole said cheerfully. 'Nice day for it?'

Amy looked up at the darkening sky. Heavy rain was forecast during the morning.

'Might as well be at work on a day like this. At least the wind has dropped.'

Amy fell in alongside her friend as they made their way down the hill and past the heavy privet hedge that marked the boundary of the factory grounds.

The Mill was a good quality clothing factory and had acquired its nickname because, at one time, it had actually been a cotton mill, powered by a long-redundant water wheel that had been built on the river at the back of the premises.

The changing room was a hive of gossip as Amy and Carole walked in.

Big Nose Beryl, so called because of her inability to keep it out of anyone else's business, had the ears of the rest of the workforce as she pronounced on the weekend's events.

'He was found stark naked with a carnation in his teeth. I mean, come on, there's a lot more to this than meets the eye. I always said he was a wrong 'un.'

Her voice stuttered to a halt as Amy caught her eye.

'You ought to be a reporter for the scandal sheets, Beryl,' Amy said, giving her a stern, warning look. Amy had had many a run in with the gossip machine that was Beryl.

'I was just saying...'

'Beryl, as my mother says, if you can't say anything nice about someone, don't say anything at all. Especially if they've passed on and can't answer back. Anyway, I'd like to know where you got this information? Was it from your mother by any chance?'

'Keep my mother out of this, Amy.'

'I only asked because she was on the phone to the rest of the town while the poor, dead vicar's body was still warm.'

Amy took off her coat, hung it on her peg, then opened her bag and fished out a headscarf turban which she tied expertly in place without needing to use the mirror. After pushing her bag under the bench, she turned to face Beryl, who had become unusually quiet.

'The police haven't yet released any details of the murder but let me give you this snippet from someone who was at the scene yesterday. The vicar was fully dressed, there was no flower of any kind on, or close to, his body and, before Beryl tries to convince everyone that he was involved in something illegal, he wasn't. The poor man has been murdered and the last thing the police need is to hear people like her spread the sort of nasty, malicious gossip that can only get in the way of their investigations.'

Beryl glared back at Amy.

'Ooh, someone got out of the wrong side of the bed this morning.'

'I don't have a wrong side of the bed, Beryl. I'm always as bright as a button until I get to work and hear your whining voice.'

Having said everything she thought she needed to say, Amy nodded to the rest of her colleagues, pushed open the door and strode quickly across the factory floor to her machine. By the time Carole walked down the same aisle to her own machine a few places in front, Amy had already completed her first garment of the day.

At lunchtime, Amy had just sat down with her mug of tea and opened her sandwich box when she received a nudge in the ribs from Carole.

'Ooh, look, Amy, lover boy is in. Has he come to woo you or arrest you?'

Amy followed Carole's gaze to the canteen doors where she saw the tall figure of Bodkin waving to her. Picking up her tea and sandwiches, Amy shrugged to Carole and to the sound of cat calls and whistles, she walked as nonchalantly as she could, across the canteen.

'Hello, Bodkin,' she said as she approached the doors. 'This is a pleasant surprise.'

Bodkin grinned. 'It's not really a social call, but it's always nice to see you. I know you'll be interested in what I've got to say. Shall we sit in my car, it's still drizzling.'

Amy hurried out of the loading bay doors and followed Bodkin to the black, Morris Ten car that was parked just along from the Mill gates. Once they were settled inside, Amy opened up her sandwich box and offered it to Bodkin.

'Go on, take a couple, I know you won't have eaten today.'

Bodkin grinned and took two triangle cut sandwiches from the box. Peeling back the top slice from one, he took a look at the contents, then took a huge bite.

'Ooh, that's nice, my stomach thinks my throat's been cut.'

'Leftover ham from last night's tea,' Amy said. 'There's a slice of cake too, we can share that after.' Amy took a long sip of tea and passed the cup to Bodkin. 'Go on. Share and share alike.'

'I could do this every day,' said Bodkin, handing the cup back. 'It's nice to be pampered.'

'Drop that thought now, Bodkin,' Amy said seriously. 'I'm going to be the talk of the factory when I go back in as it is. Big Nose Beryl would have me marked down as the prime suspect for the vicar's murder if you came back again tomorrow.'

Bodkin laughed. 'I know what workplace gossip is like. I worked in a canning factory for a few months. It's not a lot better at the station either.'

Amy finished her sandwich and wound down the window an inch to let the air circulate and allow it to clear.

'They'll be watching, I don't want them wondering why the windows have suddenly steamed up.'

Bodkin shook his head and wound down his own window a touch.

'You think of everything, Amy,' he said.

'I know,' she sniffed, 'I should be the detective really.' She broke off a piece of cake using a paper napkin and handed it to

Bodkin. 'So, what brings you to the Mill? It can't just be my vivacious company.'

'It's partly that, but I've come to tell you that I've set up a meeting with Mrs Gatting at the vicarage tonight. I remembered your father saying he'd like his sermons back if possible. Well, I'd like to have a look in his study, and those sermons would give me the perfect excuse to do just that.'

'Where do I come in?' Amy asked.

'I'd like you to chat to her while I have a good rummage around. I don't really want her looking over my shoulder while I do it. I'd like to get a look at his bedroom too, just to see if everything is as innocent as your dad claims it is. It's easy to spot if a room is occupied by more than one person.'

'I'm game,' Amy replied, brightly.

'I thought you might be,' said Bodkin trying to keep a straight face. 'It's perfect cover if Laws gets to hear about it too. You were picking your dad's sermons up and there were far too many of them for you to be able to carry home, so I said I'd give you a lift after I'd finished questioning Mrs Gatting.'

'Bodkin, you really are becoming quite devious. I'm getting rather worried about you.'

'The people I deal with every day must be having an influence on me.' He winked at Amy. 'I don't just mean the criminals either.'

Amy frowned. 'I do hope you're not including me in that statement.'

Bodkin raised his eyebrows, then laughed. Amy snapped the lid onto her sandwich box and placed it on her lap before continuing the conversation.

'So, Bodkin, have you found a suspect yet? Has anything new turned up?'

'Not really, but then I've spent all morning tidying up the paperwork from the Gillingham raid on Saturday night.'

'Raid? That sounds exciting.'

Bodkin pulled a face. 'They were investigating an armed robbery; we had to raid half a dozen addresses to try to find the man responsible.'

'Armed robbery? My goodness, Bodkin, you do put yourself in harm's way, don't you?'

'The job can be a bit scary at times but on this occasion, it wasn't. Once I knew the suspect was Bungling Bill Bosworth, I knew I wouldn't be in any danger.'

'Bungling Bill Bosworth, what a fabulous name for a criminal.' Amy almost applauded the description.

'I must have arrested him a dozen times over a three-year spell before I moved up here. The moment I heard his name I knew there wouldn't be a lot of risk in arresting him. He's quite famous down there.'

'What did he do this time?'

'He robbed a chip shop and threatened the owner with a gun. The gun in question turned out to be his ten-year-old son's cap gun. The lighting in the shop wasn't that good apparently.'

Amy snorted, then laughed out loud.

'A cap gun? Oh my goodness.'

'It didn't even have any caps in it,' Bodkin sighed.

Amy giggled. 'Oh, Bodkin, you are so funny.'

'Well, it cost me a Saturday night out and a Monday morning writing a report about a child's toy being used in a robbery. It was a catalogue of disasters for Bungling Bill too. We actually picked him up at home and his son wanted us to charge him with stealing his Roy Roger's Colt 45.'

Amy's whole frame shook as she laughed.

'Oh, poor Bungling Bill.'

'We're calling him, Wild Bill now.'

Amy shook her head slowly, then checked her watch.

'Oops, I'd better be getting back, they'll be thinking we've run off to Gretna Green by now.'

Bodkin started the car engine and leaned across the passenger seat as Amy got out of the car.

'Thanks for lunch. You just saved me from a curly edged sandwich at the station canteen.'

Amy smiled and put her hand on the door handle as she readied herself to slam it shut.

'What time are you picking me up?' she asked.

'Seven-ish. I'm hoping to get the doctor's interim report this afternoon and the post mortem results should be ready by four, so I'll be having a busy time of it. Thankfully, I don't have to attend the post mortem this time. Laws has given DC Stanley the job. I hope he didn't eat in the canteen before he sets off or it will all be coming back.'

Amy grimaced. 'I always thought I'd like to be a detective, but the more I learn about the job the less I think I want to do it.' She stepped back onto the pavement and slammed the car door shut.

'See you at seven,' she said with a wave.

CHAPTER EIGHT

After work, Amy said goodbye to Carole and a few other friends at the Old Bull and crossed the road to the red telephone box at the end of Long Lane. She lifted the receiver, shoved two bronze pennies into the slot and dialled Alice's number. She tapped her foot as she waited for Alice to come through from the kitchen to pick up. When she heard her voice in the earpiece, she pressed button A on the panel.

'Hello, Mollison Farm, Alice speaking.'

'Hello Alice speaking this is Amy speaking,'

Alice groaned.

'Do we have to go through this every time you call?'

'Oh course, it's part of the fun,' Amy replied brightly.

She could visualise Alice smiling on the other end of the line.

'Right, darling, I've got some hot news for you.'

'Ooh, is it about the...' Alice lowered her voice to just above a whisper, 'murder?'

'There's no need to whisper, Alice, it's a private conversation. No one is listening in.'

'Ah, but those girls at the exchange sometimes do. Greta Colback does it all the time and—'

'Alice, the pips will go soon, do you want my news or not?'

'Couldn't you just come down here and tell me in person?'

'No, silly. I can't, because that's a bit of the news.'

'Oh, I see... well, get on with it then?'

Amy sighed.

'Right. Well, the reverend was poisoned, most probably with strychnine but we won't know that until the toxicology results come back.'

Alice laughed. 'We?'

'Oh, shush, do you want this news or not?'

'Sorry, of course I do.'

Amy knew that Alice wasn't the slightest bit sorry, she could picture her biting her lip as she waited for her to speak.

'Hmmm it's hard to tell at times. Right. The vicar may also have been bashed on the back of the head but, WE! That's Bodkin and I, won't know that until the results of the post mortem are in. In other news, WE, are going around to see Mrs Gatting at the vicarage tonight.'

'Haha, so you managed to wheedle your way in then?'

'I'm not wheedling anything. I'm an important part of the investigating team.'

'Did Bodkin call you that?'

Amy coughed.

'Not in as many words, no, but he must have meant that or he wouldn't have invited me this evening.'

'There is that,' Alice replied.

'Okay I'm off now, I've got to get ready. Oh, I wish Dad would get a telephone in, this is so much faff.'

'Keep working on him, he'll give in eventually, Amy, he always does.'

'Oh, before I go, where do you get those little cards you use to promote the farm? You know, they used to be called calling cards in the olden days.'

'They call them business cards now. I get mine done at Walton's printers, they're on the Gillingham Road, about half a mile out of town, right next to the scrap yard, you can't miss it.'

'Are they expensive?'

'They work out about a penny each so...'

Alice's voice was cut off as the pips sounded and Amy was left with the choice of putting in more coins or ending the call. She decided she'd got enough information and placed the receiver on the cradle.

Outside the phone box, two people were waiting. The first in line was one of the cleaning staff from the Mill. She glowered at Amy as though she had been on the call for an age.

Amy smiled sweetly at her, then after nodding to the man waiting in the queue behind her, she crossed the road and walked the short distance home.

At six-thirty, Amy, tapping her foot to the rhythm of Al Donahue's Jeepers Creepers, put the finishing touches to the light make up she had applied, then slipped into a white floral print dress she'd bought for twelve shillings from Brigden's nearly new, fashion store in the town. After slipping on her black Oxford shoes, she stood away from the mirror and examined her reflection critically. Finally satisfied, she took the precious record from the gramophone turntable and slipped it back into its sleeve and went downstairs to greet her father who had come home from work while she had been getting ready.

'Hi, Dad, how was your day?'

'Hello, dear,' Mr Rowlings gave Amy a hug. 'My day was the same as always. Are you going out again? You're looking rather glamorous.'

'I'm going to pick up your sermons from the vicarage. Bodkin's giving me a lift back with them.'

'That's very kind of him but there was no hurry.'

'It's not putting him out, he's going there anyway, he's questioning Mrs Gatting tonight.'

Amy cringed as she realised what she had said. She knew what her father's response would be before he opened his mouth.

'Amy, please don't get involved in this. Let Detective Bodkin sort it out, he's the professional after all.'

Amy blew out her cheeks. 'I'm not getting involved, Dad. I'm only going there to pick up your sermons.'

Her father gave her one of his looks. 'Make sure that's all you do too. I know you of old, Amy.'

Amy plonked herself down on the sofa as Mrs Rowlings bought in her husband's dinner.

'Amy's already had hers.'

Amy pulled a face when she looked at her father tucking into his meal.

'I didn't have tripe, either.'

'There's nothing wrong with tripe, it's good for you.'

'What is it anyway? Sheep's brains or something?'

'This particular tripe is the lining of a cow's stomach?'

Amy grimaced and shook her head. 'Ugh!'

'It's called, offal,' Mr Rowlings said, chewing hard on his rubbery looking food.

'It's awful you mean,' Amy replied.

'You really don't know what you're missing.' Mr Rowlings smacked his lips and bit into another forkful.

'Speaking of things I'm missing out on. Have you had a chance to think again about having a telephone installed? It would make life so much easier.'

'For you, possibly. You could spend even more of your time talking to Alice, but I can't see how I'd be any better off. I'd be a telephone call away from putting an extra shift in at the factory.'

'Mum would use it; she could talk to her sister. It would save her writing all those endless letters, then having to wait a week to get a reply.'

Mr Rowlings shook his head.

'The answer is no, Amy.'

'But, Dad, it seems that half the town has a telephone now. You're behind the times you know?'

'Behind the times is just where I like to be.' Mr Rowlings smiled and scooped up another forkful of tripe. 'And you're exaggerating as usual, the vast majority of people in this town can only just about afford to use a telephone kiosk and they only use those if they're lucky enough to know someone with a telephone. Most would rather put their tuppence towards a glass of beer than a telephone conversation.'

'Oh, you're impossible.' Amy threw up her hands.

Any further argument was stifled when they heard a sharp rap on the front door.

Amy got to her feet and smoothed down her dress.

'That'll be your date,' said Mrs Rowlings.

'It's not my date, it's Bodkin.'

Amy tutted as she checked herself in the hall mirror. Satisfied with her appearance she grabbed her coat, picked up her bag and opened the front door.

'Hello, Amy,' Bodkin took a step forward but Amy put a hand on his chest and pushed him back.

'Dad's eating tripe,' she said. 'It's not a pretty sight.' She ushered the detective down the path to the front gate. 'Please tell me you're not a lover of tripe, Bodkin.'

'I hear too much of it in my daily life to ever want to eat it,' Bodkin replied.

In the car, Amy didn't waste any time in asking about the post mortem. Bodkin was expecting to be quizzed and immediately gave Amy a distilled version of the findings.

'The doctor's report marked it down as a suspicious death. He suspects poison, but of course he can't give a definitive cause of death, and even after the post mortem, it's still not clear what he died of. He was poisoned for sure, the pathologist said that in his opinion, strychnine was the agent used, but he can't be a hundred percent certain until he gets the toxicology results back from the lab. That might be next week now as the lab is in Gillingham and they hardly ever prioritise our tests no matter how important they are.'

'You said not clear? What do you mean?'

'He bashed the back of the head with some force so that may have been the cause of his death or at least contributed to it.'

'So, the head wound was caused when he was thrashing around in spasm?'

'More than likely.'

'Hmm.' Amy thought for a moment. 'Any news on the missing wine bottle?'

The detective shook his head.

'Maybe the killer took it with him.'

Bodkin nodded slowly. 'We can't be certain it's a him. Because we're dealing with poison there's a fair to middling chance that a woman was involved.'

'But he was carried to the bench after he died, so it may not have been the modern equivalent of Lucrezia Borgia.'

'There are many more instances of female poisoners, Amy. It was rife in the Victorian age.'

'Well, thank goodness we're no longer living in the Victorian age and women can be trusted to leave the arsenic in the fly paper,' she retorted, tipping her head to the side as she looked at Bodkin. 'Having said that, Agatha knows a thing or two about women taking revenge. She isn't averse to using a dollop of poison in her stories and she builds many of them around true cases.'

Amy smiled to herself, then returned to the subject of the wine bottle.

'Where were we? ... oh yes, the killer, be it him or her, probably disposed of the evidence then?'

'That's the theory we're working on. We think whoever it was, didn't want to leave the bottle lying around if the strychnine had been mixed with the wine. There may have been prints on it.'

Amy rubbed her hands together. 'Ooh, a proper mystery. Something to get our teeth into?'

Bodkin rolled his eyes to the heavens and breathed in deeply.

'I just hope Acting Superintendent Laws has had an early night. I dread to think what he'd have to say if he saw us arriving together.'

The vicarage was a large, early eighteenth-century building set back in grounds that bordered the yew-flanked wall of the churchyard.

'It's a big place for two people,' Bodkin said as he took in the impressive Neo-Classical frontage. 'It must cost a fortune to maintain.'

They stepped into the Adam style square porch and Bodkin rattled the iron door knocker. It was a full minute before Mrs Gatting opened the door.

She was an attractive woman with high cheek bones and full lips, her brown hair was parted in the centre with soft curls hanging down to her neck. She wore a plain black knee length skirt with a white blouse.

'Mrs Gatting? I'm Detective Sergeant Bodkin, I telephoned earlier.'

Mrs Gatting suddenly began to shake. She put her hands to her mouth and stared wide eyed at Bodkin.

'I didn't do it! It wasn't me,' she cried.

CHAPTER NINE

'No one is accusing you of anything, Mrs Gatting,' Bodkin said quietly. 'I'm just here to check a few details.'

The housekeeper nodded, then looked at Amy quizzically.

'This is Miss Rowlings, she's come to collect the sermons I mentioned.'

'I've seen you in church, dear.' Mrs Gatting stood back to allow the pair to enter.

The hall was spacious but shabby, with faded, plaster walls and a carpet square sat on dingy looking grey tiles. On the right-hand side, a staircase with a rounded banister and a threadbare, red patterned carpet led upward. Built into the wall at the bottom of the staircase was a peeling, green painted door. In contrast, on the left-hand side of the hall were three, new-looking, varnished oak doors. A fifth door that had been left ajar, faced them from the far end of the hall.

'Please, come this way,' Mrs Gatting said nervously as she led them across the carpet square, past a side table with a black telephone and a thin telephone directory sitting on its highly polished surface.

'Can I offer you a cup of tea? I was just about to make one.'

Bodkin shook his head but Amy nodded.

'That would be lovely.'

Mrs Gatting took them through the open door and into an oblong, lime green, kitchen. She held out a hand to offer them a seat at the large pine table, then picking up the kettle from the Aga range, she shook it before holding it under the tap to add more water. Placing the kettle on the hotplate, she turned back towards them with a sad smile.

'It's all very strange. I keep expecting to see the vicar sitting there waiting for his supper.'

Bodkin nodded, a sympathetic look on his face.

'This must have been a big shock to you.'

'Devastating. It's a terrible thing to have happened. I don't know how anyone could do something like that to him.'

'Like what, Mrs Gatting?'

'The poison, oh, I've heard the rumours, I've had telephone calls from a few friends. Are you saying they were wrong?'

'We've said nothing official yet, because to be honest we don't know what happened, and we won't know until the test results come back.' Bodkin was silent as the housekeeper spooned tea into a large, brown pot. 'But, while we're on the subject of poison, do you keep any on the premises?'

'Yes, we've got rat poison. We keep it in the cupboard under the sink.' Mrs Gatting pointed to a cupboard door.

'Do you mind if I have a look?'

Mrs Gatting crouched down, opened the cupboard then moved out of the way while Bodkin bent down to look inside. Reaching in he pulled out a red tin with the words, RAT GONE!

on the front. Holding it carefully, he read the printed information on the back of the tin.

'Sodium Cyanide,' he read.

'We mix it with water and brush it onto pieces of fruit, generally apples or pears but we sometimes soak grains in it and leave a saucer on the floor.'

Amy shuddered.

'Do you get them in the house too?'

'Sometimes, yes, they try to get into the food cupboard but we tend to find most of them in the cellar. We searched and searched to find out how they get in but despite blocking a few things off they still manage to find a way.'

'Do you ever use any other sort of poison?' Bodkin asked, peering a little deeper into the cupboard.

'Not any more. The reverend told me they'd tried arsenic but the rats seemed to get to know the smell and wouldn't go near it after a while.'

'Have you ever used strychnine?'

'When I first came here, about six years ago. He had a tin of it in the cellar, but I couldn't bear to see them suffer like that. I came down one night after hearing a screeching noise and found two of the poor things having convulsions on the kitchen floor. I told the vicar I wasn't happy about it. Look, I know they're only rats but if we're going to kill them, they deserve a better death than that. They're God's creatures after all. Cyanide seems to be quicker and less painful for them.'

'Do you still have the strychnine container?'

'No, Harold... Mr Villiers disposed of the tin. I'm not sure what he did with it.'

Bodkin placed the canister carefully back into the cupboard, closed the door then washed his hands thoroughly. After drying them on a towel that was hanging from a drawer handle, he walked across to the table and watched as Mrs Gatting poured tea for herself and Amy.

'If you have no objections, I'll like to take a quick look in the vicar's study. Just in case there's anything in there that might give us a clue as to what happened to him. I'd like to see his bedroom too.'

'His bedroom?'

Bodkin nodded. 'I have to check. There could be a threatening letter up there. Victims often get warning notes before they are attacked and they don't tend to let the people around them know about them.'

'I see, well, I suppose that will be alright, you being a policeman and all. I'll show you the way.'

'There's no need, Mrs Gatting. You enjoy your tea. Just point me in the general direction.'

'The study is the first door on the left as you came into the hall. His bedroom is up the stairs, third door on the left. Don't go into any of those rooms on the right-hand side. A couple of them aren't safe.'

'Really?'

Mrs Gatting rubbed her palms together then locked her fingers and pushed her hands out in front making her knuckles crack.

'When I first came here the house was a disgrace, it had hardly been touched since it was built a couple of hundred years ago. The last time it had been decorated was in Victorian times. There was only a very rudimentary bathroom, the lavatory was out the back, you could sit there listening to the river lapping on the banks on quiet nights. Anyway, when I moved in, they decided that they'd do something about the state of the place, so they refitted the kitchen, installed a bath and lavatory in one of the bedrooms upstairs and redecorated two bedrooms and three of the five rooms downstairs. Basically, as you come in, if it's on the left-hand side of the house it's been refurbished, if it's on the right, it hasn't. Some of the floorboards up there are rotten. There was a leak in the roof that was only partially mended. The wallpaper is falling off the walls and the glass is broken in one of the bedroom windows.'

'Why didn't they finish it, it's such a lovely house?' Amy asked.

'I'm not sure if they ran out of money or they thought that as there were only two of us living here, they would just do enough to make us comfortable.'

When Bodkin had left the room, Amy picked up her cup and sipped at her tea.

'What was he like, the reverend? Was he a difficult man to look after?'

'Not a lot different to any other man I would imagine,' the housekeeper replied. 'Why do you ask?'

'Oh, I'm sorry, it's just that he did have a bit of a feisty reputation. My father got on with him really well though, he won't have a word said against him so it's a bit of a paradox.'

'He had his faults, that being one of them.' Mrs Gatting nodded towards a side table underneath which was a wooden crate that had been stamped with a wine producer's logo. 'He couldn't get enough of that.' She looked up at the clock on the wall then got to her feet. 'Excuse me for a moment, it's time for my insulin shot.'

The housekeeper crossed the kitchen, opened a drawer and lifted out a china dish containing a large steel tipped syringe. Placing it carefully on the counter she put her hand in the drawer again and pulled out a small glass bottle. Removing the top, she dipped the needle into the bottle and drew out a measured amount. Turning her back on Amy, she pulled her blouse from her skirt and injected herself in the stomach. Placing the syringe carefully on the counter she adjusted her clothing and turned back to face Amy.

'I'm sorry about that. I generally do it in private but it's been half an hour since I had my tea. I have to do this three times a day, it's a bit of a pain but it keeps me alive.'

'It must be a bit of a faff. How long have you been diabetic?' Amy asked.

Mrs Gatting tipped hot water from the kettle into a saucepan and set it on the hotplate, then picking up the syringe with a pair of tongs she placed it gently into the hot water.

'I have to sterilise it every evening,' she explained. 'Erm, I was diagnosed in nineteen-twenty-seven, the year before my Alfred was killed. I was lucky, the boffins had discovered insulin about five years before and it had just made its way over here from America. Had I become ill any earlier I'd almost certainly have died. Diabetes was a death sentence.'

'Oh my goodness, I had no idea they'd discovered it such a short time ago,' Amy said. 'Do you get your prescription from the local chemist?'

'Yes, I pick it up every week with the reverend's indigestion powders. My sister makes up the prescriptions for us... She's a pharmacist,' she added, proudly.

'That's good news for you,' said Amy with a smile. 'Do you get a discount?'

The housekeeper snorted. 'Sadly not, although she's a trained pharmacist she only works for Mr Hales, she doesn't own the business.'

'That's a very handy relative to have.'

'Oh yes, she can make up a remedy for anything from back-ache to a hangover. She helped me such a lot when I lost my Arthur. I had pretty much given up on life.'

'That must have been an awful time for you. Reverend Villiers suffered a bereavement too, I believe.'

Mrs Gatting nodded.

'The poor man. He lost the love of his life to the Spanish flu, he never really got over it.' She leaned towards Amy and her voice dropped to little more than a whisper. 'I think that's why he turned to drink in the end. He couldn't cope.'

Before Amy could reply, Bodkin walked back into the kitchen.

'Do you know, I think I might have that cup of tea after all.'

As Mrs Gatting turned away, Bodkin looked at Amy, then shook his head as he sat down.

'Nothing,' he mouthed.

CHAPTER TEN

Mrs Gatting poured out tea for Bodkin and another cup for Amy and herself, then sat down at the kitchen table opposite the detective. Bodkin took a sip of his tea and nodded in appreciation.

'Mrs Gatting,' he began cautiously. 'I know what I'm about to ask may seem intrusive and upsetting and I'm sorry about that but I do have to ask these questions. If I don't someone else will.'

Mrs Gatting fiddled with her wedding ring as she nodded.

'That's fine, Mr Bodkin, I've got nothing to hide.'

'Firstly, could you tell me about your relationship with Reverend Villiers?'

'There's not a lot to tell really,' the housekeeper said. 'I cooked and cleaned for him, ironed his clothes, that was about it really.'

'Did you get on?'

'As well as anyone can under these circumstances, I

suppose. He wasn't an easy man to live with, really, especially when he was in drink.'

'So, it was merely a working relationship?'

'Of course, it was!' Mrs Gatting snapped. 'What are you trying to insinuate?'

Bodkin leaned forward and placed his hands on the table.

'I'm asking if your role was more than just a housekeeper, Mrs Gatting.'

Amy shot him a quick glance but Bodkin ignored it and kept his eyes on the housekeeper's face.

'No! and I'm really not happy with this line of questioning.'

Bodkin leaned back in his seat.

'I did say the questions might be uncomfortable. So, you are saying that you were not in any sort of physical relationship with Mr Villiers?'

'That's EXACTLY what I'm saying.'

'What about emotionally. Did he confide in you, discuss things about his personal life?'

'No, he was a very private person. He did mention Emily a few times when he was still coherent, but never when he was completely sober. I've heard him muttering her name when he's fallen asleep in his armchair a few times and I've heard him scream out in the middle of the night more than once.'

'Emily was his fiancée I take it? The girl who died of the flu?'

Mrs Gatting nodded.

'He had no other personal problems that you knew about? No arguments, no enemies, no one who would want to get back at him for any reason?'

'No, I can't think of anything. He did rub people up the wrong way at times. He wasn't universally liked, but I'm sure no one actually hated him, certainly not enough to kill him.'

Bodkin sipped more tea, then holding his cup in front of his chest, he looked into it as though reading the tea leaves.

'Did the Reverend Villiers ever try anything on with you?'

Mrs Gatting's head shot back, she glared at Bodkin.

'NO!'

'He didn't accidentally brush against you. Get closer than you'd like him to get? You never found him hanging around the bathroom door?'

Amy rolled her eyes to the ceiling.

'Bodkin!' she hissed.

'You people have very sick minds, Sergeant Bodkin,' Mrs Gatting said with a steely edge to her voice.

'Please answer the question.'

'No!' the housekeeper spat. 'Nothing like that ever happened.'

'Thank you,' Bodkin waved his tea cup and smiled encouragingly.

'Any chance of a refill?'

Mrs Gatting sniffed.

'I don't know if you really deserve one after that.'

Bodkin sighed.

'Mrs Gatting, I repeat, I did warn you that the questioning was going to be uncomfortable. It's one of the reasons I wanted Miss Rowlings here with me.'

The housekeeper's shoulders slumped.

'It's all right, I suppose you do have to check these things.' She looked at Amy and smiled softly. 'Thank you for coming along. I do feel a little more relaxed with you here.'

Amy smiled back. 'I'm happy to help in any way I can.'

They sat in silence while Mrs Gatting took the pan off the hotplate and placed it on the work surface to cool.

'What are you cooking?' Bodkin asked, sniffing the air.

'Nothing edible,' Mrs Gatting replied. 'It's my insulin syringe. It has to be sterilised regularly.'

'I'm sorry, I didn't mean to—'

'Intrude? It's a little bit late for that.'

'That told you,' Amy whispered, prodding Bodkin on the arm with her finger.

When the kettle was back on the hotplate, the housekeeper turned around to face the policeman. She clasped her hands and held them in front of her stomach and pursed her lips.

'Is that the last of the personal questions?'

Bodkin shook his head.

'I'm afraid not, but it's the last of the questions regarding your relationship with Villiers.'

Mrs Gatting sighed and emptied the tea pot into the sink.

'What now?'

'Are you in any kind of relationship at the moment?'

The housekeeper rocked her head slowly from side to side.

'No, but, yes, possibly.'

Bodkin looked puzzled.

'Was that a yes or a no?'

'It's complicated. Things haven't really got very far to be honest. Peter is keen, I know that, but he doesn't really understand women.'

Amy tipped her head and looked at Bodkin.

'He's not alone in that, Mrs Gatting. Not many of them do.'

The housekeeper gave a quick laugh. 'Hopeless, aren't they? I could see there was something between you two as soon as Mr Bodkin sat down.'

Amy looked shocked. 'THERE ISN'T!' she said, too quickly.

'It's the way you look at each other. The little smiles, the glances. There's something there, even if he doesn't realise it yet.'

Bodkin coughed; Amy blushed.

'So you see, that's how it is with Peter and me. He's a lovely man, very caring and considerate. He's polite, not the slightest bit pushy, but he doesn't know how to move things on to the next level.'

Bodkin, who had recovered his poise, looked up with interest.

'Okay, who is Peter and how long has he been stuck on this level?'

'Peter is the church groundsman, gravedigger, window cleaner and general handyman. Not all of those things are in his job title, he's only employed to look after the graveyard, dig new graves when needed. Basically, he keeps things looking tidy but he does help out around the place if we need him to. The vicar isn't... wasn't a very practical person when it came to things like that.'

Mrs Gatting spooned tea into the pot and added the boiling water.

'Oh, and he's been stuck on this level for about three months. I've dropped a few hints that I'd be happy for it to get a little bit more involved, but as yet, he either hasn't noticed them or he's ignoring them.'

'He won't have noticed,' said Amy. 'You could hold up a big sign saying, What are you waiting for? and he'd think you wanted him to cut the grass or something. He sounds a typical bloke.'

Bodkin massaged his forehead with the fingers of his right hand.

'Does Peter come into the house often?'

'Every morning and most evenings. I cook him breakfast every day before he starts work and he pops in to say goodnight before he heads off home when he's finished for the day.'

'Did the vicar have breakfast?'

'Oh my goodness, no. He could never face food in the morning, not after the drink. No, he used to have his indigestion powder in a glass of warm water and that would be it.'

'Indigestion powder?' Bodkin raised one eyebrow.

'He'd been taking them for just over a week. My sister makes something up for him. She called it an antiacid or something like that. I pick them up along with my insulin. I was telling Amy about it while you were looking around the place. To be honest, I think he was developing an ulcer because the powders didn't seem to help much. They made him worse if anything, but my sister insisted he persevere with them for another week or so before trying a different remedy.'

'What were the powders made up of? How were they presented? Were they in a jar, a packet?'

'They came in a paper bag. The powders were measured out and placed in little paper wraps. As to what's in them, I have no idea, you'll have to ask my sister.' The housekeeper got to her feet. 'There are still a few in the drawer, I keep them with my insulin.'

Bodkin followed Mrs Gatting across the room and waited as she opened a drawer.

'There.' She pointed to a paper bag with the Hales logo printed on the side. Inside was a small stash of paper wraps, each one about two inches long and an inch wide.

The detective picked up one of the paper wraps and sniffed at it. Pulling a face, he sniffed again, then dropped it back into the bag and slipped it into his pocket.

'More testing for the lab,' he said, almost to himself.

Mrs Gatting slid the drawer shut, then picked up the teapot and carried it to the table where she set it down on a grey, wicker coaster in the centre.

Bodkin returned to his seat and resumed the questioning.

'So, back to Peter. He has breakfast, says goodnight before he goes home, do you see him at any other time?'

'He occasionally drops in when he's on his way to the pub.'

'How occasionally would that be. Is he a big drinker too?'

'I don't think he's that big a drinker, at least I've never seen him the worst for wear. He goes out most Saturday and Wednesday nights.'

'He sounds even more like you, Bodkin,' Amy said grinning. 'They're your nights out too, maybe you should get together, have a lad's night.'

Bodkin pursed his lips as he looked across at her.

'He might not like the idea of going to the pictures with another bloke,' he said, turning back to Caroline. 'Does he live nearby? Does he have to pass the church to get to or from the pub?'

'No, he lives on the estate, Rushton Street. He walks back along Main Street to get home. On the opposite side of the road to the church. He only comes over to say hello on his way out. Sometimes he'll try to persuade me to join him, but pubs aren't my thing. I don't drink much... the odd sherry at a wedding, that sort of thing. It's the atmosphere of the pubs I don't like. They're too smoky and there's way too much tension among the men for my liking. You know a fight is going to break out before long.'

Bodkin waited for the housekeeper to pour the tea, then he added two spoons of sugar, a splash of milk and stirred it absentmindedly as he thought.

'Was Peter here last Saturday evening?' he asked.

'Yes, he popped in before going to the Dragon.'

'Was the reverend here too?'

'He was as it happens. There was a meeting at the church

hall. They were kicking around ideas for a new local children's charity, they were discussing setting up a fund to provide medication for poor children with long term medical conditions.'

'What time did that break up?'

'About eight. They came back here afterwards for a glass of wine, from what I could gather, they hadn't come to any decision on the fund.'

Bodkin leaned forward again.

'Who attended the meeting? How many people were there?'

Caroline narrowed her eyes as she concentrated.

'There were six of them including my sister.'

'Could you list their names for me?' Bodkin produced a notepad and a silver ballpoint pen from his pocket.

'Let me see. There was Doctor Frazier, he's retired now but he likes to get involved in things like this still. Mr and Mrs Brown from the café on Cherry Steet, they have an invalid daughter, hence their interest. My sister, that's Agatha Walker, her boss, Eugene Hales, the owner of the pharmacy and Constance de Vere, the councillor, it was all her idea in the first place; if I were to be cynical, I'd say she is hoping for some good publicity out of it. She's up for election again next year. She telephoned him on the Friday before the meeting, he took the call in his study. It was a long conversation too. Mr Villiers wasn't too happy about things when the phone call ended either. He ended up being couped up in his study for the rest of the night. The weather outside was foul so he couldn't take his usual after supper walk.'

Bodkin finished listing the names, then looked up and tapped his notebook with the point of his pen.

'How did these people get on with the vicar, was there any animosity at all between them?'

'Not as far as I'm aware, but then, Agatha, my sister, apart, I don't really know any of them that well. Just to nod to in passing.'

'I see,' Bodkin tapped the notebook again. 'So, all in all there were nine of you here, including the vicar. Where did they have their drinks? In his study?'

'Not at first, they were all in here to start with.'

Bodkin looked around the room.

'It must have been quite a tight squeeze.'

'They weren't here long. Mr Villiers gave them his cheap wine. I think they were hoping for some of his good stuff. There was a bottle already open from Friday night over on the table over there, but they were to be disappointed. He gave them the 'house white' as he calls it, then they all went into his study to work out a date for their next meeting.'

'I see.' Bodkin screwed the top back onto his pen, then began to tap his notebook again. 'And what was Peter doing while they were here, did he join in the conversation?'

'No, and to be honest, nor did I. The vicar made it obvious by his body language that the sooner they were gone the better he'd like it. He wanted to make a start on his own wine I think.'

Bodkin looked across the room as if picturing the scene.

'So, you and Peter were standing where?'

'Over by the side table. Peter was a love. He put my syringe on to sterilise while I sorted out some decent wine glasses for the guests. I'd just taken my insulin before they arrived.'

Bodkin folded his fingers together and rested his chin on them.

'So they left about what time? Eight-thirty...nine?'

'They were only here for half an hour or so, they were gone well before nine.'

'And what about Peter?'

'He left at the same time. But he went out the back door while they were all congregated at the front wishing each other a good night and telling each other they must get together socially.'

'You know that because?'

Mrs Gatting looked at him oddly.

'Because I was standing in the porch while they were chatting. Peter waved to me as he slipped along the side of the house.'

'Now, this may sound a strange question, Mrs Gatting, but do you have any sticks of chalk on the premises?'

'Chalk?'

Bodkin nodded.

'Yes, there's a blackboard in the church hall, Mrs Rosegarden uses it on a Sunday, there's always a couple of packets of it in there... oh, and there's a small one in the church foyer, the vicar uses... used it to list any upcoming events.'

'What colour is it?'

'The blackboard?'

'The chalk.'

'Oh, of course, sorry, it's white.'

Bodkin got slowly to his feet, stretched then yawned.

'I beg your pardon,' he said tiredly. 'Could you warn Peter that I'm going to have to have a chat with him.' He tapped his coat pocket. 'I'll get around to your sister and the rest of the committee soon.'

Mrs Gatting smiled nervously at the detective.

'So, have you done with me? You believe me when I say I had nothing to do with it?'

Bodkin nodded to her.

'I may need to speak to you again to clarify a few things, but yes, for now at least, that's it.'

Amy got to her feet and smiled at Caroline.

'It's been lovely to meet you at last. I've seen you in church so many times.' She walked out into the hall alongside the housekeeper. 'Could I get those sermons now or would you like me to call back at another time?'

'Oh goodness me, I'd forgotten all about those.' Caroline turned towards the stairs. 'They're up here, follow me.'

She led them up the stairs and along the threadbare, red carpeted corridor, pointing out the unsafe bedrooms as they passed. At the fourth door on the right, she stopped and twisted the brass door knob.

'It's a bit stuffy in here, the damp has got into the wallpaper,' she advised. She opened the door, flicked on a Bakelite switch and an old-fashioned tungsten bulb flickered into life.

Amy immediately caught her breath. She looked around the room at the intricately patterned, faded green, flock wallpaper with is huge areas of blackish damp. The fabric was peeling from the walls in many places and large patches of mould were clinging to the bare plaster where the paper had come away. At the far end of the room a window with a broken pane, was open.

'We have to keep that open or you can't breathe in here,' Mrs Gatting said. 'I used to sit in that bay and read when I first arrived but after half an hour or so I'd start to get a headache. We leave the window open to get a bit of air circulating.' She held a hand over her mouth and pointed to three piles of cardboard box files. 'Let's grab them and get out of here. No wonder the workmen didn't fancy working on this side of the house.'

There were twenty-one files in all, one for each year and one containing speeches. Amy stuck her chin on top of the seventh of her share of the boxes and carried them out of the room. As soon as she was in the cleaner atmosphere of the corridor, she took a deep breath and let the air out slowly.

'Thank goodness we haven't got to go back in there any time soon. The air is foul.'

They carried the box files down the stairs and Amy and Bodkin loaded them into the boot of the black Morris.

The housekeeper stood in the doorway and waved to them as they bid her a good night. Once they were inside the car, Bodkin switched on the lights and fired up the engine.

'You were incredibly hard on her, Bodkin,' Amy said sternly as the detective pulled away from the forecourt. 'You could have been a little more subtle with your questioning. I know you have to get answers but surely you can be a little more... nuanced in the way you approached it.'

Bodkin looked askance.

'We'd still be there tomorrow morning if I'd been more nuanced about it. Why go around the houses to get to the point? It only prolongs the agony. No, I tend to favour the direct approach. You can tell a lot by the way they respond to a difficult question.'

'So, do you think she had anything to do with it?'

'I'm not convinced she didn't, let's put it that way. She had the opportunity and she also had the means. I just can't figure out a motive at the moment. That syringe would be very handy if you wanted to inject something through a wine cork, and those powders are troubling.' He tapped the side of his head. 'Something is niggling away at me but I can't quite put my finger on what it is.'

'So, you'll be coming back then?'

'I think you can count on that, Amy.'

CHAPTER ELEVEN

On Tuesday, after tea, Amy sat in her room listening to Bing Crosby sing, You Must Have Been A Beautiful Baby, as she laid out another sheet of her father's typewriter copy paper on her dressing table, and tried for a fourth time, to design a simple business card. Two sheets had been screwed up into balls on the floor before she hit on a design she liked. Smiling to herself, she folded the sheet, stuck it in the pocket of her cardigan, took Bing's recording off her gramophone, then went down to the hall and grabbed her coat from the hook on the wall.

'Mum, I'm off to Alice's for a while, see you later, I won't be late back.'

Alice was trying to placate a clearly irritated Martha when Amy stepped into the kitchen at the farm.

'Hello, dearest, you're looking a tad stressed,' Amy said as she took off her coat and hung it on the big hook on the back of the door.

'She's been grumpy all day. It's not just me this time, she's annoyed with everyone.'

Alice had had a difficult relationship with her baby from day one. Her labour had been long and traumatic, Martha finally arriving as Alice lay sprawled on the huge oak kitchen table. After steadfastly refusing to breast feed, Martha had finally settled on formula milk but for some reason, that Alice found incredibly frustrating, her baby seemed to prefer anyone else's company but hers.

'Do you want me to take her for a few minutes?' Amy asked, holding out her arms.

Alice shook her head.

'No, thanks, love. I'm determined to get Martha to realise that I'm her mum and I have the right to hold and feed her.'

Amy gave her a sad look.

'Good luck with that, my darling. She's ten months old now, you think she'd have picked up on that by now.'

'She's not as bad as she used to be,' Alice said defensively. 'She puts up with me these days, she just prefers to spend her time with other people.' Alice looked over her shoulder to Miriam. 'Like Miriam for instance. Mind you, she's got the knack with babies, she had four of her own.'

On hearing Miriam's name, Martha began to grizzle, then began to perform a forced, angry cry. Alice held her to her shoulder and patted her back, making soothing noises but Martha wasn't about to give up that easily. Eventually, the angry yells turned into angry sobs and the tears began to roll down her cheeks as she kicked at Alice's stomach.

'Come on, pass her over,' Miriam said softly. 'No point letting her work herself into a state.'

Alice sighed and passed her baby to Miriam. She was right. Martha wouldn't give up until she got her way. At least she would spend half an hour or so with Alice now and if she knew they were alone in the house and couldn't be passed on to anyone else, she was happy to stay in her mother's arms even longer than that.

Alice walked to the sink and filled the kettle.

'So, what's the latest news? How did it go at the vicarage last night?'

'It was very interesting as it happens,' Amy said and began to relate everything that had happened.

'I'm lucky to be alive, I think. That bedroom stank. I could hardly get my breath.'

'Damp is a terrible thing, it causes a fungus to spread and the spores of that can cause real harm,' Miriam said as she rocked Martha in her arms. Miriam was in a relationship of sorts with a local builder. 'John says a lot of the older houses in the town are riddled with it. That's why so many kids have breathing problems.'

Amy shook her head.

'If it's anything like that bedroom, I'm surprised they can breathe at all. It was horrible.'

Alice poured out three mugs of tea, put Miriam's on the wooden tip on the arm of her chair, then passed a mug to Amy and sat down herself, holding hers between both hands.

'You mentioned a Peter Kissman when you were telling your story. If it's the same man I'm thinking of, he moved here about ten years ago. He's been working at the church for a while now but he worked for Connors' before that. He helped do some road works on the lane when he was with them. Mum used to make tea and sandwiches for them when they were installing the new drains. He seemed to be a very nice man.'

Alice's mother had been weakened by Alice's birth and had finally succumbed to her frailties a couple of years previously.

Her father had been devastated by her death and had turned to drink, dying of broken heart a year later.

Amy suddenly remembered her business card design and pulling the sheet of paper from her pocket she laid it out in front of Alice with a flourish.

Alice picked it up, studied it, then looked over the top of the sheet with the sort of look on her face that Amy clearly thought meant she was impressed with the design.

'It's lovely. I really like it.'

'Thank you, dear heart, it took me all of twenty minutes.'

'ARIA Investigations. Agent Amy Rowlings,' Alice read from the sheet. 'I like that, but what does, ARIA stand for. Isn't it something they do in opera?'

Amy's face lit up.

'It stands for... are you ready for this, it's absolutely brilliant?'

Alice nodded.

'AMY ROWLINGS INVESTIGATIONS AGENCY! Isn't it sublime?'

Alice nodded again.

'It really is very clever.'

Amy looked smug.

'But...'

'Oh-oh, there's a but?'

'I was just thinking,' said Alice slowly, 'that you used the word investigations, twice.'

Amy frowned.

'No I haven't.'

'Yes you have.' Alice pointed to the sheet of paper.

'It says, AMY ROWLINGS INVESTIGATIONS AGENCY, then underneath you used the word, INVESTIGATIONS again.'

'Ah, but I didn't use it on the first line, that just says, ARIA, so it reads, ARIA INVESTIGATIONS, you see?'

'Not really,' Alice looked puzzled.

'ARIA is just an acronym of Amy Rowlings, blah blah blah. I doubt anyone will ever ask what it stands for, so ARIA INVESTIGATIONS will be all anyone ever sees really.'

'Ah, I get it now.'

Amy patted her best friend on the arm.

'Well done.'

'I think it sounds great,' added Miriam as she stood up to carry Martha through to the parlour to put her in her downstairs cot.

'There's another thing,' said Alice suddenly.

Amy sighed.

'Now what?'

'There's no address and no telephone number. How is anyone ever going to find you?'

Amy sighed again.

'You've hit my bent nail right on the head, darling. That's the only flaw in my reasoning. I can't put my address down because someone might just turn up at the front door and Dad would have a fit. As for the other, well, I don't have a telephone number so I can't put one on the card.'

'You can use mine,' said Alice, brightly.

'No, I couldn't... could I? Do you mean it? Oh, Alice you're the brightest star in the heavens.' She threw herself at Alice and grabbed her in a bear hug. 'But, are you sure you don't mind, it's for farm use really.'

'Of course I don't mind. Just don't put my address on it. I don't want people turning up at my door asking for an investigator to spy on their wayward husband either.' She pulled a face at Amy, then continued. 'I don't mind being a telephone answering service for you though and I'm sure Miriam won't mind either if I'm out with the pigs when the call comes in.'

Amy hugged her again. 'You really are the best friend a girl could have.'

'There is one more thing I just thought of,' Alice said. 'Sorry.'

'Go on then, where else does my master plan fall down?'

'Well,' Alice said slowly. 'Where are you going to meet your clients to hear about their sordid affairs?'

'I doubt there'll be any clients to be honest, Alice. I'm only really setting this up so I can get inside the police station without that big bully Laws having a go at me. I'm not going to hand the cards out willy-nilly. I've got my job at the Mill to think about, I'm not going to give that up any time soon so if anyone does want me to find their missing pooch or uncover details of their spouse's meanderings, I'd have to explain that I could only ever work on the case at weekends, and no one would want to pay me for that. No, this is just for Laws' benefit. Bodkin told me that the police use trusted private investigators to help them solve cases and I'm going to get myself on that list of trusted investigators one way or another.'

'It's a good plan, but why bother buying a stack of business cards if you aren't going to hand them out?'

'Credentials, my dear, credentials. He's not going to believe I work as a gumshoe unless I can hand over a card. They all do it in the movies. Charlie Chan has his credentials and Agatha writes about Poirot handing out his business cards all the time. It's the done thing in the detective world, all the pros have them. In theory I only need one card and possibly one as a spare in case the girls in Laws' office lose the original. No one is going to print just two cards for me though, so I'm going to have to get them done in bulk. One lot should last me the rest of my life, unless I do make it big and can afford to give up working at the Mill.'

'Gumshoe, I love that. Amy the gumshoe.'

Amy grinned. 'Only my shoes will be clear of gum and will preferably be of the Oxford variety.'

'So, when are you getting them done, are you using Walton's? Use my name as a reference if you like, though I doubt they'll remember me, I've only ever had one batch of two hundred and fifty from them.'

'Yes, I'm using them, I like the way they did your cards. Bodkin's looks very similar to that so they may print for the police too. I'm nipping over on Saturday morning after I've checked out Brigden's for a new dress and been to see my uncle Maurice. He's got a new stock of records in.'

'Ooh, that's exciting. I wonder if he's got that Bing Crosby, Alexander's Ragtime Band? I read about it in the Photoplay magazine you lent me last month.'

'I really don't know what he's got until I get there. If he's got it, I'll grab a copy for you. He might well have it, he knows I love a bit of Bing.'

Alice grinned.

'Do you want the money now?'

'No, dear heart. I'll take a risk and trust you for it.'

After more tea and a chat about the farm and its workforce, Amy grabbed her coat and set off back up Long Lane towards home.

Lying in bed that night she pulled the card design from under her pillow and read the words aloud.

'ARIA INVESTIGATIONS. Agent Amy Rowlings.'

Still holding the sheet of paper in her hands, she fell fast asleep.

CHAPTER TWELVE

On Saturday morning, Amy got up early and caught the eight-thirty bus into town so that she could be first in the queue outside Brigden's. There was always a queue, Saturday was the day that the new stock was put on the rails.

Brigden's Nearly New Fashion Store was a small shop just off the High Street. It was set up like one of the posh designer stores in London and carried a stock of 'labelled' items, many of which had only been worn once, sometimes, not at all. The items marked seconds, were as good as most garments from lesser factories that had been marked as perfect.

Once inside, Amy hurried to her favourite bargain rail where most of the dresses had been worn at least once but you'd never have been able to tell.

To her disappointment there was nothing she really liked in her size, so she wandered around the store looking at the other rails although she knew she'd never be able to afford the prices. On the rail marked factory seconds (labels) she found a blue patterned, mid-calf length, bias cut dress that she knew would accentuate her waist and fit nicely over her hips. She had lusted over one very similar to it last summer but it had eventually been sold for just under two pounds.

Amy held the dress of her dreams in front of her as she looked into the full-length mirror, then closed her eyes and imagined herself wearing it. When she opened them again, she found Sharon, a girl who worked in the store and who had become something of a friend over the last eighteen months, standing behind her.

'It's lovely, Amy. It really suits you.'

'Thank you, Sharon, but I can't afford it.'

'You haven't even checked how much it is yet.'

Amy laughed.

'I know, but I don't have to, it will be way out of my price range.'

'Do you want to know; it might surprise you?'

'No, I'll only get upset about it.' Amy turned to hang the dress back on the rail.

'It's thirty shillings.'

'Thirty? That is a good price but still way beyond what I can afford to spend on a dress. Ten shillings is more my level, fifteen tops.'

'I'm sure we can find a way around it, Amy.'

'How do you mean?'

'Well, we can put it aside until you've paid it off. Say, three weeks at ten shillings or four weeks at eight. I know that's two shilling more but you know what Madam is like.' Sharon flicked her head to where the owner of the store was working on her books at the counter.

Amy sucked on her bottom lip.

'No, honestly, I can't afford it, and even if I could, I wouldn't be able to wear it very often. I mean, where would you wear a dress like that around here?' She hung the dress back on the rail. 'It was just nice to dream for a moment.'

When Amy left Brigden's she walked smartly around to the post office and drew out a pound from her savings account. She was desperately saving up to buy an HMV, electric powered radiogram. Her uncle Maurice had told her he could get a good quality second hand model for about thirty-five pounds. Amy had eighteen in the bank now that she had taken out the pound to pay for the business cards.

From the post office, Amy went to her favourite café on High Street and sat for twenty minutes sipping an espresso and watching the Saturday shopping crowds passing by on the pavement. From there she walked around to her uncle Maurice's house. Amy loved visiting her uncle. He was an importer of sheet music and 78 records from the USA. He let Amy buy what she wanted at cost price and often made a present of a record to his favourite niece.

When Amy asked him about the new Bing Crosby record, he grinned and pulled a copy of it from behind his back. Amy gave him a hug and told him that the record was in fact for Alice. She then told him about the business cards and the birth of her new sleuthing enterprise.

'So, I can't afford a record for myself this week, Uncle Maurice. I really do have to buy these cards if I want to realise my dreams and help the police solve major crimes.'

Maurice hugged her again and told her he was absolutely positive that with her energy and drive she could achieve whatever she wanted in life. Then he gave her the copy of the Bing Crosby record for Alice and a copy of the Jimmy Dorsey version of Change Partners that she had been desperately trying to get hold of for months. She had been offered the Fred Astaire version but liked the Dorsey one much better.

'Pay me in a week or two when you're not trying to build a business empire,' he said with a smile.

'Uncle Maurice, I can pay you for Alice's record because she'll give me the money as soon as I hand it over. It's just my own money I've got to be careful with. I've just seen the most beautiful dress in Brigden's and they offered to save it and let me pay over a month but I'm still saving up for my radiogram, and the Mill are shutting for a week over Easter to get some maintenance work done so I'll be short of my production bonus the week after. They'll pay our basic hourly rate but that's all.' She opened her purse and handed her uncle the five shillings Alice owed for her Bing Crosby record. 'Not that I'm complaining. It will be lovely to have a whole week off, we normally only get the two-week shutdown at the end of July.'

Uncle Maurice slipped the two records into a paper bag with his own company logo printed on the side and handed it to her.

'Pay me when you have it. Don't leave yourself short. Okay?'

Amy gave her uncle another hug and with an effusive thank you, almost skipped out of the house to make her way along the half mile stretch of the Gillingham Road to Walton's Printers.

The print works was much smaller than Amy had expected it to be. It was a one storey, red brick building with a large pair of steel doors built into the side and a small office bolted onto the front. When Amy pushed open the door and walked in, she found that there was no one around. She waited a good five minutes before slipping past a walnut desk and stepping through the open door at the back, into the workshop. She was again disappointed to find that instead of a clanking, grinding series of conveyor belts, wheels and pulleys that she'd seen used by the newspaper presses in the movies, there were just four small machines on the factory floor, all of which lay idle.

She took another step into the factory, then almost screamed as a deep male voice broke the silence.

'What are you doing in here? It's a workshop not a beauty parlour.'

Amy spun around to find a thirty something man, wearing a blue pin striped suit with a white shirt and yellow spotted tie, glaring at her.

'I'm sorry, I waited for ages in the office but no one came.'

The man looked Amy up and down and then suddenly changed his tone.

'I'm sorry, I didn't mean to make you jump. I wouldn't want to startle such a beautiful young lady.' He held out his hand. 'I'm Murray Walton. I'm a partner in the company.'

Amy forced a smile as she took his hand and shook it. She'd heard similar simpering, fawning, flattery like that on many occasions from men of all ages in the Old Bull.

'I've come to see about getting some business cards printed. You come highly recommended. Alice from Mollison Farm said she wouldn't go anywhere else.'

'Alice... Alice... is that the movie star lookalike, what's her name now?'

'Alice,' Amy repeated.

'No... whosit... Rita, that's it, Rita Haywood.'

'Hayworth,' Amy corrected.

'Whatever. She's bloody gorgeous I know that.'

'She is, they both are,' Amy replied. 'Now about these cards.'

'Do you fancy a night out. Me and my mate would show you both a good time.'

‘No, I’m sorry, I’ve come to get some cards printed not to be chatted up.’

Murray’s tone suddenly changed again.

‘Suit yourself. You don’t know what you’re missing though.’

Amy fought back the urge to tell him she knew exactly what she’d be missing and both she and Alice would be relieved to have missed out on it, but she kept her fixed smile and tried to return the conversation to the matter in hand.

‘Erm, the cards.’ Amy fished out her design and handed it to Murray who glanced at it before handing it back.

‘Standard print job, nothing special there.’ He thought for a moment. ‘Standard price too seeing as my offer of a discount was refused, so that will be a pound for two hundred and fifty.’

Amy opened her purse and pulled out a pound note.

‘Minimum print run, five hundred.’

‘But I don’t need five hundred. That’s far too many,’ Amy said with a frown.

‘It’s not worth my while otherwise,’ said Murray. He looked around as a young man about Amy’s age walked into the workshop. He was a scruffy looking lad with tousled red hair. He wore a pair of inky overalls with a collarless shirt underneath.

‘Anything I can do to help, Mr Walton?’ he asked.

‘Just get the bloody Armstrong job on the presses will you, Jacobs. I want it printed and boxed by the time you leave at five.’ He looked at his watch. ‘I’d better run. Lunch date won’t wait.’ He took a long look at Amy again as if she might change her mind about the night out he had offered her. When she didn’t, he put his hand on her back and pushed her gently towards the steel doors.

‘Maybe come back when you have enough money, eh love.’

He followed Amy out of the doors, then, after treating her to a lecherous grin, he climbed into a green sports car, fired up the engine and revved it until Amy's ears hurt, then, with a wink and a wave, he shot out of the gates onto the main road.

Amy stuffed the pound note back into her purse and began to walk towards the yard gates. She stopped abruptly when she heard a voice behind her.

'Never mind that smarmy sod. Did he try it on with you? I bet he did, didn't he?'

Amy turned around to face the young man.

'He tried; he didn't get anywhere.'

'Good for you.' He held out his hand.

Amy took it and shook it. 'Jacob, is it?'

'Jacobs, first name Noah,' he replied.

'Ah, I'm sorry, I misheard. I'm Amy, Amy Rowlings.'

Noah grinned a toothy grin. Amy found herself liking him already.

'What did you come for anyway?'

'I wanted some business cards printing, but I didn't need five hundred of them so my order was refused.'

'How many do you need?'

'To be honest, two.'

Noah's laugh sounded almost melodic.

'You can't do a run for just two. It really can't be done. It's just a waste of materials.'

'I was willing to get two hundred and fifty, but he said you had a minimum print run.'

'He does, I don't,' said Noah, grinning again. 'How much did he want for the five hundred?'

'Two pounds,' Amy replied.

'And how much do you really want to spend?' Noah asked.

'As little as possible,' Amy replied. 'I'm only just starting out on this enterprise. I don't have a lot of money.'

Noah thought for a moment.

'What if I were to say I'd do you fifty for five bob.'

'Five shillings, are you serious?'

'I wouldn't offer if I wasn't.'

'And you're not going to say I have to go on a date with you to get the deal?'

'I daren't,' Noah replied seriously. 'My Denise would murder me.'

'Good for her,' Amy replied. 'I would too.'

Noah held out his hand. 'So, do we have a deal?'

Amy thought about it. 'I'm not sure, Noah. Wouldn't it be stealing?'

'Noooo,' Noah shook his head. 'I'm doing the Armstrong job this afternoon and I can use the cut off card from that job to do yours, there should be just about enough. It will only get thrown out anyway.'

'What about the ink?'

'For fifty cards. I could spit more ink than that would use up.'

Amy thought again. 'But I don't want you to get into any trouble on my account.'

'There'll be no trouble. He won't be back to lock up until five-thirty at the earliest and I'm supposed to finish at five, so he'll be getting at least half an hour out of me for free and that, surprisingly enough, is about how long it will take for me to set up your little print run.'

Amy made a quick decision, stuck out her hand and when Noah took it, shook his vigorously.

'How will I collect them and when do I pay you?' she asked.

'I'll be in the Bell tonight, about half eight with Denise, do you know it? It's great in there on a Saturday they have a jazz band on. You ought to give it a go anyway. You'd really enjoy yourself. There's a dance floor, so you could kick your heels up.'

'I know the Bell, it's on Stoney Street just off Middle Street, isn't it? I've only ever been in during the week.'

'You honestly don't know what you're missing.'

Amy frowned then laughed.

'That's the second time a man has told me that in the last few minutes.' Amy thought for a moment. 'I can't guarantee bang on eight-thirty because I'm going to the pictures with my friends. I can pop in on my way home though.'

'I'll be there until chuck out,' Noah replied. 'It's nice to meet you, Amy. When you're ready for some more you'll know where to find me.'

'I doubt I'll ever need any more to be honest.'

'Well, there's always letterheads, receipt slips, invoices. We do the lot here.'

'That sounds wonderful, thanks so much, Noah. I'll see you tonight.'

Amy started to turn away but Noah called her back.

'Erm, it might be better if I knew exactly what I was supposed to be printing.'

Amy rolled her eyes heavenwards and pulled her design from her pocket.

'The top bit on the front and the telephone number on the back with the address, please.'

Noah studied the sheet of paper and nodded to himself.

'Just, Long Lane? No building number?'

'Just Long Lane,' she repeated.

'Right, I'm on it. See you tonight,' Noah waved his hand and turned back to the workshop.

CHAPTER THIRTEEN

As Amy passed the police station on the way to the bus stop on Middle Street, she decided to call in and see Bodkin as she'd heard nothing from him at all since they left the vicarage on Monday evening.

PC Ferris was on the desk as she walked in. He was a tall man with a thin frame, friendly eyes and neatly parted brown hair. He greeted her warmly, then asked what they were all going to see at the pictures that night. Bodkin and Ferris always made up a foursome with Amy and Alice on a Saturday evening.

'It's Fred Astaire and Ginger Rogers in Swing Time, I'm really looking forward to it, Fred and Ginger are so good together on screen.'

Ferris nodded.

'I saw it in London when I went back to see my parents. Spinton is always at the back of the queue when it comes to movie releases.'

Suddenly Amy heard Bodkin's voice booming out from the offices behind Ferris.

'Cranston! Is that forensic report back from Gillingham yet? They promised we'd get it first thing.'

Amy grinned. 'Is that His Master's Voice I hear?'

Ferris grinned back. 'I'd hate to hear that coming out of my gramophone speaker.'

'Do you think I could have a quick word? It's not really that important if he's too busy though.' Amy gave Ferris her best smile.

Ferris walked around from the back of the desk and opened the door to the wating room.

'You know where his office is. It should be all right. Laws isn't around today, at least, I haven't seen him.'

Amy gave Ferris a quick peck on the cheek, then walked three quarters of the way down a long narrow corridor lined with photographs of long retired policemen. She arrived at Bodkin's office just as he stuck his head out of the door to shout for Cranston again.

'CRA... Oh, hello, Amy, this is a pleasant surprise.' He looked up and down the corridor nervously. 'Laws is in the building,' he said in a stage whisper.

Amy pulled a face. 'Oops, I'd better get back to the right side of the waiting room counter,' she said, quietly.

'No, it's all right. He's in a meeting with Chief Superintendent Grayson. He was called in urgently, I'm not sure what it's all about.'

'Shall I risk it then? I don't want to get either of us into any trouble,' she said.

Bodkin looked up and down the corridor again.

'Come in, I'm just about to make a cup of tea.'

Bodkin stood back to allow Amy to enter, then walked

around the back of his desk where an electric kettle was steaming away. He pulled two mugs from the top of a filing cabinet, then dropped two cloth tea bags into the mugs leaving the Lipton's tag hanging over the top edge and poured the boiling water directly into the cups.

'It's not as elegant as making leaf tea but it tastes the same,' he said.

'It doesn't bother me how it comes,' Amy agreed. 'They use tea bags all the time in the café in town and some of the older ladies won't use the place because of it. Alice won't use tea bags either even though I'm always nagging her to join the modern world. Tea leaves are such a faff.'

Bodkin handed her a mug and offered the sugar bowl but Amy shook her head.

'Sorry, milk's off.' He lifted a yellowing bottle from the top of the filing cabinet, sniffed at it and pulled a face. 'If you can't take it without milk we can always nip down to the canteen and get a drink there,' he sniffed the milk bottle again, 'but you're probably better off putting some of this in your mug than being that desperate.'

Amy bobbed her tea bag up and down a few times then lifted it out of the mug by the tag. She looked around for somewhere to dispose of it. Bodkin offered his waste paper bin and she dropped it on top of a few pieces of crumpled paper.

'What did you want to see me about,' Bodkin asked eventually. 'Not that it isn't a pleasure to see you for any reason.'

'I've been dying to know what's happening with the Villiers's case,' she said, sipping at her steaming mug of tea.

'The answer to that is not a lot,' Bodkin replied, taking a long glug of his own drink. 'We're still awaiting the toxicology report, we can't do a lot without it because we don't know exactly what we're looking for. It was supposed to be here first thing but it's late, as usual.'

Just then, the figure of Acting Superintendent Laws appeared in the doorframe. Amy spilt her tea on her shoes as she quickly got to her feet. Bodkin got slowly to his and nodded to this superior officer.

'Don't get up on my account,' Laws said jovially. He bowed his head towards Amy. 'Miss Rowling, it's always a pleasure.'

Amy's jaw hit her chest. This wasn't the bullying police officer she knew and loathed.

'I've just dropped in to say goodbye, Bodkin. At least for a while. I've been asked to take over as Acting Superintendent down in Maidstone. Three months initially, but we'll see how it goes. You may not have seen the last of me yet.'

'We'll all be sorry to see you go, sir,' Bodkin said with more of a grin than a smile on his face.

Laws preened. 'The Chief Superintendent will be along shortly. He'd like a word with you.' He turned to leave, then looked back at the sergeant. 'Oh, the toxicology reports are in. I believe the Chief Super had them on his desk a few moments ago. Right, I'd better be off. I've got to drop Mrs Laws at her mother's before I go, she won't be accompanying me.'

Laws turned into the corridor and began to whistle a jaunty version of, Happy Days Are Here Again as Bodkin and Amy exchanged shocked glances.

'Well, that's a turn up for the books. He was very nearly human,' Amy said.

Bodkin was still staring at the empty door frame. 'I've never seen him like that before, ever.'

Amy grinned. 'I bet Mrs Laws is dancing a merry jig too.'

Before the conversation could be turned towards Laws'

marital situation, another uniformed figure entered the office. Bodkin shot to his feet immediately.

'Chief Superintendent Grayson. Hello, sir.'

Amy swivelled in her seat, then began to stand.

'Please don't get up on my account, my dear.' He smiled at her warmly.

Grayson was a broad-shouldered man and stood at a little under six feet in height. He had a round welcoming face with a wide nose and a pair of almond shaped eyes. His uniform, although clean and well pressed, was what Miriam would describe as, lived in. He slapped the buff file he was carrying onto Bodkin's desk and sucked air through his teeth.

'Do you want the good news or the bad news, Bodkin?'

'Oh, I er, I always like the bad news first, sir, that way there's something good to follow that will cushion the blow.'

'Well, that report is the bad news. You're going to be tested to the limits with this case. It's not going to be a simple murder investigation by any stretch of the imagination.'

'I had a feeling you were going to say that, sir.'

'Now the good news. I always like handing out the good news.' Grayson beamed at Bodkin.

'You took your inspector's paper last year I believe?'

'Yes, sir. I have been offered an inspector's role, but it was down in Maidstone and I didn't want to move again so soon after arriving in Spinton.'

'Well, you're being offered it again, on an acting basis for now. You're all moving up a grade now that Laws is heading south. Harris will be Acting Chief Inspector; I know you get on with him so you'll make a good team. You're Acting Inspector, Stanley will move up to Acting Sergeant, we just need to find a new detective constable now. We're a bit light in that area.'

'Could I recommend Constable Ferris, sir. He's done his

sergeant's exam and flew through it, he's been trying to get out of uniform since before we moved up here from Gillingham, we're well blessed with beat officers and I think he'd be ideal.'

'Ferris, Ferris,' Grayson mused. 'Is he the chap on the front desk today, the one who sings at the Christmas concert? He's got a hell of a voice for a policeman; he could charm the criminals in with that voice. The female ones at least.'

'That's him, sir, I'm sure he won't let you down.'

'I'll take a look at his service record, thank you, Bodkin.' He pointed to the file on the desk and frowned. 'Nasty business that. He was a vicar for pity's sake. Be very careful with this one; it could be quite sensitive.' Grayson turned away from the desk and smiled at Amy who had just got to her feet.

'Now, young lady to what do we owe the honour?'

'This is—' Bodkin began, but was interrupted by Amy.

'I'm Amy Rowlings... from ARIA Investigations. I help the police now and then. I provide a lot of background information and I'm well known in the area so people tend to talk to me when they might not trust a police officer.'

Bodkin looked puzzled. 'ARIA?' he mouthed.

Grayson clapped his hands, then thrust his right one towards Amy.

'Excellent, though I can't say I've heard of you,' he said, as his huge palm engulfed Amy's.

'She helped us a great deal with the Handsley murder case a few weeks ago,' Bodkin put in.

'Ah, yes, I seem to remember Laws mentioning someone, wasn't she—'

'Miss Rowlings really is an asset to us, sir. ARIA are a new agency,' Bodkin said, desperately trying to derail his boss's train of thought.

Grayson beamed at Amy again.

'Good, good. Just make sure she's fully accredited, Bodkin. We don't want headquarters questioning why she's getting involved in an investigation, do we? Make sure she's registered with us.' He beamed at Amy again.

'That means you get to have a line on your business card that says Kent Police Accredited. It won't get you into a murder scene but it will allow you some leeway if we require your services.'

Grayson turned and headed for the door leaving Bodkin and Amy staring at his back, open mouthed.

'I like him,' Amy said when Grayson was out of earshot. 'He seems to be a very sensible man. I have no idea what he's doing in the police force.'

Bodkin shook his head at her, then picked up the toxicology report.

'You'd better get some cards printed. The office staff will need one when they register you. ARIA indeed.' He looked up from the buff file cover.

'AMY ROWLINGS INVESTIGATIONS AGENCYI' she said proudly.

'Very clever,' chuckled Bodkin as he opened the file. 'Very clever.'

Amy gave Bodkin a full two minutes before her curiosity became too hot to handle.

'So, what does it say, Bodkin? Come on, share and share alike, I share stuff with you remember?'

Bodkin looked up from the file as if only just realising that Amy was there.

'It's complicated,' he said.

'I can handle complicated. Come on, Bodkin, please?'

Bodkin tossed the buff file onto his desk.

'To put it simply. He was poisoned.'

'We already knew that, Bodkin. Blimey, I thought these people were exp—'

'He was poisoned by strychnine as we suspected.'

'So, what's so complicated about that?'

'He was also poisoned by arsenic.'

'Gosh!' Amy exclaimed.

'And Hemlock,' Bodkin added.

'Good grief! Someone really wanted to see the back of him, didn't they?'

'Exactly, Amy. People keep saying he had no enemies but this tells a completely different story.'

Amy took a deep breath, her eyes sparkled as she spoke again.

'This really is something to get our teeth into, isn't it? We have... eight suspects already.'

'That list will almost certainly be added to by the time we finish this investigation,' Bodkin said, wearily.

'But we've got a start, Bodkin. There were eight people in the kitchen with the vicar and the already opened bottle of wine that night. It must have been one of them if it was the wine that caused him to spasm like that.'

'Not necessarily, Amy. We don't have the wine bottle and even though the post mortem said there was wine in his stomach, we can't say conclusively that poison was administered that way. We don't have the bottle, so we can't test it.'

'It's a thesis though, Bodkin,' Amy said. 'Have you had any word back about those paper wraps yet?'

'Yes, I got that yesterday. 'Basically, it's sodium bicarbonate. Simple baking powder plus dried papaya plant. It's a common remedy for stomach complaints, the thing is, three of the five wraps were contaminated with arsenic.'

'Oh my goodness... the vicar hadn't been taking them for very long, had he? Mrs Gatting said she suspected that he had an ulcer.'

Amy rubbed her hands together as she thought.

'The powders were an excellent means of getting arsenic into him. How many people knew he was taking them, and who had access to the wraps?'

'That shouldn't be too hard to figure out, but God alone knows how they got the hemlock into him too.'

'Bodkin!' Amy held up a warning finger. 'I've told you before. Don't blaspheme.'

Bodkin waved away her complaint and rubbed his forehead with the palm of his right hand.

'Right. We can get going on this investigation at last.' He got to his feet. 'Wait here, Amy, I'm just going to catch up with Acting Sergeant Stanley, I'll be back in five minutes.'

'Could I use your phone, please, Bodkin? I need to make a quick call.'

Bodkin nodded. 'Dial nine for an outside line.'

When Bodkin had gone, Amy picked up the phone and dialled for the operator.

'Could you put me through to Walton's Printers, Gillingham Road, Spinton, please?'

It took a full three minutes before Noah answered the phone.

'Hello, Noah, it's Amy Rowlings. We spoke this morning?'

'The job's not done yet, Amy, I'm still on the Armstrong print.'

'Oh good, I'm not too late then. Listen, Noah, I've got a slight change to the wording on my design.'

CHAPTER FOURTEEN

A few minutes later, Bodkin walked Amy to the reception area, putting his finger to his lips as Amy was about to congratulate Ferris on his forthcoming promotion.

'Wait until the Chief Super has offered him the job,' he whispered. 'It will be a nice surprise for him.'

Amy grinned. 'I can't wait to see his face. He's always telling us how he'd be the new Poirot if he ever got into the CID.'

Bodkin opened the main door to the station and held it open while Amy stepped out onto the pavement.

'I'd offer you a lift but I'm going to be tied up until at least five o'clock,' he said, apologetically.

'That's all right, Bodkin. I'll get the bus.'

'I was going to get a bit of shopping in, but there's no chance of that now,' he said. 'I'll have to risk a sandwich in the canteen before I leave.'

'Oh, I'd forgotten all about you moving into your new flat. I'm so sorry, Bodkin. How did it go?'

'It went smoothly enough, thanks, Ferris and Barker helped me out. All my stuff is still in boxes though. I'm going to have to wear this suit tonight, though I think I've got a clean shirt somewhere.'

'Come to tea with us, Bodkin. Don't go risking food poisoning in the canteen. I don't want you throwing up over me in the cinema tonight.'

'I don't want to impose on your mum and dad, Amy.'

'You wouldn't be an imposition, Bodkin. Mum and Dad are always happy to see you, in fact, I'm pretty sure that Mum has plans to marry us off. I'll tell you what. Bring your shirt and I'll iron it for you. I don't want to be seen with a scarecrow when we go into the Bell tonight.'

'The Bell?'

Amy nodded. 'I've got to meet someone in there after the film ends. We don't have to stay long but I think you might just enjoy the experience. There's a jazz band on, you like jazz, don't you?'

'It's all right, yes, I don't mind it.'

'Good, it's all sorted then. Come around to mine as soon as you get out of work. I'll tell Mum there'll be one extra for tea.'

At four o'clock, Amy had her bath, then sat in her room listening to her new Jimmy Dorsey record as she dried her hair. By the time Bodkin knocked on her door at twenty-five past five, she'd applied her make-up, done her hair and had laid out the clothes she would be wearing that night. Slipping into the dress she'd worn earlier in the day, she hurried downstairs, reaching the bottom step as Mrs Rowlings opened the front door.

'Hello, Sergeant Bodkin,' she said, cheerfully.

'Mrs Rowlings,' Bodkin greeted her as he stepped into the hall.

'Call me Elizabeth,' she said, looking over her shoulder at Amy. 'You're a family friend now. What's your first name? Sergeant Bodkin seems so formal.'

'Bodkin,' Bodkin replied. 'Just call me Bodkin.'

'He won't tell you his first name, Mum, he's embarrassed by it.' Amy took Bodkin's arm and led him into the living room where Elizabeth had already laid the table.

'Right, give me your spare shirt, I'll run the iron over it now. I've got the ironing board set up in the kitchen.'

Bodkin handed over a paper bag and Amy pulled the creased white shirt out and held it up.

'Have you been using it as a floor cloth, Bodkin. I've never seen anything so creased.'

Bodkin shrugged.

'It must have got creased up in the move.'

'And you were going to go out wearing it tonight?'

'I'd have had a go at it before I put it on. I honestly didn't realise how bad it was, sorry.'

'And look at those trousers, Bodkin. They look like you've been sleeping in them.'

Bodkin looked down at his trousers unhappily.

'I–'

'Leave the poor man alone, Amy. He's working on a murder case; he hasn't got time for ironing.' Mr Rowlings put his newspaper down and pushed himself out of his chair to hold out his hand. 'Good evening, laddie.'

Bodkin shook Rowlings' hand and mouthed, 'thank you.'

Amy tucked the shirt under her arm and held out her hand to Bodkin as her mother came in from the kitchen carrying plates laden with sandwiches.

'I'll take the trousers too.'

'What? I, er, I can't take them off here.'

'Amy, leave the poor man alone,' Mr Rowlings repeated.

'Dad, I'm not going out in public with a man wearing trousers that look like they were stolen from a tramp.'

'Amy!' Mrs Rowlings gave Amy a horrified look.

'I mean it, Bodkin. Off with them. It will take me ages to get them looking even half decent.'

Bodkin looked around desperately. 'I can't, not... I mean... I can't.'

'I seem to remember we've been in this situation before,' said Amy sternly. She pointed to the door.

'Upstairs first room on the left. Pass them out through the door when I shout.'

Bodkin sighed.

'All right.'

'You can't do them now, Amy, we're just about to have tea. Poor Bodkin can't be expected to eat in his underwear.'

'They need pressing, properly pressing, that means steam. They'll take at least an hour to dry out and we're supposed to be getting the bus at seven.' She held out her hands, then clapped them together. 'Come on, chop chop.'

'Oh you'll make a proper shrew of a wife,' Mr Rowlings said, pulling out a seat at the table. 'Beware, Sergeant Bodkin.'

Elizabeth began to giggle, then covered her mouth with her hand. Amy gave her a seething look before turning back to Bodkin.

'I'll be up in thirty seconds. Be ready.'

Bodkin obediently left the room; Amy could hear his feet as they slowly clomped up the stairs.

Turning to her mother she held the shirt up.

'This isn't too bad really; it will only take a minute. It's those trousers. Did you see the state of them?'

Amy went into the kitchen and draped the shirt over the ironing table, then walked back through the living room and shouted up the stairs.

'Bodkin, I'm coming up, ready or not.'

By the time she got to the top, an arm holding a pair of navy-blue trousers was reaching out from behind her bedroom door.

'Thank you, now, that wasn't so difficult, was it?'

'Amy, the tea is getting cold and the sandwiches will start to curl if they aren't eaten soon,' Mrs Rowlings called out.

'We're coming down, Mum,' Amy shouted.

'How can I possibly come down?' hissed Bodkin.

'You'll just have to put my dressing gown on, Bodkin. It's hanging on the back of the door. I'd get you a pair of Dad's trousers but they wouldn't come close to fitting you and his dressing gown only got washed today, it's still soaking wet out on the line.'

Amy set off down the stairs carrying Bodkin's rumpled trousers. As she reached the bottom step, she heard a small voice calling to her from the top.

'It's PINK!'

Amy let out an exasperated sigh.

'Who else is going to see but us? Mum and Dad have seen me in it lots of times. Hurry up, Bodkin, your tea is getting cold.'

Amy slung the trousers over her shoulder, picked up a small plate, loaded a handful of sandwiches onto it and carried it out to the kitchen.

'Pour his tea, Mum, he's on his way,' she said.

A couple of minutes later, Bodkin's face appeared around the living room door. Flashing a look towards the kitchen and holding the edges of a dressing gown tightly across his chest, he slipped into the room and sat quickly down at the table.

'I'm so sorry about this,' he said quietly as he accepted a china cup and saucer from Mrs Rowlings.

'Think nothing of it, laddie,' said Mr Rowlings. 'I'm sure we've seen worse.'

'Speak louder,' Amy's voice floated in from the kitchen. 'Don't leave me out of the conversation.'

After tea, Bodkin remained with his bare legs stuck underneath the table while Mrs Rowlings cleared the crockery and Mr Rowlings poured a generous amount of whisky into a crystal tumbler.

'So, laddie, are you any closer to finding the reverend's killer?'

'We know how he died, pretty much, but we don't know who the perpetrator was or what reasons were behind it,' Bodkin replied as he stretched his neck to look into the kitchen.

'So, was he poisoned? What with? And how was it administered?'

'At this stage we don't know much at all, Mr Rowlings. I obviously don't want to go into a lot of detail here, it would be very upsetting for you. Let's just say it wasn't accidental, someone meant him serious harm.'

'I can't think of anyone who would even think of doing such a thing.'

'Are you on any of the reverend's committees?' Bodkin asked.

'No, I don't have time for anything like that. By the time I get home from work I only ever want to relax for the evening. He did chat to me about what went on in one or two of them though.'

'Do you know anything about this new committee he chairs? The poor children's medication fund?'

'He did mention it once or twice. He couldn't see the need for it.'

'Really? Poor children's medication?'

'There was already a similar fund in place, Mr Bodkin. They didn't need another one.'

'Who ran the original fund?'

'Councillor de Vere.'

'But she was the...'

'She was the woman who was pressing so hard for the new committee,' Amy said as she stood in the kitchen doorway.

'She was pushing hard for funding too,' Mr Rowlings said. 'She wanted to send a letter out to some of the larger local businesses asking for their support. But not the really big firms, she'd already milked their charity funds dry with her last appeal.'

'What was that for?' Bodkin asked.

'The medication for the poor, fund,' replied Mr Rowlings.

'That sounds very similar,' said Bodkin.

'It was pretty much identical from what the reverend told me,' said Rowlings.

'But why didn't they just continue with the old fund and run a new campaign?'

'Apparently, there were issues with cash flow because some of the money had been syphoned off to another charity account, so Mrs de Vere had closed the fund at the bank. The reverend, Mr and Mrs Brown, and as far as I know, the pharmacist, were never part of the de Vere council run campaign. She closed down her committee before she approached the vicar for help.'

Just then, Amy came in from the kitchen holding a freshly

ironed shirt on one hand and a pair of pressed, but obviously damp trousers over her right arm.

'All done,' she said draping the trousers over the back of a dining chair and hanging the shirt over the back of another. She looked at Bodkin appraisingly. 'Pink suits you. Men should wear pink.'

Bodkin closed his eyes and groaned.

'Don't take the mickey, Amy, it's bad enough having to wear it.'

'I was being serious, actually, Bodkin, that light shade of pink really suits your colouring. If I were to bring out my own range of men's shirts, I'd definitely have a light pink shade in the collection.'

Bodkin looked down unhappily at the dressing gown.

'It could have been worse, Bodkin. Mum's was the only alternative and that's got hundreds of pretty little flowers on it.'

At ten to seven, they heard a knock at the door.

'That'll be Alice,' Amy said, getting to her feet.

Bodkin was panic stricken.

'Quick, pass me my trousers. She can't see me like this.'

Amy picked up the trousers and felt the legs in two or three places. Satisfied that they were dry enough she handed them to him, then took the shirt off the back of the chair and passed that to him too. Before she had the chance to get into the hall, Bodkin had rushed out of the door and was half way up the stairs, the pink dressing gown flapping behind him.

CHAPTER
FIFTEEN

At nine fifteen, Amy and Alice, along with Bodkin and Ferris, walked down the steps of the picture house and began the short walk along Middle Street towards the bus stop. Amy seemed particularly excited as she chatted with the others about the film they had just seen.

'That was hilarious, wasn't it? When Fred was at the piano and Ginger came in while he was singing a love song to her. His face was a picture when he looked up and saw that her head was covered in shampoo.'

'Anyone for fish and chips?' Alice asked. 'I'm not really that bothered myself tonight.'

'Bodkin and I had tea before we came out,' Amy replied.

'Well, I wouldn't mind some, but I can get by seeing as no one else is eating,' Ferris said. He looked up the street to where their bus had just turned the corner at the top of the hill. 'The bus is here anyway, no time for chips.'

'I've erm, got to meet someone in the Bell,' Amy announced.

'I said I'd be in there for nine. We don't have to stay long. We can easily catch the next bus.'

'A change is as good as a rest,' Alice said, taking Amy's arm. 'I've never been in the Bell. I hope it's not too rough.'

'We've got these fine specimens of manhood to protect us if needs be,' said Amy with a grin.

They walked past the chip shop and took the next turn on the left onto Stoney Street. The Bell was about a hundred yards along.

The atmosphere in the long bar was smoky but no worse than any other pub in town. At the far end of the room was a stage on which a band of five, white-coated jazzmen were playing a Charlie Parker tune. Bodkin looked around, then smiled at Amy as Ferris began to shimmy and click his fingers in time to the music.

'Why haven't we been here before?' he called over the music. 'I love it here.'

'I didn't know they had a band on every Saturday or I'd have suggested it,' Amy replied.

While Bodkin ordered the drinks at the bar, Amy scanned the room looking for Noah. She eventually spotted him in the corner, with his arm around a dark-haired girl wearing a light blue, floral print dress.

He looked up from their conversation as Amy approached.

'Hi there,' he said, as he began to rummage around in his pocket.

'Hi,' Amy looked from Noah to the girl. 'You must be Denise, it's lovely to meet you.'

If Denise was happy to meet Amy, she didn't show it. Her eyes narrowed as she looked her up and down. Amy decided it was probably best not to push her luck, so she turned back to the printshop worker, pulled out her purse and counted out one florin and three, one shilling pieces. She handed the coins to Noah, and in return, he handed her a small cardboard box with the Walton's logo on top. Amy's hands were shaking as she flipped the box open and pulled out the top card.

'Oh it's wonderful, I love it... and it's PINK! Thanks so much, Noah.' Amy leaned forward to plant a kiss on Noah's cheek but pulled away as Denise's eyes narrowed to mere slits. Instead, she dropped the box into her bag along with her purse and held out her hand instead. 'I can't thank you enough, Noah.' She gave the green-eyed monster that was Denise her sweetest smile. 'I'm sure I'll be back for more.'

'Toodle-oo.' Amy waved her fingers, then turned away and returned to her friends who, unable to find a table, had moved away from the busy bar and had found a space on the left-hand side of the room, next to the coat hooks.

Amy sidled up to Bodkin who was watching Ferris intently. It was obvious that his colleague was bursting to get onto either the dance floor, or the stage. Amy opened her bag, flipped the box of cards open and after pulling out four, she closed the lid and snapped her handbag shut.

'You found your man I take it?' Bodkin said as he dragged his eyes away from Ferris. He leaned close to Amy's ear. 'I bet you a pound he'll be up on that stage when the band finishes this song.'

Amy laughed. 'No takers here,' she said. 'I'm not silly enough to throw money away on banker bets.'

She bit her lip and fidgeted with the cards in her hand.

'I've got something for you all,' she said, nervously. 'I hope you like it.'

Amy passed a card to Alice and to Ferris who took a quick glance, slipped it into his pocket, then turned his attention back to the band.

Alice held the card in front of her face, then gave Amy a big hug.

'Well done, you. They're gorgeous, aren't they? I love the pink.'

'It's what he had left over from another job. I'll tell you all about it later.'

Bodkin studied the face of the card, then flipped it over.

'Very nice,' he said. 'Very pink too. You don't see pink cards very often, in fact I can't remem—'

'All right, Bodkin,' Amy gave him a stern look. 'But, apart from it being pink?'

'It looks very professional. I'm only teasing.'

'Well don't,' Amy replied with a twinkle in her eye. 'I can tease about pink things too, namely a dressing gown, I'm sure Alice would love to hear all about it.'

Bodkin shook his head quickly.

'Now, now, there's no need to go that far.' He grinned at Amy. 'Seriously, these are very good quality cards. Where did you get them made?'

'Ah, that would be telling,' Amy said with a wink. 'But, seeing as you like them so much, you can have two. One for you and one for the office girls, so they can register me as a trusted consultant.'

Bodkin took the second card and glanced down at it.

'ARIA Investigations,' he read. 'Agent Amy Rowlings.'

Amy grinned. 'It's fabulous, isn't it? Do you like the bit at the bottom?'

'Kent Police Accredited,' Bodkin chuckled to himself. 'You didn't even know you were accredited until this morning. You work fast.'

'You can't afford to let the grass grow under your feet,

Bodkin, or before you know it it's round your knees and you can't find your garden shears.'

'Very true,' Bodkin agreed. 'There is just one thing'

'Oh no, not you too. What?'

'If ARIA stands for Amy Rowlings Investigations Agency, why do you need the word, investigations, underneath. Aren't you using the same word twice?'

Amy stamped her foot. 'AAAAARGH! Do I have to explain this to everyone? First, Alice, now you? I thought you were an intelligent man, Bodkin, but I'm having my doubts. Alice has an excuse because she's got a baby screaming in her ears all day and night but you...'

She tapped her foot and took a deep breath.

'I'll explain this once more, then I don't want to hear another word about it. Okay?'

Bodkin winked at Alice, then nodded to Amy, all the time trying to keep a straight face.

'No one will ever read the information that way. What they'll see, and what they'll read,' her voice slowed down, 'is, ARIA INVESTIGATIONS. NO ONE WILL USE THE WORD INVESTIGATIONS MORE THAN ONCE WHEN THEY READ THE CARD. AM I MAKING MYSELF CLEAR?'

Bodkin nodded, a serious look on his face.

'Perfectly.'

'GOOD!' Amy said, exasperated. She turned her gaze on Alice and raised one eyebrow. 'And YOU?'

'Oh, I got it this morning when you explained it,' Alice replied, cheerfully. She turned her gaze to the place where Ferris had been standing a few moments before, but he was gone. She looked around the bar and saw him climbing the steps to the stage at the far end of the room. He leaned in to speak to the trumpet player and said something in his ear. The trumpeter patted him on the back, then spoke into the microphone.

'Ladies and gentleman. We have a special guest singer this evening. He is going to give you his version of the Fred Astaire song, The Way You Look Tonight.' He turned to his band and said, 'after three.'

The room hushed to an almost perfect silence as Ferris's rich baritone voice swept across the room. All eyes were fixed on him as he performed a pitch perfect rendition of the song that the four friends had seen Astaire singing in Swing Time only an hour before. A few lines into the song, a couple stepped onto the dancefloor and took each other in their arms. Two young girls joined them a few moments later.

'Come on, Bodkin,' Amy said, almost dragging the detective to the dance floor.

'I'm hopeless at dancing,' he hissed into her ear.

'Nonsense,' she hissed back. 'Any fool can waltz.'

Bodkin sighed and took Amy in his arms, albeit a little stiffly, but by the time Ferris was into the second verse of the song the pair were gliding around the dancefloor, performing a slow waltz as well as any of the other couples who had decided to join them.

When Ferris finished the song, he was treated to riotous applause. The girl next to Amy shouted to her friend. 'We know him, he's the copper who sings at the bus stop.'

To shouts of encore, Ferris had a quick word with the band leader, who turned again to the band and called 'Begin the Beguine... after three...'

The girls in the audience screamed out their appreciation as Ferris, note perfect as ever, belted out the popular Artie Shaw song. Amy and Bodkin moved around the floor elegantly, keeping perfect time with the music.

'This is Alice's favourite song; it's a shame Ferris is singing it because he could have...'

Her voice tailed off as she saw Alice glide by in the arms of a young man wearing a neatly pressed pin striped suit.

Amy gave her a fingers wave as they passed each other on the edge of the dancefloor. Alice smiled back quickly, then gave her full attention to her dance partner.

Ferris gave the chanting crowd two more songs before he stepped down from the stage and joined Alice, Amy and Bodkin by the coat hooks.

'Well done! That was wonderful. Thank you so much for Begin the Beguine,' Alice said, giving Ferris a quick peck on the cheek. Ferris blushed as he always did when Alice showed him any sort of affection. He was still keen on her despite the fact that she'd told him nicely, but firmly, that they didn't have a future together.

Bodkin looked at his watch then across to Amy.

'The bus will be here in a few minutes; we'll have to get a move on if we're going to finish the night off at the Old Bull.'

Alice finished her drink and put the glass on the shelf above a cold radiator.

'I'm ready,' she announced.

Amy drained her glass and put it next to Alice's. She had just turned towards the door when a man of about forty, strode across the room towards them. He was wearing a knitted jumper and a pair of dark trousers. He had an oval face and brown eyes with a thick mono-brow above them.

'Are you Sergeant Bodkin?' he asked, looking directly at the policeman.

'Acting Inspector Bodkin, for my sins,' Bodkin replied. 'What can I do for you?'

'I was passed a message saying that you wanted to speak to me. I'm Peter Kissman.'

Bodkin rubbed his chin, thoughtfully.

'This really isn't the best place for the discussion we need to have,' he said.

Kissman shrugged.

'Well, it's like this. I'm out of town for the next few days. I'm going to stay with my parents for Easter, they live down at Leysdown on the Isle of Sheppey. I won't be back until Easter Monday, possibly the Tuesday if the buses aren't running on the bank holiday.'

'I see, that does make it a little awkward,' Bodkin said.

'There's a snug on the other side of the pub,' Kissman replied. 'It's always empty when the band is on.'

Bodkin looked at his group of friends and grimaced.

'Sorry, folks. It looks like it has to be done now.'

'That's all right,' Ferris said, happily. 'We're fine here aren't we, Alice?'

'Absolutely, we can always get the last bus back. It won't hurt us to give the Old Bull a miss for once.'

Ferris walked to the bar and was lucky enough to be served straight away. Bodkin accepted his pint and turned to Peter Kissman.

'Lead the way,' he said.

By the time Kissman had opened the door to the empty snug. Amy had caught them up, she squeezed herself through the narrowing gap as Bodkin attempted to close it behind them.

'I'm accredited now,' she whispered as he rolled his eyes to the ceiling.

CHAPTER
SIXTEEN

Kissman put his half empty pint glass on a small round table and sat down on the bench seat behind it. Bodkin and Amy pulled out a pair of wooden stools and sat down facing him.

'Anything I can get you folks?' a man in shirtsleeves asked from behind the bar.

'Police business,' Bodkin replied sharply. 'Can you make sure we aren't disturbed?'

The man gave a boy scout salute and disappeared into the main bar.

Bodkin took a sip of his beer and gave Peter a long look.

'Peter, this is Amy Rowlings, she's an, erm she's helping in our inquiry. Do you have any objection to her sitting in? I can...'

'No, I have no objection. I've got nothing to hide. Caroline said that Amy had been kind to her when she was being questioned.'

Amy looked at her drink and said nothing as Bodkin pulled out his notepad and pen.

'So, Peter, how long have you lived in Spinton?'

'I moved here from Sheppey in nineteen twenty-nine. I'd been working on the sea defences down there but I fancied a change and we moved up here.'

'We?'

'Yes, I was married back then. We had a daughter. Sadly, it didn't work out and we got divorced a year later.'

'I'm sorry to hear that. What job were you doing at the time?'

'I was working with the road crews, it was hard, back breaking work and I was never in the best of moods when I got home. I was so tired I didn't want to do anything with the family. I spent too much time in the pub with my workmates. Marriages don't really survive that sort of thing. Well, mine didn't at least.'

Bodkin nodded slowly. It wasn't an unfamiliar story. Drink destroyed many a marriage. His parents' included.

'How well did you know Reverend Villiers? Have you been working for the church very long?'

'I've been working there for about seven years now. I started the year before Caroline arrived. As for the vicar. I don't think anyone knew him that well. He was a pretty insular person really.'

'Did the two of you get on?' Bodkin asked.

'I didn't see a lot of him to be honest. My job was outside unless there was a bit of maintenance needing doing. His was pretty much always inside, unless he was conducting a burial service, and there wasn't much time for a chat at those.'

'But you did talk to him now and then?'

'We got on pretty well, if you call chatting about how to get rid of moles or being given an order for a grave to be dug or headstone to be erected, getting on.'

'Moles?'

'Yes, a strange topic of conversation for a vicar, but he was asking advice for one of his committee members, a councillor... de something or other... Vere, that's it. She's got a big place just off the Gillingham Road, employs her own gardener. They had a big mole problem by all accounts.'

'And you sorted it for her?'

'I don't know, I gave them some advice about the best measures to tackle the problem. We used to have them here a few years ago, but I haven't seen a single one in about six years now.'

Bodkin sat up straight on his stool.

'What did you use to kill them, Peter.'

'The vicar had an old tin of strychnine that he used to use for rats, but Caroline didn't like what it did to them so he handed it over to me. I used what was left in the tin and it did the job, as I said, I've not seen one since.'

'But if the reverend knew it would kill moles, why did he ask for your advice when Mrs de Vere had a similar problem?'

Peter shrugged.

'I don't suppose he knew what I'd used it for. He gave it to me because it killed rats and there were plenty of the little buggers around the churchyard. They used to eat the grass seed when I put it down in Spring and Autumn. There were lots of them in the crypt under the church too. He wasn't sensitive about how a rat died. He just didn't want Caroline nagging him.'

'You say you used the lot. Every last bit?'

'Every last bit. I washed out the empty tin with the hose on the waste land at the back of the vicarage, then I tossed it in the dustbin.'

'You seem to remember it all very clearly after all this time.' Bodkin lifted his own glass to his lips.

'I'm very careful with poison,' Kissman said. 'You have to be.' He took a sip from his pint. 'I've never used strychnine since. I use cyanide or arsenic compounds for the rats these days, depending what's cheapest.'

'But never strychnine?'

'I would, it works well, but it's twice the price of arsenic.'

'Do you have to purchase the stuff yourself then?' Amy asked.

'No, but the reverend was extremely careful with the church funds and he had a memory like an elephant. He could remember to the penny what we'd paid for a certain item, even if it had been a year or more since we last bought any.'

Bodkin's pen was poised above his notepad.

'Where did you buy the stuff from when you did purchase it?'

'Hales, the pharmacist on the High Street. They're as cheap as anywhere and they have a licence to sell it, so it's all legit. They record the amounts purchased.'

Bodkin jotted down a few notes, then looked up from his pad.

'I take it you wouldn't object if I took a look around your sheds?'

Peter opened his hands.

'Feel free.'

'What might I find there, poison wise, Peter?'

'Arsenic trioxide, potassium cyanide, I've got that in two forms, one a powder and one an insecticide. You mix it with water to make a fine spray. You have to be really careful with that one as you can easily breathe it in, but it's good for wasp nests and the like.'

Bodkin gave Amy a sideways glance and was silent as he made more notes.

'Hemlock, Peter. Have you got any hemlock?'

'What would I need hemlock for? I don't even know if it would work with pests. How would you administer it?' He laughed suddenly. 'Make them a cup of hemlock tea?'

Bodkin didn't join in the laughter.

'Is there any hemlock in the churchyard, Peter?'

'No, I don't think so. I've heard there's plenty on the river-bank at the back though and there's some on the wasteland up by the cement works. I know that because I remember hearing that a young lad was poisoned by it when he was playing with his mates. They tried to make peashooters out of the stalks. They thought it was cow parsley, I think.'

'So, you do know what hemlock looks like, Peter?'

Kissman laughed again.

'I wouldn't know it from cow parsley either.'

Bodkin studied the man for signs of nervousness but he seemed to stay quite calm throughout the questioning.

'Can you take us back to last weekend, Peter. How did you spend it?'

'The day? I spent Saturday morning digging a grave with Abel Crossley and we had a bloody nightmare of a time doing it too.'

Bodkin made a note.

'Abel Crossley?'

'He's on the council staff, he works for the parks and cemeteries department. He helps me out if I get a particularly tough digging job. Like at the boggy bottom end of the churchyard, where the trees overhang the wall. There are a lot of tree roots there.'

'Why do people buy plots down there then?' Bodkin asked. 'I mean, if the ground is boggy, it's not the nicest place to be buried.'

'It's cheaper down there,' Kissman said.

Bodkin nodded in understanding.

'Ah yes, I see. Please carry on.'

'As you may remember, it tipped it down on the Friday, the rain was torrential for most of the day. It eased off overnight but there was a lot of standing water around and even though the part we had to work on is on a steep slope, there hadn't been time for the water to run off. It was a bit of a quagmire.'

'And the job had to be done on the Saturday?'

'It had to be done over the weekend, but neither Abel nor I fancied coming in on Sunday, so we did it on Saturday morning. We didn't finish it until gone three. We were digging lumps of clay out, not soil.'

'I saw it on Sunday morning,' Amy said. 'I was thinking that I wouldn't fancy having your job doing the backfilling after the funeral. You broke a spade digging it out, didn't you?'

'I did, yes. Thankfully it was right at the end of the job. I only have two shovels.'

'Did the vicar ask you to get Abel in?'

'No, I asked the vicar. He was very good about it. Mind you, he didn't have a lot of choice. Mrs Constadine's funeral was booked for Tuesday.'

'I see,' Bodkin mused. 'So, what time did you finish work?'

'Just after three. The church bells chimed the hour as we were covering the grave with the tarp.'

'Then what did you do?'

'I made us a cup of tea in my workshop. Abel had a hip flask with whisky in it so we warmed our insides up with that.'

'And after the tea?'

'I went home. Abel would have gone straight to the pub to put his bets on.'

'I'm going to forget you said that, Peter,' Bodkin said quickly.

'I'm sorry, I'm glad about that. I wouldn't like to drop him in it. I know off course gambling is illegal.'

'What did you do?'

'I went home, had a strip wash at the sink, then went up for a bit of a kip. I was knackered.' He looked across at Amy and held up his hand in apology. 'Sorry, miss.'

'I've heard a lot worse,' said Amy.

Bodkin swilled his beer around in his glass then took a long drink from it. Seeing the glass was almost empty, he swallowed, then finished it off.

'Now, Mr Kissman. Let's get back to Saturday. What did you do in the evening?'

'I didn't wake up until after six. I put my glad rags on and had a bit of tea, then I walked round to the vicarage to see Caroline. I generally drop in on my way to the pub.'

'What time would that have been?'

Kissman thought for a moment.

'It would have been about a quarter to eight. The vicar's meeting broke up at eight, I remember that because the committee came into the kitchen to get a glass of wine?'

'The vicar's good wine?' Bodkin asked.

'Ha! No. He wouldn't let them near that. He gave them some stuff he bought locally.'

'Did you have a glass yourself?'

'I wasn't offered one, so no.'

'Right, now, think carefully, Peter. Can you remember seeing an open bottle of the vicar's good wine on the counter before or after the committee appeared?'

'There was a bottle of his French stuff on the side, whether it had been opened or not I really couldn't say.'

'Okay, so what were you doing when the committee arrived?'

'Just chatting to Caroline. I was a bit annoyed when they all turned up because I've been trying to pluck up the courage to ask her out for weeks, but the moment never seemed right. Well, on Saturday, the moment was perfect. I'd been thinking about what to say all the way over from my house and when I finally opened my mouth to ask her if she'd like to come to the pictures with me, that bloody lot turned up.'

Amy pulled a sad face. 'Oh no!'

Peter shrugged. 'And so the moment passed. The reverend asked for clean glasses and as Caroline was searching for them, I noticed her insulin syringe was lying on the counter. Now, I know she's a very private person and doesn't like anyone knowing about her illness, so I picked it up, filled a pan full of water, slipped the syringe in and put it on the hotplate.'

'You knew that had to be done every night?' Bodkin asked.

'Of course. I've seen her do that lots of times.'

'I see. Okay, what happened then?'

Peter closed his eyes and thought for a few moments.

'When Caroline had found enough glasses, the vicar pulled out two bottles of what he calls his house white, and Mrs de... de Vere, took charge of opening them and pouring the wine into the glasses.'

'Then what?'

'They chatted about this and that for a while, then they decided they needed to set a date for the next meeting, so they all went into the study.'

'What were you doing while they were sorting dates out?'

'Nothing. I stood there trying to work up the courage to ask her out again. She thanked me for putting her syringe in the pot and then there was an awkward silence. I think she was waiting for me to ask her, but I was tongue tied again.'

'Oh, poor you, Peter,' Amy said, sadly.

'Poor me all right. The next day the vicar was gone and I think my chance might have gone with him.'

'Why do you say that? She might be in need of comforting, a friendly shoulder, that sort of thing,' said Amy.

'It doesn't look that way to me. I telephoned on the Sunday after I heard the news but she didn't want to talk about it. She's got her sister if she needs comforting. I seem to have been discarded.'

Amy leaned across the table towards him. 'It's early days yet. Give it time.'

Bodkin looked wide eyed at Amy, then he turned his attention back to Peter. 'What time did the party break up?'

'It wasn't a party, but I'd say about a quarter to nine. Caroline went to the front door to see them off. I slipped out of the back and walked around the side of the house. I can use the churchyard as a short cut to get to the High Street.'

'Why didn't you go out of the front door with the rest of them?'

'They were all standing in a group in the porch. They were taking forever to say their farewells.' He hesitated then went on. 'I'm not one for socialising really, Mr Bodkin. Besides, I was gagging for a pint.'

'Who did you see in the pub, Peter?'

'Abel was there. He'd had a good win so he was cele... Abel was there. We had a chat about the football with a few other guys. The Dragon was busy that night.'

'Which other guys? Can you give me any names?'

Peter blew out his cheeks.

'Erm, Joe Proudfoot... Tony Slowman was there, and Norman Lane. Cyril the landlord will vouch for me anyway. He'll remember Abel splashing his winn... Well, he'll vouch for me.'

'What time did you leave the Dragon?' Bodkin asked, jotting down a quick note.

'Bang on last orders. The bar closed at ten-thirty officially, but Cyril sometimes has a lock in. I never bother with that and anyway, I was buggered after all that digging. So, I didn't hang about.'

'Which way did you walk home?'

'Straight down Main Road. I live on the estate. Forty-seven Rushton Street. I got home just before eleven.'

'Can anyone verify that? Did you speak to anyone on the way?'

'No. I can't remember speaking to anyone.'

'What about neighbours, were there any lights on next door?'

'I can't remember, I doubt it. Both sets of my neighbours are over seventy. I never hear a peep out of them after nine o'clock. They're up and about early though. Up at sparrow fart, as they say.'

He shot Amy another glance and winced.

Amy put her hand to her mouth to stifle the giggle that was building up. The colloquialism had always amused her.

Bodkin picked up his empty glass, turned towards the bar, then remembering he had asked not to be disturbed, he put it back on the table again while licking his dry lips.

'I've only got a few more questions, Peter, but I might need to speak to you again when you get back. Unless your parents are on the telephone network of course?'

Kissman shook his head.

'Sorry, they can't afford luxuries like that. They're both in their sixties now.'

'I believe you have breakfast at the vicarage every morning, is that correct?'

'Best breakfast in Spinton too. Much better than the stuff they serve up at the café. She's a good cook is Caroline. Villiers doesn't know what he's miss... Oh... sorry.'

'So, did Caroline ever cook for the vicar?'

'Oh yes, he had his evening meal at home, sometimes it was sandwiches, sometimes cold cuts of meat and a bit of veg, depending what's in season.'

'What about lunch?'

'He was always out and about in the day, seeing parishioners, doing God's work in the parish. I think he used to have lunch in town a few days a week. On Thursdays he probably had it in Rochester with the bishop. I can't swear to that though.'

'So, he never ate in the mornings?'

'His stomach wasn't up to it. Not after the amount of wine he put away at night. It was always at least one bottle according to Caroline. Sometimes, if the weather was bad and he was confined to his study, he'd open a second one. I can't say if he ever finished both bottles. Caroline was sure that he was developing an ulcer but I wouldn't know if that was true. I know he's been suffering with indigestion recently. He was being treated for acid reflux. His doctor prescribed some powders. The pharmacist made them up for him.'

'Who was his doctor? Do you know?'

Peter shook his head.

'How long has he been taking the powders?' asked Bodkin.

'Oh, only a week or so; he had them with a glass of warm water every morning.'

'You saw him take the powders? Where were they kept?'

'Caroline kept them in the drawer with her insulin.'

'Who mixed the powders for him? Did he do it himself?'

'No, Caroline always did that for him. I think his hands were shaking too much to do it himself.'

At that, Bodkin got to his feet and waited for Peter to do the same.

'Thank you for that, Peter. I'll be in touch if I need to speak to you again. You can probably count on it. There are always more questions in cases like this.'

Peter nodded to the detective and gave Amy a shy smile then he picked up his empty glass and walked back to the long bar.

'Well, what do you think?' Amy asked when he had gone.

'He seemed genuine enough. He wasn't on edge and he answered all of my questions without having to think too hard.' Bodkin picked up his own glass and Amy's, then followed her out of the snug.

'So, he's in the clear then?'

'Oh, I didn't say that, Amy. He's not in the clear. Not by a long shot.'

CHAPTER SEVENTEEN

On Sunday morning, Amy strolled up the hill towards the church with her parents walking arm in arm behind. The weather was a big improvement on the previous week. Easter was fast approaching and the sun seemed to have been given a kick to remind it of the fact. The misty, cold air of the previous Sunday had been replaced with blue skies and a light, warm, breeze. Amy found that she had to undo her coat and remove her knitted beret before reaching the infants school which marked the half way point on their walk.

The lychgate was open and many more people than usual were using that entrance to reach the church. A small group of worshipers stood inside the gate, reading the few messages of condolence that had been left alongside two, small flowerless wreaths on the bench seat where the vicar had been found.

At the narthex, the stand-in vicar, the Reverend Daley, wearing his freshly laundered vestments, beamed at his congregation as they filed into the church, shaking hands with parishioners, smiling and tousling the small children's hair as they passed by. He had a narrow frame with an extended neck, a triangular shaped face and long, almost feminine eyelashes. His dark brown hair was parted on the right. His smile, whilst broad, seemed to Amy, to be forced.

'Hello there,' he said as Amy stepped up to the doors of the church. 'Thank you so much for attending my first service.' He looked over Amy's shoulder to the line of people waiting to enter. 'Looks like being a bumper crowd.'

Amy took his hand which she found to be surprisingly clammy. She wiped her palm on her coat as she turned away wearing a fake smile of her own, and waited until her parents had shaken hands with their new, stand-in vicar.

'I don't like him at all,' Amy whispered as they entered the church.

'Shhh,' her father hissed. 'It matters little whether you like him or not. Judging by that smug look on his face, it looks like he's here for good.'

Inside the church, Amy smiled at Caroline and nodded to a few other acquaintances, then taking their usual seats on the right of the aisle, they sat down and waited for the service to begin.

After the service, which had been mercifully short, the Rowlings family again shook hands with the new vicar as he waited at the door of the church.

'I hope you enjoyed the sermon,' he said to Amy's father with something akin to a smirk on his face.

Mr Rowlings eyes held Daley's for a few moments longer than necessary.

'It should be commended for its brevity,' he replied, letting go of the vicar's hand and turning away in one movement.

As Amy stepped out into the sunlight, she found Bodkin waiting at the top of the gravel path that led to the lychgate.

'Bodkin, this is a surprise. I didn't have you down as a churchgoer.'

'You'd be right too,' he replied with a quick smile. 'I've been taking a look at Mr Kissman's workshop. I dropped in on him this morning to pick up the keys. I'm just waiting for Mrs Gatting, Peter asked me to give the keys to her as it will save me going back to his place later.'

'Ooh,' Amy's eyes lit up? 'Did you discover anything?'

'It's pretty much how he said it would be. There were no surprises. I couldn't see any sign of a tin of strychnine. So, unless he's got it stashed elsewhere, he was telling us the truth.'

'So, he does have both arsenic and cyanide powder then? Mind you, he did explain why he needed two different types.'

'There's not much of either poison in there to be honest but I'll have a word with the pharmacist in the week to see how often he bought it. I'll also get one of the team to pick up the church accounts for the last few years to see if they match what the pharmacist tells us. Interestingly, he has a blackboard too, he lists his jobs on it, but the only chalk I could find was white. I think he must scrounge it off Caroline.'

Bodkin stopped talking as he spotted Mrs Gatting coming out of the church door.

'Mrs Gatting?' he called. When she looked across, he waved to her and after excusing herself from the fair-haired lady she was walking with, she stepped slowly across to where Bodkin and Amy were standing.

'I've been asked to give you Mr Kissman's workshop keys, Mrs Gatting. He said he'll pick them up in the morning.'

Bodkin handed her a set of three keys. The housekeeper nodded curtly, then turned towards the chipped slate path that led between the two giant mausoleums, to the side gate in the church wall.

'Oh, while I've got you here. Could you tell me the name of the reverend's doctor? I need to have a chat with him.'

'It's Doctor Mighten. He lives on Claypole Street. I'm not sure of the number but you can't miss it. He has an extension on the side of the house that he uses as a surgery. There's a sign over the entrance.'

'How are you getting on with the new vicar?' Bodkin asked. 'Will you stay on when he moves in?'

'I really don't know what the bishop's plans are. I'll find out in the week, I suppose, he's coming up to Spinton on Friday. I believe he's going to pronounce on who will become our new vicar. I'll probably get to find out my own future at the same time. I have to say I'm hoping there's a surprise in store for us. There's something about the Reverend Daley I don't like, but I can't quite put my finger on it.' She smacked herself on the back of the hand. 'That was uncalled for. I honestly shouldn't feel any animosity towards him, but he just seems a little cold. Maybe it's because I know he was trying to get Reverend Villiers moved on, so he could take over the parish himself.'

'The, admittedly few, people I've spoken to all seem to have the same opinion of him,' Bodkin replied.

'Count me among them,' Amy muttered.

Bodkin thanked Caroline, then watched as she made her way through the gravestones towards the vicarage. After a few moments he turned back to Amy.

'What are your plans for the day?'

'I don't have any to be honest. I'll probably drop in on Alice later but apart from that I'll just be listening to music and reading my new Photoplay magazine.' She looked into Bodkin's face with a quizzical look. 'Why do you ask? Were you going to invite me to join in with a bit of sleuthing?'

'Not today, sadly. I've got a report to write up, so I'll be dropping into the station in a few minutes. After that I'm unpacking boxes and trying to make my new place look a bit more like home.'

'I could help you if you like?' Amy said.

'Thank you, but no. I'd much rather your first impressions of the place are good ones. It looks like a tip at the moment.' He smiled warmly at her. 'Oh, I'd forgotten.' The detective pulled a card out of his pocket. 'This is my card; it's got my office extension number on it so you can dial it direct and not have to go through the main desk to get in touch. I've jotted the phone number of the new flat on the back. You'll have to wait a while for me to find out I've got an incoming call though. The phone is downstairs in the lobby so someone else will probably answer when you ring. You'll be better off not using a kiosk, your money could be used up while you're waiting.'

Amy took the card and gave it a quick glance. 'What's your flat number? I know you're on the first floor.'

'Flat four,' Bodkin replied.

'I might pop by one evening in the week if that's all right,' Amy said. 'I'm off from Thursday afternoon right through until the Wednesday after Easter. They're fitting a new electricity supply at the Mill. The one we have can't take the load any longer. The machines keep conking out, mid garment. They can't do it while we're working, so we're all getting a few days off.' She grinned at Bodkin. 'Lucky you, we could have the case cracked by the time I go back to work.'

'If only,' Bodkin said seriously.

'Speaking of the Mill. Are you dropping in for lunch again tomorrow? Shall I ask Mum for extra sandwiches?' Amy asked.

'I doubt I'll have time, tempting as the offer is. I'm going to see Doctor Mighten tomorrow, then I've got a team meeting, it's down to me to hand out tasks now I'm Acting Inspector. There's no rest for the wicked. I'm also going to be arranging appointments to see Mrs de Vere and the rest of the people on the committee. Mrs de Vere interests me greatly... Well, talk of the Devil.'

Bodkin nodded towards the church where a smartly dressed, hatless woman was in conversation with the vicar. She smiled and put her hand on his arm as they spoke. The Reverend Daley's smile seemed much more genuine than it had been earlier.

Amy watched them closely for another two or three minutes until the councillor once again patted the clergyman's arm before walking slowly away.

'Well, well, well,' Amy said, almost to herself. 'That was interesting.'

'Was it?' Bodkin asked. 'I didn't see anything particularly revealing in their exchange.'

Amy shook her head as she looked at the detective.

'You're hopeless, Bodkin, you really are.'

'Why, what did I miss?'

'You mean you didn't see the way they acted around each other, the doe-eyed look she was giving him, the way her fingers lingered on his arm? You missed her eyes fluttering, the way her lips were parted slightly, the way she kept fiddling with her hair? And as for him, he couldn't take his eyes off her face, his nostrils were flaring. He listened intently to every word she said. Honestly, Bodkin, I really can't understand how you missed all that. Those two are involved romantically, or at least they're about to be. I'd put a year's wages on it.'

'Blimey!' Bodkin muttered. 'You spotted all that from one short conversation?'

'It's a woman thing, Bodkin. That's why you need female detectives in the force.'

Bodkin chuckled. 'Hang on a minute; didn't Mrs Gatting say something similar about us the other night?'

'Pfft,' she replied. 'Women don't get it right every time. Some of us are more gifted than others.'

After refusing Bodkin's offer of a lift, Amy watched the detective walk back towards the church before turning away to take the lychgate path as it was a quicker way for her to get to the main road.

As she reached the Belvedere mausoleum, she spotted something glinting in the sunlight out of the corner of her eye. Turning towards the tomb, she looked down to the narrow gap at the bottom of the weathered, almost grey, oak door and the glittering object that was protruding slightly from underneath.

Crouching, Amy tried to push her finger into the gap to retrieve the object but it was wedged in too tightly. Pulling her long-handled steel comb from her purse she wedged it into the gap and began to jiggle it about until a piece of green glass slipped out onto the stone slab she was kneeling on.

Amy knew immediately what it could mean to the investigation. Getting to her feet she began to walk quickly towards the church, hoping to catch up with Bodkin, then when curiosity got the better of her, she stopped and turned back.

'The Belvedere tomb,' she whispered to herself, her mind going back to her childhood when, following Sunday school, she and her friends would dare each other to enter the creepy crypt. The lock of the door had been broken for many a year and all the children of the area knew that with a little bit of coaxing they could force the heavy oak door open. Then it was a challenge to see who was the bravest. Oddly it always seemed to be one of the girls who would summon up the courage to step into the crypt. Once, Penny Scrivener, having been double dared by her own brother to go further inside, began to descend the steps, only to find herself plunged into pitch darkness as her mean and twisted brother slammed the door shut behind her. Luckily Amy had been on hand to rescue her and no lasting damage was done to her mental state.

Amy shivered as the scary childhood memories came back. She had never taken more than one, tiny, baby step into the crypt herself, but the horrified face of Penny Scrivener blinking into the daylight when Amy had rescued her, was never far from her mind whenever she found herself near the tomb.

With shaking hands, she slid her fingers into the gap between the door and the frame and attempted to get some sort of grip, but her fingers weren't strong enough to ease the door outwards. Refusing to admit defeat, she tried again, then, when she failed again, she picked up her long-handled steel comb from the floor and pushed it into the gap. Angling it slightly, she hit it repeatedly with the heel of her palm until she felt something give. Then, using her fingers again, she finally managed to get hold of the back of the door and tugged at it until it came away from the frame. The hinges squealed and the glass underneath scraped as the gap grew to about six inches.

Amy stopped and took a deep breath, imagining all manner of things that might be waiting for her on the inside. Then, summoning all of her courage, she took hold of the door again, dragged it fully open and narrowed her eyes as she looked into the gloom.

Thankfully, there were no ghouls, demons or creepy skeletons awaiting her. Instead, on the top step of the crypt, were the shattered pieces of a broken bottle.

CHAPTER EIGHTEEN

AMY WAS ONLY STILL FOR A FEW MOMENTS, THEN, SPINNING AROUND, she shouted for the detective.

'Bodkin... BODKIN!'

When his burly frame failed to appear within a few seconds, she pushed the door shut, then hared off up the path that led past the church entrance to the main gate. On the pavement, she looked right and left but could see no sign of the policeman so, taking a deep breath, she hurtled across the fortuitously quiet Main Road and ran as fast as her legs could carry her, up the hill to Middle Street where she took the corner almost like a motorcyclist before coming to a stop, gasping for air outside the police station.

Pushing the door open she stepped into the reception and leaned on the front desk, still fighting to get her breath.

'Bodkin... Quick...' she gasped.

The duty officer was a spotty faced constable with prematurely thinning hair and a long chin that he must have struggled to get his helmet strap over.

'I'm sorry, miss, what was that? I didn't quite catch it.'

'I need... Bodkin, now,' she said, taking in another deep breath.

'Lucky old Bodkin,' the young constable said, jealously.

'Please, just get him... it's IMPORANT!' Amy almost screamed at the man.

'Hold on to your horses. I'll have to see if he's in first.'

Amy opened her bag and pulled out a card from the buttoned-down compartment on the side.

'ARIA Investigations. KENT POLICE ACREDITTED!' she said as she held the card in front of his face.

'All right, miss, calm down, I'll see if he's in his office.' The policeman picked up the telephone handset on his desk and dialled.

If there was one thing Amy hated above anything else, was being told to calm down, but she held her tongue and waited impatiently as the constable waited for the call to be answered.

'Hello, sir, I'm sorry to disturb you but there's a young lady in reception from...' Amy held up the card again... 'ARIA Investigations. She says it's very important... You're coming out. Right, sir. I'll tell her.'

'He's on his way.' The constable smiled at her, then leaned over his desk.

'What are you do—' He stood bolt upright as Bodkin stepped smartly out of the corridor.

'Barker?'

'She's here, sir.' Barker pointed towards Amy who was shuffling her feet impatiently.

As soon as Bodkin opened the door to reception, Amy grabbed hold of his sleeve and tried to drag him to the front door.

'Come on, quickly, I've found it.'

'Found what?' Bodkin pushed his weight onto one foot to stop himself being propelled out of the front door.

'The evidence. The bottle; quickly, Bodkin, someone might be removing it as we speak.'

Bodkin suddenly became Mr Efficient.

'The vicar's wine bottle? Where is it?' He pulled back on Amy's arm as she tried to pull him across the pavement.

'It's in the cemetery, Belvedere... Hurry, Bodkin, hurry.'

Bodkin held up one hand as he made a quick decision.

'Wait here, I'll get the car, it will be quicker.'

'Hurry, Bodkin,' Amy pleaded. 'Bring forensics too.'

'On a Sunday? You'll be lucky,' Bodkin said as he hurried to the gates that led to the car park. He stopped for a moment before passing through them and shouted an order as though he was speaking to one of his junior officers.

'Go back in, tell Barker to get PC Somersby. I want him out front before I get back with the car.'

Amy did as she was told. Barker, obviously not wanting to get on the wrong side of his boss, immediately picked up the phone and dialled.

'Canteen? Yes, it's the front desk. Acting Inspector Bodkin wants Somersby out front ASAP, no, make that, he wants him here yesterday, it's urgent.'

Amy stepped back out onto the pavement and by the time Bodkin pulled out of the gates in his Morris Ten, Somersby was staggering out of the front door, his helmet under his arm.

Bodkin leaned across and opened the front door as he screeched to a halt in front of Amy. She jumped in and quickly slammed the door behind her. When she looked over her shoulder Somerby had joined them in the back of the car.

Bodkin pulled away, turned onto the main road and headed down the hill towards the church. As the tower loomed up ahead of them, Amy pointed to the wide pavement that ran along the side of the church railings.

'The lychgate entrance,' she said, hurriedly.

Amy's head almost hit the roof as Bodkin drove the Morris up the kerb and onto the pavement. Beeping his horn to warn a small group of Sunday strollers to get out of his way, he gradually slowed the car to a crawl as they approached the lychgate.

Amy had opened the door, even as the car was pulling to a halt. Leaping out, she slammed the door behind her and hurried through the ancient gateway.

'It's just up here,' she called as she heard Bodkin's footsteps close behind her.

When she reached the Belvedere mausoleum, she stopped and pointed to the weather-beaten old door.

'In there,' she said.

Bodkin pushed his fingers into the gap between the door and frame and stepped back, pulling the door open as he did so.

'Phew! It's still there. Thank goodness,' Amy said as she took a step forward and stood alongside the detective.

'How the hell did forensics miss this,' Bodkin said as he crouched down to examine the broken bottle.

'It's not their fault, Bodkin,' Amy said as she crouched down next to him. 'It was misty and murky last Sunday. I only spotted the piece of glass wedged under the door because the sun shone on it. No one would ever have noticed it otherwise.'

Bodkin grunted. 'It's their job to notice.'

The detective pulled out his handkerchief and carefully lifted the sharp corner of a large piece of the bottle. Turning it over, he showed it to Amy.

'Here's the label, Entre Deux Mers, it's his all right.'

'But how do we know it's the one from last week?' Amy

asked. 'Couldn't this be an old bottle that he dropped and kicked into here himself?'

Bodkin pointed to the bottom of the bottle which was in one piece and still had a small amount of wine in it.

'The test will tell us, but that doesn't look like it's been here too long to me. There's no dust and had it been here for any length of time, that wine would have evaporated.'

Amy clutched the detective's arm. 'Ooh, you are clever, Bodkin. I take back what I said about you the other day.'

Bodkin looked sideways at her and winked. 'There's life in the old dog yet.'

Bodkin carefully placed the piece of broken bottle on the top step and looked down into the gloom. There were three steps leading down to the dusty slabs at the bottom of the crypt. On the right-hand side, three stone coffins lay on thick sandstone shelves.

He leaned in and peered further into the tomb. 'Well, at least there are no bodies lying on the floor in there.'

'We used to go in there as kids, for a dare,' said Amy, quietly.

'You've got more guts than me then,' Bodkin replied as he straightened. 'I wouldn't like to go down there now, and I'm an adult.'

Bodkin tossed the car keys to Somersby and ordered him to drive back to the station and find something to carry all the broken pieces in. 'Make it a sturdy box, a crate would be better.'

'Sir.'

As Somersby hurried away to do his superior's bidding. Bodkin reached into the crypt and using his handkerchief again, picked up the thick, bottom piece of the bottle that contained the wine. He sniffed at it, then put it down on the stone slab at his feet.

'I'll carry that over myself. I don't want to risk spiling it in the back of the car.'

Amy turned away from the tomb and took a few paces towards a patch of ground that looked as though it had been trampled down. The grass had been flattened and the stems of the tulips that had been growing around the edges of the plot had been snapped or were lying broken on the surrounding gravel.

'This must be where he was thrashing about when the poison hit its peak,' Amy said, sadly.

'We think so. Forensics didn't miss that at least.'

Amy looked at the flattened ground with her head tipped slightly to the side.

'Even with the storm that happened the day before, that's a lot of damage.' She turned and studied the far side of the lychgate where Villiers's body had been found.

'He didn't get all the way over there on his own, did he?'

'Not in the state he would have been in, no. Someone put him there after death.'

Amy walked slowly across to the lychgate bench and then turned and looked back towards the flattened area of ground.

'He must have been making a bit of a racket in his death throes, don't you think? Someone must have heard him screaming.'

'No one's come forward to say they saw or heard anything after nine o'clock. Not yet at least. We're going to put out an appeal in the Spinton Star this week to see if we can jog anyone's memory. The thing is, the pub goers may already have passed by before this happened.'

'Well, it was planned, obviously. This wasn't a spur of the moment thing, was it?'

Bodkin frowned at her. 'Why do you say that?'

'Because of the chalked message, I can't see anyone writing that out on the spur of the moment, can you.'

'Nope,' Bodkin agreed, then he grinned. 'I had already worked that out, you know.'

'Ha!' Amy retorted. She looked through the gate to the pavement as Bodkin's car pulled up. 'Ah, here's Somersby.' Suddenly she laughed out loud. 'Oh my goodness, Bodkin, he's brought a beer crate.'

CHAPTER NINETEEN

When the broken glass had been cleaned up, Bodkin returned to the station with Somersby and after saying goodbye at the lychgate, Amy took a slow walk home, carrying her coat over her arm as she enjoyed the early spring sunshine.

At the Old Bull she waved to one or two of her male colleagues from the factory as they milled around outside waiting for the doors to open at twelve. As she turned onto Long Lane, she bumped into Miriam who was taking Martha for a walk in her Silver Cross pram.

'Are you coming to see us later?' she asked. 'Alice is dying to hear the latest news from the church.'

'Ha! If she turned up for anything other than a wedding or a christening, she'd know what was going on,' Amy replied with a smile.

'Oh, you know Alice. She's an open-air type, she gets claustrophobic inside a church.'

Amy nodded knowingly. 'She feels she's being lectured to. She was the same at school. She wouldn't have turned up then if her mother hadn't brought her to the school gates every morning.'

Amy kissed the tips of her fingers, reached into the pram and placed them gently on Martha's forehead. 'See you after lunch, little one.'

At home, Amy got changed out of her Sunday best clothes and pulled on a pleated brown skirt and a pink knitted jumper, then she sat on her bed listening to her precious records as she re-read, The Mysterious Affair at Styles, Agatha Christie's first Poirot novel. Amy had chosen it from her bookshelf because the victim had been poisoned with strychnine and she wanted to see if Poirot's little grey cells turned up anything that might help with the Villiers case.

At one, her mother called her down for Sunday lunch and she sat at the table with her head bowed while her father said a lengthy grace.

Amy was not as religious minded as her parents but still a firm believer and although the last book she would pick up to read was the bible that had taken up a permanent residence on the small round table next to Mr Rowlings' armchair, she did have a reasonable knowledge of its contents, having studied it before her confirmation at thirteen.

'I saw you speaking to Mr Jenkins outside the church. Has a date been set for the funeral yet?' she asked. Sydney Jenkins was the local funeral director.

Mr Rowlings speared a fatty looking piece of beef with his fork.

'The bishop is taking care of arrangements himself as Harold had no close relatives. The funeral has been booked for the Tuesday after Easter at eleven o'clock. I'm not sure yet who will be conducting it but we could find out on Friday as the bishop is coming up for the Good Friday service. I'm hoping to get a word with him, I'd like to say a few words myself if he will allow it.'

'I'm sure he'll allow it, Dad, after all those sermons you wrote for him.' Amy reached across the table and took her father's hand.

'It would be a cruel irony indeed if he allowed Daley to conduct the service. He hated Harold.'

'Hated is a strong word, Dad. I know they didn't get on but—'

'They hated each other, Amy. The feeling was mutual. Daley had been trying to usurp Harold for over fifteen years. He seemed to think that merely being born a Spintonian gave him the God given right to take over the parish. He conspired behind Harold's back.'

'Conspired?'

'He's been defaming Harold for years down at Rochester and a few of his old theology student friends, joined in the hunt. Harold and Daley got off on the wrong foot right from the start. He thought it was beneath him when he was sent up here as a curate not long after he was ordained. I have my own contacts down at Rochester and I've been kept well informed about his character assassination of Harold over the years. He claimed Harold was an alcoholic, that he had been stealing church funds, more recently that he had been associating with... prostitutes... None of the mud stuck but it did leave quite a large stain. Harold has been summoned to Rochester to appear before the bishop on at least three occasions. Fortunately, he had more sense than to take Daley's word over Harold's.'

'That's just what I was thinking, Dad. Surely if the bishop saw any validity in the accusations he'd have acted. I'm surprised Mr Daley is even in the frame for the job after all that.'

Mr Rowlings put his knife and fork on his plate and took a sip from his tumbler of water.

'Oh, the bishop thinks rather highly of the Reverend Daley, Amy. They share an interest in science. Both of them studied Chemistry at Cambridge before switching to Theology. I believe both keep themselves up to date with the latest discoveries. He just wasn't interested in all the jealous tittle tattle that reached his ears. He's a reasonable man and he knows how competitive some members of the clergy are. He'll know that Daley only sees our church as a stepping stone to his own job.'

Amy put her own cutlery down and leaned back in her chair, brushing a stray strand of hair out of her eyes, she studied the crucifix on the wall opposite as she thought about what her father had just said.

'And there's me thinking that members of the clergy were full of God's good grace. From what you just told me, they're every bit as greedy and grasping as the rest of society.'

'They are mere mortals just like the rest of us,' Mr Rowlings replied. 'They have the same weaknesses and suffer the same temptations. Greed and envy being just two of the seven deadly sins that the Reverend Daley has succumbed to. I think we can add pride to that list too.'

Amy thought back to when she saw Daley with Councillor de Vere earlier that morning and wondered if lust might also be added to the list. And wrath, what about wrath? Was he obsessed enough about the parish to commit murder to get his hands on it?

She was brought out of her musings when her mother placed a bowl of apple pie and custard in front of her.

'You were miles away then, our Amy. Eat your pudding before it gets cold.'

After lunch, Amy got her clothes ready for work the following morning, then took a stroll down to the farm where she spent a pleasant afternoon catching up on the rest of the town's gossip with Alice and Miriam.

At five o'clock, she returned home, and after tea, picked up her Christie novel and sat on the sofa reading Captain Hasting's account of how Poirot solved the murder of Emily Inglethorp, while the Ovaltineys performed their concert party on the radio. Just after nine, she gave her mother a hug and received a whisky scented kiss on the cheek from her father before heading up to bed.

Amy arrived at work on the Monday morning to find that the upcoming week-long break had become the hot topic of conversation amongst the workforce and the vicar's murder had become yesterday's news.

Big Nose Beryl tried her best to hijack the conversation with her unfounded allegations regarding Pauline Clarke, a young machinist who hadn't been seen since she clocked out on the previous Wednesday evening. In Beryl's mind the mystery had a simple answer. Pauline had either run off with Wilfred Parry, a married man some twenty years her senior who, as it happened, hadn't been seen since Wednesday himself, or had discovered she was pregnant and had caught the train to London to do 'something about it'.

When Carole pointed out that Wilfred had broken his leg working at the cement works the week before Pauline's apparent disappearance, instead of being embarrassed, Beryl merely said that, 'in that case, the second option must be true'.

Amy sighed and decided that for once, she'd ignore Beryl's malicious gossip, and after tidying her turban in the wall mirror, she left the staff room and walked slowly to her machine where the runner had already stacked a basket of unfinished garments.

By eleven o'clock, her machine had died three times and the maintenance crew were being run ragged. At half past, the power failed completely and the entire factory was plunged into semi darkness, the only light coming in from the narrow strip of glass panels, high up on the back wall. The stand-in foreman, Mr Bartholomew, who had been given the job on a temporary basis, came out from his office and urged everyone to remain calm. A few minutes later, the maintenance crew carrying powerful torches, walked up and down the aisles leading the machinists to safety.

At twelve o'clock, a meeting was called in the loading bay and the workers were told that the factory would remain closed until the new electricity supply had been installed. To cheers, Mr Bartholomew wished his staff a Happy Easter, then ordered the workforce to form an orderly queue, pick up their belongings from the changing room and make their way home.

'Well, that's a bonus,' Carol said as she and Amy walked past the overgrown hedge that marked the boundary of the factory. 'How are you going to spend your extra days off? Do you think you'll get to see that policeman of yours?'

Amy tucked a wayward strand of hair behind her ear and looked at her friend with a twinkle in her eyes.

'I'm counting on it,' she said.

CHAPTER
TWENTY

'What on earth are you doing home this early?' Mrs Rowlings looked up at the big, round clock on the kitchen wall.

'The factory's shut down. The power went off and they couldn't get it back on again,' Amy replied happily.

'Are the electricity company starting work early then? They weren't due to begin until Thursday, were they?'

'I'm not sure, Mum, all I do know is... I've got the WHOLE WEEK OFF!' Amy did a little dance, pulled her sandwich box out of her work bag and placed it on the thick wooden counter underneath the food cupboard. 'I'll put the kettle on, I bet you're ready for a cuppa.'

Mrs Rowlings wiped her sweating brow with the back of her hand, then pulled a sopping wet, white shirt out of the copper boiler with a pair of wooden tongs and dropped it into the half-filled Belfast sink to rinse. Once she was happy that most of the soap had been removed, she repeated the process with two more shirts, then emptied the sink and fed the soaking wet shirts through the mangle to remove as much water as possible.

'Can I give you a hand, Mum?' Amy asked, spooning tea into the pot. 'You really ought to try tea bags, they're so much easier.'

Mrs Rowlings stuck out her bottom lip and blew air up onto her face.

'No, it's all right, dear, I've almost finished now. Your clothes are already on the line.'

Refilling the sink with cold water she dropped the shirts into it again and added a little bag of Dolly Blue which would hopefully remove any greying from the shirts and make them look as white as they were when they were new.

Amy hurried across the room and wound the mangle handle as her mother fed the wet shirt through. Holding it up to check it after the press, she folded the shirt and laid it on top of a pile of washing that was sitting on a chair by the back door waiting to be hung on the line.

'Thank you, dear,' she said as she began to feed the next shirt into the mangle rollers.

After lunch, Amy decided to catch the bus into town to pay the pound she hadn't needed to spend on her business cards, back into her post office account. Still tempted by the bias-cut dress, she paid another visit to Brigden's but after holding it in front of herself in the mirror again, she fought back against the temptation to take Sharon up on her offer of paying for the dress over a four-week period, and hanging it back on the rail, she took one last, lingering look at it, then walked back out to the High Street.

The weather had turned chilly again and a brisk, northerly wind had picked up. Amy pulled the collar of her coat tight across her neck and sticking her head down, she walked into the wind until she got to the junction with Middle Street.

Resisting the temptation to drop in on Bodkin, she turned onto Main Road and made her way down the hill past the church and continued on until she got to the newsagents. A small bell tinkled a welcome as she pushed the half glass door open. A short line of men were waiting at the counter, all clutching a copy of The Sporting Life, newspaper.

On spotting Amy, the men all stood back from the counter and waited impatiently for her to collect a copy of Woman's Own which she bought now and then as a thank you gift for her mother.

Smiling at the men, she turned and left the shop, leaving the Monday punters to put their illegal bets on the afternoon race cards. Harry Oldham, the newsagent, was known to offer a 'bookies' runner' service to one of the local bookmakers. If the police knew about it, they turned a blind eye.

As she came out of the shop, she almost bumped into Peter Kissman who was hurrying, head down, towards Rufford Street, his open raincoat flapping behind him in the stiff breeze.

'Hello, Peter,' Amy said, stepping back into the shop doorway to avoid a side on collision.

Kissman lifted his head at the sound of her voice. 'Oh, it's you. Hello.'

'I thought you were going to Leysdown for Easter?' Amy said.

Kissman blew out his cheeks, then let the air escape. 'Change of plan. I'm er... well, I went to see Caroline yesterday evening. I finally managed to explain how I feel, and... well, she said, YES! We're going out on Saturday night.'

Amy grinned widely. 'I'm so pleased for you, Peter. Well done for having the courage to give it one last try.'

Peter looked up to the heavens and smiled. 'I seized the moment this time.'

'So, you're not going on holiday now?'

'Oh it wasn't really a holiday as such. I just haven't seen the old folks for ages. I'll go in the summer now. It's nice down there when the sun's out. I might ask Caroline if she'll come with me.'

Amy nodded enthusiastically. 'I'm sure she will.' Her face took on a serious look. 'I hear the reverend's funeral is set for next Tuesday now. Will you be... I mean will it be your job to dig...'

'The grave? Yes. I'll be doing that, I'll have to start on Thursday, probably. I can't work on Good Friday or Easter Sunday, and Monday is a bank holiday, so it doesn't give me a lot of time to get it dug. If I'm struggling with time, or the weather, I'll get Abel to come over again on Saturday to help me finish off.' He was silent for a moment. 'That's if the new vicar will pay him the extra to do it. Mr Villiers never queried it, he just used to cough up when the job was done. I get five bob extra for graves. Abel got the same for helping.'

He looked down the hill towards Rufford Street and pulled his mac tight around his chest.

'Well, I'd better get a move on. I'm nipping home to change my boots.' He held one foot up to show its flapping sole. 'You can't tidy graves in leaky boots.'

Amy said goodbye, then, on impulse, instead of making her way home, she turned right and headed back up the hill towards Middle Street, intending to tell Bodkin about Peter Kissman's change of plan. She was just about to enter the police station when she heard a car's horn toot. When she turned around, she saw Bodkin's Morris Ten pulling up at the kerb.

The detective wound down his window and smiled at her. 'Have they sacked you at last? Why aren't you at work?'

'The electricity finally gave out. They've shut us down until after Easter.'

'Lucky you. I wish this place would shut down,' Bodkin replied.

'Are you going inside?' Amy asked.

'I was going to, but I don't think I'll bother now. You have saved me from a police canteen lunch. Come on, hop in, we'll go to that little café on Cherry Street, we can kill two birds with one stone.'

Bodkin took off his grey hat and placed it on the oblong table as he stood waiting for Amy to sit. Their order of a pot of tea and plates of ham sandwiches was being made ready behind the counter. Mrs Brown hummed to herself as she cut the fresh bread and spread it thickly with deep yellow butter. Bodkin salivated as the smell of frying bacon wafted across the café. Two workmen wearing badly stained overalls, sat at a table by the window, waiting patiently for their greasy lunches.

Bodkin studied the menu as they chatted.

'It's quite reasonable here, and you can get a proper meal, not just the cake and sandwiches the Morning Sun Café serves up on the High Street.'

'I like the Morning Sun. I go in every Saturday after seeing what delights Brigden's have to offer.'

'Well, I think I might make this place a regular stop off in future, there's far less chance of getting food poisoning here than there is in the police canteen.'

Bodkin smiled as Mrs Brown placed a white tea pot in the centre of the table, then offloaded two white cups and saucers from her tray. After retracing her steps, she returned with two plates of thick cut ham sandwiches.

Amy thanked her and watched the cook as she returned to watch the pan of sizzling bacon.

'I've seen her in church,' she said. 'She's aways with a much older man, I think it's her father. Sometimes there's a young girl with them, she must be about thirteen or so.'

Bodkin bit into his sandwich and closed his eyes, savouring the taste. 'My Go... goodness, I'm ready for this.'

Amy gave him a warning look then picked up her own sandwich and took a dainty bite. 'Did the reverend's doctor tell you anything interesting?'

'Extremely interesting,' Bodkin replied before taking another huge bite of his sandwich.

Amy picked up the tea pot and lifted the lid to peer inside.

'Ah, tea bags. Another forward-looking woman,' Amy said as she replaced the lid and poured tea into their cups. After adding milk to both from a small, white china jug, she placed the pot back in the centre of the table, then, picking up her own sandwich again, she sighed and held it in front of her mouth.

'Well, Bodkin. Are you going to spill the beans or are you going to keep me in suspense until you've had lunch?'

Bodkin grinned and washed his food down with a big gulp of tea.

'The reverend was in good health for a man of his age, especially for a man who drank as much as he did. Doctor Mighten had advised him to cut back on the amount he consumed but he wasn't particularly worried about him.'

'So, he didn't have an ulcer then?'

'Apparently not, he was being treated for gastroesophageal reflux disease, acid reflux to me and you. Recently he had been complaining of a bitter taste in his mouth even between meals.

Doctor Mighten put that down to the acid reflux and prescribed the bicarb powders.' Bodkin took another bite of his sandwich. 'This is really good.' He nodded towards Amy's plate and pointed to his mouth, encouraging her to eat. Amy picked up her sandwich again and took another small bite.

Bodkin swallowed the mouthful, then continued, much to Amy's relief.

'This is the interesting thing. He'd only been complaining of the reflux and bitter taste on his tongue for the last week or so before he died. So, something had changed in his body, or something had been introduced to his diet to have instigated that change.'

'Had he complained of vomiting or really bad stomach cramps?'

Bodkin tipped his head towards her and winked. 'That was my very next question and the answer was no.'

Amy put her sandwich down again and took a sip of tea. 'Did he only make one visit to the surgery with this particular complaint?'

'No, he went back on one other occasion, complaining that the reflux was getting worse and his stomach was feeling bloated. He also reported that at certain times of the day, he couldn't taste anything at all. At other times he could taste food that had a strong flavour but even then, nowhere near as well as he could before the reflux started. Doctor Mighten decided that he was now suffering from Dysgeusia, or possibly, Hypogeusia, which are similar conditions that affect the tastebuds. Both conditions can just be a temporary phenomenon. Either condition can lead to either a bitter taste, a semi-permanent, sweet taste or a lack of any taste at all.'

Bodkin pushed his empty plate away and looked greedily at

the untouched half of Amy's sandwich. 'Are you going to eat that?'

Amy offered up her plate and Bodkin slid the thick pieces of bread onto his own.

'I'm so glad I don't suffer from Dysgeusia,' he said, taking a big bite.

Amy picked up her cup and held it in front of her mouth without taking a sip. 'That can't have been very pleasant for him.'

'Villiers told the doctor that he'd changed his diet and was eating a lot of fish instead of meat, and while that didn't stop the bloating or reflux, it did give him a little relief. He also took to carrying a bag of sweets around with him all the time. He said that after one or two mint humbugs or a couple of pineapple chunks, he could begin to taste them. He seemed to think they might keep his tastebuds alive while the doctor worked on a cure for the Dysgeusia.'

'What about his wine, could he taste that?'

'Now, that's one question I didn't ask, but some wines are strong flavoured so maybe he could.'

Bodkin finished his bonus sandwich, drained his tea cup, then sat back rubbing his stomach. 'That'll keep me going for a while.'

'You really should look after yourself a bit better than you do, Bodkin. I hope you're going to cook proper meals once you've settled in to your new home.'

'The road to hell is paved with good intensions,' Bodkin replied. 'But I will try to eat some healthy food. I know I can't live on sandwiches and fish and chips for the rest of my life.'

Amy reached across the table and patted his hand. 'You're welcome to come to us for Sunday lunch, or for a meal in the week. Mum always cooks too much.'

'You're very kind, Amy,' Bodkin said as the two workmen, having finished their bacon sandwiches, got to their feet.

'Thanks, Mavis, see you tomorrow,' the taller of the men said.

As the door closed behind them, Mavis came from behind the counter and began to clear the table they had just vacated. She piled the crockery onto a wicker tray and looked over to Bodkin as he caught her eye.

'Do you think we could have a word, Mrs Brown,' Bodkin said, pulling his warrant card from his pocket. 'It's about the late Reverend Villiers.'

CHAPTER TWENTY-ONE

A shocked look came across Mrs Brown's face.

'Me... What have...? I mean, I don't know why you would want to question me about his death?'

'It's not solely about his death, Mrs Brown. We need a bit of background information.' Bodkin got to his feet and pulled out a spare chair. 'Please, sit down.'

Mavis Brown was a small woman of just over five feet in height. Her light brown hair was streaked with grey. Amy put her at about forty years of age. Her face was careworn, rather than aged, her furrowed brow, making her appear older than she was. Her dull blue eyes hinted at a life of worry and sadness.

'I'd better lock up before we begin,' she said. 'Will it take long? I usually get a bit of a rush about three, before the school empties out.' She walked to the door and flipped the open sign to closed, then turned the key in the lock and pulled down the blind. 'Are the schools even open, it is Easter week, isn't it?'

'They're shut for a fortnight,' Amy said.

Mrs Brown mouthed 'of course' then smoothed down her flower-patterned pinafore and sat down.

'Are you with the police?' she asked Amy.

'Miss Rowlings is assisting us with this case,' Bodkin said quickly.

Amy dipped into her bag and pulled out one of her pink cards. 'Kent Police Accredited,' she added.

Mrs Brown seemed content with the explanation.

'How can I help?'

Bodkin gave her a reassuring smile. 'Firstly, I'd like to say how much we enjoyed our lunch. I've taken a look at your menu and I can assure you that you'll be seeing me on a regular basis. There'll be a few shillings extra in your till every week from now on.'

'Oh, it's not my till,' Mrs Brown replied. 'I wish it was. No, I'm just the head cook and bottlewasher, I'm afraid. Mr Armitage is the owner. He gave me the fancy title of manageress when he took me on, but I'm really just his skivvy.'

'There are worse jobs, I suppose,' Bodkin said. 'Do you get any help at all?'

'Young Mary comes in on a Saturday when we get busy but mostly it's just me.'

'Have you worked here long?' Bodkin asked.

'Seven years in June,' she replied. 'I've become a fixture more or less. We live in the rooms above.'

'We?'

'Gerald, my husband. He's having a nap upstairs. He needs to rest a lot more these days.'

'I'm sorry to hear that, is he ill?' Bodkin asked, sympathetically.

'He's not quite himself these days, it's just old age. He's gone downhill since he retired. He'll be seventy this year. He worked in the mines for too long and its finally caught up with him.'

'I've seen you with him in the church,' said Amy.

'Yes, we like to go when we can. We take my daughter, Violet with us some weeks.' A sad look came over her face and she studied her hands. 'She's not with us at the moment.'

Bodkin gave Amy a quick glance as if sharing a thought.

'Mrs Brown, we believe you were at a meeting at the vicarage on Friday the twenty-fourth of March. Is that correct?'

'Yes, Gerald and I attended a meeting to discuss setting up a new committee to help the poor children of the parish get much needed medication.'

'And was it a successful meeting? Was the makeup of the committee agreed?'

'No. The reverend had changed his mind about it since the last time we'd met. He didn't say why, but he did have quite a long discussion with Councillor de Vere about something.'

'She already ran a similar charity venture, I believe.'

'She did, but she was in the process of winding it up. Two of her main sponsors had pulled out leaving the fund short of money. She was hoping to get the church to invest in their place. The church had been gifted a few thousand pounds in a will and it hadn't been decided what use it would be put to. Mrs de Vere was steadfast in her opinion that at least some of the money should be invested in her fund. She's a very determined woman when she's roused.'

'Do you know how big this donation was... the amount gifted to the church?'

'I believe it was a large sum. Eight thousand pounds.'

'I'm surprised the bishop didn't step in to seize the money for dioceses' purposes,' Bodkin said. 'It really is quite a lot of money.'

'He couldn't. The will stipulated that it was only to be used for the good of the parish. He couldn't get his hands on it even if he wanted to.'

Bodkin nodded in understanding.

'The vicar didn't give any hint as to why he was reluctant to invest in Mrs de Vere's venture then. He didn't put any alternative ideas forward as to how he intended to spend the windfall?'

'No, and to be honest, I didn't expect him to. We were only there to discuss our... Mrs de Vere's proposed committee.'

'Why were you invited to be on the committee in the first place?' Amy asked. 'I'm not being snooty, but everyone else seems to be belong to a profession.'

'I know, and we were surprised to be asked. Mrs de Vere stopped us outside the church the other Sunday and invited us to take part. There was no payment involved, to us at least.'

Amy tilted her head to the side. 'Did she say why she wanted you on the committee?'

'For our experience of how the fund works. We were beneficiaries of her charity, you see. We still are, for now at least. I'm not sure what's going to happen if Mrs de Vere can't access more funding. Violet's treatment is so expensive. We could never afford it on our own.'

'So, you weren't members of Mrs de Vere's charity committee before she tried to set the new one up?' Bodkin asked.

'No. Doctor Frazier was and so was Eugene Hales who owns the pharmacy. Agatha Walker, she's the pharmacist who does most of the dispensing, wasn't a member of the original charity committee though. She was asked to join the new one at the same time as me.'

'What is Violet being treated for if you don't mind me asking?' Bodkin flashed Mrs Brown a short-lived smile.

'She has, err… she has a mental illness. She has been diagnosed as suffering from psychosis. It's got progressively worse over the last couple of years. She spends a lot of time in Hanover House, the mental institution on the Gillingham Road. She's allowed home now and then, when the symptoms ease, but we never get to keep her here too long. She's very ill… she's only fourteen, it's not fair.'

Mrs Brown wiped away an angry tear.

'You should see the things they did to her there. Hydrotherapy… they basically stood her against a wall, naked and sprayed her with freezing cold water with a hosepipe. Then they tried insulin shock therapy, which induced convulsions while in a coma. After that they made her have electroconvulsive therapy. That was probably the worst of all. She wasn't much more than a zombie when she was recovering from that. Eventually, they said they were going to give her a lobotomy, take part of her brain away. Over my dead body. I tried everything to stop that operation going ahead and eventually, they said they'd give an alternative therapy a chance before resorting to the operation. Apparently, in America, they were using an experimental medication on patients with depression and severe melancholy. The drug is called amphetamine and the makers claimed it did have some success.'

Mrs Brown slumped in her chair.

'Unfortunately, the Hanover House hierarchy refused to pay for the treatment or the setting up of the clinical trial, so our only option was to fund the treatment ourselves but we didn't have anything like that kind of money. Oh, it wasn't a fortune, don't get me wrong, but with Gerald's pension and my earnings here, we only just about survive ourselves. If the flat didn't come with the job, we'd be living in a slum somewhere.'

Bodkin leaned forward in his chair. 'So, Mrs de Vere decided to pay for Violet's treatment. That was very noble of her.'

'We tried a few charities but hers was the only one that responded to our plight. They covered the whole cost of her treatment and her share of the clinical trial. It was a Godsend.'

Amy closed her eyes for a moment. 'Poor Violet,' she whispered.

'Did the treatment work?' Bodkin asked.

'Yes and no, she did improve slightly, she still got the voices in her head but she wasn't as bad as she had been. She was getting particularly violent when she had an episode and as she was growing up, she was getting stronger. She was so hard to control.' A flash of pain shot across her face. 'Anyway, they're still trying different doses and they still give her a sedative when her attacks get really bad.'

'Have they kept her in the asy... in the hospital since she started the trial?' Bodkin asked.

'Mostly. She came home for a while a few weeks ago, but she had an attack almost immediately. We didn't want to send her straight back, so we kept quiet about it and she calmed down after a day or so. We used to take her for long, daily walks down by the river. The fresh air helped her a lot, I think. She was home for about three weeks. It was hard work but we managed. Gerald used to sit with her upstairs and I got young Mary to help out if I needed to spend time with Violet during the day.'

Bodkin clasped his hands and rested them on the table. 'Mrs Brown. Let me take you back to that meeting. Can you remember anything untoward that happened? You said that

Mrs de Vere and Mr Villiers were involved in an argument. Was it a heated one?'

'Heated? No, I wouldn't say, heated, but they were animated, that's for sure.'

'Did the argument take place in the church hall or the vicarage?'

'The church hall, I think they had agreed to sleep on it and discuss their differences at a later date by the time we got back to the vicarage.'

Bodkin leaned back in his chair and pursed his lips.

'Okay, so, can you take us through exactly what you remember after you got to the vicarage. Think very carefully, Mavis. Even the smallest detail might be important.'

Mavis put her hands on her temples as she gathered her thoughts.

'The meeting broke up about eight o'clock and the Reverend Villiers invited us all back to the vicarage for a glass of wine before we went home. When we got there, he took us into the kitchen and he got a couple of bottles of wine from the cupboard while Mrs Gatting, that's his housekeeper, found us all a clean glass.'

'Was there anyone one else in the kitchen apart from the committee and Mrs Gatting?'

'Yes, there was a man there, I've seen him around town now and then but I don't know him. He was with Mrs Gatting when we got there... OH! He put a syringe in a pan of water and put it on the hotplate, I do remember that. I thought it a bit odd.'

'Anything else. What was the vicar's attitude like? Did he seemed pleased to have you all in his house?'

'Not so you'd notice. He just wanted us to drink up and get out, I think.'

'Did you notice any other wine apart from the bottles he

got from the cupboard? Were there any other bottles lying around?'

'I can't remember seeing any.'

Bodkin nodded slowly. 'So, you are all in the kitchen drinking wine. What were you all talking about? The committee, the weather...?

'Tittle tattle mostly, but I remember saying how hot it was in the kitchen. The vicar must have agreed as he took his jacket off and hung it on the back of a chair. Mrs Gatting offered to open a window, but then someone mentioned a date for the next and probably last, committee meeting and we all followed the vicar through to his study to check his diary.'

'The study is even smaller than the kitchen, isn't it? It must have been pretty crowded in there.'

'Not uncomfortably so. We all gathered around his desk while he got his day diary out of the drawer. He proposed a date and that was it, really.'

'Which date did he propose?' asked Bodkin.

'The twenty-first, I think. Yes, it was, Friday the twenty-first at seven o'clock in the church hall.'

'Mrs Brown, I'd like you to concentrate hard on that study. Did anyone leave while you were all gathered around the desk.'

'No, no one left. We all left together.'

'Can you remember anything else, no matter how irrelevant it might seem?'

'Well, the vicar patted his pockets once, obviously expecting to find something, but then he rolled his eyes and took a boiled sweet from a bag on the desk. He didn't offer them round though.'

Bodkin closed his eyes as if picturing the scene. 'There were no sweets on the desk when I went in on the Monday evening,' he mused.

Bodkin let the train of thought lapse, then smiled up at the cook again. 'Then what, Mrs Brown?'

'We all put our empty glasses on his desk and he led us out to the front door where he wished us a good night and we all made promises to each other that we'd catch up during the week. I doubt anyone was serious about it of course. I wasn't. Gerald and I don't usually mix in those circles.'

'When you were standing around in the porch, did anyone go back into the house?'

'No... Yes, wait... Both Mrs de Vere and Mrs Walker went back in. Mrs Walker had left her spectacles on the vicar's desk and Mrs de Vere said she needed a glass of water as the wine had given her hiccups.'

'Was Mrs Gatting there at this time?'

'Yes, she was standing in the doorway, she had to step aside to allow them back in.'

'Were they inside very long?'

'No, Mrs Walker was back within a few seconds, Mrs de Vere took a little longer, but not much. She had to have time to drink the water, I suppose.'

'You've been very helpful, Mrs Brown; you have an excellent memory that's for certain, and, as that is the case, do you remember seeing the man in the kitchen again that night?'

'Yes, he must have left by the back door, he came along the side of the house as we were saying our goodbyes. He disappeared through the gate that leads to the churchyard. He waved to Mrs Gatting just before he went out of sight.'

Bodkin bit his bottom lip as he took the information in.

'Right, I think that's all, Mrs Brown. As I said. You've been very helpful. We may need to talk to you again if anything needs clarifying, but apart from that, I think we're done so please don't get nervous when you see me come through the door later in the week. I'll be chasing my lunch, not criminals. I do like the look of your menu.'

As Bodkin got to his feet, Amy had a thought.

'Speaking of menus. Did the vicar ever eat here himself?'

The question seemed to catch Mrs Brown by surprise. 'Err, yes, he did as a matter of fact. He used to come in three days a week, regular as clockwork.'

'Which days, Mrs Brown?' Bodkin was suddenly interested.

'Monday, Wednesday and Friday. He said he liked to help out the local businesses. I know he used to go to the chip shop on Middle Street every Saturday lunchtime.'

'What did he order? When he was here, not from the chip shop.' Bodkin grinned as he clarified his question.

'Until a couple of weeks ago he always had beef and two veg. Then he changed suddenly and started ordering boiled fish. He said it was to help his digestion. It didn't matter what sort, whatever we had that was fresh. He used to have a single dollop of mash and a few large spoons of parsley sauce with it. More than I'd usually dish up. I'm not a fan but he liked it.'

'Is there anything else you can tell us about the vicar?' Bodkin asked. 'Did he say anything about the committee or talk about any other local gossip while he was eating?'

'No, he hardly said a word. He used to compliment me on my cooking after every meal but that changed when he switched to fish, I don't think he actually liked it that much. The only thing I can remember him saying that last week, was something about enjoying the taste of the sauce.'

'He had developed a problem with his tastebuds, Mrs Brown,' Bodkin said. 'He could only taste foods that had a particularly bitter or sweet flavour.'

'That's why he started going to the sweet shop is it? I did

notice that. For the last week or so, as soon as he left here, he'd head straight across the road to Cavanagh's.'

Mrs Brown got to her feet and walked Amy and Bodkin to the door. After lifting the blind and unlocking it. She flipped the sign to 'open' then opened the door to let them out.

'One last thing, Mrs Brown. Do you keep any poisons on the premises, rat killer, anything like that?'

'No, we don't need to. The council look after things like that. They sent a team of rat catchers out at regular intervals; the town had a huge rat problem until they started sending in the extermination teams. I haven't seen one in two years now.'

Bodkin allowed Amy to walk out first, then, after shaking Mrs Brown's hand, he stepped out into the street.

'If you think of anything else that you think might assist us, please don't hesitate to call,' he said, passing her one of his cards.

'Where to now, Bodkin?' Amy asked as they began to walk along Cherry Street.

'I've got an appointment with Mrs de Vere at three o'clock, but I've suddenly developed an irresistible craving for a quarter pound of dolly mixtures.'

CHAPTER TWENTY-TWO

CAVANAGH'S SWEET SHOP HAD BEEN IN THE FAMILY FOR OVER SEVENTY years, but the owner was still managing to eke out a living despite the new innovation that Woolworths had brought in with its Pick and Mix counter.

The shop was dimly lit, the only light coming through a dingy, eight-pane window and from a single electric bulb that hung from the ceiling on a thin, twisted wire. Mr Cavanagh himself had worked at the shop since he was eleven and had inherited the business when his father had been gassed in the last months of the Great War.

Cavanagh was in his seventies with sparse white hair and skin like an over ripe peach. His arthritic right hand, hung almost useless at his side as he scooped a measure of acid drops from a large jar onto his metal scales. Crouching down to make sure the quarter pound measure was accurate, the old man reached into the jar with his left hand, selected one sweet between his finger and thumb and dropped it onto the scales before tipping the contents into a paper bag, twisting the top and handing it over to a tall, stringy woman, not much younger than the sweetshop owner himself.

She looked up as the doorbell tinkled and Amy and Bodkin walked in. Waving the bag at them she made for the door.

'They're for my great grandson, Horace,' she announced as though the transaction needed an explanation.

Bodkin smiled and opened the door for the elderly lady who simpered before walking out onto the pavement.

'How may I help you?' Cavanagh stretched out his arms as though he was about to perform a conjuring trick.

'This lady would like...' Bodkin held out his own hand towards Amy.

Amy looked around the dingy shop at the rows of dusty glass jars and boxes of chocolate bars.

'Ooh, you have so much to choose from,' she said, her mind taking her back to when her mum and dad used to bring her into the shop when she was a little girl. She didn't really have a sweet tooth these days, but both her parents did, and they both adored mint humbugs.

'Could I have a quarter of mint humbugs please?' she said. 'The stripey kind.'

Cavanagh reached up to the third shelf and awkwardly grabbed the large jar, pulling it expertly close to his chest to stop him dropping it. After weighing out the four ounces, he once again, took one extra sweet from the jar and dropped it onto the scale.

'There you are, that'll be thruppence,' he said with a smile as he twisted the paper bag and handed it over to Amy.

Bodkin handed over a threepenny bit and Cavanagh rang it into his till.

'Anything else I can do for you?'

Bodkin produced his warrant card and showed it to

Cavanagh. Amy smiled as the old man squinted at it in the dim light. He might as well have been showing him a bus ticket.

'I'm from Spinton police, Mr Cavanagh. I've got a couple of questions to ask if you don't mind.'

'I don't mind, son,' the shopkeeper replied. 'My scales are spot on and I don't overcharge.'

Bodkin held up his hands, palms towards the sweet shop owner.

'It's nothing to do with how your business is conducted, sir. We'd just like to know if you remember serving the Reverend Villiers in your shop.'

'Villiers? Oh, of course, he's the dearly departed, isn't he? Yes, he's been calling in recently. Most days actually.'

'What did he purchase, can you remember?'

Cavanagh pointed to the humbug jar.

'Mint humbugs, pear drops, pineapple chunks and aniseed balls, but mostly pear drops and pineapple chunks. They are covered in sugar you see. He liked his confectionary to be as sweet as possible.'

'And you say he came in every day?'

Cavanagh nodded.

'Oh yes. Two o'clock give or take a quarter of an hour.'

Bodkin pulled out his notebook and pretended to jot down a few notes as he waited for the old man to continue.

'He'd have eight ounces a day. A full pound in two eight-ounce bags on a Saturday because I don't open on Sundays.'

'And he's only been coming in recently?' Bodkin asked.

'I'd never seen him before in my life until he walked through that door about three weeks or so ago. I'm not a religious man you see. There's too much suffering in the world for me to believe in any loving God.' He looked over his narrow glasses at Amy. 'No offence, if you're a believer,' he added.

'Did you get chatting to him at all. Did he ever discuss his health?'

'Not as such, apart from saying he preferred the sweetest of the sweet. We didn't get into politics or the state of the country or anything like that.'

Bodkin thanked the shopkeeper, turned away and opened the door to allow Amy to walk out of the shop first.

'We didn't learn much from him, did we?' Amy said, stuffing the sweets into her bag.

'No, nothing new, but we have added to our knowledge of his movements over that final week. Everything we hear from any one source has to be confirmed before we can use it to build up the big picture.'

He led Amy back to the car and opened the door to let her into the front passenger seat before scurrying around to the driver's side.

'Right, Mrs Councillor de Vere, it's your turn,' he said.

'I've been looking forward to talking to her,' Amy said excitedly. 'There's definitely something going on between her and Mr Daley.'

'You, erm, won't be able to come in with me for this interview, Amy. We're going to be discussing financial issues and she's not going to be happy talking to me about her personal life, let alone someone without an official reason to be questioning her.'

Amy sighed. 'So, my police accreditation only goes so far then?'

'It's already stretched further than it's supposed to stretch,' Bodkin replied. 'Stretch it much more and the elastic will snap.'

'All right, Bodkin, you've made your point,' Amy said with a disappointed tone in her voice. 'But you will give me the gist of the conversation, won't you? You can leave out the figures, I just want the facts.'

Bodkin sighed as he started up the engine. 'Shall I drop you at home first?'

'It depends what you are doing after interviewing Mrs de Vere,' Amy said. 'I'd much rather be working on the case with you than sitting at home twiddling my thumbs, even if I'm only a bit of a hanger on.'

Bodkin shook his head and gave her a quick smile as he looked over his shoulder before pulling away from the kerb.

'After Mrs de Vere, I was going to sit in the park and think things through for half an hour,' he replied. 'I think much more clearly without the sound of telephones ringing and typewriters clacking.'

'I'll come with you then,' Amy said cheerfully. 'I can help you think.'

The de Vere residence could almost be classed as a Georgian mansion and was set in a couple of acres of gardens just off the Gillingham Road.

Bodkin parked on a tarmacked area at the side of a large pair of wrought iron gates that had been built into a high brick wall.

'Are you sure you want to wait?' he asked as he switched off the engine. 'I'll be in there at least thirty minutes, possibly a full hour.'

Amy patted her bag.

'I've got Mum's Woman's Own magazine in here. That will pass the time, though it's hardly riveting reading. If I'd have known I was going to be abandoned, I'd have brought my

Agatha book with me. Poirot is on the case of the Inglethorp murderer.'

'Ah, The Mysterious Affair at Styles,' Bodkin said. 'Good old Hercule, I wish we had him on our force. Inspector Japp didn't know how lucky he was.'

'You don't need Hercule,' Amy replied breezily. 'You've got me.'

Amy could hear Bodkin chuckling to himself as he unlatched and pushed open one of the ornate gates. When he disappeared around a bend on the path, she pulled out her mother's magazine and flicked through the pages looking for something of interest. She had just found an article which was exploring the changing role of women in the home, when she heard a tap on the window next to her head. She looked left to see a long-faced man smiling through the side window at her. Amy wound it down and smiled back.

'Hello, Joe,' she said. 'This is a nice surprise. What are you doing here?'

'I work here, for my sins,' he replied. 'I've been here a couple of years now. Didn't your father tell you?'

'No, but then that's a conversation he's more likely to have had with Mum than me,' Amy said.

'What are you doing here yourself?' Joe tucked a newspaper wrapped parcel under his arm and straightened with a groan. 'I'll tell you what. My back knows all about working here,' he said.

Amy looked sympathetic. Joe Proudfoot was in his mid-forties, about the same age as her father, who had begun to complain himself about the occasional back pain. Joe was tall with an angular, clean-shaven face. His once-brown hair was rapidly turning to grey but his eyes had lost none of their sparkle and when he smiled, they lit up. He was wearing a pair of green overalls, black wellington boots and a checked cloth cap.

'I'm waiting for Inspector Bodkin,' Amy explained. 'We're going to the park for a stroll when he's finished questioning Mrs de Vere.'

Joe's eyes twinkled. 'Really? What has her ladyship been up to now?'

'Probably nothing,' Amy said. 'But she was in a meeting with Reverend Villiers the night before he died and Bodkin wants to know if she remembers anything that might help him solve the case.'

'So, she's not a suspect?'

'Everyone's a suspect, Joe, until they aren't. That's Bodkin's mantra.'

Joe looked up the path towards the house, then back to Amy.

'As her majesty is going to be tied up for a while, do you fancy a cuppa and a chat? I've got an electric kettle in my shed.'

Amy wound up the window and got out of the car. On impulse she reached into her bag and pulled out her pen and a church leaflet that someone had handed her the week before and turning it to the blank side, she wrote.

I'm quizzing the gardener. If you get back before me, I'm in his shed. Don't worry, he won't bump me off, he's my dad's friend.

Amy

XXX

Leaving the sheet of paper on the driving seat, Amy slammed the door shut and followed Joe through the gates and across the well-kept lawn to a green painted timber shed with a broken padlock hasp.

Amy spotted it immediately.

'Did she break in to see what you're hiding away in here?' she asked, grinning.

'It wouldn't be a big surprise if she had,' he replied. 'She wants to know what I'm up to every minute of every day. She likes to get her money's worth out of me.'

Joe opened the shed door and waited while Amy stepped inside before following her in and closing the door behind him.

'We had a break in a couple of weeks or so, ago. It was a strange one. Nothing was stolen, not that I could see anyway. But the shelves had been rearranged. It was like someone had been searching for something.'

CHAPTER TWENTY-THREE

There was only one, tall, rickety chair in the shed and Joe offered it to Amy who struggled to climb onto it. When she did manage to sit down, she found that she had an excellent view through the propped open, single pane window, across the beautifully manicured grass, to the huge house that loomed up above the tall hedge that bordered the lawn.

Joe shook the kettle and after satisfying himself that there was enough water in it for the two of them, he picked up his own mug, then a dingy looking one from a shelf under his bench and took them out to rinse under the outside tap.

When he returned, Amy was relieved to see that the dirty cup now looked relatively clean.

As Joe busied himself with the tea, Amy took a look around the shelves that contained various tins of different coloured paint, a bottle of turpentine, a tray containing packets of seeds and two or three tins labelled weedkiller, rat gone and insect killer. On the floor were four hessian bags each with its own white printed label denoting which type of grass seed it contained.

Joe wiped Amy's mug on his sleeve and inspected it again. Satisfied that it was clean enough, he passed it to her, then took a sip from his own, steaming mug.

'I wonder how your Mr Bodkin is getting on with the Queen of Sheba?' he mused.

'You really don't seem to like her very much, Joe,' Amy said. 'I'm surprised you put up with her if she's that bad. There's always work for gardeners on the council.'

'I left a council job to come here, remember?' Joe said.

Amy couldn't remember ever being told. She decided that it must have been something her parents had discussed in her absence.

Joe sipped his tea again, then looked into his mug as though he had spotted a foreign object.

'It was better money than the council paid, although the hours are longer... in summer at least.'

Joe put his cup on the bench and pulling out an old crate from underneath, he flipped it on its side then sat on it.

'Life was easier when I first started but since Mr de Vere skedaddled, she's turned into a right little dictator.' He leaned closer to Amy then lowered his voice. 'She had a lot of money trouble after he vanished. I always got my wages on time, but I know a lot of the tradesmen in the town didn't get the money to clear her slate at the end of every week. Tomkins, the greengrocer and Jed Burnett at the butcher's shop were always complaining about her in the Dragon. It wasn't just them either. She owed money to everyone from the newsagent to the haberdashers.'

'Oh dear, that can't have done her reputation much good,' Amy said.

'You're not kidding. It got to the stage where the local businesses demanded cash for anything she wanted to buy. That grass seed for instance...' Joe kicked the hessian bag nearest to him throwing up a small cloud of dust. '...I had to pay for that with my own money and get it back from her with my wages.' Joe picked up his tea and took a long sip. 'To be fair to her, I always got paid, every Friday afternoon. Four o'clock on the dot.'

'Do you know if she has any personal income, Joe? A family trust, that sort of thing, A house like this must take some keeping up.'

'I wouldn't know about that, Amy. I do know that she had to sell her car at one point. She still hasn't replaced it. Oh, and I also know that she's had the house valued at least twice. I actually saw her arguing with the valuer from Hoskins, the Estate Agent. I honestly don't know what price he put on the old pile but I know it was a couple of thousand pounds less than she was hoping to get. I heard her berating him about it... Have you added the lovely gardens, the extra car parking area, the triple garage, etc?' Joe emptied his cup and waved it at Amy. 'More tea?'

Amy shook her head. She'd hardly touched the first one. The state the mug had been in was still worrying her.

'That'll be just me then,' Joe said as he shook the kettle again before placing it onto the paraffin stove.

'So, she's still in financial difficulty, is she?' Amy asked, trying to get the conversation back on track.

'No, I think she's come into some money. Maybe she won the football pools, maybe her husband's had a change of heart and is providing her with an income, but in the last few weeks she's cleared all her local debts and she's started using taxis to get around, so she must have money in the bank. Jed Burnett and Alf Tomkins have restored her lines of credit. She's even got her slate back at the hardware store so I can order stuff without forking out for it myself now.' He pointed to the newspaper wrapped parcel. 'That's a new set of blades for the mower.'

Amy leaned forward to put her mug on the bench and almost tipped the tall chair over. Joe hurried forwards to steady her. She laughed to cover her embarrassment. 'I'm so clumsy.'

When she was settled again, Joe carried his fresh cup of tea back to his upturned crate and plonked himself down on it again.

'Joe, you said you had a break in. When was this, can you remember exactly?'

'It was the week she settled all the debts... and it happened on a Tuesday night. I remember because I wanted to buy a new hasp for the padlock on the Wednesday, but I wasn't going to shell out for it myself and the hardware store wouldn't give her any credit. Then on the Friday, she settled up and all was fine and dandy.'

'You didn't get a replacement hasp though?'

'Oh, yes, I've got one. It's in the drawer there.' Joe nodded towards an old dressing table drawer that was perched on top of a bag of sand, under the bench. 'I just haven't had the time or inclination to fit it yet.'

'Did you report the break in to the police?'

Joe shook his head. 'No, madam wouldn't hear of it. She said there was no point as nothing had been stolen.'

Amy rubbed her cheek gently with her finger tips as she thought.

'That's so strange, why would you go to all the bother and risk of breaking into somewhere and then not steal anything?' Amy looked up at the long, high shelf that held all the tins and bottles. 'You said things had been disturbed. How could you be sure? I mean, it doesn't look like the items on the shelf have been particularly organised.'

'You wouldn't see any order to it, Amy, but I do. I have a sort of obsessive, compulsive character. I like things to be in some sort of order. Those items on the shelf might look like they've been put up there at random but they're actually in alphabetical order.' He pointed to one end of the shelf where a tatty box had the word Alpha Slug Bait, printed on it in fading yellow letters, at the other end was a tin labelled, Ziegler Rooting Powder.

'When I checked, a few of the items were in the wrong place, so someone had obviously been messing with my system.'

'What had moved, Joe? Can you remember?'

'The poisons were in the wrong place. The cyanide I use to make a solution to destroy insect infestations was next to the strychnine-based crystals I used to kill off the moles, and they should have been a long way apart.'

'You said earlier you wouldn't be surprised if she'd broken in herself to see what you had in here, were you serious about that?'

'I was half-joking. I said I wouldn't put it past her. She used to come in sometimes with the invoices when they arrived and check it with what I had in the shed. She couldn't just leave you to get on with things. She's a bit of an autocrat. She has to have control over every tiny thing. I think that was down to the money worries because she wasn't like that when I first came. She didn't seem to care what anything cost back then.'

'Does she have many visitors, Joe? You know, male friends?'

'Not until recently. I don't think she'd have answered the door to a man in case it was the bailiffs up until a few weeks ago, but she has had one regular visitor that I know of. Now,

I'm not saying there's anything untoward going on, but she is still a youngish woman and a very attractive one. With the property she owns, she might be seen as a bit of a catch in some quarters.'

'Who, Joe? Who was it?' Amy leaned forward eagerly and again forced the rickety chair to wobble about alarmingly.

'That Daley fellow. The stand in vicar. He's been here a few times recently. NOW! I can't say if he spends the night. I'm not going to accuse him of that, but I have seen him calling just before I finished work... and... well he was here once when I arrived, that would have been at eight o'clock in the morning, so he either arrived before I did for some reason, or...'

Before Amy could ask any more questions, she heard voices coming from outside. Slipping off the high chair, Amy crept to the shed door and eased it open. On the path, on the left-hand side of the shed, stood Bodkin and Mrs de Vere. They had their backs to her as they chatted.

'So, you are sure there's nothing more you can tell me about Mr Daley?' Bodkin asked.

'I told you, Inspector. I hardly know him. We've spoken once or twice that's all. The last time I saw him was at church on Sunday, we had a brief chat, nothing important, I can't even remember what the conversation was about. It might just have been the weather.'

'And before that?'

'I think I might have bumped into him in the street... or at some meeting or other. I honestly can't remember. I meet so many people at so many different events, it's hard to keep up.'

Bodkin handed her one of his cards. 'If you can think of anything else, no matter how seemingly irrelevant. Give me a call,' he said.

Mrs de Vere took the card, turned and walked across the

lawn towards the house. When she had disappeared between the gap in the big hedge, Amy pulled the door open and then turned to Joe.

'Did you hear all that, Joe?'

Joe nodded. 'She's lying through her teeth for some reason best known to herself. The Reverend Daley came to call on her last Friday. He was still there when she brought my wages out at four o'clock and I didn't see him leave before I went home at five-thirty.'

Amy gave the gardener a hug and a peck on the cheek.

'You must drop in and say hello to Mum and Dad, Joe. They'd love to see you and have a proper catch up.'

Joe smiled, happily. 'I will, tell them I'll pop in at the weekend.'

Amy stepped out of the shed and after a quick look across the lawn towards the house, she crouched low and scurried across the lawn towards the main gates.

CHAPTER TWENTY-FOUR

As she walked through the big iron gates, Amy saw Bodkin standing by the driver's side of the car. He waved the hastily written note at her as she stepped towards him.

'We won't have to dig up the lawns looking for your body then?' he said with a grin.

'HA! You might have if Mrs de Vere had found me lurking in the shed,' she replied.

Bodkin opened the passenger side door to allow Amy to climb inside, then slammed it shut and walked around to the opposite side of the car.

'Are we off to the park then?' Amy asked as the detective started up the engine.

'No, I've changed my mind about that,' Bodkin replied. 'Something's been niggling away at me. How do you fancy a walk along the river instead?'

Bodkin reversed out of the parking bay, then performed an untidy three point turn before driving back up the Gillingham Road towards Spinton. As they passed Hanover House Hospital,

Amy bowed her head and sent up a quick prayer for Violet Brown. When they reached the Welcome to Spinton sign on the outskirts of the town, Bodkin shot her a quick glance.

'Are you ill or something? I thought you'd be nagging me for details of my interview with Mrs de Vere, long before now.'

'I didn't think you wanted to share,' Amy said, giving him a quick glance back. 'I do have my own news. I've learned several things that might be of interest to you over the last couple of days but I haven't had chance to talk to you about them.'

Bodkin glanced across again, then concentrated on the road. 'Go on then?'

'Share and share alike, Bodkin. I tell you something, then you share something with me. It's only fair.'

Bodkin sighed.

'I told you I can't share her personal or financial details with you, not that I've learned that much about them, she's a very cagey lady is Mrs de Vere. I will say this though. I'm going to arrange a meeting with the financial top brass at Skellinghouse Industries tomorrow. She's been trying to lead me up the garden path, I know it.'

Skellinghouse were one of the area's biggest employers and had three factories making home appliances in the Kent region.

'Why, what have they got to do with anything?' Amy asked.

'They pulled their money out of her charity venture, or are at the point of doing so. I'd like to know why. I'm also going to see if I can have a word with her bank manager, though that's never an easy thing to arrange.'

'That's a big one, it has to be worth two of mine,' Amy replied, thoughtfully.

'Well?' Bodkin said after a few moments.

'Okay,' Amy held up a finger. 'One. This is a bit of info you might have heard about but as you haven't mentioned it, I don't think you have.' She looked right towards the detective as she spoke. 'Dad told me yesterday that the vicar's funeral is going to take place next Tuesday. Were you aware of that?'

Bodkin nodded. 'I did read something about it. There was a note on my desk this morning.'

'Did the note tell you that the bishop is coming to Spinton for the Good Friday service?'

'No, it didn't.'

'Well then you won't be aware of the fact that Reverend Daley has a meeting scheduled with the bishop just after the service. That's when he'll find out whether he's got Saint John's church or not. Dad's fuming about it in case the bishop allows Daley to conduct Villiers' funeral service too. He's going to the Good Friday service with Mum of course. He's being allowed a short meeting with the bishop as well, because of all the work he's done in the parish.'

'What time is the service being held?' Bodkin asked.

'Eleven. But the meetings will take place after that in the church hall.'

Bodkin nodded to himself. 'It looks like Saint John's is the place to be on Friday morning. I'll clear my diary. I'd like a word with both of those people.'

Bodkin leaned forward and looked through the passenger window before taking a sharp right-hand turn that led to a piece of empty wasteland from which a narrow, much trodden path led down to the river bank.

'You said you'd got more to tell me?'

'Oh yes, of course I have.' Amy held up another finger. 'Peter Kissman is still in town.'

'Really? I thought he was taking some time off to spend with his parents.'

'There's been a change of plan. He finally plucked up the

courage to ask Caroline out and she's accepted so he's staying now. He's actually going to be digging the vicar's grave.'

'That's good news. It's nice to know that the main witnesses are handy if we need quick answers.' He was silent for a moment. 'There's something... No I can't quite put my finger on it. But I think it's more to do with Mrs Gatting's evidence than Peter's.'

'Your turn, Bodkin. I've got lots more to tell you, but come on, share and share alike.'

'Well, for what it's worth. I think Mrs de Vere told me a pack of lies about how well she knows Daley. I've been thinking about what you picked up on at the church. They were talking about more than just the weather last Sunday.'

'He's been calling on her at her house for the last few weeks. He may even have stayed over,' Amy confided.

'Really! How do you know that?'

Amy took him through everything she'd learned from Joe about Councillor de Vere's financial problems, the abandonment by her husband, her sudden influx of money and her bourgeoning relationship with Daley. When she mentioned the break in, Bodkin's ears pricked up.

'That's interesting. She wouldn't let him inform the police, even though some poison may have been stolen?'

'No, she wouldn't hear of it.'

'Good work, Amy,' Bodkin said, rubbing at his stubble covered chin. 'We'll make a detective of you yet.'

They got out of the car and walked along the narrow, well-trodden dirt path that led to the river. The strong wind from earlier in the day had eased to a slight breeze. Amy tucked the annoying strands of hair that blew across her face, behind her ear and smiled at the swans and mallards as they glided elegantly across the river towards them. She ran her hand through the tall reeds at the side of the river, then tucked her arm through Bodkin's and fell in with his stride.

'It's lovely down here. I really ought to come more often.'

'Do you know what hemlock looks like?' Bodkin asked.

Amy shrugged. 'I haven't got a clue. I know it's a tall weed and that it's highly poisonous, that's about all I do know.'

Bodkin reached into the inside pocket of his mac and pulled out a black and white photograph.

'This is what we're looking for,' he said.

'Pity it's not in Kodachrome,' Amy said, as she examined the page. 'Hey, where did you get this from? Don't tell me you tore it out of a book. Bodkin, that's sacrilege.'

'Just don't tell them at the library,' Bodkin replied, quickly.

'And you're a policeman. There really is no hope for society,' Amy said, giving him one of her looks.

They walked along the bank, stopping now and then to compare plants with the picture in Amy's hand but though they found a few similar looking plants, none of them were quite right in every detail. After another five minutes, Amy stopped at the side of a thick hedge that screened a property from the riverbank. Growing through the hedge were large clumps of eight-foot plants with thick, purple blotched stalks that were especially colourful near the base.

'This looks like it, Bodkin,' she said, bending down to examine the bottom of the plants a little more closely.

'Blimey,' Bodkin replied. 'They're big enough, aren't they? There must be enough to poison the whole town's water supply here.'

'It's growing all along the other side of the river too,' Amy pointed across the water towards a long line of plants that stretched for a good thirty yards.

Bodkin looked around trying to work out where they were in relationship to the buildings in the town, but couldn't see through the hedge and he wasn't the slightest bit inclined to get too close to the deadly hemlock plants.

'Let's move along a bit further.'

A hundred yards on they found another clump of the deadly weed but on this occasion, there was a gap in the hedge close by. Bodkin ducked and climbed into the space, holding back a sharp hawthorn branch so that Amy could follow. When they came out on the other side of the hedge, they looked across a well-kept lawn to a wide, imposing, red brick building.

Bodkin looked up the garden towards the back of the house, then left towards the huge oak and the line of yews that grew next to a high, brick wall.

'If my eyes aren't deceiving me, that's the vicarage,' he said.

Amy looked down at the flattened scrub that ran through the hedge to the riverbank.

'And someone has been through here quite recently.'

Bodkin stood silently for a while as he took in the old vicarage with its oak-panelled back door and the six, eight pane windows that ran across the length of the house on the ground floor. Then his eyes followed the dirty brickwork up to the first floor where another row of casement windows ran, although on this floor some of the windows had been bricked up, most likely to escape the crippling window taxes that the government had brought in at some point in the house's life.

On the left of the building, one of the upper windows hung slightly ajar and the bottom corner pane was missing. Bodkin stared up at the black hole that made up the bottom corner of the casement, his mind straining to grab hold of the elusive picture that was sitting right on the edge of his imagination, just waiting to be plucked and dragged in.

'There's something...'

'What, Bodkin? What have you spotted,' Amy asked eager to join in with the detective's train of thought.

'The window,' Bodkin muttered. 'It's broken.'

'That will be the one that Caroline used to sit in front of when she first moved here. Remember? She said they used to leave the window open to get some air into that room because of the damp and mould.'

'The wallpaper! Of course. Now I'm seeing the real picture.'

'Wallpaper? What are you going on about, Bodkin?' Amy stood in front of the detective and waved her hand in front of his face.

'BODKIN!' she snapped. 'What on earth—'

'A hell of a lot of Victorian wallpaper was made using arsenic in the process. It gave it that lovely green colour in the pattern, but any room that has it on the walls can be a death trap if the damp and mould sets in.'

'Really?' Amy was puzzled. 'Oh, of course. Our famous Victorian lady poisoners used to use it when they'd run out of flypaper,' she said.

Bodkin nodded absentmindedly.

'You saw for yourself how bad that bedroom was. It was making us feel ill and we'd only been in it a few minutes.'

'So, what are you saying, Bodkin? Do you think Mrs Gatting is in the frame again?'

'She was never out of it,' Bodkin replied. The detective looked back at the hedge, then up at the broken window again.

'Two out of three,' he muttered.

'What is? Oh, Bodkin you can be so obtuse at times.'

'Okay, I'll explain,' Bodkin looked directly into Amy's face. 'Just try to follow what I'm saying, don't jump in and ruin my reasoning. It's not a fully formed theory as yet.'

'You mean shut up while you prattle on, don't you? All right, I get the message.'

Bodkin held up a finger.

'What do we know so far? We know that three poisons were used on Villiers. Hemlock, arsenic and strychnine. After tonight, we know that Mrs Gatting has access to hemlock, we know she has access to arsenic, albeit by a more complicated method of acquiring it. We also know that at one time at least, she had access to strychnine, although that link might be more tenuous.'

Amy opened her mouth to speak, then put her hand over it to silence herself.

If he had noticed that she had been about to interrupt, he ignored it.

'So, she had means, she had the opportunity, all we're lacking is a motive.'

'I was about to ask if we can prove a motive,' Amy replied after ten seconds of silence. 'We don't have an inkling of why she would do it. Anyway, would she really go to all the trouble of manufacturing her own arsenic when she knew there was a tin full of it in Peter's shed? She was trusted with the keys, remember?'

'I did say the theory wasn't a fully formed one,' Bodkin said with a smile. 'I knew you'd pick holes in it straight away.'

'I'm not disputing the main part of your theory, Bodkin, but it isn't just the fact that she could have got the arsenic from Peter's store. Would she know how to remove the arsenic from the wallpaper in the first place? Would she even know it was there? And,' she looked back to the bushes behind her, 'would she know hemlock from cow parsley? We didn't until you tore that picture from a precious work of literature.'

Bodkin screwed up his face as he thought.

'Maybe not, but her sister certainly would. She'd know everything there is to know about hemlock and arsenic, not to mention the strychnine. Maybe they were in it together.'

CHAPTER TWENTY-FIVE

When Amy came down from her room for tea that evening, she found Mr Rowlings sitting in his armchair reading the paper.

'Hi, Dad.' Amy crossed the room and planted a kiss on her father's cheek. 'How was your day?'

'The same as always,' he replied. 'What have you been up with your unexpected afternoon off?'

'Oh, not a lot. I went into town. I bumped into Bodkin and we drove down to Mrs de Vere's house on the Gillingham Road. I saw Joe Proudfoot, he does her gardening. He passed on his best wishes and said he'll try to drop by at the weekend.'

'Did you hear that, Lizzie? Joe Proudfoot is going to pay us a visit at the weekend.'

Mrs Rowlings stuck her head into the living room and wiped her brow with the back of her hand.

'That will be nice, dear. We haven't seen him in ages. We'll have to get something nice in for tea.'

'Speaking of meals,' Amy said. 'I was going to ask Bodkin round for dinner on Thursday evening, would that be all right?

The poor man isn't eating properly. He needs a decent meal inside him now and then.'

'We'd love to have him,' Mr Rowlings replied. 'As long as it's not too much extra work for your mother.'

Mrs Rowlings wiped her brow again as she turned to walk back into the kitchen.

'It won't be a problem; I've got some nice beef mince. I can make a shepherd's pie. We might need a few more potatoes and a bit of cheddar for topping though, oh, and a couple of tins of tomatoes. We're right out. I'll have to nip into town tomorrow.'

'Speaking of tomorrow, what are your plans?' Mr Rowlings asked.

Amy shrugged. 'I haven't got a lot planned. I was going to see if Bodkin needs a hand with anything, then I was going to go to the library. I need some more Poirot. I fancy reading Peril at End House again. I haven't read it in years.'

'I much prefer Evelyn Waugh to Agatha Christie,' he replied, looking over his paper. 'I still don't approve of you interfering in Bodkin's investigations but if he finds you useful, I suppose it's all right. Before you do any of that though, you can help your mother with the laundry.'

'But Dad I–'

'No buts, young lady, your mother is rushed off her feet. She's cooking dinner and folding today's big wash while we sit here, idling.'

'It's all right,' Amy heard her mother call from the kitchen. 'I've almost done. It just needs ironing and putting away now.'

'So, that's your task for tomorrow, Amy, you can help with the ironing.'

'But, Dad, it's my day off.'

'Your mother doesn't get a day off, Amy. Think about that.'

'Why don't you help her, Dad? You're just sitting there reading the paper.'

'I've been to work, young lady. It's my job to provide for the family. Your mother's job is to look after us at home and you should help her do that.'

'But I work too,' Amy said, hotly.

'I'm aware of your contribution to the upkeep of the house, Amy, but we don't ask a lot of you really. Anyway, you should be learning how to run a house. You'll be married with children one day and then you'll have to know how to look after your husband or it will be a short-lived marriage.'

Amy's mouth dropped open.

'Women weren't put on this earth with the sole objective of making a man's life easier,' Amy snorted. 'When... if... I ever do get married; I can assure you that my husband will do his share around the place. Times are changing, Dad. Women are demanding more out of life.'

'Times are not changing in this house, Amy. Not while I live in it anyway.'

Amy shook her head in frustration. 'Dad. The way things are going in Europe, there may well be another war soon, then women will be expected to do the men's jobs again, just like they were asked to do last time. That eventually led to us getting the vote. We'll expect a lot more this time around.' She walked towards the kitchen door, then looked back as her father opened his paper again. 'Men won't be waited on hand and foot forever. Enjoy it while you can.'

Mr Rowlings looked up over his paper with a sad look on his face.

'I'm not going to get into a heated argument with you, Amy. I know you're a high-spirited young woman with your own ideas about the way life should be and I have never tried to stifle your enthusiasm but you are sounding more and more like a Suffragette. I thought we'd left them behind when women won the vote.'

Amy snorted. 'They never went away, Dad. They never went away.'

Mrs Rowlings shook her head and put her finger over her lips as Amy walked into the kitchen.

'Don't bother arguing, dear, it's just the way things are at the moment,' she said quietly.

'Well, it shouldn't be like that, Mum.'

Mrs Rowlings patted her on the arm. 'I know, dear, but I honestly don't mind. This is my job. I'm a housewife. Your dad works extremely hard to bring in enough money to give us a comfortable life. When I think of how other families suffer... Just thank God your father doesn't spend all his money on the horses or in the pub, that's all I can say.'

Amy sighed deeply. 'I know, Mum. Dad's a good father and a good husband. I'm not disputing that. He just got me so wound up just then. Looking after the house is women's work. It's beneath a man to do anything to help.'

'Your father is of that generation, love. It's how they expect things to be done. They're the head of the household and what they say goes.' She winked at Amy and flashed her a quick smile. 'Let's just leave them wallowing in that fantasy while we get on with running things, eh?'

Amy gave a short laugh. 'All right, Mum, I'll say sorry to him. I suppose it's up to my generation to make change happen.' She gave her mother a hug. 'Never think I don't appreciate what you do for us, Mum, because I always have and I always will, even if I don't show it.'

'You do show your appreciation, dear. You bought me a copy of Woman's Own today. I'm going to get stuck into that when we've had dinner. There's a lovely knitting pattern inside this week.'

Amy suddenly remembered the sweets Bodkin had bought at Cavanagh's and hurried to the bottom of the stairs to get them out of her bag. She carried them behind her back into the living room and walked slowly across to her father.

'Sorry, Dad. I know we have our differences on a few issues but I do appreciate what you and Mum do for me. Of course, I'll give her a hand tomorrow.' She gave him a kiss on the forehead and produced the bag of mint humbugs.

'Ooh what a rare treat,' Mr Rowlings beamed. 'Thank you, my dear.'

'Bodkin bought them for you. They're for Mum as well,' Amy warned, 'so don't go scoffing the lot.'

The next morning Mrs Rowlings let Amy have a rare lie in and didn't call her for breakfast until eight o'clock. By the time Amy got downstairs, she had already put two eggs in the pan to boil and was just about to drop two thick-cut pieces of bread into the toaster.

Amy looked at the mountain of ironing that had been stacked in precarious piles on the two chairs near the back door. Another pile was stacked, leaning like the Tower of Pizza on the draining board next to the sink. Her face fell. That lot was going to take the best part of the morning to clear.

Mrs Rowlings sensed her distress.

'I'll do the ironing, dear, I find it quite soothing, really. It would be a great help if you could nip to town for me though. I've left a list on the dining table. It's mostly tinned stuff, but I would like another fresh loaf.'

'If you're sure, Mum. I'm willing, if not over eager to do my share of the pressing.'

'I'll tell you what. I'll pile up the ironing in the living room as I do it and you can help put it all away when you come back. Just make sure you're here well before your father gets home. I told him I'd get you to help me with this lot.'

Amy gave her mother a hug, then carried her breakfast through to the living room and put it down on the table. Picking up the shopping list, she skim-read it, then folded it and put it in the pocket of her skirt.

'Tinned peaches, tinned pineapple chunks, sugar, evaporated milk? We'll all be needing a trip to the dentist after that lot.'

'I thought I'd get something sweet for Mr Bodkin after you said he wasn't eating properly. That will help boost his energy levels. Anyway, you know your dad has a sweet tooth.'

'He's got a mouthful of sweet teeth,' said Amy, spitting toast crumbs as she spoke.

Mrs Rowlings laughed as she unfolded the ironing board.

'Oh, Amy, could you add some aspirin to that list. I'm out of them and I always get a headache after steam ironing for any length of time.'

Amy pulled out the folded paper from her pocket, picked up her father's crossword pen and jotted, aspirin down at the bottom of the list.

'Alice will be dropping in with our fresh milk soon,' Mrs Rowling's called, as Amy repocketed the list and opened the door to the hall. 'Are you going to hang on for her?'

'No, I'd like to get it all done early, Mum. Tell her I'll drop by in the week.'

'All right, dear. Oh, I've left my shopping bags hanging on the front door handle,' she said.

Town was busy for a Tuesday morning but Amy was able to get everything on her mother's list in reasonable time. The biggest queue was at the grocers where she had to join a long queue to order and pay for her goods. There were two people behind the counter to pick items from the shelves and pack them into brown paper bags for the customers if required but they both seemed to take an eternity in performing the tasks. Even when they had finished picking the order, they'd chat to the customer about the weather, the state of the grass verges or the health of their respective families.

After a quick trip to the greengrocer to buy onions, potatoes and spring greens, Amy strolled across to the chemist, pushed open the door and held it as an elderly lady left the shop. She was greeted by a middle-aged woman with a pale skin and grey-flecked hair. She stood at around five feet nine inches tall with a thin frame and a small bosom. She wore a long white coat which had an enamel badge on the right-hand lapel with the word Pharmacist written on it. Around her neck was a thin silver coloured chain that held a pair of round-lens spectacles. She lifted them to her eyes as she turned towards Amy.

'How may I help?'

'I'd like some aspirin please,' Amy said.

The woman turned away and reached up to a shelf on the wall behind her and picked up a clear bottle, sporting a yellow label with Bayer Aspirin printed on it. She handed the bottle to Amy who passed over a shilling to pay for the medication.

'It's nice to see a woman running things,' Amy said, brightly. 'It's nearly always men, isn't it?'

'Oh, I don't own the shop,' the woman said. 'I'm merely the pharmacist. Mr Hales is the owner.'

'Merely? Don't underestimate your value,' Amy said. 'I

think it's wonderful that women can be doctors and pharmacists these days. There just aren't enough of them.'

The woman nodded her head slowly as she smiled at Amy.

'And what do you do, my dear? Please tell me that you're studying at university and aim to become a scientist, a lawyer, or some such thing.'

Amy shook her head. 'Sorry to disappoint you but I'm a machinist at the Mill. I'd love to be a police detective but they don't allow women into the CID. Not around here at least. We are too emotional to be able to think with enough clarity to crack complex cases by all accounts.'

'I'm sure the law says that women are allowed to serve in the police force, in fact I know it does. But I know what you mean. It's one thing being a policewoman, it's another thing altogether getting onto that promotion ladder, isn't it?'

Amy felt herself taking an instant liking to the pharmacist. Stuffing the aspirin bottle into her bag, she stretched her hand across the counter.

'I'm Amy Rowlings,' she said.

'I'm Agatha Walker and it's a pleasure to meet a fellow equal rights campaigner,' she replied.

'Oh, I don't campaign, I'm not really political, I just get angry when I'm told I can't do something just because I'm a woman,' Amy said firmly.

'Well, maybe you should campaign, Amy Rowlings. I don't mean to sound disparaging but I do think you might be wasting your talents working in a factory. Have you ever thought of trying to get into university?'

'People like me don't go to university,' Amy replied. 'I was thinking of doing a few night classes at college though.'

'People like you are exactly the people who should be going

to university,' Agatha said. 'The day is coming when that will happen and it can't come soon enough.'

Amy looked past Agatha to the wall where two certificates were hanging in wooden frames.

'Is Mr Hales a pharmacist too, or does he just own the business?' Amy asked.

'He is, but between you, me and the gatepost, he's a bit past it now. He's not up with all the new medicines and treatments. He's in his seventies, and his hands aren't really steady enough to measure out minute portions of dangerous chemicals.'

'So, do you run the shop and do all the dispensing? That must be a lot of hard work?'

'We women are used to hard work, aren't we?' Agatha said with a grim smile. 'As it happens, Mr Hales is usually in charge at the front of the shop. He does the book keeping too. He takes every Tuesday morning off to get all the paperwork done. I'd hate to do that side of things. I'm much happier with a Bunsen burner and a test tube. I get to have Tuesday afternoons off but I have to do all the day's dispensing before I leave.'

'I met your sister the other night,' Amy said. 'It's Mrs Gatting isn't it? I was over there collecting my father's old sermons. He used to write them for the vicar. There were about twenty years' worth of them.'

'Ah, so you're the young lady she told me about. She said you were a nice young girl. I can see what she means. I'm going over to see her after lunch as it happens.'

'Really? I was going to drop in this afternoon too,' Amy said, desperately trying to think of an excuse as to why she might have to visit the vicarage. 'I picked up stacks of box files the other night, there was a year's worth of sermons in each file but when Dad checked them, there was one year missing. Nineteen twenty-nine, I think it was. I told him I'd drop in to see if Caroline could find it.'

'Well then. I look forward to seeing you again, Amy Rowlings,' Agatha said with a smile. 'I should be there around about two o'clock.'

CHAPTER TWENTY-SIX

When Amy left the shop, she hurried along the High Street until she got to the top of Middle Street where she jumped on a bus that would take her to the Old Bull at the end of Long Lane. She had considered dropping in at the police station to let Bodkin know that she was going to visit Agatha Walker at the vicarage but she soon pushed the idea away. Bodkin had told her that he had been trying to make an appointment at Skellinghouse HQ and with Mrs de Vere's bank, so he probably wouldn't be around for most of the afternoon.

When she got back home, she unloaded the shopping and passed the bottle of aspirin to her mother.

'I've got to nip out again, Mum,' she said. 'Something's come up.'

'Well, whatever it is, it can stay up until those clothes are packed away,' Mrs Rowlings replied, washing down a couple of tablets with a glass of water. 'Do ours first, that will be the bulk of them. You can leave your laundry on your bed and pack it away tonight if you like. Dad won't go in your room.'

Amy looked at the huge piles of freshly pressed clothes and sighed inwardly, but then realising that her mother had let her get away with so much already, she forced a smile, grabbed the first pile and hurried up the stairs with it.

At a quarter to two, Amy, having changed into a pleated navy skirt and white blouse, pulled on her black jacket and stepped smartly out of the house.

She took her time walking up the hill towards the church as she didn't want to risk arriving before Agatha, and by the time she skirted the church railings on her way to the vicarage it was almost ten past two.

As she walked through the gates into the vicarage courtyard, she noticed a familiar black Morris Ten parked under the shade of a thick, densely-branched yew. Amy rattled the lion's-foot knocker and a minute or so later, the door opened and she saw Agatha Walker, framed in the doorway.

'Hello, again,' she said, stepping neatly aside to allow Amy to enter into the hall. 'We're all in the kitchen, it's turning out to be quite a party.'

Bodkin got to his feet as Amy, followed by Mrs Walker, entered the kitchen.

'Amy... Miss Rowlings, this is a pleasant surprise,' he said, as he narrowed his eyes and tipped his head slightly to the right in a questioning motion.

'Hello again,' Amy said. 'It's nice to see you—'

'Could we please cut the pretence,' Agatha said, frowning at Amy, then at Bodkin in turn. 'It's patently obvious that you two are colluding, at least to some extent. You are in the presence of two, intelligent women. Caroline saw though your little act the last time you were here. There really is no need to continue the performance. If we want to watch bad acting, we can go to an amateur dramatic society presentation.'

'Miss Rowlings is—' Bodkin began, but was cut off by Amy.

She pulled one of her pink cards out of her bag and handed it to the pharmacist.

'ARIA Investigations,' she read.

'Kent police accredited,' Amy added, quickly.

'What does that mean?' Mrs Walker asked with a confused tone in her voice.

'It means she can assist us with our investigations under certain circumstances,' Bodkin said, carefully. 'Miss Rowlings has a vast amount of local knowledge. She has been of great assistance to us over the last few months.'

Agatha looked up from the card to Amy. 'I knew there was more to you than meets the eye,' she said. 'Do you mind if I keep this? I may have need of your services, one day. I'm sure you are very discreet.'

'It's not all subterfuge, I promise you,' Amy said quickly, noting the initial look of disappointment on Agatha's face. 'I really did come around to pick up my father's sermons the other night. Inspector Bodkin was kind enough to give me a lift home with them. I admit, I did know him before we came here that night, but I swear, I was here to pick up the old files.'

'And the supposedly missing box file, the one you've come over to find today?'

Before Amy could admit to misleading the pharmacist, Bodkin came to her rescue.

'It's still in the back of my car. It must have slipped off the seat when I was driving you home the other night. I meant to drop it in to your father but I just haven't had the time.'

'Good! That's that settled then.' Mrs Walker gave Amy a

curt nod. 'I'm so glad you haven't attempted to mislead me. I'd have been so disappointed in you.'

The chemist turned away as Amy looked down at her feet.

'Right, Caroline, get that teapot filled and put plenty of water in the kettle for a top up. I think we're in for a session, here.'

When they were all seated around the table with their filled mugs of tea in front of them, Agatha put the palms of her hands flat on the table and looked across it to Bodkin.

'So, Inspector, where would you like to begin?'

'Firstly, I'd like to ask about the poor children's medicine committee. When were you asked to join, who invited you? And was there any reason given for your invitation seeing as they already had one pharmacist in the shape of Eugene Hales?'

'Eugene was asked to join because of his contacts in the pharmaceutical industry. I, on the other hand was asked to join for my pharmaceutical expertise.' She held out a hand towards Amy. 'As I was telling young Miss Rowlings earlier. Eugene hasn't kept up with recent developments in medicine. Oh, I've no doubt he can still conjure up a cough remedy of some description, but he really isn't au fait with the latest drugs and treatments. I am, I dispense them every day of my life. I know what works for what condition and I know which medication a young patient is likely to tolerate best.' She held up her head, proudly. 'I'm not only a qualified pharmacist, Mr Bodkin, I'm also qualified to perform clinical research, to conduct medicine trials. In short, I am far more highly qualified than any GP in the area.'

Amy almost applauded as she looked across the table, sparkly-eyed at the chemist. Agatha, noticing her look of approval, inclined her head slightly towards her.

'I'm sure you'd be a huge asset to the committee,' Bodkin

replied. 'But if Hales was there purely for his contacts, what was Doctor Frazier's role? He's been retired for over five years.'

'Ah, Doctor Frazier,' Mrs Walker clasped her hands across her chest and bit her bottom lip. 'He was a bit of a conundrum, I have to say. He was and I suppose, still is, well respected around the area and I suppose anyone with the letters VC after their name can't fail to add something to the committee's standing.'

'I met him this morning,' Bodkin replied. 'He seemed... a little full of himself. What did he get his VC for? He showed it to me but he didn't say how he got it, which I was a little surprised at given his enormous ego.'

'I didn't get on with him either. The only one who did was Eugene, but he's known him for years. I believe they were in the Boer War together at the turn of the century. Apparently, Frazier saved his general's life somehow. I think it was with the use of a gun, not the use of a piece of medical equipment. He was quite the hero it seems.'

Bodkin picked up his mug and turned it around in his hands, pushing a finger in and out of the space in the handle. Suddenly he looked towards Caroline Gatting, who had added little to the conversation so far.

'Do you spend much time on the riverbank, Mrs Gatting?' he asked.

'What a strange question... No, not really. I've probably only taken a few short walks in all the time I've been here. I think the last time was a few weeks ago. Agatha and I took our niece, Gloria down to feed the ducks.'

'Do you know what this is?' Bodkin pulled the black and white photograph from his pocket and pushed it across the table towards her.

The housekeeper picked up the glossy sheet and studied it carefully.

'No idea. Sorry, but then I don't claim to be a botanist.'

'Mrs Walker?'

The pharmacist took a quick glance at the picture then pushed it back across the table.

'Conium maculatum, commonly known as poison hemlock, all parts of the plant are highly toxic, in fact it is the most poisonous plant in the United Kingdom.' She looked directly at Bodkin. 'Do not eat it.'

'I try to avoid it,' Bodkin replied.

'The plant contains toxic alkaloids, the worst of which is coniine. It is particularly deadly at this time of year. The leaves give off a foul scent when crushed which is a blessing because most animals will keep away from it. Oh, and it's a member of the carrot family of plants, believe it or not.'

The chemist handed her empty mug to her sister. 'Any chance of a top up, dear?'

Caroline got to her feet, picked up the teapot and carried it over to the sink. After emptying its contents, she poured in a bit of hot water from the kettle, swilled it around, then emptied it again before tipping in four spoonsful of leaves from a grey patterned, china caddy.

Agatha meanwhile was warming to her task.

'Did you know that back in the day, Christians believed that the hemlock plant became poisonous after growing on the hillside where Jesus was crucified? When his blood touched the plant, it became forever toxic.' She looked from Amy to Bodkin. 'Now, is there anything else you'd like to know about it?'

'Do pharmacists dispense it?'

'Tiny amounts were used as sedatives or antispasmodics.

We tend to steer clear of it these days but I do know that homeopaths still use it in their concoctions.'

'Do you have any at the dispensary?'

'No, we don't keep stocks of coniine.'

'Thank you for that,' Bodkin replied with a nod. 'So, as you are familiar with the plant, you must be aware that there is a large colony of them on the other side of the hedge just behind the house.'

'I did notice it, yes.'

'But neither you or your sister, ever collected any?'

'I'm not that stupid and Caroline would have had no idea what it was.'

'Thank you,' Bodkin replied. 'Now. As you are probably aware, there is a readily available, arsenic supply, hanging off the walls of the upstairs bedrooms. How easy would it be to extract it?'

'Relatively simple,' Mrs Walker replied. 'Just chuck some of the paper, the mould, or both, into a pot, boil it up, then skim off the sludge. Anyone could do it really.'

'You did know about the old wallpaper in the back rooms then?'

'Of course. Caroline took me up there when she first noticed the effect the air in the back rooms was having on her. I explained what it was and told her that if she had any sense, she'd keep out of them.'

'I do have to ask this question. Caroline, have you ever used any of the materials in the upstairs rooms to extract arsenic?'

'Don't be ridiculous, why on earth would I want to do that?' Caroline replied, almost scalding herself with the boiling water from the kettle.

'Inspector,' Agatha cut in. 'I'm not sure where these questions are leading, but I have to point out what a nonsensical line of questioning you have embarked upon. If either Caroline, or I, wanted to procure arsenic, there are far easier ways of obtaining it than boiling old wallpaper in a witch's cauldron. I can put my hands on enormous amounts of it any time I choose, and if I can, it follows that Caroline can too. Neither of us would have to get the wallpaper scraper out.'

Amy suddenly found herself biting her lip to stop herself bursting out laughing. She shot Bodkin a quick glance, but if he found Agatha's response amusing, he wasn't showing it.

He was about to ask another question when Agatha spoke again.

'Now, you have either wittingly, or unwittingly, given me a clue as to how the vicar was killed. Can I assume that one, or both of the poisons we have been discussing was found in his system when he died?'

'I'm not at liberty to say, Mrs Walker.'

'I'll take that as a yes, then.'

She leaned back in her chair to allow Caroline to place the teapot in the centre of the table.

'Are there any other poisons you want to discuss?' Agatha continued as Caroline picked up the mugs and carried them over to the sink to rinse out. 'I have access to all of them.'

Bodkin held up his hands.

'I am well aware of that, Mrs Walker. Now, as you are the expert, what would you say is the easiest way to administer a lethal dose of strychnine?'

Agatha pursed her lips as she thought.

'Strychnine... well, you could mix it into a solution and inject it into a vein, into food, or a drink, but I suppose the simplest way would be to top up a sugar bowl with it as it looks almost identical.'

Bodkin took out his notebook and flipped through it. 'And, you have access to strychnine of course?'

'Of course. We sell it as a vermin killer.'

Caroline poured more tea and handed the mugs around. Bodkin added milk to his, then two spoons of sugar.

'Now, can I take you back to the night of the committee meeting. I have been told that there was something of a row between Mr Villiers and Mrs de Vere, is that correct?'

'I wouldn't call it a row, but they were on opposite sides of a... let's call it an earnest discussion.'

'Regarding the large donation the church had recently received?'

Agatha nodded. 'Correct.'

'Was the money discussed at committee level?'

'Not really... well, yes, but not in any real detail on how the money would be used. I can tell you that Mrs de Vere was requesting a specific amount and that she required the money to be transferred quite soon or the charity would run out of funds and would therefore have to be wound up.'

'How much?'

'Four thousand pounds.'

Bodkin whistled.

'That's a lot of money, how many children would benefit from the charity.'

'Less than a hundred, but they would be among the poorest in the town. There are other charities that do a similar thing, usually through the free hospital. In this case, the money wouldn't be used directly for the purchase of medicines. The bulk of the donation would be used to invest... buy stocks and shares and the interest accrued would be spent on the medicines and treatments.'

'So, was she looking to expand the charity? I thought she had ample funding from Skellinghouse?'

'They were pulling out. According to Councillor de Vere, they had changed their priorities when it came to charity funding. I honestly don't know who they were thinking of sponsoring next, just that it wouldn't be her fund.'

'Before that meeting, had the vicar intimated that he was interested in using the church's money to invest?'

'I believe so.'

'So, what do you think happened to make him change his mind?'

'I can only guess at that.'

'Please, feel free to hypothesise,' Bodkin said.

'She was struggling financially. Everyone in the town who knows her, knew it. She hadn't been paying her bills, not even her local ones. Then in the blink of an eye, she was solvent again. It doesn't really take a genius to work out that her good fortune and the sudden need for an injection of funds into her charity, might be related.'

CHAPTER
TWENTY-SEVEN

Amy sipped at her tea as she thought about Agatha's revelation. It matched perfectly with the information that Joe had given her. All that was missing was his news about the Reverend Daley. Amy looked through the steam rising from her mug towards the pharmacist and wondered whether she knew all about that as well. She wouldn't be the slightest bit surprised.

Bodkin pretended to study his notebook again.

'A little later on that night, the committee came here, to this very kitchen for a glass of wine. Did you notice anything at all that was out of the ordinary?'

'Not that I can think of. Peter was here of course, standing by the back door. I saw him put Caroline's syringe into the pot on the stove to sterilise it, which was very kind of him.'

'The wine you consumed was what he called his 'house white', did you see any other wine on the worktops that night? Any of his own French wine for instance.'

Agatha nodded.

'There was a bottle of his more expensive stuff on the counter. I thought he was going to offer us some of that for one wild moment, but I ought to have known better. We got the vinegar, the three shillings a bottle stuff.'

Bodkin smiled.

'Did you see anyone go near his own bottle at all? Did anyone pick it up to read the label or anything?'

'No, not that I recall. I think he'd have snatched it out of their hands if anyone had tried.'

'I had a drink from it,' Caroline said, holding up her hand as if she was asking for permission to speak.

'You had a drink from it?' Agatha's mouth fell open. 'But you don't drink? And when was this? Certainly not when I was in the kitchen.'

'It was before you all came in. Peter picked it up and took a swig straight from the bottle, then he passed it to me. "Go on, be a devil," he said. I only had a mouthful, then I handed it back and he pushed the cork in and put it back on the counter. We didn't drink much, just a mouthful each. I think Peter was going to ask me out and he was trying to summon up the courage. It was just a light moment. It seemed to lessen the tension between us. As it was, he didn't ask me anyway... not that night at least, because suddenly the room was filled with committee members.'

Bodkin made a few notes.

'Why didn't you mention this the last time I was here, Mrs Gatting?'

'Oh, I don't know. I didn't want to get into any trouble over it, I suppose. There seemed to be so much attention on that blooming bottle of wine.'

'It may be the thing that poisoned him, Caroline,' Bodkin said sternly.

'Well, I'm still alive, and so is Peter.'

Amy brushed away a stray strand of hair and looked over at Bodkin.

'Well, we know the wine hadn't been poisoned before the committee members turned up. So that's something new.'

'Indeed. I only wish we'd been informed earlier,' said Bodkin, staring directly at the housekeeper.

Mrs Gatting dropped her eyes.

'I'm sorry,' she muttered.

'Back to the wine drinking,' Bodkin said, tapping his notebook with the tip of his pen. 'Agatha. You seem to have an eye for detail. Can you tell us what you remember, describe what you saw, where everyone was standing, did anyone say anything out of the ordinary? Was there anything out of place? Did anyone apart from Mrs de Vere, hold a grudge against Mr Villiers for even the slightest reason?'

Agatha pursed her lips as she thought.

'First off, I don't know about any individual grudges. When we first came into the kitchen, Peter and Caroline were by the back door. She was looking a bit red faced, now I know why. She was waiting for Peter to pop the question.'

'Oh, I wasn't. He was just about to ask me out, that's all. I could sense he was on the verge of asking me, he was very nervous.'

'Whatever. Anyway. The bottle of wine was on the counter, near to where they were standing. His evening meal was on the table, here. Slices of cheese and beetroot, I seem to remember. It was quite warm in here, Mrs Brown commented on it. The vicar made a show of wiping his brow with his handkerchief, then he took his jacket off and hung it on the back of the chair.' She looked round the table... 'That one,' she said, pointing towards her sister. 'Then Caroline was ordered to find some clean glasses. I think Mrs de Vere asked us to raise a toast to the success of the committee and we all did, apart from the vicar. He didn't drink from his glass at all. He put it on the counter, then just left it there.'

'And that was it? What were you all chatting about?'

'Oh, this and that, idle chatter, nothing relevant to this inquiry.'

'Then what?'

'Mrs de Vere asked the vicar to pick a date for the next meeting. The vicar didn't seem particularly keen to do that. I think as far as he was concerned, there wouldn't be another one. But then he shrugged and marched us all out to his study.'

'And everyone followed?'

'Except Peter and Caroline... Oh, Eugene and Doctor Frazier were a bit late arriving in the study, but not by much.'

'Did they stay in the kitchen longer than the others?' Bodkin shot Caroline a quick glance.

'There were still one or two milling around as I gathered the glasses. I had to wait to take Eugene's glass from him. Doctor Frazier was holding onto his too. I think he was hoping for a top up. Mrs Brown put her empty glass down and grabbed the full one the vicar had left before Frazier could get hold of it, then she followed her husband out of the door.' Caroline paused. 'He's a strange one, Mr Brown, he doesn't seem with it all the time, if you know what I mean. I think he's going senile.'

'What was Peter doing?'

'He took the empty wine bottles out to the bin for me. It's near the back door.'

'So, are you sure you saw everyone leave the room?'

'No, I can't say that for certain because I followed Peter out to the bin. I'd had bangers and mash for my own tea and the potato peelings were sitting in the foot-pedal bin, wrapped in newspaper, so I took that out before they started to smell. There was no one else in the kitchen when Peter and I came back, I do know that.'

Bodkin made a few more notes, then rubbed behind his ear with the top of his pen.

'Right, back to the study. Tell me what you remember, Agatha.'

Agatha closed her eyes and concentrated her thoughts.

'We were all grouped around his desk, one or two were still sipping wine, most not. The vicar pulled his desk diary out of his drawer and opened it at the yearly calendar inside the front cover... then... oh yes, then he patted his pockets, or where his pockets would have been had he been wearing his jacket. I think he was looking for his pen... then he grabbed a couple of pineapple chunks from the bag of sweets on his desk. I thought he might offer them around but he didn't. I wouldn't have minded one. It would have taken the taste of that disgusting wine away.'

'Then you all settled on a date. The twenty-first?'

'You are well informed,' Agatha said.

'What happened next?' Bodkin asked.

'The vicar made a note in his diary to confirm the date.'

'Where did he get a pen from?' Amy asked. 'Wasn't he patting his pockets, searching for one?'

'Oh you clever thing,' Mrs Walker flashed her a beaming smile. 'Well spotted. There was a fountain pen on his desk, a red one with a silver cap, so he must have been looking for something else in his pockets. Well done!' Agatha stuck her thumb up to Amy then turned to Bodkin. 'I can see why the police accredited her.'

Bodkin gave her a tired smile.

'Then, everyone went home, is that correct?'

'We had a chat at the front door. Caroline had opened it and was standing by, bidding us all a good night.'

'But you didn't go, did you, Agatha? You went back inside, as did Mrs de Vere.'

'Do you know, you're right. I'd left my glasses on the desk in the study. I went back to retrieve them.'

'And Mrs de Vere?'

'She was going into the kitchen as I came back out of the study. She was hiccupping, that cheap wine probably caused it, I think she needed a glass of water.'

'How long was she in there?'

'A couple of minutes, no longer than that.'

'And did the drink of water work? Did it cure her hiccups?'

'I assume so.'

'What about Peter Kissman, did you see him again?'

'Yes, before I went back in, he walked up the side of the house and went through the gate into the churchyard. He waved to Caroline as he passed.'

'And Reverend Villiers. What did he do after his guests had gone, Mrs Gatting?'

'Mmm. Let me think...' The housekeeper was silent for a few seconds, staring at the wall behind Bodkin as she concentrated.

'He came into the kitchen, ate a little bit of his tea, not more than a couple of bits of cheese, really. Then he grabbed his wine and went back to his study, I believe he was working on the sermon that Mr Rowlings had dropped in on Thursday evening.'

'How long did he stay in there?'

'He came out about ten, maybe a few minutes, after. I'd just tapped on his door to tell him I was going up to bed.'

'Was he drunk?'

'No, I don't think so. It looked like he'd eaten quite a few of the sweets from the new bag on his desk. He wasn't slurring or wobbling about.'

Bodkin made a few more notes before speaking again.

'What did he do then, Mrs Gatting?'

'He was carrying his bottle of wine when he came back into the kitchen. He put it on the table while he pulled his jacket on, then wished me a good night, picked up his wine and went out of the back door.'

'And that was the last you saw or heard of him?'

Caroline nodded.

'Yes, I went up to bed. There was no sign of him the next morning. I assumed he'd gone for a walk to clear his head.'

'Was the back door still unlocked?'

'Yes, but it would have been if he'd got up early and gone for a walk.'

Bodkin closed his notebook and slipped it back into his inside pocket, then clipped the pen to the top pocket seam.

'I'm nearly done,' he said with just the hint of a smile. 'Mrs Walker, did you or your sister bear any grudges against the vicar? Do you know anyone who might have, for any reason?'

Amy flicked her eyes towards Bodkin as Caroline shot Agatha an equally quick glance.

Agatha squirmed a little in her seat as her confident air dissipated momentarily.

'Someone's been gossiping. Who was it?'

'I'm afraid I can't tell you that,' Bodkin replied.

'All right. I'll give you the real story, not one built on Chinese whispers.'

Amy rubbed her hands together under the table as she leaned forwards eagerly.

'The Reverend Villiers denied me my one and probably only chance of landing my dream job and Hell will freeze over before I'll forgive him for it.'

CHAPTER
TWENTY-EIGHT

'WHAT WAS THE JOB?' AMY ASKED, AS SHE RESTED HER ELBOWS ON THE table and sat her chin in her cupped hands.

'I would have been working in medical research at Cambridge University, running clinical trials on new drugs and treatments. They have opened up a new department and they wanted a team leader. I was overqualified for it if anything. I have my degree in chemistry and my pharmacy qualifications but I also have two years of toxin research behind me. All that made me a shoo in for the job. All I needed were three professional referees. I asked Eugene, as he could give me a rock-solid career reference. I've worked for him for almost twenty years after all. I've also known the coroner for many years so I asked him. I made my big mistake when I asked Villiers. I was a fool for asking him in the first place, I could have gone to the Mayor, I know the Chief Constable very well, but like an idiot, I asked Villiers.'

'Why him?' Bodkin asked.

'He married us, Christopher and me, and he christened

both my children. We've known each other a long time. Caroline got her job here because I had recommended her. I thought he would give me a glowing reference, especially after helping him sort out his sleep issues. He's had problems with that since his fiancée died back in nineteen-nineteen. She comes to him in the night but it's never a friendly visitation. He says she blames him for her death. I think that's the main reason you see him cursing the dead in the churchyard. That and the drink of course.'

Bodkin took a sip of cold tea, grimaced, then put the mug back on the table.

'He gave you a bad reference? When did this happen, and why would he do that? Are you sure it was him? How do you know it was the reference that put the kibosh on any chance of you getting the job?'

'I got the rejection letter just over a month ago. As for how I know, I have a contact within the research department. She couldn't get to look at the actual references but she did tell me that the selection panel, whilst being very impressed with my qualifications, couldn't take a risk on my temperament. The reference stated that I was unreliable, overly emotional and indecisive.'

'And how do you know it was Villiers' reference that sealed your fate?'

'It had to be him. The coroner and I are as thick as thieves. I'm regularly invited over to dinner and whenever he has a tricky issue that concerns drugs, toxins or chemicals, he always seeks my advice, so he's hardly likely to write anything like that about me. Likewise, Eugene Hales. He knows how well I perform under pressure; I've kept that place going pretty much on my own for years now. Besides which, when I told him I was applying for the post, he offered to write me the best, most glowing reference that Cambridge had ever seen, and he did. He showed it to me. So, I'm afraid there was no doubt about who the culprit was.'

'Had you fallen out with him recently? Villiers that is?'

'We did have a difference of opinion about the sleeping draughts I was supplying him with. They were barbiturate based and he was becoming addicted to them. I told him he needed to come off them for a few weeks but he wasn't happy at all. He went to Doctor Mighten to try to get him to change my mind and dispense them, but Mighten was of the same opinion as me.'

'So, he got his own back by giving you the lousy reference.'

Agatha nodded.

'He was still on the sleeping draughts when I asked him to provide one, but by the time he'd written it and sent it off, we'd had our altercation.'

'Did you threaten him at all, or did he threaten you in any way?'

'I may have said, something silly like, "I'll kill you for this," but it was only a throwaway comment. I didn't mean it. I've taken a personal oath to protect life.'

'Was it in public?'

'No, it was in the back of the shop. Eugene might have overheard. Villiers might even have asked him to overrule me, but if he did, he didn't mention anything, certainly not to me.'

'What a shame. You would have been perfect for that job,' Amy said. 'Who got it in the end, did you ever find out? I'd put a month's wages on it being a man.'

'And you'd win your bet, Amy,' Agatha said. 'It was between him and me. We were the final candidates, whittled down from a shortlist of six. My qualifications knocked his into a cocked hat, but they counted for nothing in the end.'

'Maybe it wasn't the reference then,' Amy said. 'Maybe it was simply down to misogyny.'

'I think that played a big part, Amy. But the reference was the final nail in my coffin.'

'Won't you be able to apply again at some stage? Surely a similar job will come up before too long.' Amy said.

'With that reference in my file? No, I won't get another chance like that one.'

'Well, I think that is despicable,' Amy retorted. 'Both the vicar and the selection board deserve to be horsewhipped.'

Agatha reached out her hand to Amy, who took it and squeezed it gently.

'It's the way of the world, Amy. Nothing can be done for my generation, it's up to yours to make sure things change. Don't sit back while the next generation of men take over from their fathers. Fight them tooth and nail. Women can't just be the equal of men anymore. We have to be better than them to get anywhere.'

At four-thirty, Bodkin got to his feet and thanked the sisters for their time. When they were back out in the courtyard, he asked Amy if she would like a lift home.

'Only if it's on the way.'

'Your house isn't on the way to anywhere,' Bodkin replied.

'It's just a saying, Bodkin, don't try to get smart, it doesn't suit you.'

'Okay, it is out of my way, but it doesn't matter, it will only take five minutes and I'm happy to drop you off.'

Amy grinned as she climbed into the car.

'Gotcha, Bodkin. I made you feel guilty again.

'So, what do you think of their new stories,' Amy asked as

Bodkin pulled out from under the big yew. 'Do you think they could have done it. Revenge is a really strong motive, isn't it?'

'It's one of the strongest,' Bodkin replied, 'and she had the means and the opportunity too. Her sister may have helped, they are very close, that pair.'

'Could an intelligent woman like that possibly commit murder though, Bodkin?'

'It's usually the clever ones that do it, Amy, and our Agatha is a very clever woman. She'd know how to cover her tracks. She actually told us the easiest way to administer strychnine. A spoonful of sugar in his tea and he's a goner.'

'So, are we ruling the wine out now?' Amy asked.

'Not likely. That broken bottle was hidden for a reason and I think we both know what that reason was.' Bodkin drove in silence for a few seconds, then continued. 'No, the wine is still our best bet. Mrs de Vere had access to it as did Eugene Hales and the hero that is Doctor Frazier, then again, so did the sisters, or at least one of them, the other could just be the provider of the poison.'

'It gets more confusing the more we discover, doesn't it?' Amy said.

'There's nothing unusual in that, Amy. But, just as in the Handsley case we worked on, there will be a breakthrough. Someone will slip up.'

Bodkin brought the car to a halt outside Amy's house, then performed an untidy three point turn so that he faced up the hill towards the Old Bull.

'Are you going back to the station?' Amy asked.

'No, I'm going home to study my notebook. I need to refresh my memory about the Bungling Bill case, he's up before the beak tomorrow so I've got to give evidence.' Bodkin scratched his stubbly chin as he looked out of the windscreen.

'I was going to drop in on Eugene Hales before he closes the shop for the night. I'd like to know just who he's been selling strychnine to and what he actually heard when Agatha and Villiers were arguing, but that will have to wait for now. I'll drop in on Friday after I've spoken to Mr Daley and the bishop.'

Just as Amy was about to get out of the car, she remembered Bodkin's dinner invitation.

'Oh, Mum and Dad have asked me to invite you round for dinner on Thursday. It will be a proper meal, not just sandwiches. Mum thinks you need feeding up. She's making a shepherd's pie.'

'Shepherd's pie...' Bodkin was almost salivating, '...is my favourite meal. Thank them both for me will you. What time should I arrive?'

'About six, but Bodkin...'

'Yes?'

'Don't bring any ironing with you this time.'

CHAPTER TWENTY-NINE

'If you're going to the library today, could you take your father's book back and pick him up something suitable. He likes Evelyn Waugh and he has a new book out, I think your dad said it's called, Stoop, or Poop, something like that. They didn't have it in the last time he tried to get it.'

'It's Scoop, Mum, it's a satire on the newspapers. I read a review about it in my magazine.'

'That's the one, he's left the book he just finished on the table.'

Amy picked up the novel and slipped it into her bag with the Agatha Christie she had just read. 'I think I'll give Murder on the Orient Express another outing,' she said.

'Oh dear, another book about murder. Wouldn't you like a nice love story instead?'

'Murder mysteries are far more interesting,' Amy replied. 'And Agatha is the queen of murder.'

'I'll stick to my love stories, thank you,' Mrs Rowlings said. 'Mind you, you have to be careful, I got a book out by Daphne de Maurier, it was called Rebecca, but it wasn't a love story at all, it was about a ghost. I was too frightened to get out of bed when I was reading that one. I was hearing strange noises all night.'

Amy put her hand to her mouth to stifle a laugh then picked up her bag and walked to the front door.

'Bye, Mum, I won't be too long,' she called.

Spinton public library was an orange-brick building with a sandstone dressing and a central round-arched doorway. Between the first-floor windows was a series of carved stone art nouveau panels.

Amy felt the thrill she always felt as she climbed the seven stone steps and pushed open the oak panelled door that led to the treasure trove inside. She joined a short queue at the counter and handed both books to Reanie, a fresh-faced girl who had been at school with Amy. Reanie put the book on a pile, sorted through the tray of little beige ticket holders until she found the ones belonging to the Rowlings and handed her back her tickets. Both Amy and her father had two but had only used one on the last visit.

Stuffing the tickets into her pocket, Amy walked to the nonfiction section of the library and walked between two rows of shelves until she found the Natural History section, then after running her finger across the spines of a long line of books, she stopped at a thick, glossy-covered tome, titled Kent. A Botanical Heritage, by an aptly named author, C.D Planter. Amy took the book to a reading table, flipped open the cover and ran her fingernail down the table of contents until she found a chapter about hemlock.

'Bodkin, you hooligan,' she said as she turned to the listed page, only to find that the glossy black and white plate that should have been showing the plant in all its glory, had been torn out. Shaking her head at what, to her, was a wanton act of vandalism, she focussed on the page that followed the missing photograph and began to read.

Apiaceae, commonly known as the carrot or parsley family contains nearly 3,780 species and is distributed worldwide. Hemlock, or poison hemlock (Conium maculatum), contains the poisonous alkaloid, coniine in all parts of the plant and is deadly to both humans and livestock...

After reading the entire chapter, Amy put the book back on the shelf and made her way to the fiction section where she was delighted to find that not only, Murder on the Orient Express was on the shelves, but there was also a copy of the Waugh novel that her father was so keen to read.

Amy took the books to the counter and waited while Reanie stamped the date indexes with a small rubber stamp, then put her tickets into a pair of little cardboard pockets and placed them back into the 'books out' tray.

Wednesday was half day closing in Spinton and all the shops in the town complied with the law that had been brought in during the early part of the century. Shoppers were well aware of the early closing rules and the High Street and Main Street were almost empty as Amy walked along, looking into the unlit shop windows.

With Bodkin giving his evidence in court, Amy found herself at a loose end, so caught the bus home and after placing her father's new book on the arm of his chair, she went out into the garden where she could hear her mother singing one of her favourite traditional folk songs, Greensleeves.

'Did you know that Henry the Eighth has been credited with that song, Mum?' Amy said as she stepped onto a thin line of paving slabs that bisected a neatly cut lawn. 'He is supposed to have written it for Anne Boleyn but it's doubtful that he did.'

'I don't care who wrote it, I just love the melody,' Mrs Rowlings began the first verse again. She had a good singing voice and Amy used to love listening to her singing lullabies when she was a child.

'Do you need any help before I go up to play my records, Mum?' she asked as her mother, having forgotten the words in the middle part of Greensleeves, began to hum it instead.

'No thank you, dear. I gave the lawn its first cut of the year earlier on. I'm just pottering today. I might prune the rose bushes this afternoon.' She put her secateurs onto a small round iron table, sat down on a matching chair and looked up at her daughter. 'Are you in for lunch? I've got some nice potted beef on the cold shelf.'

Amy rested her hand on her mother's shoulder and gave her a kiss on the top of her head.

'I'll make lunch today, Mum. I'll give you a shout when it's ready.'

After lunch, Amy went up to her room and played a selection of records by Tommy Dorsey, Billie Holiday, Benny Goodman, and the Andrews Sisters, but her thoughts were concentrated on what she and Bodkin had learned from the sisters at the vicarage the day before. Amy couldn't quite put her finger on it, but something was niggling away in the back of her mind. Frustrated that she couldn't pin down her reservations about the evidence they had heard, she picked up a notepad and listed everything she thought relevant.

Wine bottle!!! Is that the only solution?

Arsenic in the digestive powders, added while dispensing or after, if after, who put it there?

Hemlock... where from? How did it get into his stomach?

Acid Reflux!

Evening meal. Cheese and beetroot, did he actually eat it?

Sugar in tea!

Syringe? Is it relevant or a red herring?

Who was alone in the kitchen with the wine bottle?

Would revenge over a job opportunity be a reason to kill? Possibly.

Mrs de Vere!!!

Mr Daley, not present at the meeting, where was he?

What will Bodkin find out at Skellinghouse?

Eugene Hales? What will he reveal?

Mr Brown, suspect or not? Ask Bodkin.

Peter Kissman drinks in the Dragon… so does Joe Proudfoot. What does Joe know about him?

At five-thirty, almost dizzy with the unanswered questions spinning around in her head, Amy went down to the kitchen where her mother was busy making cheese on toast. 'This is for us, dear,' she said. 'Dad's having his tripe again.'

After tea, desperate for news about the case and wondering if Bungling Bill had got his just desserts, Amy pulled on her coat and stuck her head into the sitting room where her parents were seated at the table discussing the vicar's funeral.

'Dad just opened a letter, Amy. It's from Wilson, Kendall and Beanney solicitors. He's been named in Mr Villiers' will. He's got to go to the reading of it after the funeral on Tuesday.'

'Ooh, that's exciting, Dad. I wonder what you've been bequeathed? We could be rich.'

'Harold didn't have a lot of money, Amy. He was a vicar, not a businessman.'

'He could afford to buy posh wine by the crate, so he wasn't particularly poor, either,' Amy replied.

'We'll see on Tuesday,' Mr Rowlings said before biting into a stringy length of tripe. 'But don't get your hopes up.'

'Hey! We could get a phone installed if he leaves you

enough,' Amy said excitedly.

Mr Rowlings sighed, deeply. 'Where are you off to?'

'I'm going to drop in on Bodkin at his new flat. I haven't seen it yet.'

Mr Rowlings narrowed one eye as he studied her. 'Be careful, Amy. I'm not sure I like the idea of my daughter being alone with a man in his apartment. I know romance is a big thing when you're young, but...'

'It's BODKIN, Dad,' Amy replied with a puzzled look on her face. 'He hasn't got a romantic bone in his body.'

'Hang on a moment, Amy. I've got something for Mr Bodkin. It's a house warming present. It isn't much but I hope he likes it.' Mrs Rowlings hurried to the kitchen and returned carrying a muslin covered dish. 'It's only an apple pie. I was going to give it to him tomorrow night but he might not have had time for his tea, what with him being away in Gillingham all day.'

'That's so lovely of you, Mum,' Amy said, taking the dish from her mother's hands. 'Okay, I'm off, I won't be late back.'

'Amy!' Mr Rowlings tipped his head to the side as he gave her a warning look.

'Yes, Dad, but you don't have to worry about me. It's only Bodkin.'

'It's Bodkin I'm worried about,' Mr Rowlings said with a dry laugh. 'He has no idea what he's letting himself in for.'

Amy caught the bus outside the Old Bull and with Bodkin's gift on her lap, travelled the short distance to Middle Street where she got off outside the police station. Sticking her head inside reception, she waved to Constable Barker to get his attention. 'Is Bodkin in residence?' she asked.

Barker laughed. 'No, miss, he went straight home when he got back from Gillingham. He'll be over at his flat.' He sniffed the air as the smell of apple pie wafted across the reception area. 'If any of that is going spare you know where to find me.'

Amy waved goodbye, then crossed the street to Farley Lane, soon to be Constabulary Way, and turned left into the car park of the newly constructed, Bluecoat House. The building was almost perfectly square and was built out of rough faced, yellow-tinted London bricks. The entrance door was made from one sheet of tempered glass, set in a dark-oak frame, and had clear, full length glass panes on either side. Amy looked through into the entrance hall. On the left was a set of stairs that rose from the ground, then took a sharp right turn to the second flight. At the bottom of the staircase was a door marked with the number 1. On the opposite side of the entrance hall was a matching door with the figure 2 on it. On the floor, outside the door was a pair of brown, men's shoes. On the back wall, facing her was a telephone.

Amy studied the four-button buzzer panel, none of which had yet been given name cards, pressed the buzzer for flat four and waited. When there was no sign of Bodkin coming down the stairs, she pressed again, when there was no response to that, she got angry with it and pressed the buzzer repeatedly.

'It can't be connected yet,' she muttered to herself, 'either that or he's having a nap after a long day in court.'

She decided to give the buzzer panel one more chance and pressed the button for flat two. A few seconds later, the door to the flat opened and a blonde woman a few years older than her, stepped into the lobby. Frowning at Amy, she wriggled, model-like, across the tiled floor and opened the front door.

'Yes?'

She was a large breasted woman with a strong frame and an oval shaped face. Her lips were full and red painted, her eyes were almost almond shaped and stunningly blue. Her platinum hair was parted in the middle and hung in tight curls over her ears. She wore a black pencil skirt, black Oxford shoes and white blouse which had two triangle darts sewn under the bust to help highlight her already impressive bosom. Amy thought she was a dead ringer for the Hollywood Actress, Mae West.

'I want to go up to flat four but no one is answering,' Amy said, unable to take her eyes from the woman's bust.

'No, they wouldn't be,' the woman stated in a matter-of-fact way.

'Do you know where he's gone?' Amy asked.

The woman held onto the door with one hand as if waiting to slam it shut should Amy try to set foot inside.

'I do, who wants to know? that's the question.'

'I'm his friend, Amy Rowlings.'

The woman looked Amy up and down and then sniffed as if not really liking what she was seeing. 'Is it important? He's busy at the moment.'

'Not vital, no but hey, if he's in why isn't he answering the door, is his buzzer connected?'

The blonde woman stuck her head out of the foyer, reached across with her right hand and pressed the button for flat four. A faint buzzing noise could be heard coming from upstairs. 'It seems to be working,' she said.

Amy tapped her foot impatiently. The woman ran her hands over her hips and narrowed her eyes at Amy. 'A friend, hey?'

'Yes, but I don't see why I should have to explain myself to you. Are you going to let me in or not?'

'Not, actually,' the woman said, then began to close the door. Suddenly Bodkin appeared in the doorframe of her flat.

'Trixie, is something wr—'

'Bodkin?' Amy's jaw dropped as she saw the detective step

into the hall and reach for his shoes.

'It's all right, Trixie, Miss Rowlings is a friend of mine. I'll see to it.'

Trixie stepped back and treated Amy to a scowl, then as she turned towards Bodkin his face suddenly lit up, her red lips formed a pout and she breathed in sharply, which had the effect of pushing her huge breasts out even further.

Bodkin managed to get one shoe on but was struggling with the other. He hopped across the floor as he tried to drag it onto his foot. 'Come in, Amy,' he said. 'I'll show you up.'

Trixie and Amy exchanged looks, the blonde curling up her lip as Amy stepped into the foyer. Turning away from her, she focussed on Bodkin again, who had now successfully managed to cram his foot into his shoe. 'I'll wash up,' she said, running her long-painted fingernails gently across his cheek. 'If there's anything else you need, you know where I am.' The busty blonde wiggled her way back to her front door, then turned and gave Bodkin a spectacular wink.

Bodkin blushed, muttered,' thanks' then held out his hand towards the stairs, inviting Amy to climb.

Bodkin's flat was still in a mess, with pairs of trousers, odd socks and crumpled shirts thrown over the back of the chairs and sofa. Piles of unopened cardboard boxes and wooden crates were stacked randomly about the living room.

'I haven't had much chance to do the unpacking,' he said, quietly.

Amy flicked her head towards the staircase. 'I can see why,' she said.

'Now, Amy...'

'If there's anything else I can do for you,' Amy mimicked as she wriggled her hips.

Bodkin groaned. 'She invited me in for dinner, I couldn't

refuse, really.'

'Oh yes you could, Bodkin.'

'I couldn't, Amy, honestly. She works at the station, she's Laws' secretary.'

'How come she didn't follow him to Maidstone then?'

'It's too far for her to travel, she's going to be re-assigned.'

'What as, a hat rack? You could hang a couple of helmets on those—'

'AMY! That's uncalled for. She only invited me down for a meal because she knew I'd been in court all day. There's no need to get jealous.'

'JEALOUS! I'm not jealous, Bodkin, how could I be jealous of a... a... FLOOZIE like that?'

'Amy there's really—'

'That hair and those pouty lips,' Amy pulled a fish face. 'And those... BOSOMS! For goodness's sake, Bodkin the woman is deformed.'

Bodkin held up his hands palms out. 'Amy, I promise you, that's the first time I've been in her flat. She invited me for dinner as a neighbourly gesture. It would have been churlish to refuse.'

'Bodkin, it is of no consequence to me. I don't care if you're in her flat from morning till night. I don't care if she cooks for you, if she washes your socks or if she irons your... underpants... I'm just disappointed in you that's all. I thought you had better taste than that.'

She spun around on one heel before suddenly turning back again. Stuffing the apple pie dish into his still protesting hands, she walked as demurely as she could towards the door, then slamming it behind her, she stomped down the stairs and after a quick glare at flat number two, she let herself out and hurried back to Middle Street to catch the bus home.

CHAPTER THIRTY

'Is there anything else I can do for you?'

Amy pouted her lips, put her hands on her hips and stuck her bottom out.

'I mean... Has she no self-respect? I honestly thought Mae West was opening the door, mind you, that bosom of hers got there a long time before the rest of her did... I still can't believe it... and she works in a police station... I mean, they actually let her turn up for work looking like that.'

Amy put her right hand on her hip and began to swing it.

'I really thought she was going to ask him to 'Come up and see me sometime.''

'You mean, down,' Alice said, biting her lip. 'She lives downstairs, Bodkin is upstairs. He'd have to—'

'Yes, yes, stop nit-picking, you know exactly what I meant.'

Alice bit her lip again and then mouthed, 'oh dear' to Miriam who suddenly began to study her knitting pattern, intently.

'It looks like the little green-eyed monster has found you,

Amy,' she said, shooting her a quick glance before resuming her knitting.

'JEALOUS! Of HER! What is there to be jealous of? I mean, she's just so, so... blousy.'

'She does seem to have got under your skin,' Alice said, fighting hard against the giggle that was threatening to sneak out of her mouth.

'Under MY skin? HA! You're assuming that I give a damn about her, which I don't.'

'No, of course not,' Alice replied as she picked up the teapot and carried it over to the sink. Closing her eyes, she screwed up her face and almost succeeded in holding in a laugh. 'Perish the thought.'

Amy glared at the back of Alice's head.

'You haven't seen her. Honestly, I really thought Bodkin had better taste than that. I mean... all that make-up, those pouty lips, she looked like a trout... that shade of lipstick didn't help her... and her hair... that platinum shade, it's all right in Hollywood, but it just doesn't look right on Farley Lane... Jean Harlowe has a lot to answer for... and that bust... sticking it out the way she does... If I had a chest like that, I'd be doing all I could to hide it.'

Amy began to pace backwards and forwards as she continued to rant.

'What's that phrase they use in America? BIMBO... that's it. While I'd usually defend any woman from being called derogatory names, I can't bring myself to do it in her case. The tag just fits so well.'

Alice held up the refilled teapot.

'More tea—'

'It's not just the way she looks, she has to flaunt it...' Amy struck the pose again and swung her hip as she did another impression of Mae West. 'I've been on more laps than a napkin,' she cooed.

Miriam snorted, unable to hold the laughter in any longer.

'Oh, Amy, you are funny.'

'That's EXACTLY how she is though,' Amy retorted. 'You can just see her saying it,' she pouted again and cupped her hands about a foot in front of her chest. 'And that chest... Honestly, I'm so disappointed in Bodkin. Of all the people to canoodle with, he chooses that, hussy.'

Amy looked down at her own chest, then across to Alice.

'I mean, I've got a chest, haven't I? It's not as though I'm lacking in that department.'

'You have a perfectly good chest,' Alice replied, trying to keep a serious tone to her voice.

'It's not as nice as yours, I'd love to have a bust like you, but I do have one. I can do cleavage.'

'Maybe he was telling the truth, love,' Alice said, soothingly. 'Perhaps he did feel it would be churlish to refuse her dinner invitation. That's probably all there was to it.'

Amy slumped down on a chair and sighed, deeply.

'I know. It's Bodkin we're talking about here, isn't it? I doubt he'll have even noticed her giving him the come on. I bet he noticed those—'

'That's more like it. It is Bodkin we're talking about,' Alice said, putting a mug of tea on the table in front of Amy. 'There, drink your tea, it might help lift your spirits.'

Amy sighed again and picked up her mug.

'He's supposed to be coming around for a meal tonight. Well, if he as much as mentions her name, he'll be wearing his shepherd's pie, not eating it.'

. . .

Amy was already in the living room when Bodkin arrived at six. Pretending to be captivated by her book she remained on the sofa, leaving her mother to answer the door.

'Hello, Mr Bodkin. Amy's in the living room, she's engrossed in her murder story, she didn't hear you knock.' She took the detective's damp mac and hung it on a hook then reached for his hat. 'Is it raining?'

'Cat's and dogs,' Bodkin replied. 'I'm glad I came in the car. I think I might have had to swim down the lane.'

'Mr Rowlings... Amy,' Bodkin nodded to them each in turn as he entered the living room.

Mr Rowlings beamed at him from his armchair. Amy glanced up and said nothing.

'Sit down, laddie,' Mr Rowlings said in his strange, Scottish brogue. 'Dinner's ready, Lizzie is just dishing it up.'

'I hope you like shepherd's pie, Mr Bodkin,' Mrs Rowlings said as she placed a plate of steaming food in front of him.

'Just Bodkin, Mrs Rowlings. Shepherd's pie is my favourite meal, I was only saying so to Amy yesterday, wasn't I?' Bodkin shot Amy a nervous glance.

'Uh-huh,' Amy muttered without looking up from her book.

Mrs Rowlings shot her puzzled look.

'Come on, Amy, never mind murder stories. Your dinner is on the table.'

Amy snapped her book shut, walked to the table and pulled out the chair next to Bodkin. After a quick sideways glance, she tossed her head, put her hands together and prepared for her father to say grace.

It was left to Mrs Rowlings to try to keep the stilted conversation going throughout the meal; Mr Rowlings seemed oblivious to the tense atmosphere. When they had finished the main course, she carried the empty plates through to the kitchen, then, looking around the half-closed door, she crooked her finger towards Amy and made a loud 'psssst' sound. When Amy glanced across, she beckoned her to come into the kitchen.

'Have you and Bodkin had words, our Amy?'

'No. Well, not exactly.'

'What does, not exactly mean?' Mrs Rowlings hissed. 'You could cut the atmosphere out there with a knife.'

'It's something and nothing, Mum. Don't worry about it. I'm a little bit peeved with him that's all.'

'Is it because he doesn't share all the evidence with you? You can't really expect him to, Amy, you're not a policeman.'

'No, it's not that. It's something and nothing. I just expected him to... well, I expected better of him, that's all.'

'Oh dear, that doesn't sound too encouraging. I've always found Bodkin to be a very considerate young man.'

'Leave it, Mum. It honestly doesn't matter.'

Mrs Rowlings placed her hand on Amy's arm and smiled, softly.

'Sort it out between you before he goes home, dear. Don't let things fester. It's always best to have things out in the open.' She patted Amy's arm again, then opened her utensils drawer. 'Now, where's that tin opener.'

After dessert, Mr Rowlings poured himself a large whisky while Mrs Rowling sipped at a glass of lemonade. Amy and Bodkin sat awkwardly on the sofa, giving each other occasional glances but saying nothing.

'Whatever it is, Amy. It's not worth all the angst,' Mr Rowlings said, after a full two minutes of silence. He looked Bodkin in the eyes and flicked his head towards the kitchen. Bodkin got to his feet and walked through the door before he turned to look at Amy, holding his hands up as if to say, 'it's not my idea'.

Amy sighed, shot her father a look, then got up and walked slowly into the kitchen, closing the door behind her.

'Well?' she said.

'Amy... I'm sorry, whatever it is I've done, I apologise. Can we just forget about it now?'

'Whatever it is? You don't even know what you're apologising for do you, Bodkin?'

'To be honest, no. But I've been miserable all day, if that helps.'

'Oh, Bodkin, you have no idea when it comes women, do you?'

'To be honest. No. I do my best, but most of the time I'm just floundering around, worrying if I'm saying, or doing the right thing.'

Amy laughed softly and put her fingers on his face as he looked earnestly down at her.

'Poor Bodkin.'

'You mean I'm forgiven, for whatever it was I did? Look, Amy, there's nothing going on between—'

Amy put one finger over his lips.

'Shh. You're forgiven, don't go dragging it all up again. I know you weren't up to anything underhand. It's just not you, but... don't ever expect me to ever make friends with that... woman.'

'I'll try to avoid her, but it won't be easy, living and working at the same place. She's hardly the shrinking violet type. She can be rather, overfamiliar.'

'That's one way of putting it,' Amy replied. 'Look, I know you can't avoid her, living where she lives, but if you must go around for dinner, at least keep your shoes on. When you take them off at the door like that it looks like you've become part of the furniture.'

'No more dinners,' Bodkin replied. 'She's not even a good cook. Not a patch on your mum.'

'I don't think her culinary abilities will ever be seen as her main attraction,' Amy replied rolling her eyes. 'Look, Bodkin. I'm sorry too, I overreacted to the situation. It was her attitude towards me as much as anything.'

'You did get a bit feisty,' he said. 'I've never seen you like that before.'

'You should see me when I'm really riled,' Amy replied. 'Though maybe you should hope you never do.'

'So, how did it go at court? Is Bungling Bill behind bars again?'

Amy and Bodkin sipped tea as they sat on two wooden chairs at the side of a small, pine, kitchen table.

'He is. He got two years.'

'And the world is a safer place,' Amy said with a smile. 'Poor Bungling Bill.'

'The bulk of the sentence was for stealing his son's cap gun. That's what I told the lad at least. He came to court with his mother. I think she's going to be looking to get a divorce soon. Quite right too, it's no way to bring a child up. He's a bright young thing. I told him to apply to the police when he grows up.'

Amy brushed her lips against Bodkin's cheek, then sat back nursing her mug of tea.

'You've got a big heart for a copper, Bodkin,' she said. 'Come on, let's go back in or Mum will start to listen at the door.'

. . .

'Did you hear I've been mentioned in Harold's will, laddie?' Mr Rowlings asked before taking the tiniest sip of whisky.

'I hadn't, no. Who is handling it?'

'Wilson Keppel and Betty.'

'Wilson, Kendall and Beanney,' Amy corrected. 'Wilson, Keppel and Betty are the music hall act that do the Egyptian sand dance.'

'Ah, that's right,' Mr Rowlings said with a smile. 'We saw them at the Empire in Canterbury a few years ago, didn't we, Lizzie? Very funny.' Mr Rowlings flattened his hands and made a jabbing motion with them. 'Very funny.'

'The letter was from Godfrey Wilson. He's the man Alice calls her Gangster Lawyer because of that car he drives, I think you met him once, Bodkin.' Amy said.

'Oh, yes, I remember him. It was during the Handsley murder case. He was George Handsley's solicitor, wasn't he? Drove an Alvis as I recall.'

'That's the one. He's a nice man. Alice thinks the world of him.'

'What will you do with your windfall?' Bodkin asked.

'Oh, I doubt it will amount to much,' Rowlings replied. He shot a quick glance towards Elizabeth. 'I'll probably donate it to some charity or other.'

Amy's jaw dropped. 'Dad! You deserve that money after writing all those sermons, however much it is. You should spend it on a holiday or something.'

'The something being a telephone, I presume.'

'Well, it would make life easier.' Amy grinned.

Mr Rowlings smiled fondly at his daughter, then gave his wife another quick glance before shifting his eyes to Bodkin again.

'Are you any closer to catching his killer, Mr Bodkin?'

'We get closer by the hour, Mr Rowlings. Don't worry, we'll get our man... or woman, as the case may be.'

'Are we really any closer to catching the killer, Bodkin?' Amy asked as the pair sat in the front seats of the detective's Morris Ten.

Bodkin took off his hat and scratched his head.

'No closer than we were yesterday,' he said. 'But it's strange how all the loose ends can suddenly pull together. I'll be glad when we finally get the lab reports back on that wine bottle, I'll tell you that much. I dropped in and had a strong word with them today. Apparently, Acting Superintendent Laws has got them prioritising one of his murder cases. They promised me both sets of results by Saturday.'

'Results? I thought we were only waiting on the wine bottle?'

'Nope, we haven't had the fingerprint results back from Villiers' digestive powder wrappers yet, though I have been told there are at least four sets of good quality prints on both the outer bag and at least one of the wraps. One set will probably belong to me. One set will more than likely be Mrs Gatting's as she actually mixed the powders for him every morning, and one set will presumably be Agatha Walker's, as she dispensed the medication.'

Amy sat bolt upright; her face lit up with excitement. 'So, the fourth set could belong to our killer?'

'It's possible, Amy. It's possible... But when it comes to murder, nothing is ever that simple.'

CHAPTER THIRTY-ONE

SAINT JOHN'S CHURCH WAS MORE THAN HALF FULL FOR THE GOOD Friday service which was a good turnout, according to Mr Rowlings. A rare appearance in the parish by the bishop had obviously boosted the numbers.

Reverend Daley conducted the service and although it was generally well received by the congregation, more than a few noted an air of arrogance about him. Rowlings began to wonder if he had already been given the news about his future role in the parish.

After the service, Daley stood in the foyer, shaking hands and wallowing in the warm words he received from many of the parishioners. When the bishop arrived in the narthex, Daley bobbed his head in deference, then held out his hand to accept congratulations from his boss.

Bishop Warrington was a stout man of around seventy years of age, with flabby jowls and a collection of chins underneath a pair of almost womanly lips. He wore a white surplice over his purple cassock. His head was bare, his long, white combed-over hair attempting to hide an almost monk-like bald spot on the crown of his head. He was followed by a group of four other clergymen, all dressed in black cassocks with white surplices over the top.

Despite the pomp surrounding him, Rowlings found the bishop to be an engaging man. His eyes sparkled in genuine delight as the engineer strode forward to welcome him.

'James! I'm delighted to meet you again, it's been far too long,' he beamed.

Rowlings lowered his head in deference.

'Ten years, Bishop. I remember it as though it was yesterday.'

Warrington took his arm and they walked around the side of the church together.

'I always meant to write and thank you for your service to the church, James. Both myself and Harold valued your assistance.'

'He passed the thanks on, Bishop, no letter was needed.'

'And how is your good lady wife... Elizabeth, is it?' Warrington looked across the body of Rowlings towards Mrs Rowlings who was walking alongside.

Elizabeth bobbed her head quickly.

'I'm very well, thank you, your Emi... Bishop,' she replied, nervously.

Amy had taken up a position just behind her father and listened eagerly to the conversation as they walked around the side of the church towards the meeting room that had been bolted onto the back of the old church some eighty years before.

As they turned the final corner and the church hall came into view, she saw Bodkin waiting at the entrance. He stood to the side and held out his hand as Rowlings introduced him to the bishop.

'Ah, yes, Detective Inspector Bodkin. My clerk advised me that you had requested an interview. Can you give me twenty minutes while I announce the name of the new vicar of Spinton?'

Bodkin smiled as he nodded.

'I'll need a word with Reverend Daley too.'

Bodkin stuck a thumb up to Amy as she entered the hall, then stepped inside himself and stood with the Rowlings family as the bishop walked up to the dais and the room began to fill up.

In all, there were fifty-three invited guests and dignitaries in the hall. Bodkin watched them enter from his vantage point about half way down the aisle. As Mrs de Vere swept up the red carpet towards the stage alongside Reverend Daley, Bodkin took a pace to the side and held out his hand to the new vicar.

'Reverend Daley, I don't know if the bishop passed on my message but he has agreed that I might ask you a few questions when the speeches are over.'

Daley muttered something Bodkin couldn't quite catch and put in two quick extra paces to step around the detective.

'You too, Mrs de Vere,' Bodkin said as she came along side. 'Wait for me near the doors, if you would.'

Bishop Warrington got to his feet to a warm ripple of applause and stepped up to the lectern.

'Ladies and gentlemen, it is with a mixture of pleasure and regret that I find myself standing before you today. Pleasure because it's always a delight to stand before such a loyal and passionate congregation. Regret, because of the circumstances that lie behind this visit. Reverend Villiers was a good friend and a very able member of the clergy. I will miss both his company and his counsel...

The bishop warmed to his topic, praising both the parish and the church volunteers who had raised money for the many good causes the diocese had supported over the time he had been in charge.

After almost twenty minutes, he looked up at the big clock on the back wall, then began to wind up his speech.

'... And so, the moment you've all been waiting for. I am delighted to announce that Reverend Villiers successor and the new vicar of Spinton, will be...' he paused for effect, '...The Reverend Michael Daley.'

Daley stepped onto the stage with the sound of enthusiastic applause ringing in his ears. He shook hands with the bishop, then holding his arms aloft like a winning prize fighter, he stepped up to the lectern.

'Ladies and gentlemen... fellow parishioners... nay... friends... I am delighted to have been chosen to be the new shepherd of the Spinton flock...'

If the bishop's speech was filled with many warm tributes for the dead vicar, Daley's speech only mentioned him once. Rowlings fought back a mixture of anger and tears as he heard his new vicar, the man he would have to pray alongside, speak about the bright exciting future that lay before the parish. The speech was mercifully short, and after just five minutes at the lectern, Daley stepped down from the stage to be slapped on the back and verbally congratulated by the town's elders. Amy watched Mrs de Vere closely as she shouted out her congratulations, applauding as though Daley had just won the hundred-yard sprint at the Olympic Games.

Amy looked around for Bodkin and found him standing by

the stage waiting for the bishop to step down. As Daley turned to look at him, the detective pointed to the clock and held up five fingers, then pointed to the far corner of the hall where two, leaflet covered tables had been pushed together.

Amy hurried up to Bodkin's side and stood quietly as the detective began his questions.

'Thanks for giving me the time, your... I'm sorry, how do I address you without causing offence?'

'Bishop will be fine,' Warrington said, warmly. 'I'm not sure how I can help, but I'll do my best.'

'Thank you,' Bodkin said as he pulled out his notebook and pen. Turning to a clean sheet, he scribbled on the top corner to get the ink flowing, then wrote, Bishop Warrington, 7/4/39 in large letters across the page.

'I don't have many questions for you to be honest, Bishop, but I would like to know about your relationship with Harold Villiers.'

'Harold and I have been both colleagues and friends for over twenty years, I am... was aware that he had been battling his demons for much of that time, but to his credit, he didn't let them get in the way of his ministry. He wasn't the easiest man to love, but he was an effective minister. He did his job well and he did it... mostly, with dignity.'

'You were aware of his drink problem then? How long had you known?'

'All the time I've known him, pretty much... no, that's not fair. I think it only began after he lost the love of his life to the Spanish flu. He was about thirty years old then, but it hit him hard. He took some time off to try to sort his problems out. I believe he had some spiritual counselling too. After a few months he returned to the church and was sent here to Spinton, it was thought that having his own flock to look after would help him. Give him a new focus as it were. He was here for twenty years and I can honestly say I personally never regretted giving him the position.'

'I believe he was hauled over the coals a few times though,' Bodkin said, glancing up from his notes.

'Hauled over the coals? That makes it sound as though he was dragged before me to be summarily punished. That wasn't the case.'

'No?'

'No. I can assure you Inspector, that Harold was never hauled over anything. There had been complaints from some quarters about his behaviour, but not from the people of his flock. The complaints always arrived by anonymous means. No one would ever put a name to the poison pen letters. I had my suspicions of course. The clergy is just as competitive as any workplace.'

'Was Reverend Daley one of the people you suspected of planting rumours?'

'I'm not willing to answer that question, Inspector Bodkin, as I have no proof, and suspicion, in my profession at least, isn't enough to hang a man.' The bishop gave Bodkin a tight smile.

Bodkin returned the smile and nodded in acknowledgement of the reprimand.

'Nor is it in my profession, Bishop.'

The detective tapped his notebook with the tip of his pen and furrowed his brow.

'What were these accusations exactly?'

The bishop waved the question away with his hand.

'I'm not prepared to answer that, it is confidential information. I think you are more than aware of that. Priests, lawyers and doctors have an understanding with their flock, patients and clients. I cannot abuse that trust.'

'The man is dead, Bishop. I'm the person who has been given the responsibility of finding his killer. You won't be betraying his confidence now that he's no longer here.'

'I'm sorry, my son. I really can't help you with this line of questioning.' He smiled and offered his hand. 'Now if that's all...'

'Why Daley?' Bodkin burst out. 'Why him, when we all know he was the prime source of the rumours against Villiers? Aren't you disrespecting his memory by handing the parish over to him?'

'Daley is a very capable and intelligent man, Inspector. I'm sure he'll do very well here, but to speak honestly. I don't think my reasons for choosing him are any of your business.'

Warrington nodded curtly, then turned away and beamed at Mr Rowlings who was standing only a few feet away.

'Now, James, let's have that chat about the eulogy you've written for Harold.'

Bodkin ran his hand over his chin, then, clearly frustrated, he turned away from the stage and crossed to the far corner of the hall where Daley was chatting to Mrs de Vere. Amy quickly followed him.

'Ah, Reverend Daley, at last,' Bodkin said holding out a hand. 'I'm Inspector Bodkin, I've been trying to get hold of you all week.'

Daley gave the detective's hand a half-hearted shake.

'Yes, well, I'm a busy man these days, I've been preparing to take over the parish. It's not just a matter of standing up on a Sunday, you know. There are going to be lots of changes around here.'

'Will one of them include recognising the new charity committee and making a donation to it?'

'That's none of your concern, Inspector Bodkin.'

Bodkin looked squarely at Councillor de Vere.

'I think you might find that it is.'

Amy edged closer so that she was standing right behind Bodkin. She shot a glance over his shoulder at the councillor who was visibly shaken by Bodkin's remark.

'I can assure you that you'll find nothing wrong. Everything to do with the charity is legal and above board,' she said, though Amy noticed she was unable to hold Bodkin's eye.

'We'll come to that shortly, Mrs de Vere,' Bodkin replied, firmly. 'I'd like to hear more from the new vicar at the moment.'

Daley shuffled his feet and forced a smile. 'How may I be of assistance?'

'Firstly, I'd like to know why you disliked Harold Villiers so much. Was it all down to professional jealousy? He had something you wanted, namely this parish?'

'There was no jealousy involved. I was the best man for the job and we both knew it.'

Bodkin pursed his lips. 'So, what would you call spreading malicious rumours about a rival? Was that done out of a sense of comradery?'

'Firstly, they were not unfounded rumours. Secondly, the reports didn't come from me.'

'But you were the only one who would benefit from them, Mr Daley, no one else, just you.'

Daley shrugged. 'If Villiers had conducted himself better, he wouldn't have been under so much pressure from Rochester.'

'But he wasn't under pressure from Rochester or anywhere else,' Bodkin said. 'I've just been talking to the bishop about that very thing.'

Daley shot a quick look at the bishop who had now finished his conversation with Mr Rowlings and was laughing at a weak joke, shared by a member of his entourage.

'How long have you been back in Spinton, Reverend Daley?'

'Three months, give or take.'

'That's a long time to be away from your duties, isn't it?'

'Look, my mother is recovering from pneumonia. I've been helping to look after her.'

'Very laudable,' Bodkin replied. 'I hope she's recovering well.'

'She's on the mend,' Daley replied.

'But the fact remains, that three months is a long time to be away from your clerical duties.'

'I've been administering to four small parishes that aren't big enough to warrant a full-time vicar. One of them has a population of only a hundred, so, I flit between them, holding services at each one on a monthly basis instead of a weekly one.'

'Ah, I see,' Bodkin replied. 'Someone else will have to do that now I take it, or will you be merging all five parishes?'

'No, Spinton is too large a concern. I'll just be looking after this one.'

'You were born here, I believe?'

'Yes.'

'So, have you always had this searing ambition to look after this parish?'

'Since I first came to the church, yes. What's wrong with th—'

'You always wanted to become a priest? You never had any other ambition when you were growing up?'

'What a strange question.' A puzzled look came across

Daley's face. 'No, I wanted to be an engine driver, then a fireman or a wild west sheriff, like most boys.'

'Or a scientist? You studied chemistry at university I believe?'

Daley nodded.

'How long did you study chemistry for?' Bodkin asked.

'About two and a half years.'

'So, you would have studied heavy metals during that time. You'd have known all about lead, mercury, cadmium... arsenic?'

'Yes, amongst many other things.'

'Why did you change courses so suddenly? I mean, that's two and a half years of your life, wasted.'

'I don't see it as a waste. Learning is learning. We should all strive to increase our knowledge throughout our lives.'

'Indeed,' Bodkin replied. 'But why switch, and from classic science to a ... theoretical degree?'

'I had a calling,' Daley almost snarled. 'But I suppose you're going to sneer at that.'

Bodkin shook his head.

'Not at all. I had a calling when I joined the police force. I had an unremitting desire to see thieves, embezzlers and murderers locked up.' Bodkin smiled at the vicar. 'So, I know all about callings.'

'Look, Inspector, I really don't like this line of questioning. If you're going to accuse me of something then do it and let's get it out of the way.'

'All in good time, Reverend,' Bodkin said, smiling again.

The detective looked at Mrs de Vere for a few seconds, then focussed his attention on Daley again. Pulling out his notebook, he flipped to a page that contained an old shopping list and pretended to study it.

'Tell me about your relationship with Mrs de Vere,' he said, suddenly.

'Relationship?'

'How close are you?'

'Now listen here,' Daley spluttered.

'It's a simple question, Mr Daley, are you in a relationship with Mrs de Vere? Either sexually or professionally?'

'No to both,' Daley spat. 'We hardly know each other. We only met a few weeks ago for Go... goodness's sake.'

Bodkin nodded and made a note in his book.

'So, you haven't had any private meetings with her? You haven't spent a lot of time alone in the last few weeks... at her house for instance... you have never stayed for the night?'

'NO! and I resent the implication. You are listening to unfounded rumours.'

'Isn't that odd,' Bodkin replied. 'The Reverend Villiers suffered in a very similar way, didn't he? The only difference is, you were the one spreading those malicious rumours, this time you're on the wrong end of them.'

'The stories about Villiers were the truth!' Daley shouted. 'He was an alcoholic, he stole money...'

'LIES! All LIES!' Mr Rowlings almost pushed Bodkin aside to get to the new vicar. 'Harold never took a penny from the church. He may have liked a drink in his own time, but he was no alcoholic. I knew him for over twenty years. He was a better man than you'll ever be.'

'HA!' Daley exploded. 'And what about the young girls? What about the prostitutes. DENY THAT!'

Rowlings didn't reply, instead, he pulled back his fist and hit Daley squarely on the chin, then, turning away, he took hold of his wife's arm and marched her towards the door.

CHAPTER THIRTY-TWO

'I WANT THAT MAN ARRESTED,' DALEY SAID, RUBBING BLOOD FROM HIS mouth with his handkerchief.

'I'll arrest him if you insist,' Bodkin said. 'Though I don't think it would be a very good way to start your new career. He's one of the church's stalwarts. He has a lot of friends in the parish.'

Daley spat into his handkerchief, then checked to see if he had any loose teeth.

'Maybe you're right. But I want an apology.'

'Don't hold your breath on that one,' Amy muttered to herself.

'Do you want me to call for a doctor?' Bodkin asked. 'There's one just down the road from here.'

Daley dabbed at his mouth again, there was no fresh blood.

'No, I'll be fine.' He looked past Bodkin to the group of guests who were watching the proceedings intently. 'Go home, everyone, the excitement is over. Things just got a bit heated.'

As the guests began to disperse, Bodkin checked his notebook again, then continued his questioning of Daley.

'Are you all right to carry on? I won't be long now.'

Daley nodded and slipped the bloody handkerchief into his pocket.

'Where were we... Oh yes. You were about to tell me about your relationship with Mrs de Vere?'

'There is no... Look, Inspector. My private life is my own and I do understand you are conducting a murder investigation, but please. Don't keep picking away at this, it really is irrelevant to your investigation.'

'I'll tell you what is, and what is not, relevant, Mr Daley,' Bodkin replied. 'We could be looking at a conspiracy charge at minimum here.'

'Conspiracy? To what end?'

'Embezzlement... Fraud... Murder...'

'Murder! What in blazes?'

'Where were you on the night the Reverend Villiers died, Mr Daley?'

Daley's mouth dropped open.

'You can't think I'm responsible for that. We had our differences; we really didn't like each other but I would never have gone that far. I'm a man of God.'

'You had a motive for wanting him out of the way, Reverend.'

'Motive? That's ridiculous, Mr Bodkin. Of course I wanted the parish; any local lad would want to serve his own community. It doesn't mean I'd kill someone to get it.'

Bodkin's eyes never left Daley's.

'I ask again, Mr Daley, where were you on the night of the twenty-fifth of March? Let's say between nine and eleven o'clock?'

'I was... at home, probably, swotting up on my sermon for the following day, most likely.'

'You're not sure?'

'Let me think... I was at Pucklebury on Sunday the twenty-sixth, so I would have been at home. I got a lift from the verger, Mr Conway.'

'Can you provide a witness who can corroborate this?'

'No... no, I can't. I was at home with my mother, she was asleep from seven o'clock, she takes some medication.'

'So, you didn't see Mrs de Vere that night... at any time?'

'No, I don't think so... possibly late afternoon, but not in the evening. My mother's nurse leaves at seven, after she's given my mother her knockout drops. I have to be home before then on a Saturday. She doesn't work late at weekends.'

'Do you know where Mrs de Vere lives, Mr Daley?'

Daley became agitated all of a sudden.

'N... oh, all right, yes, of course I do.'

'Did you pay her one or more visits during the week prior to Villiers' death?'

'Yes.'

'Did you stay overnight on at least one occasion?'

Daley flashed Mrs de Vere a glance.

'Yes,' he whispered.

'Was that a yes?'

Daley nodded. Blushing furiously, he shot a panicked look towards the bishop who was still chatting to a pair of local aldermen.

'You won't tell the bishop... he doesn't have to find out, does he? It could be the end of me here. Constance isn't divorced yet, you see.'

'I think that depends on what we find out, Mr Daley. Now,

did you ever go into, or have cause to break into, the garden shed at the de Vere property?'

'Break in? Why would I—'

'Just answer the question please.'

'No, I didn't break into the shed... I may have gone in there once, with Constance when she was hunting for a pair of secateurs or something. What relevance does this have?'

Bodkin smiled and snapped his notebook shut.

'Thank you, Mr Daley, you've been very helpful. We may need to speak again so, just be aware of that.'

The bishop waved across the hall to announce that he was leaving and Daley scurried across the parquet floor. Pulling an instant smile, he shook hands with the two aldermen before taking the bishop by the arm and leading him past the watching Bodkin, to the hall door.

Bodkin watched them leave before turning towards Amy.

'Well, that rattled his rafters.'

Amy nodded. 'He's still hiding something,' she said, softly.

Bodkin opened his notebook again as he turned to a nervous-looking Councillor de Vere.

'You don't let the grass grow under your feet do you, Councillor?'

'I beg your pardon?'

Bodkin flicked his head towards the door.

'You and the new vicar? Was it love at first sight? It must have been close to it; he's only been here five minutes.'

'My private life is of no concern of yours, Inspector.'

'Ah, that's where you're wrong, Mrs de Vere. In normal circumstances I'd agree with you, but these are far from normal circumstances.' Bodkin studied his notebook. 'When did you first meet?'

'It was at an art council event, about two months ago. Michael had bought a ticket. He loves anything related to the arts. We're hoping to open our own gallery here in Spinton, one day. We got talking and our friendship blossomed from there.'

'Were you still having money troubles at the time?'

'Mr Bodkin, I—'

'It's Inspector Bodkin when I'm on duty, madam.' Bodkin narrowed his eyes at her. 'And, I can assure you, I am on duty at this moment, so be careful how you answer, as anything you say, might be used as evidence later. You wouldn't want to be caught out making a silly mistake.'

'Am I to be charged with something then?' Mrs de Vere asked, with wide eyes.

'That remains to be seen, Councillor. It depends on your answers.'

Bodkin looked around the hall, then back to Mrs de Vere.

'Is this where that last committee meeting was held?'

'The medicines for the poor committee? Yes.'

'You had something of an altercation with the vicar that night, didn't you?'

'It wasn't an altercation... we had a difference of opinion.'

'On whether or not to continue with the committee and invest church funds into your charity.'

'Yes.'

'How much were you asking for, Mrs de Vere?'

'Four thousand pounds. I needed a quick injection of funds. One of my main backers was pulling out and it would have totally destroyed the charity's shares portfolio.'

'Skellinghouse being the backer?'

'Yes.'

'How big was their investment?'

'Two thousand pounds.'

'What reason did they give for pulling out?'

Mrs de Vere shuffled her feet and looked down at her bag.

'They said they were reassessing their charitable donations. I think they wanted to spread the money more widely.'

'They were about to pull all their money out. None of the new money they were about to spread, would find its way into your fund.'

'No.'

'Why do you think that was? I mean, they might possibly want to cut back on the donation but to withdraw it completely... that's a bit drastic, isn't it?'

'You'd have to ask them.'

'Oh, I already have, Mrs de Vere.'

The councillor's head dropped and she swayed slightly.

'Mr Barlow, Skellinghouse's chief accountant was very informative when I called in yesterday. Do you know what he told me?'

Mrs de Vere shook her head.

'He said that he believed the company had been a victim of fraud. That you had deliberately misused charity funds to line your own pockets. Apparently, he'd had a tip off from your bank. Your personal account was suddenly in credit to the tune of two thousand two hundred pounds. You had been running a large overdraft prior to that, hadn't you?'

Mrs de Vere began to visibly shake.

'You cashed in the bulk of the charity's portfolio and paid it into your own bank account, didn't you?'

'I was desperate, Mr Bodkin.' The councillor grabbed hold of Bodkin's arm. 'I had no choice; I was about to be bankrupted. I couldn't allow that to happen... A woman in my position in society... I would never have made enough out of selling the house to cover my debts; it's mortgaged to the hilt. That swine of a husband of mine left me in the lurch.'

Bodkin led the councillor over to the leaflet tables and pulled out a small, round-backed chair.

'Please sit down, Mrs de Vere.'

Pulling out a second chair, Bodkin sat down himself, facing the stricken woman.

'You intended to use the new church funds to replace the missing money, I take it?'

Mrs de Vere nodded.

'Villiers had pretty much promised me the money. He thought it was a great idea. To be fair to him he did like to help the poor of the parish. Especially the children.'

'So, why do you think he changed his mind?'

'I think he got someone to look into the fund for him. He had a friend in the city.'

'So, he realised that there was no money left in the fund and that Skellinghouse were demanding money that the charity no longer had. You couldn't pay them back, even if you wanted to.'

Tears rolled down the councillor's face. She pulled out a flowered handkerchief and dabbed at her eyes.

'It was all such a perfect solution, you see. If Villiers had handed over the money, I could have paid Skellinghouse back and would have had two thousand to invest in the shares. It was a win, win situation, really. No one would have suspected a thing.'

'The committee would have wanted to take a look at the charity accounts every year, surely?'

'No one ever studies them properly. Hales and Frazier were both members of my original committee. I used to give them a report at the AGM every year but they were more interested in the top-quality brandy I was plying them with. They only ever glanced at the headline figures, they never actually read the report.'

'And you thought you could do the same with the new committee?'

'I knew Villiers and Agatha Walker might be a problem but as for the rest...'

'How did you intend to get around that. If either of those two queried the accounts next year?'

'I was going to say we'd had a bit of a bad run. The stock market is up and down at the moment. I could have easily invented some share losses. My husband taught me how to hide bad news in annual accounts. He did it for years, that's why I was in such a mess when he left. Then again. If I made a few riskier, high profit investments, I might easily have made the money back and no one would have been any the wiser.'

'Your plans were scuppered when the vicar said no, though.'

Mrs de Vere nodded. 'I was up the creek without a paddle.'

'So, you turned to Mr Daley. He must have seemed like a knight in shining armour.'

'He'd already told me he was working on getting Villiers removed and that he was after the parish himself.'

'So, you hatched a plot to bump off Villiers between you?'

'No, it wasn't like that.'

'What was it like, Councillor? Please, enlighten me.'

'Michael said he had proof that Villiers was seeing a child prostitute. He was going to confront him with the evidence and if he didn't resign, he was going to the bishop with it.'

'Blackmail is a despicable crime, Mrs de Vere.'

'So is child molestation, Inspector. Villiers wouldn't have been an innocent victim.'

'Getting rid of him completely would have worked just as well. I mean, if the evidence about the prostitute didn't stack up...?'

'It would have stacked up. Michael was convinced of it.'

'Are you sure you didn't take a tiny bit of strychnine from your garden shed and drop it into Villiers' wine after the meeting? You had the opportunity. You were in the kitchen alone.'

'I was never in the kitchen alone.'

'Really? You went back in for a glass of water after the meeting broke up. Are you saying there was someone else in there at the time?'

'Oh, I'd forgotten about that.'

'Was there anyone else in the kitchen when you went to get a drink?'

'No... no there wasn't. But I didn't put anything in his wine. I didn't want to dispose of him that way. We had a perfectly good plan in place.'

'You do realise that conspiracy to blackmail is a prisonable offence, Mrs de Vere?'

'Yes, but... look, it wasn't my idea, and anyway the plan was never put into use. He died before Michael could talk to him about it.'

Bodkin stretched out his leg and felt his knee click.

'Take me back to the meeting,' he said. 'You're all in here. How long did it go on for?'

'Not long. I think we all had our say about the benefits the charity would bring to the town, we all thought the idea was going to come to fruition, but just after I'd finished speaking the vicar dropped his bombshell. He was going to put some money into a new charity that would benefit the prostitutes in the area. Pay for their medical needs, help them leave the sordid industry if they wanted to.'

'How did the committee take that news?'

'Some welcomed it, but they asked if both funds could be run at the same time, there was plenty of money to invest after all.'

'But the vicar wasn't about to change his mind, was he?'

Constance shook her head.

'Was that when you had the private discussion?'

'No, that was after the meeting broke up. It started off in here but ended outside.'

'Take me through that.'

'I got hold of his sleeve as he was about to leave and asked him to hold back. Everyone else left. I tried to put a bit of pressure on him, asking why the prostitutes were so important to him, but all he would say was, "my mind is made up." I followed him out of the door, Hales and Frazier were hanging about outside. I tried to carry on with my reasoning, but all he did was pat his pockets looking for his keys so he could lock up.'

'Did he find them?'

'No, he realised he'd left them on the table with the bag of sweets he'd been munching all the way through the meeting. He was just about to go back inside when Eugene held up a hand and said he'd get them for him. So, he nipped back inside and picked them up.'

Bodkin's eyes lit up.

'How long was Eugene inside the room, Constance? Think very carefully, it could be very important.'

'A minute or so, no longer than that.'

'And when he came back out?'

'He passed the sweets to the vicar, who slipped the bag into his pocket. Then he locked the door and we all walked back to the vicarage. The rest of the committee were waiting for us on the path.'

Bodkin got to his feet and slipped his notebook and pen into his inside pocket.

'Mrs de Vere, I have to warn you that I am awaiting confirmation of your fraudulent activities. Early next week I will be receiving a report from your bank. When I get that report, and if it contains evidence of fraud, I will be coming to arrest you. As it stands, that is all you will be charged with, but believe me when I tell you that further charges of conspiracy to blackmail may follow. Don't leave the area. If I were you, I'd get my affairs in order before you see me again. A prison sentence almost certainly awaits.'

Mrs de Vere got unsteadily to her feet and sobbing into her handkerchief, made her way slowly to the door.

Bodkin ran his hand over his mouth as he smiled across at Amy.

'The plot thickens,' he said.

CHAPTER
THIRTY-THREE

'Where to now?' Amy said as the pair walked out of the village hall.

'I'm off to see Eugene Hales. I didn't think he was in the frame but that revelation does mean he has a question or two to answer,' Bodkin said, thoughtfully.

'Can I come too?' Amy asked. 'I'll wait outside if you like.'

'No, come in with me, I don't think he's going to tell us anything you shouldn't be hearing.'

The pair took the longer path that led to the main gate, past the tarp-covered, newly dug grave that awaited the Reverend Villiers. Amy stopped for a moment and looked along the line of headstones that edged the slabbed path.

'They gave him a nice spot. The sun will be on his grave all day long.'

She turned away from the grave and fell into step with Bodkin who had waited for her.

'I reckon the bishop had a hand in that. Unless he'd already bought the plot, of course.'

'You can't buy plots like that, Bodkin, they're reserved for the great and the good.'

Bodkin unlocked the car and opened the passenger door for Amy, then walked slowly around the vehicle until he came to the driver's side.

'I've been thinking,' he said.

'I wondered what that rattling noise was,' Amy replied with a grin.

'I think we just put two more people in the frame. It could easily have been more than blackmail they were plotting.'

'Are you going to arrest them both?'

'Not yet. I'll have Mrs de Vere in the cells by Tuesday anyway. She won't last five minutes in there. If she has been holding back, she won't be for much longer. As for Mr Daley, we only have her word on the blackmail plot at the moment and, if he didn't get to approach Villiers before he died, then I don't think we could show a court that a crime has been committed and conspiracy is a very difficult thing to prove. It will be her word against his at the end of the day.'

'They could be the guilty ones, Bodkin. I know you've probably worked this out already, but can you bear with me to see if I'm thinking along the same lines as you?'

Bodkin laughed and nodded.

'Go on then.'

'Right. Well, as I see it. She claims they had a plan to blackmail Villiers, but what if they had already tried it and he had refused to play along? I'm not sure the bishop would have believed yet another set of rumours about him, after having dismissed all the other ones that were brought to his attention.

'It's obvious that they were in cahoots, it's just a matter of how far they were willing to go. He was desperate for the job and she was desperate for the money, or she knew she was finished. So, what if she hatched a backup plan in case plan A didn't work? She knows she has to get rid of Villiers, and soon.

'But, could she really trust Daley to carry out plan B? He's a sly one and he doesn't really want to get his hands dirty. Rumour and innuendo are his trademarks, not violence. You saw the way he reacted when Dad hit him just now, he didn't even try to defend himself. I know that Christians are supposed to turn the other cheek and all that, but he took it to the extreme.

'I don't think he'd see what he was intending to do as blackmail, either. He's an egotist, bordering on the narcissist. He believes the vicar's job should be his by right, so, threatening to go to the bishop with yet more allegations, however disgusting, would be seen as eminently justifiable to him. I doubt he's got the stomach for murder.

'Constance has a different mindset. She has to make sure Villiers is finished, so she fakes the break in, and pilfers a bit of the strychnine, then dilutes it and keeps it in something small, like an empty bottle of scent, something like that anyway. Then, when she finally realises that he's never going to change his mind about the money, she nips back into the kitchen and tips the stuff into his wine.'

'It's a bit of a long shot. Would you really carry that stuff around in your pocket all night on the off chance that an opportunity would arise?'

Amy shrugged. 'But what if you haven't got it with you and your one opportunity does arise? You might never get another chance.'

'True enough,' said Bodkin. 'But I'm not fully convinced. Something doesn't quite fit. I agree with you. I'm not sure he has the courage to be a partner to murder. She was definitely looking for a quick way out of her money problems though. She might have done it on her own.'

'Well, we know she had the motive, but so did he. In Peril at House End. Poirot listed the suspects and gave them all a motive. Many on his original list had the word 'none' written against them because he didn't know enough about their connections to the victim at that point. But a few had one of four motives written against their names. Gain... Jealousy... Revenge... Fear... Now, Constance's motive was definitely gain and Daley's was surely jealousy.'

Amy was quiet for a moment. Then she gave a long sigh.

'But then, Agatha Walker could be marked with revenge. We only need fear for a full set.'

Five minutes later they arrived at Hales' pharmacy. Bodkin held the door open to allow Amy to enter first. They found Eugene Hales, on the shop side of the counter, laughing along at something with an overweight, elderly man, sporting a neat moustache and bushy eyebrows that were long overdue for a trim. It was obvious from the start that he had been drinking.

'Inspector Bodkin,' he slurred. 'Are you here to arrest us?'

'Not unless you've done something wrong, Doctor Frazier,' Bodkin replied, amiably.

'And who's this little filly?' Frazier zigzagged towards Amy and pushed his face right into hers. 'What a beauty,' he said, as he struggled to keep his balance.

Amy could smell whisky on his breath. She pulled her face away from his, then took a step back. Frazier grinned lecherously.

'What are you doing later, pretty lady? Come out with

Eugene and me. We'll show you what a good time really means, eh, Eugene?'

Frazier suddenly reached out and made a grab for Amy. Bodkin stepped in front of her to shield her from his drunken advances.

'That's enough of that, Doctor,' he said, firmly.

'Leave the poor girl alone, Enoch. She's with the inspector,' Hales told him.'

'Are you going to arrest me?' Frazier wobbled as he asked.

'Carry on like you are and you'll be on a drunk and disorderly charge, if not an assault charge,' Bodkin said, grabbing the old man's shoulders and gently pushing him across the shop until the back of his legs hit a seat and he collapsed onto the chair.

'What can I do for you, Inspector?' Eugene asked. 'Do you want to speak to Agatha again? She's in the back.'

'You have a pretty face,' Frazier slurred. 'Are you sure you don't want to come with us?' He pushed his hand into his pocket, pulled out a handful of coins and offered them to Amy. 'See, I can pay.'

Amy glared at him. She was just about to tell him where he could stick his money when Bodkin put his hand on her arm and shook his head. 'Not now,' he mouthed.

The detective turned back to Hales.

'It's you I've come to see, Mr Hales.'

Hales looked past Bodkin as the doorbell tinkled and a middle-aged woman walked in.

'Just give me a moment, Inspector. We'll talk in my office. I'll just get Agatha to take over on the counter.' He opened the door that led to the dispensary and called the pharmacist. 'Customer, Agatha, can you look after her, I've got a visitor in my office.'

Agatha gave Amy a half smile, then focussed her attention on the customer.

'Ah, hello, Mrs Perkins, have you come for the usual?'

Hales walked around the counter and opened a panelled door on the left-hand side of the shop.

'This way, Inspector.'

When Amy began to follow, he shook his head.

'Not you, my dear.'

'If you think I'm staying out here with that old sot, you've got another think coming,' Amy said, angrily.

Hales looked at his friend, slumped on the chair and relented.

'Oh, come on in then.'

'Just shout when the action starts, Eugene, don't be greedy.' Frazier leered at Amy again.

The office was small, with only two chairs, one either side of the desk. Hales sat down and put his palms on a large, grained leather blotter that took up a good portion of the desk's surface.

'How can I be of assistance?'

'I just have one or two questions for you, Mr Hales, just to tidy up a few things we've been told during the course of the investigation. It won't take long.'

'Fire away,' said the chemist.

'What was your involvement with Mrs de Vere's medicines for the poor committee?'

'Committees,' Hales corrected him. 'I belonged to two, the latter being a very short lived one.'

'Regarding the original committee. Who else was involved?'

'Mrs and Mr de Vere, Doctor Frazier, and me. That was it,

really. It was down to three when Mr de Vere suddenly vanished without trace. Doctor Mighten was on the fringes but he didn't attend meetings. He just put forward patients who might benefit from the scheme, let us know which medicines they needed, etc. Constance would then get in touch with me, pay for the treatments and I'd get Agatha to dispense the medication.'

'How were you involved though, what did you actually do?'

'Not a lot if I'm honest with you. Mrs de Vere did the vast majority of the work... all of the bookwork. I introduced her to my contacts in the pharmaceutical industry. She'd ask them if they had anything going cheap, or better still, for free.' He paused for a moment as he looked across the desk at the detective. 'They did let us have some medicines at a reduced cost, we never got anything for free.'

'Did you ever hand out any medicines for free?'

'Noo,' Mr Hales replied. 'It's only a one shop business, Inspector. I can't afford to give things away. We did used to pass on any savings the drug companies gave us though.'

'And the new committee... you would have had the exact same role?'

'Pretty much, yes.'

'How long did the old charity run for?'

'Two and a half years, I believe.'

'What did the doctor do?'

'He didn't do anything, he's a VC, just there for decoration.'

'Did you ever examine the company accounts?'

'I was at a meeting where they were presented. I only ever signed them off, I didn't really study the accounts. We trusted Mrs de Vere; she ran the show.'

'What about Doctor Frazier? Did he ever study the accounts?'

'He had no interest in them at all. As I said he was there purely for decoration.'

'So, the accounts could have shown a loss, a large loss even, and you wouldn't have known anything about it?'

'As I said...'

'Are you and Doctor Frazier good friends?'

'The best. We've known each other for many years.'

'Do you spend a lot of time in each other's company?'

'A fair bit. We go out together most Friday nights, sometimes on a Saturday.'

'Where do you go? What do you get up to?'

'We go out on the town, Inspector. We enjoy the fleshpots. We sometimes get the train to London and hit the casino, though that's less often these days.'

'You're both in your seventies, aren't you?'

'I'm seventy-one next year. Enoch is seventy-four.'

'A bit old for burning the candle at both ends, aren't you?'

'We're making up for lost time, Inspector Bodkin. We were both in the military in our youth, so we didn't have much of a social life. We're playing catch up while we still have the energy to do it.' He furrowed his brow as he spoke. 'Do you think there's something wrong with that?'

'Not at all, but for men in your position...'

'We are very discreet about it all, Inspector. We both value our reputations.'

'Tell me about the last meeting you had with the committee. I understand Mrs de Vere and the reverend had a bit of a disagreement.'

'That's putting it lightly. She was furious with him.'

'So, it was a blazing row they had, not a mere disagreement?'

'It wasn't a stand-up fight, let's just say she was upset at his decision.'

'Had she asked you to try to persuade him to sign up?'

'Yes, she asked most of us, we all had our say during the meeting. We were all pretty unanimous in our views... When I say all, the vicar obviously disagreed. He wanted to set up a fund for the town's prostitutes instead. We all said we'd agree to another meeting with that item on the agenda, at a later date.'

'Mrs de Vere agreed?'

'Yes, she said she'd help out with it, but only if her own charity was to benefit too.'

'When they were arguing outside, you went back into the church hall to pick up something for the vicar, I believe.'

Hales thought hard.

'No... Oh, yes, the keys to the hall, and those blooming sweets of his. I was nearest to the door, so I volunteered to go back in to retrieve them for him.'

'How long were you in there?'

'A minute, two... not long. I couldn't find the blooming light switch at first.'

'And after you handed the keys and sweets over?'

'He locked the door and we all went up to the house.'

'You were in the kitchen when the wine was handed out?'

'Yes, awful stuff. Cheap, nasty. He keeps a good French wine hidden away, we never got to try it out though.'

'Did you see any of that French wine while you were in the kitchen?'

'Yes, there was a bottle on the side, Enoch was eyeing it up, but as I said, we never got to try it.'

'When everyone went out to the study, you were left behind in the kitchen, is that correct?'

Hales furrowed his brow again as he thought.

'Only for a few seconds. Enoch was hoping to snag another glass of wine, his stomach is stronger than mine. He'll drink anything as long as it contains alcohol.'

'When the meeting finally broke up in the study, did you and Doctor Frazier go straight to the front door?'

'We did. We were going to hit the town straight after, we were eager to get away.'

'Did anyone else go back into the house while you were hanging about saying goodnight?'

'I think Agatha did. And Florence, but they weren't inside for long.'

'Speaking of Agatha. Is it true you wrote a reference for her, with regard to a research post?'

'Yes, but sadly for her, fortunately for me, she didn't get the job.'

'Fortunately for you?'

'I didn't want to lose her. Who could I find to replace her? She practically runs the place.'

'Did you give her a good reference?'

'Oh course.'

'I can, and will check, Mr Hales.' Bodkin stroked the stubble on his chin, his eyes narrowing slightly as he spoke.

Hales looked uncomfortable.

'Maybe it wasn't quite as glowing as I told her it was.'

Amy's eyebrows shot up.

'Do you mean to say you were the one who accused her of being unreliable, overly emotional and indecisive?'

Hales hung his head.

'I'm not proud of it, but as I said. I couldn't risk losing her. I can't dispense any more. Not with this.' He held up a shaking hand. 'I have the early symptoms of Parkinson's disease. It will only get worse. I need the income from the shop, Mr Bodkin. It might have gone under if I'd lost her.'

'I'm sorry to hear about your illness,' Bodkin said, sympathetically.

'It's incurable,' Hales said. 'It's why I'm living life to the full while I can. I doubt I'll be able to hold a glass of whisky without spilling it all over myself in a couple of years' time.'

'You do know she blames Harold Villiers for her failing to get the job, don't you?' Amy said, bitterly. 'The least you can do is admit it to her. I'm sure she'll understand the reasons you did it. I doubt she'd ever forgive you, but then neither would I. It was her dream job. You pretty much ruined her life.'

Hales gave Bodkin a desperate look.

'You won't tell her, will you?'

'It's not up to me to tell her, Mr Hales. But as a supposed man of values, I think you should.'

Bodkin opened the door to the office and Amy stepped out into the shop to find Doctor Frazier spreadeagled across three chairs, snoring loudly.

Amy and Bodkin climbed back into the car and the detective reversed into a side road before pulling out onto the High Street.

'What do you make of that?' Amy asked.

'He's not the pillar of the community that many think he is, that's for sure,' Bodkin said with a shake of his head. 'Out on the town, gambling and carousing with a lecherous old drunk like Frazier? At his age, too. I doubt his reputation is as rock solid as he thinks it is. People must see them when they're out and about.'

'How could he do that to someone he's worked with for so

long? It's despicable,' Amy said with a frown. 'As if she didn't have enough hurdles to jump over merely by being a woman.'

Bodkin tipped his head and nodded in agreement before pulling up outside the police station.

'Just think, had she known the truth, it might be Hales lying in his coffin, not Villiers.'

Bodkin pulled on the hand brake and switched off the engine.

'I've just got to check my desk before I give you a lift home. Do you want to wait here or are you coming in? It will be quite safe, it's Friday afternoon, the Chief Super will be playing golf.'

As Amy and Bodkin stepped into reception, they saw the slumped, unhappy figure of Mr Rowlings sitting on a long dark wooden bench. He stood up when he saw Bodkin.

'I've come to give myself up, laddie. What I did was unforgivable and against the law.' He held out his arms. 'I'll come quietly if you want to arrest me.'

Bodkin patted Rowlings on the shoulder.

'There won't be any charges, James. Daley just wants an apology, that's all.'

'Really!' Rowling's relief was palpable. 'I'll happily do that, much as I'll hate the moment.' He pulled a sad face as he looked at his daughter. 'I'm sorry, dear, I let you down.'

Amy pulled him to her and gave him a hug.

'You didn't let anyone down, Dad. I think he had it coming after saying what he did about Mr Villiers. He knows you were just about the only friend he had. Why come out with a pack of lies like that? The poor man hasn't even been buried yet.'

'That's the trouble, Amy,' Rowlings said sadly. 'They weren't all lies. Harold used to visit prostitutes... and young ones at that.'

CHAPTER THIRTY-FOUR

'Let's talk about this in my office,' the detective said, nodding at the constable behind the counter to open the reception area door. Once inside, Bodkin led them along a long photograph lined corridor until he got to the door of his office. He was just about to step inside, when Trixie, wearing ridiculously high heels, a blue pencil skirt and white blouse, appeared in the doorway.

'Hello,' she said, giving the detective a beaming smile. 'The report has come in from Gillingham. I've left it on your desk.'

'Thank you,' Bodkin acknowledged her with a nod.

Trixie pursed her lips as she looked down her nose at Amy.

'Oh, it's you.'

Amy brushed past Trixie and stepped into the office without saying a word to her.

'Come on, Dad. We need to hear all about this.'

Trixie stepped into the corridor to allow Bodkin and Mr Rowlings to enter the office. As soon as her father was inside, Amy slammed the door on the scowling blonde.

'Who was that?' Mr Rowlings asked. 'She looked nice.'

Amy looked to the heavens. 'Men,' she muttered.

The detective grimaced.

'I do hope she hasn't been reassigned as your secretary, Bodkin,' Amy said. 'Or Doctor Frazier won't be the only one to be given a position purely for decorative purposes.'

Bodkin rubbed his forehead and sighed.

'Sit down, Mr Rowlings.'

'James, please, laddie, call me James... or Jimmy if you prefer.'

Amy's eyebrows rose in shock. Only her mother had permission to call him, Jimmy.

Bodkin picked up the kettle and waved it towards the Rowlings'.

'Tea?'

Amy looked at the yellowing fluid in the milk bottle on Bodkin's filing cabinet and shook her head.

'We're fine, thank you.'

Bodkin shrugged and put the kettle down before pulling out his chair and sitting down behind his desk. He picked up a large, manila envelope, checked the handwritten note that had been stapled to the front, then put it down again.

'So, Mr... James... This shocking revelation about Mr Villiers and prostitutes. How sure are you about it? Could it just be yet another disparaging rumour?'

'No, laddie. I saw it with my own eyes. He gave the young lassie money, then they stepped off into an alleyway together.'

'When you say young, how young are we talking here?'

'Fourteen, fifteen at best.'

'Oh, Dad,' Amy said, quietly.

'This may seem a strange question as you are his best

friend, but are you sure it was him?' Bodkin leaned over his desk. 'It might have been an innocent incident, a one-off occurrence.'

'I saw him three times, laddie. There was nothing innocent about it. She was a child, Inspector.'

'Let's start at the beginning, James. How did you come to spot Mr Villiers with the girl?'

'It was a couple of months ago. We had an emergency project on at the factory so I was asked to work on the afternoon shift to see the final stages of it through to completion.' He turned to his daughter. 'You remember, Amy? I wasn't getting in until ten-thirty every night.'

Amy nodded.

'Well, the first time I saw him was on a Friday night. I had just got off the ten o'clock train from Gillingham. I picked up the evening paper as I walked through the foyer and when I got out onto the pavement, I saw him with her. He had his back to me, but I knew who it was. At first, I thought he was just talking to the street girls, but then he asked one of the women where Sadie was. The woman pointed down the alleyway and said something that the other girls laughed at. Harold didn't laugh as far as I remember, but he stood, shuffling his feet nervously as he waited. I was going to walk over and have a word with him, but then this young girl... as I said, a child really, came out of the alley with a scruffy looking man who beat a hasty retreat when the other women began to taunt him.'

'What did they say to him?' Bodkin asked.

'Oh, they called him, headmaster amongst other things I'd rather not repeat here.'

'Headmaster?' Amy was horrified.

'I think it was their nickname for him, I'm not really sure, but if he is a headmaster, he didn't dress like one and I know for certain he doesn't work at any school around here. I know them all.'

'What happened then, James?' Bodkin asked.

'Well, the young girl, this Sadie, obviously knew him. She stretched on her tiptoes and gave him a kiss on the cheek. He pulled a ten shilling note out of his pocket and handed it over, then she took his hand and led him off down the alley.'

'How long was he there, do you know?'

'I hung around for fifteen minutes or so, standing in the shadows under the arch of the station, but then my bus came so I hurried across the road and caught it.'

Bodkin rubbed at his stubbly chin.

'You say you saw him three times?'

Rowlings nodded quickly.

'Yes, I saw him at the same time the following Friday, then again, the Friday after that.'

'And he always left with the same woman?'

'Girl, Inspector, there's no way on earth you would describe her as a woman. She may only have been thirteen. She wasn't very well developed at all.'

Amy's shoulders slumped.

'Oh, Dad, that must have been a terrible thing to witness. Didn't you ever say anything to him?'

'No, I should have and I regret not doing now. I don't know if it would have stopped him though. I wrote a sermon about lust, but just like the sermons on the evils of drink, he would almost certainly have ignored the message himself.'

'Why didn't you tell us about this before, James? There might be a connection with his death.'

Rowlings hung his head.

'I almost did, on two occasions, but Amy was there both times, as was my wife and I didn't think that particular topic of conversation was the thing for the dinner table.'

'This girl, Sadie. Can you describe her?' Bodkin asked, reaching for his notebook.

'As I said, she's very young. Mid length brown hair. Very slight in build, she hasn't developed in... he held his hands in front of his chest. She looks like Amy did at twelve, thirteen.'

'What sort of clothes was she wearing, did she try to make herself look older than she was?'

'On the contrary, Mr Bodkin. Every time I saw her, she was wearing a school uniform.'

After fifteen minutes of questioning, Bodkin got to his feet and held his hand across the desk towards James Rowlings.

'Thank you for the information, James. I wish you'd have come forward sooner but we are where we are.'

Rowlings shook Bodkin's hand, then turned to leave.

'Are you coming, Amy?'

Amy nodded and looked at her watch.

'The bus will be here soon.'

'If you wait in reception I'll give you a lift,' Bodkin said, picking up the envelope and tearing away the gummed seal.

'That's very kind of you, laddie,' Rowlings said as he reached the office door.

'See you out there,' Amy said as she got hold of the door handle.

Bodkin didn't respond as he re-read the two sheets of paper in his hands.

'Bodkin?'

The detective was suddenly roused from his musing.

'It's the lab report we've been waiting for,' he said quickly. 'The wine sample was clean. It hadn't been tampered with. We've been barking up the wrong tree.'

CHAPTER
THIRTY-FIVE

AMY GASPED.

'So, if the poison wasn't in the wine, what was it in? Oh my goodness, the SWEETS! They were in his sweets.'

Amy walked back to Bodkin's desk and brushed a stray hair out of her eyes.

'Our list of strong suspects just got longer,' she said.

'Has it? Yours may have, Amy but as I've said many times, everyone is a suspect until they're not. They're all still on my list. Every single one of them.'

'Yes, I know... but can I extrapolate? I was just thinking out loud.'

Bodkin sat down and put the envelope back on his desk.

Amy held up a finger.

'One, Mrs de Vere is a strong candidate, she had motive... gain... and she had the opportunity. She went back into the kitchen, knowing that the vicar's coat was hanging on the back of the chair, and she knew the sweets were in his pocket and she could easily have got hold of the strychnine from her garden shed, so she also may have had the means and definitely had the opportunity.'

She looked down at the desk as she concentrated, then she held up a second finger.

'Two, Mr Hales had the opportunity when he went back into the village hall to collect Mr Villiers' keys. We know he actually handled the bag of sweets before passing them to the vicar, so he had the opportunity. He definitely had the means, as his shop sells arsenic and strychnine. I'm not sure whether he has a motive though, I really can't see one.

'Three, Agatha Walker went back into the study where the vicar had left the sweets he had put aside for Sunday. He had started on them that night though, we know that because Agatha told us. She could quite easily have emptied some strychnine into his packet of pineapple chunks, which are covered in sugar, so it was perfectly camouflaged. She also knows everything there is to know about hemlock, and that was readily available to her. She could also easily have added arsenic to the stomach powders. She had the motive; revenge, and she had the means. Did she just take the opportunity when it arose?

'Four, the Reverend Daley. He could well be mixed up in the murder plot with Mrs de Vere. He had motive... jealousy, he may have had the means but not the opportunity, so at best, he was involved in a conspiracy.

'Five, Doctor Frazier. As far as we know he had no motive and no means of acquiring the poison, I can't see how he had the opportunity either.

'Six, Peter Kissman. He had the means and opportunity to poison the powders with arsenic, but he didn't have any strychnine, nor is there a motive that we know of, but he had access to the hemlock on the riverbank.

'Seven, Mrs Brown. No motive, no access to any of the poisons used and no real opportunity.

'Eight, Mr Brown. The same as Mrs Brown really, no motive, means or opportunity, but then we don't know anything at all about him, apart from the fact that he's away with the fairies a lot of the time.

'Nine, Caroline Gatting. She had access to hemlock and she cooked his meals and made up his powders every day. Claims she had no access to strychnine, but she used to have, and her sister definitely had. She may have motive as she would have been upset about the vicar's alleged lousy reference and her sister's failure to get her dream job. She was with the vicar, or around him most of the time and had plenty of opportunity to poison his sweets. So, her motive would be revenge, she had the means via her sister and they may have colluded.'

Amy counted up on her fingers and mentally checked against her list.

'That's the lot, I think.'

'Nicely summed up. Could you type that out for me, Amy? It would save me a lot of work,' Bodkin said with a smile.

'Did you think all that up yourself, dear?' Mr Rowling's asked.

'I had some help from Poirot, Dad,' she replied. 'Agatha Christie is the master of the murder mystery.'

'Mistress,' Rowlings corrected, 'she's a woman.'

'I don't like that word, it's so often used in a different context,' Amy replied.

Bodkin shuffled about in his seat.

'There are still a few things that puzzle me, apart from who actually committed the murder,' Bodkin said, thoughtfully. He raised a finger of his own. 'One, why did someone go to all the trouble of hiding a broken wine bottle in a crypt, if it wasn't the way the poison had been administered?'

'GOOD POINT!' Amy yelled, excitedly, before blushing and adding, 'sorry.'

'Two,' Bodkin raised a second finger. 'I keep saying that poison is a woman's weapon, and there are four women on your list, Amy, but I'm not sure a women could carry the dead weight of a body across the graveyard and pose it on the lych-gate bench in that way. Two women could do it, or a single woman and a man. I'm not ruling out men of course. One man could have easily moved the body by himself, even two elderly gentlemen could have managed it.

'Three,' Bodkin raised a third finger. 'What on earth happened to the bag of sweets, nay, both bags of sweets? The one that was supposedly in his pocket when he went outside that night, wasn't in his pocket when the forensic team searched the body, and the packet of sweets that we know was on his desk on the night... the pineapple chunks... was not there when I searched his study on the Monday evening.'

'Oh, Bodkin, you are clever. I can almost see your little grey cells working overtime,' Amy said, enthusiastically. 'I hadn't thought of any of that.'

Bodkin held out his hands as if he'd just performed a magic trick. 'Voila,' he said.

'Very Poirot,' said Amy.

Bodkin clapped his hands and got to his feet, then abruptly sat down again as if he had suddenly remembered something important.

'Could you wait in reception please? I have to make a telephone call to the Gillingham lab and my language may not be as proper as it might be. They still haven't sent the fingerprint file.'

. . .

Five minutes later, Bodkin pulled away from the kerb and turned onto the Gillingham Road, heading towards the Old Bull at the top of Long Lane.

'Did they manage to locate your files, Mr Bodkin?' Rowlings asked.

'They're in Sittingbourne,' Bodkin said with a shake of his head. He looked left towards Amy who was just about to open her mouth.

'Don't ask,' he said.

'So, what are you up to tomorrow, Bodkin?' Amy asked as they stood on her doorstep, Mr Rowlings had just gone in to give his wife the good news that there had been no charges laid against him.

'I'm going down to nip to Gillingham to pick up that file,' Bodkin said. 'They're getting in touch with Sittingbourne, they'll send it back overnight. What will you be up to, as if I didn't know?'

Amy grinned.

'Brigden's first thing. I haven't bought anything new for weeks now. They have this lovely... oh, you won't want to hear about that... I'll see what's new in there, then go for my usual coffee at the Morning Sun Café. My uncle is at a sheet music auction in Canterbury so sadly, I can't drop in to see what new records he's got hold of this week. I'll catch him next time.'

Bodkin smiled.

'Your usual Saturday then? Oh, I meant to tell you, Ferris didn't get the CID job. The Chief Super didn't think he was experienced enough. He'll get it one day, maybe in a couple of years' time.'

'Oh, poor Ferris,' Amy replied. 'I'm so glad you stopped me congratulating him. He'd have been devastated if he'd known he was up for the job but didn't get it.'

'It's not all bad. At least we'll get to hear him sing again tomorrow night. If he'd got the job he'd have been sent away on a series of courses.'

'Saturday night wouldn't be the same without Ferris singing,' Amy replied. She got onto her tiptoes and planted a kiss on Bodkin's cheek. 'I love our Saturday night's out.'

'Me too,' Bodkin replied, leaning towards her in the hope of getting a proper kiss.

Amy turned away with an impish grin on her face.

'Just make sure you turn up this week, Bodkin. It's Born To Dance, Eleanor Powell and James Stewart. It came out about three years ago but it was never shown here.'

'I've never heard of it,' Bodkin said.

'You'll know at least one of the songs, or at least Ferris will. Cole Porter wrote the music, you must know, I've got You Under My Skin?' Amy hummed the tune as Bodkin shook his head.

'You'll know it when you hear it... and, we might hear it more than once tomorrow if Ferris is on form.' Amy opened the front door, then turned back to Bodkin. 'See you tomorrow,' she said.

Bodkin smiled back at her.

'Missing you already,' he said.

'Good,' Amy replied. 'That's how it should be.'

As Bodkin opened the door to his car, she called his name, then blew him a kiss.

'Cook your own dinner, Bodkin,' she said.

CHAPTER
THIRTY-SIX

When Sharon, the sales assistant at Brigden's Fashion Store opened the front doors on Saturday morning, she found Amy waiting patiently on the pavement. Three other women, keen to see the latest bargains, had formed a neat queue behind her.

Once inside, Amy hurried across to her favourite bargain rail where the latest collection of nearly new dresses had been hung. Disappointed that her first choice, a yellow, short sleeved, shift dress wasn't available in her size, she moved along the rail, sliding hangers and pulling out likely looking dresses as she went.

Her eyes lit up when she spotted a white, cotton summer dress, with a red rose print.

Snatching it from the rail before Nora Beckinsale could get her hands on it, Amy hurried across to the full-length mirror and held it up in front of herself.

'Perfect,' she whispered, holding the dress tight against her body.

'I thought you might like that one,' Sharon said as she

walked along the rail, stepping aside to allow an obviously peeved Nora to get by.

'Ten shillings!' Amy exclaimed. 'Bang on my budget.'

'That bias dress hasn't been sold yet,' Sharon said, teasingly. 'It's been reduced to twenty-five shillings now.'

Amy made an O shape with her mouth.

'Get thee behind me, temptress,' she said with a short laugh. 'Let me know when it's a pound and you've got yourself a sale.'

At the counter, Amy waited patiently while Sharon neatly rolled the dress up to prevent creasing, before slipping it into a Brigden's bag. Handing it to Amy, she rang the ten shilling note she handed back into the till.

'Take a look in the sale bin,' she said as Amy took her receipt. 'There's a pair of black slingbacks for five bob, one of the heels is hanging off. Taylor's will fix that for you for half a crown and you've got a really nice pair of shoes at a bargain price.'

Amy hurried across to the sales bin, that was actually a wooden crate. It only took her a minute to find the black, sling back shoes. Flipping them upside down, Amy immediately spotted the damage to the right shoe; the heel, whilst not exactly hanging off, was definitely loose. The soles looked brand new and there was no real sign of scuffing. Making an instant decision, Amy grabbed the shoes and hurried back to the counter while Sharon was still there.

'Thanks for the tip off,' she said. 'I'll buy you a port and lemon in the Bell, the next time I'm in.'

Amy dropped the shoes into her Brigden's bag and walked out of the store humming Greensleeves.

'What a great start to the weekend,' she said to herself.

Amy's next stop would normally have been the Morning

Sun Café, but she decided to go straight to Taylor's shoe repair and key cutting kiosk, housed in Blundell's Arcade, a narrow strip of small, retail businesses, that included a newsagent, a costume jewellery outlet and a picture framing stall.

Amy handed over the shoes to Jack Taylor's apprentice, young Harry Ogden.

'How much to fix these, Harry, and when could you have them done by?' she asked.

'Two and thruppence, seeing as it's you, Amy, I'll do the job now if you like, we're not over-busy today.' Harry examined the damage. 'A couple of thin heel nails, a bit of glue and it will be as good as new. I wouldn't walk on them for an hour or two though. Give the glue time to set.'

'Can I pick them up in an hour or so then, Harry?'

'They'll be ready,' he replied, giving her his best smile. 'I saw you in the Bell, last week. Are you in again tonight?'

'I don't think so, Harry. I think we're at the Old Bull again this week.'

'Are you going out with that tall bloke? He seems a bit old for you.'

'Bodkin? No, we're just good friends, Harry.'

'You seem to see him a lot. I thought you might be an item. If you're not... well, maybe I could buy you a drink.'

Harry was three years younger than Amy but had attended the same school.

'That's very sweet of you, Harry, but I'm honestly not looking for a boyfriend at the moment. I've got too much else to think about.'

'Well, if you change your mind, you know where I am,' the young cobbler said, tossing the broken shoe in the air and catching it in his other hand.

'I do,' Amy said with a short smile.

Back out on the High Street, Amy began to make her way towards the Morning Sun Café but on a whim, changed her mind and turned right into Cherry Street and walked the few yards up the hill until she came to the dingy looking exterior of the Town Tea House. Pushing open the door, she stepped inside to find a girl of about sixteen, washing plates in a sink behind the counter. She looked up as Amy entered.

'I'll be with you in a second,' she said, wiping her hands on a worn tea towel.

The café was empty, so Amy pulled out a chair at the table nearest to the counter.

'Can you make me an espresso, please?' she asked.

'Sorry, we don't do those. It's either instant coffee or a pot of tea.'

'I'll take the tea then,' Amy said.

'Do you want anything with it? We've got a fresh baked jam sponge or I could make you a sandwich.'

'Just the tea, thank you,' Amy replied.

The girl poured boiling water into a pot and put it on a tray with a cup, saucer and a milk jug.

'The sugar is in the bowl on the table if you want it.'

'You must be Mary,' Amy said, as she set the cup and saucer in front of her.

'Who's been talking?' the young girl said with a laugh.

'Mrs Brown mentioned you when I was in the other day.'

'Ah, was you the one with the policeman?'

Amy nodded. 'I was, yes.'

'Nasty business that,' Mary said, flashing a look towards the door behind the counter.

'The vicar's death? Yes, it was.' Amy followed Mary's glance. 'Isn't Mrs Brown at work today?'

'She's having a few minutes with Gerald. He's a bit lost this morning, bless him.'

'What's he like?' Amy asked.

'Gerald? He's a lovely man, but he's not quite with it some days.' Mary made a circling motion with her finger next to her temple. 'Lovely man though.'

'It must have been hard for them, trying to run this place with Violet being the way she was.'

'Tell me about it. Mind you, I used to get extra hours whenever Violet was home. She was never here long though. Mad as a box of frogs, poor girl. Did you know they were going to cut her brains out?' Mary shuddered.

'Her mother was trying to stop that happening, wasn't she?'

'Yeah, but they had tried everything else, the lobster operation was the last resort, but then that charity stepped in and she's on the clinical trial now.' She looked back towards the door again. 'Between you, me and the gatepost, I don't think it's working though. She's just as bad as ever.' Mary tapped on the side of her head. 'Demons, she's got demons in there.'

'I don't think she has demons, Mary,' Amy said with a frown. 'She's just mentally ill. She might even grow out of the worst of it as she gets older.'

'Well, Mrs Brown thought she had demons, she got the vicar in to try to drive them out.'

Amy, who was in the process of pouring tea into her cup, froze.

'I'm sorry, what did you say?'

'Demons, Mrs Brown got the vicar in to drive them out.'

'Are you sure about that?'

'Absolutely sure. I was here, I heard it all. She made a right racket. Screaming, yelling, cursing. Her mum and dad couldn't bear to listen to it. They cleared off while the vicar was throwing the holy water at her or whatever it was that he did. Don't touch me, stay away... don't do that... stop it, she'd scream at the top of her voice. I'm surprised they didn't hear her at the asylum she was so loud.'

'When was this, Mary? How long ago?'

'Late November and into December. He was up in her bedroom at least twice a week. Then she got really bad again and had to go back to the loony bin.'

'Did this happen after he'd had his meal or did he come around specially to see Violet.'

'I'm not sure if he had a meal or not. I used to get called in before he started on her, so they could clear off out. It was a racket mind you. The customers thought someone was committing murder up there.'

'Did no one say they were going to report it to the police?'

'No. Once I'd told them who it was and what was happening, they lost interest. Everyone knows about Violet's demons.'

'Did he ever come back again, just to see Violet? After December, I mean.'

'No,' Mary leaned forward, her voice dropped to a whisper. 'I think the nut house got wind of what was going on. They told Mrs Brown to stop messing her about, or they'd cancel the home visits completely.'

'So, Mr Villiers never saw Violet again after that last session in December?'

'No, but then Violet's only been back twice since then, and never for longer than a couple of days. As soon as she starts to go off on one, they send her straight back. Two men turn up in a van with a straightjacket.'

'Poor Violet,' Amy said, finally pouring tea into her cup.

'Mavis must have been desperate, the poor woman. I've

seen him leave here at lunchtime, staggering across the street, drunk as a lord. I don't know why she trusted her only daughter with a drunk, vicar or not.'

'He was drunk?' Amy asked, furrowing her brow.

'Staggering around like a new born giraffe,' Mary said.

'Where did he come from, the Crown and Anchor? That's the only pub up this end, isn't it?'

'I never saw him go in the pub. I only live two doors up the road. He came out of here, then teetered and tottered his way over to Cavanagh's.'

'The sweet shop?'

'Yep.' Mary got to her feet and hurried back behind the counter as she heard the floorboards creaking above her head. Amy got up herself, and leaving two pennies on the table as a tip, walked out of the café and made her way across the street to Cavanagh's.

'Hello again, young lady,' old Mr Cavanagh called out as she entered the shop.

'Hello, Mr Cavanagh,' Amy eyed the rows of jars on the shelves behind the counter. Thinking it would be mean of her to ask more questions without buying something, she pointed to a jar of pear drops. 'Could I have a quarter of those, please?'

Mr Cavanagh dragged the jar off the shelf with his good hand. Tucked it under his arm, then gave the lid a twist. After carefully checking the scales, he reached into the jar and added one extra sweet to the pile.

'That'll be thruppence, my dear,' he said as he tipped the sweets into a small paper bag and twisted the corners.

Amy handed over the money and dropped the sweets into her handbag.

'We were chatting about the vicar the other day, Mr Cavanagh,' she said, carefully. 'I wonder, can you remember anything about the last time he was in?'

'What do you mean? I'm sure I told you everything I remember.'

'I know, but someone just told me that the vicar used to be drunk when he came in here. Is that right?'

'Drunk? No, I don't think he was drunk. He didn't sound drunk at least. His legs were a bit rubbery. He had to hold onto the doorframe on the way out. But that might be his age. My knees tend to go on me if I've been on my feet all day.'

'So, he wasn't staggering about, he spoke clearly?'

'He wasn't slurring his words if that's what you mean... as for staggering... he was a bit wobbly on his feet. As I said, he had to hang onto the doorframe on the way out.'

'Thank you, Mr Cavanagh,' Amy said. 'Oh, do you know where the nearest telephone box is? Would it be that one on the High Street? I've got to make an urgent call to Inspector Bodkin.'

'You can use my telephone if you like,' Cavanagh said. 'It's in the back.'

'Are you sure?' Amy said. 'I'll pay for the call.'

'You'll do no such thing, young lady. It's about time someone used it. My daughter is the only one who ever calls me on it and there's no one I want to talk to particularly.'

He led Amy into a tidy, if old fashioned back room. The curtains were partly open, allowing a ray of light to reflect off an empty crystal vase that was sitting in the centre of an oval, wooden table.

Along one wall was an ancient, horsehair sofa. On the opposite side of the room was a matching, much used, armchair. On a small, round table, next to the chair sat a black telephone.

'I'll leave you to it,' Cavanagh said, pointing towards the table.

Amy sat down on the old chair, sinking so far into the base that she could feel the wooden frame against her backside.

She dropped the Brigden's bag at her feet, flipped open her handbag and fished around for the card that Bodkin had given her, with his work extension number on the front and his apartment phone number on the back. Picking up the handset, she dialled the work number first. It rang three times before it was picked up.

'Inspector Bodkin's office, how can I help you?'

'Ferris? Is that you?'

'Hello, Amy, yes, it's me. I'm waiting for an important call from Gillingham. The boss asked me to hold the fort while he nipped home for a few minutes. He left his notebook in his other jacket.'

'Will he be long do you know?' Amy asked.

'He told me he might make himself a sandwich while he's over there, said he'd be thirty minutes, max, that was about ten minutes ago.'

'Okay, I'll try to get him there. Thanks, Ferris, see you tonight.'

'You're through to Bluecoat House, this is Trixie speaking, how may I help you?'

'It's Amy Rowlings, I need to speak to Bodkin, urgently.'

'Oh,' Trixie replied.

'It is rather urgent,' Amy repeated.

'Well, I'm not sure if he's in. He went over to Gillingham this morning.'

'He's in. Ferris told me ten seconds ago.'

'Ah, right, I'll just go and have a look then, but I'm sure he's not here.'

Amy waited as she heard Trixie put the handset down on the shelf, then she heard the sound of stamping feet followed by a stifled giggle. Thirty seconds later she was back on the line.

'No, he's not here, sorry, bye.'

'Don't you dare hang up on me,' Amy shouted into the mouthpiece. 'I know you didn't go up the stairs just then, I heard you giggling.'

'So, what if I didn't. What are you going to do about it?'

'I'll tell you what I'll do about it,' Amy spat. 'I'll report you to Bodkin for obstructing a murder investigation. I'm not sure you'll still be employed by the police after that. NOW! As I said. I have an URGENT message for Inspector Bodkin. Get him to the phone, NOW!'

Trixie didn't reply, but Amy heard her heels tapping on the stairs as she ran up to the first floor. A full minute later, she heard footsteps again, then Bodkin's voice on the line.

'Amy?'

'Bodkin, you have to come into town, quickly. There's been a development.'

'What sort of dev–'

'It's about the vicar, he was drunk, or maybe he wasn't, but Mary said he was. I'm calling from the sweet shop, Mr Cavanagh said... Oh, fiddlesticks, that's not the urgent bit, the urgent bit concerns Mrs Brown, she was lying to us... well, not lying, but she didn't tell us everything. She—'

'Amy, calm down. Just give me the headline.'

'Oh, right. Well, Mrs Brown was convinced that Violet was possessed by a demon and was so desperate to save her from the lobotomy operation that she got Mr Villiers in to try to drive the demons out of her. He was up in her room alone with her for an hour at a time. He visited her at least four times. Her mum and dad used to get out of the place when he was with her, they couldn't bear to hear her screams.'

'Good God.'

'BODKIN!'

'Sorry, Amy… I'm on my way, I'll be there in five.'

Amy put the handset on the cradle and pulling four pennies from her purse she dropped them onto the table next to the phone to pay for her calls.

'Thanks for the use of your phone, Mr Cavanagh,' she said as she walked back into the shop.

'I'm just glad to see it's still working,' Cavanagh said. 'I can't remember the last time I actually dialled out on it.'

Amy waved to him as she left the shop, then she strolled the short distance to the Town Tea House. As she got close, she saw Mary standing on the pavement looking into the café through the window.

'Hello again,' Amy said. 'Have you finished for the day already?'

'No,' Mary replied. 'I've just been sacked.'

CHAPTER THIRTY-SEVEN

Bodkin was as good as his word and arrived some five minutes later. Parking his car, half on, half off the pavement on the narrow street, he jumped out of his car and hurried over to where Amy was standing with Mary.

Amy gave the detective a full account of everything she had learned and after asking a few questions of Mary, to clarify, he pushed open the door to the café and stepped inside.

'I was expecting you,' Mrs Brown said quietly, looking down at her pinny.

Bodkin pulled out a chair and gestured for Mavis Brown to sit before pulling out a second chair, turning it around and sitting astride it.

'Why didn't you tell us about the reverend and Violet, Mrs Brown?' he asked, firmly.

'It's not the sort of thing you boast about, is it?' she replied with a tremor in her voice. 'Would you tell anyone you'd organised an exorcism for your child? I was ashamed.'

'Nonetheless...'

'Are you a father, Inspector Bodkin? If you are, you'll know that any parent would have done the same. I was guilt ridden for what I'd done... but I was just so, desperate. If... if she was possessed by a demon and it could be cast out, it would save her from that terrible operation. There might be nothing left of the real Violet after they carry that out.'

'I'm not a father, Mrs Brown, I hope to be, one day, but I do understand your concern for Violet. The thing is, you have knowingly attempted to obstruct a murder investigation by withholding evidence. You could face a charge for doing that. Do you understand me?'

Mrs Brown nodded and looked down at her clasped hands.

'Now, I'm going to go through this quickly, because I already have most of the facts.' Bodkin nodded towards Mary.

'Exactly when did you ask the Reverend Villiers to carry out this... this, casting out?'

'Last November. He was very reluctant, but I begged him. As far as I knew it was my last chance to save her from the lobotomy. Villiers finally agreed during the last week of that month.'

'Did you pay for his services?'

'No, he wouldn't accept payment. He didn't think it would work anyway. He told me not to get my hopes up.'

'So why did he go ahead if he knew it wouldn't be of any use.'

'He hoped that she might feel God's grace, that the experience might calm her at least.'

'And did it.'

'Yes, to a degree, but then she was always a lot calmer after one of her episodes.'

'She suffered an episode when he was here then?' Bodkin asked.

'Oh, yes, a huge one. I've never seen her so bad. It almost convinced me that the demons inside her were fighting the vicar. She kept screaming, leave them alone, they're my friends, I don't want them to go.'

'She heard voices?'

'A lot of the time, yes. When she was ill. When she wasn't having an episode, she didn't hear anyone.'

'So, you were there when this was happening? I thought...'

'Only the first time, and even then, only for the first twenty minutes or so. Violet wouldn't listen to him, she just held out her arms and screamed, Mummy, Mummy...' Tears streamed down Mrs Brown's face.

'And after that first session?'

'Gerald and I used to go for a long walk by the river. I'd get Mary in to watch the café.' She wrung her hands and shook her head. 'We shouldn't have left her on her own.'

'Mary told us she used to scream at him to let her go, to get off her, begging him not to touch her. Is that correct?'

Mrs Brown nodded and wiped her eyes on her pinafore.

'How many times was he alone with her in the bedroom?'

'Four, no... five times, for at least an hour, sometimes a little bit longer. She was always quiet by the time we got back. She'd be on her bed, sleeping, the whole thing just tired her out.'

'Did she say anything about the experience after the event?'

'Only that she didn't like it when he touched her. She doesn't like men, Mr Bodkin, she even backs away when Gerald gets too close, and he's the gentlest of men. The people who carried out all those dreadful experiments on her were all men. The nurses used to be the ones quietening and soothing her. In her mind, men inflict pain. She won't let them near her, not after what happened with the vicar. She has a female psychiatrist at the hospital now. She just crawls into a corner and tries to hide if any men enter her cell.'

'They keep her in a cell? That's barbaric,' Amy exploded.

'It's for her own good. She gets violent, not only to others but to herself. The walls are padded and they put her into a straightjacket. She's not in there all the time, only when she's ill.'

Amy dropped her head.

'Poor Violet.'

'I've only got one or two more questions, Mrs Brown,' Bodkin said, rubbing his chin. 'Please answer them truthfully this time.'

Mrs Brown looked from under her lashes and nodded.

'Was the vicar ever drunk when he visited?'

'Drunk? No, I don't think so.'

'Did you ever suspect him of doing anything... untoward, when he was with Violet?'

Mrs Brown hesitated.

'No, not to begin with, but then... Oh, what can I say, I was the one that invited him to spend time with her. It's all my fault. She might not be as troubled as she is, if not for me...' She dropped her head into her hands and began to sob.

Bodkin pulled out his notebook and made a quick note.

'Now Mrs—'

'BODKIN! She's upset. Haven't you got enough out of her?' Amy hissed.

The detective nodded and got to his feet.

'I'm sorry that was so traumatic for you, Mrs Brown, but if you had told us all this in the first place, I might not have had to be so hard on you.'

Mrs Brown stuck her head into her pinafore and continued

to sob. Mary stepped forward and put her arm around her shoulders.

'I'm going to have to visit Violet, Mrs Brown. There's no way around it. I need to hear what she has to say about this.'

'She won't... talk to you...' Mrs Brown said between sobs. 'Even if she's lucid. She won't talk to a man. She'll just back away into the corner and try to hide.'

Bodkin put his hand on her shoulder.

'Then I'll make sure she'll hear my questions via a woman, Mrs Brown.' He glanced across at Amy. 'Miss Rowlings will accompany me.'

Mary held the door open for Bodkin and Amy to walk through, then closed it behind her.

'What will you do for a job now?' Amy asked.

'Oh, I'll be back working here by next week. She's sacked me twice before, but Mr Armitage, the owner, always takes me back.' She lowered her voice and winked at Amy. 'He's got a thing for me, you see. He told me I'll be running the place myself in a few years' time if I do as I'm told.'

Amy shook her head and put her hand on Mary's arm.

'Just be careful, Mary.'

'So, what happens now?' Amy asked as she climbed into Bodkin's car.

'I'm going back to the station to ring Hanover House and make an appointment to see Violet and her doctor. I doubt they'll allow us in at the weekend, so it looks like it will have to be Monday... that's a Bank Holiday, isn't it? Damn. I might have to put my foot down a little. It can't wait any longer than that.'

'Do you think... do you really think the vicar... well, you know?'

'After what we heard from your father yesterday, Amy. It's looking that way.'

'Oh dear. This is awful. I didn't think this is where the investigation would lead.'

'If, and it's still an if, he did have a thing for young girls... well, I think an early grave might be the best place for him,' Bodkin said.

'Oh, Bodkin.'

'It might sound harsh, Amy, but imagine if your daughter was one of the kids he'd been messing with. What would you feel about him then?'

'I'm still not sure he did anything wrong,' Amy replied, smartly. 'And I won't believe it until I hear the evidence with my own ears. He was a hard man to like, but this...? I'm really not sure he could do anything so, so... unchristian.'

'We'll find out on Monday, Amy. You haven't got long to wait.'

CHAPTER THIRTY-EIGHT

AT JUST AFTER TWELVE O'CLOCK, AFTER A QUICK STOP AT THE SHOE repair kiosk, Bodkin dropped Amy off at her gate.

'I'll see you later. Five-thirty, as usual?'

'Thanks for the lift, Bodkin. I might wear these tonight.' Amy waved her shoes to the detective, then stood on the path and watched him drive away.

Amy spent the afternoon in her room playing records by Tommy Dorsey, Fats Waller and Billie Holiday. She had just finished playing one of the first records she ever bought, Minnie the Moocher, by Cab Calloway, when her mother knocked on her bedroom door to tell her that her bath water was ready.

'Don't stay in too long, Amy, I'm in after you, don't forget.'

Amy sighed. She had received the same instructions every week since Mr Rowlings had agreed to have the bathroom extension built onto the kitchen the previous year. The hot water was supplied by a gas-fuelled Ascot heater that had been fitted when the bathroom was built. Mr Rowlings kept an eagle eye on the gas bill when it dropped onto his doormat each month, so bathing was limited to the once a week, Saturday afternoon, soak. Amy would have liked to bathe every night, but the new system was so much of an improvement over the tin bath in front of the fire regime they used to have, that she rarely complained about it. If she ever did, her father would remind her of the awful, winter's-night bath in the tin tub in front of the fire, and all the trouble it took to both fill and empty it.

'You can't have everything, Amy. Be honest now, would you rather have the tin bath and a telephone or your lovely hot water, Saturday soak and no phone?'

'I'd like both,' Amy would reply.

Mr Rowlings always laughed at that.

'I bet you would. I can imagine you now, lying in your rose scented water for hours on end while you chat to your best friend, Alice, who lives a mere four hundred yards down the lane.'

After her bath, Amy went back to her room and sat in front of her dressing table mirror as she towel-dried her hair. Then, still wearing her pink dressing gown, she picked up her copy of Murder on the Orient Express and began to read.

At five, her mother called her down for tea, so Amy pulled on the black skirt and cream top that she'd worn earlier in the day and stepped out onto the landing, tucking her blouse into the waistband of her skirt. As she walked into the living room, she was greeted by Joe Proudfoot who was already sitting at the table, eyeing up the plate of shrimp paste sandwiches that Mrs Rowlings had placed there a minute or so before.

'Tea's up,' Amy's mum called as she came in from the kitchen carrying a huge, white tea pot.

'I've made extra sandwiches in case Mr Bodkin is hungry,' she whispered into Amy's ear.

'He's not incapable, Mum,' Amy said. 'He's just... I don't know, forgetful is probably the word. He thinks more about his job than his personal wellbeing.'

After tea, Rowlings and Joe sat opposite each other in two comfortable armchairs while Amy and her mother sat on the sofa on the other side of the room.

'It's lovely to see you, Joe. We thought you'd forgotten all about us,' Mrs Rowlings said.

'You know me, Lizzie, I don't like to intrude. Since I lost Marie, I've found myself spending more and more time on my own. I go to the Dragon for a couple of pints every night, but that's about it for my social life.' The gardener rubbed his stomach. 'Mind you, I don't think I'll leave it this long again if that's the welcome I get. That cake was sublime.'

Mrs Rowlings simpered.

'There will always be a welcome for you in this house, Joe Proudfoot,' Mr Rowlings said in his usual North Kent accent.

'How's the new job going? You're working for Councillor de Vere now, aren't you?' Mrs Rowlings asked.

'I was... I won't be there much longer.'

'Why's that, Joe?' Amy asked. Already knowing the answer before it came.

'She put me on a week's notice on Saturday. She says she's going away for a while, possibly for years.'

'Is she selling up?' asked Rowlings. 'Maybe the new owner will take you on?'

'I don't know what's happening, James. She's obviously had some bad news; her eyes were puffed up like she's done a lot of crying.'

'I'm so sorry about that, Joe,' Amy said. 'What will you do now?'

'I'm going to see Abel in the Dragon tonight. He'll put a word in for me at the council. I should be able to get my old job back. They always need good gardeners. It's like a gardener's convention in there at times, what with Abel, Peter Kissman, George Drake and myself chatting about cuttings, planting, pest control and what have you. If there's a job going, one of them will know about it.'

'Do you get a lot of pests up there, Joe?' Amy asked.

'It's not a big problem now, we get the odd insect infestation, but since I got rid of the moles, nothing worse than that.'

'Moles?' Mrs Rowlings said. 'You kill moles? Oh, that's so sad. Whenever I hear them mentioned I think of Mole in the Wind in the Willows story. He was such a gentle character.'

'They ruin the lawns, Lizzie,' Joe replied. 'I was really struggling to get rid of them, nothing I tried, worked. They got used to the smell of arsenic and used to dig their way around the bait.'

'So how did you manage it in the end?' James Rowlings asked.

'Mrs de Vere got a tip from the vicar. Peter Kissman works for him, and he had a similar problem. He advised that I use a strychnine-based poison, I tried it, and the moles were gone inside a month. The daft thing was, I could have asked Peter myself, I see him every week in the pub. I did ask him if he had any spare strychnine, the weekend after I received the advice, but he said he hadn't used it for years, as the moles had never come back.'

Just then, Bodkin arrived, looking, for him, quite presentable. His trousers had a nice sharp crease and his shirt had been neatly ironed.

Amy introduced the detective to Joe.

'We were just talking about Peter Kissman, Bodkin. He drinks with Joe at the Dragon on Saturday nights.'

'Really?' Bodkin held out his hand and introduced himself. Joe leaned forwards to shake it, then leaned back in his chair.

'Do you mind if I quiz you a little about Peter?' Bodkin asked. 'Nothing too serious, we just need to check on his movements around the time of the murder.'

'That was the twenty-fifth, wasn't it...? The Saturday night?'

Bodkin nodded and eased himself into the space on the sofa between Amy and her mother.

'Was he in the pub that night? What can you remember about it? Was he agitated or maybe a little self-absorbed?'

'Let me think, that would have been the night Abel had his big win. He was splashing the money about like nobody's business. Hmm, no, I can't remember anything out of the ordinary, apart from that. Peter arrived at his usual time, had his usual two and a half pints and left bang on last orders. He never bothers with last orders. He is always very careful about the amount he drinks.'

'He used to be a problem drinker, didn't he?' Bodkin asked.

'He had a big problem with drink back in the day. That was when I first met him. I don't think I ever saw him sober. He was banned from just about every pub in Spinton at one time or another for his behaviour. He'd start drinking straight after work and not finish until they chucked him out at closing time. He'd spend all his wages on drink, it cost him his marriage in the end. You couldn't so much as glance at him without getting a punch in the teeth. He wasn't a nice person back then, ask any of the women who knew him. He couldn't keep his hands off them.'

'So, he was an alcoholic?'

'Or well on the way to becoming one at least. He never missed an hour's work though, and it was a tough job, working on the roads.'

'How did he manage to kick the habit, Joe? You say he's so careful with the amount he drinks now. Most alcoholics can't go near the stuff or they'll jump right off the wagon.'

'The Salvation Army saved him, Mr Bodkin. They used to trawl the pubs on a Saturday night back then. They don't come up this way since their HQ was demolished to make way for the new school. They're based in Gillingham now. Back in the day though, they'd try to save a few souls. They managed to save Peter's soul. It was too late for him to save his marriage though.'

'So, he joined the Salvation Army?'

'No, he never became a soldier for Christ, but he did used to go to the weekly meetings they held to help alcoholics, drug users, etc. It did him a lot of good. They gave him his confidence back. He stayed off the beer for years. Never touched a drop. Then, about three or four years ago, he started to come in again. Just the odd half pint and a chat with his fellow gardeners. He gradually built that up to his two and a half pints, but he never has a single sip more than that, not even if someone offers to buy him a drink, and he never gets involved in the regular after time lock-ins. He says his goodnights at last orders and that's the last we see of him until the following Wednesday.'

'That takes a lot of willpower,' Bodkin said.

'I think God helps him out a bit. This is how it works with Peter. He always starts off with a full pint, and he'll sip away at that while the rest of us drink two or three. Then he'll have three half-pint top ups that last him the rest of the night. I mention God because he puts his hand over his heart, closes his eyes and mutters to himself when he's getting near to the end of his drink. I think he's asking God to help him stick to his limit.'

'What does he mutter, have you ever heard what he says?'

'No, it's barely audible. I think it's some prayer or other he learned at the Sally Ann. Whatever it is, it works for him.'

'On that Saturday. Did Peter go home on time?'

'Ten-thirty on the dot, as always.'

'What about Wednesday evenings?'

'Just the same,' Joe replied. Two and a half pints. Wednesday is darts night. Peter scores for the Dragon team.'

'He doesn't play himself?'

'Good heavens, no. He couldn't hit a barn door with a banjo.'

Bodkin nodded to the gardener.

'Thanks for clarifying that, Joe. You pretty much back up what he had to say, but now we know a lot more about him.'

'Is he a suspect?' Joe asked.

'Everyone is a suspect until they're not,' Amy said, quickly.

Bodkin smiled, then jerked his thumb towards her as he looked across the room towards Joe.

'What she said,' he said.

At six, Amy hurried upstairs to get ready for the night out, leaving Bodkin chatting to Joe and her parents.

At twenty-five past, Alice arrived. Amy, wearing her new dress and shoes, beckoned her to come upstairs as Mrs Rowlings stepped back into the living room.

'That's nice,' Alice said. 'It's new, isn't it?'

'Brigden's,' Amy said doing a twirl. 'I beat Nora Beckinsale to it by a whisker.' She bent her knee to lift her foot. 'I got these too, five bob, and a couple of shillings to fix, they had a loose heel.'

'They're fabulous. I do like those,' Alice said.

'You'll have to come up with me next week. You could do with a few additions to your wardrobe,' Amy said.

Alice laughed. 'I'll still be cleaning out the pigs while you're running your hand down the sales rail.'

Suddenly Amy became serious, she brushed her rose patterned dress down and stood sideways on to her best friend.

'What's my bust like in this?'

'It's fine, same as always.'

'It doesn't make them look small, then?'

'You look very attractive, just like you always do.'

'Yes, but I mean...' she looked down at her breasts, then placed the palms of her hands underneath and gave them a push.

'I was thinking of putting a couple of darts underneath, to see if it would make them look a bit bigger.'

'Amy, why are you suddenly so bother... Ah. Trixie... I get it now.'

'It's not that. I've worried about it for ages now. Everyone else seems to have such a full bust and mine is... well, like that.'

'You have a lovely bust, Amy. Most women would sell their souls to have a figure like yours. And you don't have a small bust anyway. It's perfect.'

'Do you really think so?'

'What was it that dirty minded so and so, Jeb Murray used to say at school? "More than a handful is a waste." He was probably right about that.' She held her own breasts in her hands. 'Yours aren't that much smaller than mine anyway. I really don't understand why you want to change the way you look. I'm sure Bodkin appreciates them just the way they are.'

'Bodkin?' Amy rolled her eyes as she reached for her brush to give her hair a final touch up. 'What's he got to do with anything?'

CHAPTER THIRTY-NINE

'I love James Stewart,' Alice said as the four friends walked down the hill towards the bus stop. 'I didn't know he could sing.'

'You can't beat a Cole Porter score,' Ferris added as he began to hum, I'm Easy to Love, one of the songs from the film which had originally been released in 1936.

'Who's for chips? We've got plenty of time before the bus,' Alice said.

There was only a small queue at the chip shop and they were soon sitting on the wall outside with their packets of fish and chips wrapped in the week's newspapers.

Amy picked a chip from her bag, blew on it to cool it down, then took a dainty bite.

'So, where is it tonight. The Bell or the Bull?'

'I liked it in the Bell last week,' Ferris said, 'but I'm happy to go with the flow.'

'The Bell was a bit loud for me,' Bodkin said, swallowing a

piece of battered fish. He looked sideways at Ferris. 'Particularly when a certain copper hit the microphone.'

Ferris's jaw dropped in mock shock.

'You wait until you hear what I'm singing tonight.'

'I bet it's from Born to Dance,' Alice said.

'Correct, give the lady a cigar,' Ferris said, wafting his hand in front of his mouth after swallowing a hot chip, whole.

After depositing their empty newspaper wrappers in the rusty, iron waste bin that sat on the pavement outside the chip shop, the four friends took a vote on where to go for a drink. The Old Bull won by three votes to one.

'Never mind, Ferris,' Amy said, patting him on the arm. 'We'll do the Bell next week. I promise.'

'Oh, I don't care particularly,' Ferris replied. 'I just liked being on stage with the band.'

The Old Bull snug was busy. Some of Amy's friends from the Mill were sitting in a group on the old church pew benches in the corner. They waved and hooted at her as she walked in.

'Watch it, girls, they might be wielding their truncheons,' Edna Rowe, a fellow machinist shouted, drunkenly.

Amy stuck her tongue between her teeth and shook her head gently.

Bodkin, who was standing between Amy and Alice while Ferris got the drinks, wagged a finger in the women's direction.

'Now, now, girls, keep it clean,' he said.

'You can handcuff me to the bedpost anytime you like, love,' Edna said.

'Me too,' said Betty Scholar, who had been married for almost forty years. 'Just as long as you lock my Fred in the pub until Sunday morning. I wouldn't want him disturbing us.'

After Ferris had passed the drinks from the bar, Bodkin led them across towards the fireplace where a log fire crackled and spat out a welcome. The early April clear skies outside, promised a deep frost by morning.

Amy chinked glasses with each of her friends in turn, then took a long sip of her port and lemon.

'Did you manage to book an appointment at Hanover House for Monday? You haven't mentioned it,' she asked.

'They took a lot of persuading, but yes. Even though it's a bank holiday, they'll allow me to see her on Monday. She has a lady psychiatrist... a Doctor Fuller. She'll be in attendance just in case Violet reacts badly to having a man close by. There will also be a nurse there too, more for reassurance than anything else. I told them that you were going to act as my mouthpiece if she refused to answer my questions directly. They're fine with that, in fact, they welcome the idea.'

'What time?'

'I'll pick you up at home at twelve-fifteen. The meeting is set for twelve-forty-five. She has her lunch at one-thirty, she tends to get a bit sleepy after food.'

'Righto,' said Amy. She turned away from Bodkin to look at her workmates who were all on their feet, banging on the table, trying to encourage Ferris to sing.

'Ferris, Ferris...'

Feigning reluctance, Ferris held up his hands for silence before delivering a note-perfect rendition of, I've Got You Under My Skin, a song that Virginia Bruce had sung in the Born to Dance film the friends had just seen. As he hit the last note, the women began to applaud frantically.

'More! More...'

Amy eased up close to Alice as Ferris began to croon, 'I'm in the Mood for Love,' a song originally sung by Frances Langford in the film, Every Night at Eight.

'Are you in the mood for love, Alice?' she asked as her best friend rocked slowly to Ferris's singing.

'Not with Ferris, he's not right for me,' she replied without taking her eyes from the singing policeman. 'He's a lovely lad and he can sing me a lullaby at bedtime if he likes, but he will have to sleep in the next room.'

'Have you seen anything of Godfrey, lately?' Amy asked.

Godfrey Wilson was Alice's Gangster Lawyer who dressed like Edward. G. Robinson and drove the sort of car that any Hollywood gangster would have been proud of. Although he was much older than Alice and was married, they had become more than just friends.

'I had a quick chat with him on the phone yesterday as it happens,' Alice said. 'He's reading the vicar's will on Tuesday. He said he might nip over afterwards as he has a bit of time on his hands. He's got to track down someone the vicar left money to, apparently, so he'll be away from his desk for the next few days.'

'Well, it won't take him long to find my dad,' Amy said with a laugh. 'He's going over for the reading after the funeral on Tuesday. He doesn't know if he's been left anything, but you don't get asked to a will reading unless there's something in it for you.'

'I wonder how much he's been left? Are vicars usually very rich?' Alice asked. 'You might get that telephone yet, Amy.'

'There's no chance of that,' Amy replied, sadly. 'Unless he's left Dad enough to retire on, he won't get one installed. As I told you, he thinks he'll be at the beck and call of his boss if he does.'

. . .

At ten-forty-five, they left the pub and walked slowly past the red telephone box towards Amy's house, about a third of the way along Long Lane. At Amy's gate, Alice said goodnight and she and Ferris continued to walk down the unlit lane to Alice's farm, where he knew he would only receive a perfunctory peck on the cheek for his troubles. Ferris wasn't the least bit put out. He and Alice knew exactly where they stood with each other.

'What's the plan for tomorrow?' Amy said when Ferris and Alice were out of earshot.

'A lazy day, I hope. I've got a few bits to see to in the morning, but that's it for the day,' Bodkin said. 'Next week might end up being a bit hectic, so I might put my feet up for a few hours in the afternoon. What about you? Are you going to church?'

'On Easter Sunday! Good grief. My Dad would drag me up to the church by my hair if I even thought about not going. As it is, I like to go. It will be different this year with Daley doing the honours though.'

'I'll see you outside the church when it's all over then,' Bodkin said.

'On the lychgate path? Who are you spying on this week?'

Bodkin laughed his deep, throaty laugh.

'Oh, I'd like to see how Mrs de Vere and Mr Daley react to last Friday's questioning. Providing she shows up of course... and, I want a quick word with Caroline Gatting about those missing sweets.'

'Oh yes, I'd almost forgotten about those,' Amy said.

'She may have put them in a drawer and forgotten about them. Maybe she ate them herself... if she did it will prove they hadn't been poisoned, I suppose.'

'She's diabetic, Bodkin. I don't think she'd have scoffed them herself.'

'So she is. She might be allowed one or two now and again though. Maybe she gave them to her niece if she dropped by. I'll find out one way or another tomorrow.'

'Talking of kids. I was thinking about the conversation you had with Mrs Brown today, when she asked if you were a father or not. You looked a bit sad when you replied.'

'Time's passing me by, Amy. I'm thirty now. Being tied to the job as I am... well, let's say it gets in the way of a family life.'

Amy looked him in the eyes and smiled warmly.

'You'd make a good father, Bodkin. I think you'd be great around kids.'

'Do you really think so?' Bodkin asked, looking back into Amy's eyes. 'I would like to have children one day. What about you?'

Amy held his eyes for a few seconds, then turned her head away quickly and looked down the lane towards the farm.

'I don't know why you're bringing me into this conversation, Bodkin. It's your kids we're talking about.'

The overnight frost had vanished from the graves by the time the worshippers walked out of the church at the end of the Easter Sunday service. Bodkin, standing alone on the lychgate path opposite the church entrance had mumbled along to the final hymn, Amazing Grace, and was still humming the tune to himself as Amy walked along the gravel path towards him, having avoided shaking hands with the new vicar.

'Happy Easter, Bodkin.'

'Good morning, Amy,' Bodkin replied. 'What brings you here?'

Amy pulled a face at the detective. 'A bit of religion would do you good, Bodkin,' she said with a resigned tone in her voice.

'It would cloud my judgement, seeing only good in people,' Bodkin replied. 'Besides which, I have you to fill me in if I ever need advice on the subject.'

'Purgatory awaits you, Bodkin,' Amy said with a grin. 'And you'll be there a long time with that attitude.'

'I never have been one for harp music,' Bodkin replied. 'Ah, here's Mrs de Vere.'

It was painfully clear that the closeness of the week before was not going to be repeated. Daley could hardly hold her eye as she stood before him, desperately trying to engage him in conversation.

Bodkin seemed agitated as he watched the couple, continually running his hand over the dark stubble on his chin.

'Even I can see that the body language has changed,' Bodkin said. 'He can't even bring himself to look at her.'

In the foyer, Daley shuffled his feet and looked about for a friendly face. Seeing Bodkin eyeing him, he suddenly took two paces forward and almost brushing the councillor aside, thrust out his hand towards Amy's father.

'I'd just like to apologise for the other day. I got angry and I was wrong,' Rowlings said.

Daley beamed a wide smile at him as he pumped the engineer's hand.

'Think no more about it, Mr Rowlings, or may I call you James?' Flashing Mrs de Vere, a quick glance, he put his arm around Rowlings' shoulders and led him away towards the main gate. 'I believe you write incredible sermons...'

Mrs de Vere stood alone for a few moments, then with a look of sheer hatred on her face, she followed the vicar along the path.

'Ah, Mrs Gatting,' Bodkin said as the housekeeper stepped onto the stone chip and gravel path that led towards the vicarage. 'Just the person I was looking for.'

'What is it now?' Caroline asked.

'It's only a little thing. I'd like to know what happened to the bag of pineapple chunks that were on the vicar's desk on Saturday night. Only they weren't there on Monday when I searched the study.'

'Oh, those. I threw them in the bin when I was cleaning up on Monday morning.'

'Why did you throw them away so quickly?'

'Because I would have been tempted to eat them, and if I had started, I wouldn't have been happy until the last one had gone,' she replied. 'I've always had a sweet tooth, Inspector, but my body can't take sweet, sugary things any more, even with the insulin shots. I asked the vicar not to leave them lying around the place, and to be fair to him he did keep them in his pockets, or in the drawer of his study most of the time,' she paused. 'Why are you so interested in them anyway?'

'Because we now believe that the poison that killed Mr Villiers was sprinkled over his sweets, whether it was the packet in his pocket or the bag on his desk has yet to be determined.'

'Goodness me. It seemed that all your questions were aimed at who had access to his wine.'

'The investigation has moved on, Caroline. We know for sure now that the wine hadn't been tampered with. The sweets however...'

'I didn't touch his sweets,' Mrs Gatting said, firmly. 'And I didn't go anywhere near his study until the Monday morning.'

'No, but your sister did,' Bodkin replied.

Bodkin took off his hat and scratched his head as he watched the housekeeper walk away. Turning back to Amy, he let out a deep sigh.

'What's the matter, Bodkin? You seem a little on edge this morning,' Amy said, laying her hand gently on his sleeve.

Bodkin sighed again.

'Gillingham... well to be more precise, Sittingbourne, have lost the fingerprint evidence.'

'What do you mean, lost? I thought they were sending it back.'

'They were supposed to, but it has been misplaced again. The desk sergeant seems to think it might have been sent to Scotland Yard by mistake.'

'Scotland Yard? My goodness, but can't you get it sent back from there? They must know the file doesn't belong to one of their cases.'

'I was on the phone to them for an hour this morning. They can't find it and are adamant that they never actually received it.'

'So...'

'So, it has disappeared... for now at least. Oh, it will turn up one day, maybe in five years' time, some detective or other will find it lying at the bottom of his in-tray, but for now, it's gone, vanished without a trace.'

'Oh dear, Bodkin... But, can't they just take another set of prints from the wrappers and the bag they came in?'

'No, because they are inside the envelope with the photographs of the fingerprints. They sent the whole lot off together.'

Amy shook her head.

'That means we might never know the identity of the

fourth person that picked up those wraps. The killer could get away with it.'

Bodkin rubbed at his stubble again.

'It was our best piece of evidence to date, but you're right. If it doesn't turn up soon it could well mean that our poisoner might walk free.'

CHAPTER FORTY

Bank Holiday Monday always meant a lie in at the Rowlings household. Even Mr Rowlings, who was up at six every morning, didn't get out of bed until seven.

Amy woke up at seven-thirty with the smell of frying bacon wafting up the stairs. After resisting the temptation for fifteen minutes, she got out of bed, pulled on her dressing gown and after a quick visit to the downstairs lavatory, she stepped into the living room, sniffing the air.

Mr Rowlings was sitting at the table tucking into bacon and eggs.

'I hope you left some for me, Dad,' she said, walking around the table to plant a kiss on her father's cheek.

'I heard you get up, love, I just put yours in the pan,' Mrs Rowlings said as Amy walked into the kitchen.

'Morning, Mum,' Amy replied, giving her mother a quick hug. 'That smells so good.'

'Eggs and bacon, or a bacon sandwich?'

'Ooh, eggs, I think.'

'There's toast and tea on the table, I'll just get the eggs going.'

Amy walked back to the living room and sat down opposite her father. Mr Rowlings looked over his newspaper at her, then resumed reading.

'The paper boy doesn't get a bank holiday lie in then?' Amy said.

'Nor should he,' Rowlings replied, holding the paper up to show a torn front page. 'He won't be getting his sixpenny tip next Christmas if he doesn't take more care with the papers.'

Amy took a half slice of toast from the rack and covered it with a thick layer of butter. As she was about to bite into it, her mother placed a plate in front of her containing two fried eggs and three crispy rashers of bacon. Amy broke the yolk of one of her eggs with the corner of her toast, then crunched on it.

'Oooh, that's delish. We should have eggs and bacon every morning for breakfast.' It was normally only served up as a once a week treat, usually on a Sunday.

'I'll get Alice to put aside a pig for us, shall I?' Mr Rowlings said, lowering his paper again. 'She's already kind enough to let us have fresh eggs. I'm sure she wouldn't mind butchering a pig for us as well. The only problem would be...' his face appeared over the top of his Daily Herald, 'paying for it.'

'I was only saying,' Amy replied, cutting into a rasher of bacon.

'What are your plans for today, Amy?' Mrs Rowlings asked.

'I'm going to Hanover House with Bodkin,' Amy replied through a mouthful of toast.

'What on earth are you going there for? It's probably the last place I'd choose to go on a bank holiday.'

'It's to do with the investigation. I can't go into details, it's a bit hush-hush.'

'Well, just you be careful, our Amy, there are some strange sorts in there.'

Hanover House was a huge, sandstone and yellow brick building that had once been a notorious Victorian asylum. Set in pleasant gardens behind high walls and a secure gatehouse, it was now controlled by the local authority and had garnered an excellent reputation among the mental health fraternity for its pioneering work with the mentally ill. Although some of the methods used were still quite brutal, the doctors and staff cared deeply for the welfare of their patients.

'It looks more like the gateway to a castle than a hospital,' Amy said as Bodkin pulled up at the huge stone arch that was built into a twelve-foot-high wall.

'Those Victorians knew how to build, didn't they? This place was as secure as any prison. We couldn't build anything like this these days, it would cost the earth.'

A uniformed man came out of a room built inside the arch, carrying a clipboard.

'Inspector Bodkin from Spinton police, and Miss Amy Rowlings from ARIA Investigations,' Bodkin said after winding down his window.

Amy tried her best to keep a grin off her face as the guard looked into the car to get a good look at her. Satisfied, he signed two chits and handed them to the detective, then, producing a large iron key from his trouser pocket, he unlocked the ornate gates and pushed them open.

Bodkin nodded to him as he drove into the beautifully kept grounds. Amy looked around as they drove along the single-track tarmacked road towards the main building of the hospital. Immaculate lawns, recently dug flowerbeds and neatly trimmed shrubs, lined their route.

'Blimey, they must employ as many gardeners as hospital staff, to keep it looking like this,' Amy said. 'It's like the grounds of a stately home, isn't it?'

'The local authority run it, so they probably use some of their own workers,' Bodkin said. 'It is beautiful though. My old dad could never get his lawn to look like that.'

At the main doors of the hospital their chitties were checked by another security man, who got them to sign a log book before leading them along a short, painting-lined corridor to the governor's office.

'Bodkin and Rowlings, sir,' he announced. 'Here to see Violent Violet.'

Mr Whittingham was a portly man who wore an expensive, if ill-fitting, suit. He had a blotchy, podgy face and a wide nose on which was perched a pair of round, wire-framed spectacles. Rolls of fat hung over the crisply starched collar of his shirt. He remained seated as Bodkin and Amy walked in.

'So, you're Bodkin are you?' the governor said, ignoring Amy completely. 'I hope you realise this is highly unusual. Bank holidays ought to be respected.'

'It is a very urgent matter,' Bodkin replied.

'It had bloody well better be,' Whittingham spat. 'I have a lunch engagement.'

'We won't be here long. We just need to ask one or two questions.'

'Violet Brown? Good luck with that. She doesn't talk to men at all.' He glanced up from reading Violet's file. 'Don't start her off, for God's sake, Bodkin. It'll take the staff two days to calm her down again.'

'Miss Rowlings is here to assist me with the questioning,'

Bodkin replied, moving to the side to allow Amy to step forward.

Whittingham's face lit up.

'Hello, my dear, forgive me, I didn't notice you at first. What a pretty little thing you are. If you ever fancy a secretarial job, just give me a call.'

'I have a job,' Amy said, firmly. Her eyes narrowed as she stared down the governor.

Whittingham held her fierce look for a few seconds, then waved them away with a waft of his flabby hand.

'Back along the corridor, wait in reception. I'll get Doctor Fuller to collect you.'

'What a horrible man,' Amy said as they reached the waiting room. 'He could do with a long walk, not another big lunch.'

Doctor Fuller was an attractive woman in her mid-thirties with straw coloured hair and a welcoming smile.

'I see you survived your first meeting with our glorious leader,' she said to Amy as she led them along a series of passageways until they came to a wide staircase. 'Top tip, don't get within an arm's length of him, he's like an octopus.'

'Someone should do something about it,' Amy said with a scowl. 'He should be reported to the authorities.'

'It's just your word against his,' Doctor Fuller replied. 'Who are they going to believe?' She held her arm out towards the staircase. 'The lift is out of action again, sorry.'

She led them up two flights of stairs to a wider corridor with at least a dozen doors leading off it. About half way along, she stopped, and turned towards a white-painted door on the right-hand side.

'She's calm today, so far. She did have a rather serious episode yesterday evening in the dining room and it took quite a lot out of her. We're hoping she doesn't have another one today or she'll be back on the sedatives.' She turned to face Bodkin. 'If she starts to become anxious, back away. Please don't push her too far with the questioning. She's a bright little thing but she becomes distressed very easily.'

Violet was a pretty, red-headed girl with a freckled face and a pair of piercing, green eyes that seemed to be able to look deep into your soul. Bodkin had held the eyes of some of the most vicious, hardened criminals in the area, but he found himself looking away as the young girl focused her unblinking attention on him. She was dressed in a knee-length cotton smock and a pair of navy slippers with a white fur trim. She was standing by the window, at the side of which was a young woman in a nurse's uniform. Amy recognised her immediately as Connie Broughton, a girl both she and Alice had been at school with. She smiled as Amy entered and gave her a finger wave.

'Violet, this is Inspector Bodkin and Amy Rowlings, they've come to ask you a few questions, is that all right?'

Violet said nothing, but continued to stare at Bodkin. After a full minute she turned her attention to Amy.

'I'm having pilchards for tea if I'm good. Do you like pilchards?'

Amy nodded. 'I love pilchards.'

'Are you staying for tea?' Violet asked.

'No, I don't think I can, maybe next time.'

'It might not be pilchards then though.'

Doctor Fuller motioned for Bodkin to sit down on a seat by the door. Bodkin did as he was asked, then cleared his throat as he looked at the young girl.

'Hello, Violet. I'm Bodkin.'

The girl ignored him and turned to Connie. 'There's a man here.'

'I know, Violet, but he's a nice man, he's just come to talk to you.'

'I don't like men, they hurt.'

'Mr Bodkin won't hurt you, Violet,' Amy said, softly. 'He came with me. I wouldn't let anyone hurt you.'

'Mum did,' Amy replied sulkily.

'That's what I've come to ask you about, Violet,' Bodkin said as he leaned towards her.

Violet immediately backed away, flattened herself against the wall and tucked her head under her arm.

Bodkin held up both hands.

'I'm sorry, Violet. I'll just be quiet, shall I? Amy will ask you the questions.'

Violet shot him a hateful glare, then nodded.

The detective beckoned towards Amy, then whispered something in her ear. Amy listened intently, then crouched down next to Bodkin's chair.

'We don't want to keep you too long, Violet, but we do need to know what happened when the vicar came to see you. Was he a nice man? Was he friendly?'

Violet shook her head quickly.

'Did he speak to you? What did he say?'

'He waved his book at me. We didn't like it. He told them to leave... I didn't want them to leave.'

'Them? Oh, the friends who talk to you, the ones no one else can see?'

Violet nodded.

'Are your friends here now?' Amy asked.

Violet tossed her head nonchalantly.

'No, they're not here today.'

'Do you miss them when they aren't here?'

'No, not really, they can be a nuisance. They only come back when they feel like it. Sometimes I tell them to go away, but then I miss them when they do.'

'The vicar tried to make them go away, but they didn't want to, is that right?'

Violet nodded again. 'He kept telling them to leave. "I CAST YOU OUT IN THE NAME OF GOD!" He used to shout that a lot.'

'But they didn't go away?'

'No, they got angry with him and that frightened me.'

'I bet it did. I'd have been frightened too,' Amy said, soothingly.

She was silent for a few moments.

'Violet, did the vicar ever touch you when he visited?'

Violet screwed up her face. 'I don't want to think about it.'

'I'm sorry, Violet, but just tell me what happened, then we'll talk about something else.'

Violet closed her eyes and grimaced.

'Did he touch you?'

'HE HURT ME! He hurt me so much... he wouldn't get off, he just kept doing it... I didn't like it, I said I'd tell Mummy, but he wouldn't stop.'

Violet began to shake, uncontrollably.

Bodkin shook his head then looked down at his feet. 'The filthy...'

'How many times did this happen, Violet? Was it just the once, or did he hurt you more than once?'

'Four times, it was four times, and I told him to stop, but he just wouldn't, it hurt so much.' She put her hands over her mouth as tears filled her eyes.

'I think that's enough for now,' Doctor Fuller said. 'It's all right, Violet, you don't have to talk about it anymore. Think about something nice now.'

Violet's demeanour changed almost immediately. 'You can see over the wall from here,' she said to Amy. 'Come see.'

Amy walked across to the window and looked out over the gardens.

'Mum's house is over there somewhere.'

'I know, I saw her on Saturday. She sends her love.'

'Is she coming to visit?'

'Soon, Violet, she's busy with the café at the moment.'

'We go for walks down by the river. I like the swans and ducks.'

'I like the swans and ducks too.'

'I like your frock, it's got flowers on it,' Violet said, taking hold of Amy's dress and stroking one of the large red roses.

'Thank you, it's new, I'm rather fond of it, that's why I wore it today. I thought you might like it too.'

'Do you like my garden?' Violet asked, pointing out over the grounds.

'I love your garden, you're so lucky to live here,' Amy replied.

'Would you like to walk around it with me.'

'Next time I come, I'll let you show me your garden,' Amy said.

'Toby looks after the garden. He's a very good gardener,' Violet said.

'You spend a lot of time in the gardens don't you, Violet?' Connie said, touching her lightly on the arm.

'It's calming for her. We let her roam for an hour or so a day,' said Doctor Fuller.

'On her own?' Amy asked.

'Well, yes, she's quite safe. It's not like she could ever

escape, is it? I couldn't get over that wall with a ladder. Violet likes to be out in the open air and it's very calming for her. She knows how to tell the time and she's never late back in. If we say an hour, she's back, bang on the hour. We do like to give her as much independence as we can. She's fourteen, after all, she'll be an adult soon.'

'It's my birthday in May. I'm going to have a party, will you come?' Violet looked pleadingly at Amy.

'I'd love to come, thank you for inviting me.'

Violet suddenly threw herself at Amy and wrapped her arms around her. 'Will you visit me when Mum can't come?'

Amy returned the hug. 'When I can, Violet, yes.'

Violet pushed herself hard against Amy, her arms encircling her.

Amy patted the young girl on the back as Violet pushed her head against her shoulder and clung on even tighter. She lifted her hand to stroke Violet's hair, but then a shocked look came over her face as she felt the hard swelling in Violet's belly push against her own.

'Oh no,' she muttered before turning her head towards Bodkin.

'She's pregnant.'

CHAPTER FORTY-ONE

'Why on earth didn't you tell us she was pregnant?' Bodkin fumed.

They stood in a group in the corridor, just outside Violet's room.

'Have you never heard of doctor, patient, confidentiality, Inspector?' Doctor Fuller said, sharply.

'Of course I have, but she's fourteen. A criminal act has been committed here.' Bodkin paced back and forth in front of the doctor.

'Given her mental condition, we thought it best to keep that information to ourselves for the time being. You saw what she's like. Can you imagine the stress she'd be under if she had to appear in a courtroom? Again, given her mental state, I doubt they'd accept her testimony. Anyway, the man is dead. You can't convict a dead man.'

'Have her parents been informed?'

'Of course they have.'

'So, Mrs Brown knows? How long has she known?'

'Since we found out, about three weeks ago.'

'How far is she along?'

'We estimate, sixteen, possibly seventeen weeks.'

'So, she fell pregnant in late November, early December?'

'It would appear so.'

'I'd like to look at her record if that's all right?'

'Follow me, my office is on this floor,' Doctor Fuller said.

She began to walk along the corridor. Bodkin started to follow, then turned back towards Amy.

'I'll see you down at reception. You don't have the authority to read her report.'

As Bodkin walked off with Doctor Fuller, Amy made her way back to the staircase with Connie.

'I'll have to leave you here, Amy; I've got to get back to her. Can you find your own way to the entrance?'

Amy nodded.

'It's been lovely to see you again, Connie, I just wish it was under happier circumstances. How long have you worked here? The last time I saw you, you were on a machine at Tomlinson's.'

'It's better money here... or it will be when I finish my training. It is shift work, but I'm getting used to that now.'

'It must be a lot of stress for you though.' Amy looked back along the corridor. 'I mean, some of the patients must be... very difficult.'

'It's hard work and it does get to you now and then, but it's all worthwhile in the end. It's an early start on the day shift, but I'm done for two o'clock. We only have to work eight hours. I was doing ten at Tomlinson's factory.'

'We should arrange to meet one Saturday night. Alice would love to see you.'

'Are you still on Long Lane?'

Amy nodded. 'Where are you living now?'

'I live with my mum, over on Garland Street.'

'Ah, I remember now. Say hi to her for me, won't you?'

Connie turned back towards Violet's room and Amy started on the long walk back to reception.

Half an hour later, Amy and Bodkin climbed into the detective's black Morris Ten on the forecourt of the hospital.

'Mrs Brown needs a severe talking to. She's been leading us a merry dance. First, she neglects to tell us about the vicar's visits then she somehow forgets to tell us that her fourteen-year-old daughter is pregnant.'

Amy raised her hands on her temples and began to rub her fingertips around in a circle.

'She'll give the same reason as before, Bodkin and to be honest, I can understand why. She was ashamed. I feel so sorry for her.'

'It gives her a motive though, Amy.'

Amy nodded. 'One of Poirot's famous four. Revenge.'

'But how did she manage to get the poison into him. She was never alone with the sweets.'

Amy was silent for a moment.

'Maybe that wasn't her. Maybe that was Caroline and Agatha working together, or another member of the committee. Mrs de Vere, for instance.'

'So, what are you thinking?'

'Just give me a moment, Bodkin. There's something... OH COME ON, THINK!' Amy slapped the dashboard in front of her in frustration. 'It's there, it's like finishing a jigsaw, but the last piece is missing...'

Bodkin started up the engine.

'Well, when you find it down the side of the chair, shout out.'

The detective put the car into gear and drove slowly towards the gatehouse. Just as the security guard stepped out of his room to open the gates for them, Amy suddenly sat bolt upright.

'SOCRATES!' she yelled.

'Who?' Bodkin said as he raised his hand to the guard and drove carefully through the arch.

'Socrates. You know, the Greek philosopher?'

'What about him?'

'He was charged with impiety and corrupting the young with his ideas. He was an opponent of democracy... anyway, he was sentenced to death, a sentence he accepted. He was ordered to commit suicide by drinking a cup of poison hemlock.'

'Okay,' Bodkin said, as he turned onto the Gillingham Road and headed back towards Spinton.

'Socrates drank the hemlock brew and described what was happening to his body as he was dying. He was told to walk around until his legs became heavy, then to lie down until the poison reached his heart at which time he'd die.'

'Okay, what about it?'

'Villiers was seen meandering around the street after leaving the Town Tea Shop, Bodkin. Mary told me that. Mr Cavanagh said something similar. He said that Villiers looked a bit rubber legged in his shop and had to hang on to the door for a while before he left.'

'But he didn't lie down and die, did he?'

'No, but he wasn't drunk either. What if Mrs Brown had poisoned his food with hemlock?'

Bodkin pursed his lips.

'Go on.'

'Symptoms can occur between thirty minutes and a couple of hours after ingesting the plant. The symptoms include muscle weakness. Just like Socrates, the numbness could have worked its way up from his feet.'

'How do you know all this?'

'Because I actually read the library book instead of just vandalising it, Bodkin. You'd have known all about hemlock if you had bothered to read the page after the one with the photograph on it.'

'Fair enough, but doesn't that stuff stink? How would she have got it into him?'

'That's easy enough. She'd been cooking him boiled fish and parsley sauce. Hemlock is often mistaken for wild parsley, it's a member of the same plant group. All she had to do was chop it up finely and sprinkle it onto his sauce. It might have tasted a little bitter, but just about everything tasted bitter to him anyway, that's why he ate so many sweets. He'd never have known anything about it.'

'It didn't kill him though.'

'She may not have given him enough, or if she cooked it in the sauce with the real parsley it might have reduced the strength of the poison. She's hardly Lucrezia Borgia. This was the first time she'd done anything remotely like this.'

Bodkin rubbed his stubble covered chin with his left hand as he steered the car with his right.

'She used to take Violet for walks along the river bank, didn't she? She'd know exactly where to find the hemlock.'

Amy nodded enthusiastically.

'That's right... Oh, I've just had a thought. Does this mean we're looking for more than one, would-be assassin?'

Bodkin pulled a face.

'Two seemingly unconnected people attempting to poison the same person for different reasons? It's a novel idea but I've never come across it before. No, Amy, I keep saying that poison is a woman's weapon and this case just goes to prove that theory is right once again. Come on. Let's see exactly what Mavis Brown has to say about all of this.'

The Town Tea Shop was locked and shuttered when Amy and Bodkin arrived, but through a gap at the bottom of the pull-down blind that covered the half pane of glass on the front door, they could see a chink of light that was obviously emanating from an electric light bulb.

Bodkin hammered on the glass until the blind was suddenly raised and Mary's puzzled face appeared. He made a twisting motion with his hand and pointed to the door handle. A few seconds later they were standing in the empty café.

'You got your job back then?' Amy said.

'Yeah, she knows she can't do without me, but she made sure I'd be punished for telling you what I knew. That's why I'm here doing the cleaning on a bank holiday Monday.'

'Is Mrs Brown at home, Mary?' Bodkin asked.

Mary pointed towards the ceiling.

'She's upstairs. Do you want me to give her a shout?'

Mrs Brown arrived downstairs with an air of resignation about her.

'I've been expecting you,' she said.

Bodkin pulled out a chair.

'Sit down, Mrs Brown,' he said firmly.

Mavis sat on the chair and placed her hands on her lap as Bodkin took a seat on the opposite side of the table.

'Mary, go upstairs and sit with Gerald,' Mrs Brown ordered.

'But I have to get on with the cleaning.'

'Just do as you're told for once!' Mavis snapped.

Mary walked reluctantly towards the door that Mrs Brown had just come though.

'And shut that behind you. I'm not having you listening in on this.'

When Mary had left the room, Mrs Brown clasped her hands and looked across the table at Bodkin.

'How was she? Was she lucid today?'

'She was, Mavis. She was fine. She's looking forward to going for a walk in the gardens.'

'She loves that garden. She really believes it belongs to her. She tells the groundsmen what she thinks they should plant, and where they should plant it, even though she wouldn't know a pansy from a foxglove.'

'Speaking of plants, Mrs Brown. Do you know what hemlock looks like?'

Mavis averted her eyes from Bodkin's fixed stare, then scratched her head and looked at her hands.

'No... why would I?'

Bodkin produced the much-creased photograph from his inside pocket.

'This is hemlock, Mrs Brown,' he pushed the photograph across the table towards her.

Mavis gave it a quick glance, then looked away again.

'It grows by the river, Mavis. There's colony after colony of it down there.'

'Is there? I wouldn't know.'

'Mrs Brown,' Bodkin said sternly. 'You have tried to lead us up the garden path on two occasions so far. Rest assured, you won't do it a third time. Did you collect hemlock from the riverbank?'

The cook began to scratch furiously at her scalp. Beads of sweat appeared on her forehead.

'You'd have done the same if it had been your daughter. She was ill, I trusted him... and he went and did that to her.' She looked at the detective through tear-filled eyes. 'She's fourteen... FOURTEEN!'

'Mavis, believe me when I tell you I have every sympathy, but you should have come to us. You cannot take the law into your own hands.'

'Who would have believed me? It was the vicar for pity's sake.'

'Vicars have been arrested before now, Mavis,' Bodkin replied.

'It wasn't just that. It was the shame. I wouldn't have been able to hold my head up in public. I couldn't bear the thought of what they'd be saying about poor Violet behind my back.'

'So, you decided to do away with him?'

'I didn't even know if it would work,' Mavis said, drying her eyes on her sleeve. 'It was all trial and error. There was an article in the local paper about hemlock a few months ago. Some kids had been poisoned when they were messing about with it over at the cement works. The article went into a fair bit of detail about how to avoid inadvertently digesting it and what it might do to you if you did. It looks just like parsley when you chop it up. Mind you, the smell was awful. It reminded me of the cellar of the last house we lived in. It was infested with mice.'

'So, what did you do to get around that?'

'I couldn't think of a way to begin with, it really stank the place out. So, I put the leaves on a shelf in the pantry while I tried to find out more about it. When I remembered it a few days later, it had dried out a fair bit and the smell had pretty much gone.'

'How did you go about harvesting it, Mavis? How much did you use?'

'I'd seen it when I was walking by the river with Violet. She used to love picking flowers and different kinds of leaves. I had to make sure she didn't pick any of that. I wore gloves when I went back to get some. I only snapped off a short stem. It had a few ferny-looking leaves on it. I hoped that would be enough to make him ill if nothing else.'

'So, your plan was merely to make him ill?'

'Not really, I wanted him de—'

'Be careful what you say, Mavis. Think clearly before you speak. You are admitting to having committed a serious offence.'

'Was it the hemlock that killed him? I wasn't sure it could have been when I heard the news that he was dead on the Sunday morning. It was a good thirty-six hours after he'd eaten it, you see, and I'd seen him over at Cavanagh's on the Saturday, so I didn't think it had worked.'

'How many times did you feed him hemlock, Mavis?'

'Twice. The first time was a couple of weeks before he died, then I gave him some more on Friday the twenty-fourth.'

'How did you prepare it?'

'I chopped the dried leaves up very finely and dropped them into the parsley sauce as it was simmering. I didn't use too much in case it tasted bad and he thought that something had gone off. The second time I tried a different approach and put the chopped leaves onto the sauce after it had finished cooking.'

'Did you notice if the poisoned food had any effect on him?'

'I didn't see anything, I assumed it would take a while to work. Mary saw him staggering across the road towards the sweet shop though. She thought he was drunk.'

Bodkin stood up wearily and asked Mavis to get to her feet.

'I'm really sorry to have to do this, Mavis but I really don't have any choice.' The detective blew out his cheeks and stepped around the table so that he was standing next to the trembling woman.

'Mavis Brown, I am arresting you for the attempted murder of Harold Villiers. You do not have to say anything unless you wish to do so, but what you do say may be given in evidence. Do you understand?'

Mavis nodded her head.

'I'm not sorry,' she said. 'I'd do it again, Mr Bodkin. She was only fourteen.'

CHAPTER FORTY-TWO

THERE WERE THIRTY OR SO MOURNERS STANDING AROUND THE GRAVE awaiting the bishop's final prayers. The cold, fine, but constant drizzle had been hanging around all morning as if waiting for the coffin to arrive at the graveside. Drips, or sometimes light streams of water fell from the brims of hats and trickled down the men's necks. Most women held black umbrellas aloft, which helped shield some of the hatless men from the worst of the drizzling rain.

The bishop, who had conducted the service himself in the church, used a white handkerchief to wipe away a misty film that had gathered on his forehead as he recited his final graveside prayer for the former vicar.

'We have entrusted this, our brother to God's mercy, and we now commit his body to the ground: earth to earth, ashes to ashes, dust to dust: in sure and certain hope of the resurrection to eternal life through our Lord Jesus Christ, who will transform our frail bodies that they may be conformed to his glorious body, who died, was buried, and rose again for us. To him be glory for ever. Amen.'

Peter Kissman, wearing a waterproof cape, leaned on his shovel as he stood, hidden from view behind a large, stone plinth, waiting for the service to end, hoping that the green tarpaulin he had used to cover the mound of earth at the grave-side, had kept out the worst of the weather.

Bishop Warrington, made the sign of the cross, then stepped away from the open grave. Reverend Daley, who had stood alongside the bishop for the graveside prayers, followed suit, leaving the mourners standing on the sodden grass at the side of the path.

Mr Rowlings moved forward to stand in the spot where the bishop had committed Villiers' body into the care of God, and offered up a silent prayer of his own, as Amy and her mother stood at his side with their heads bowed.

Back on the stone path, the bishop thanked Rowlings for his 'beautifully written eulogy' and asked if he would consider writing articles for the monthly, diocese magazine. Daley, hung around at the bishop's side, hands clasped in front as he looked around nervously.

Amy watched him closely. He had not taken any formal part in the funeral service itself, seemingly content to sit at the back of the church as the bishop led the mourners through the Christian ritual.

Caroline Gatting and Agatha Walker, stood close together sharing a single umbrella, both wore thin, black lace, half veils over their eyes, making it hard to read their emotions. Eugene Hales was absent, obviously reluctant to close the pharmacy for the morning. Amy noted there was no sign of Doctor Frazier or Mrs de Vere, either. The rest of the mourners' number were made up of representatives from the local council and the town's scouts and guides groups.

Mrs Rosegarden, the formidable Sunday School teacher had arrived at the funeral with her husband, a small framed man with a skinny neck that made his collar look like it was two sizes too big for him.

'What time is the food dished up?' he said aloud, obviously not caring who heard. 'Come on, you lot, let's get out of this bloody rain.'

Mrs Rosegarden mouthed her apologies to two elderly women who tutted at his remarks, then holding her umbrella over his head, took his arm and began to lead him away from the damp, increasingly restive crowd.

Mrs Gatting and her sister followed the Sunday School teacher back towards the church hall where the triangle-cut sandwiches and sponge cakes that she had prepared were sitting on covered plates on a long row of pushed together tables alongside a huge, steel, tea urn.

Mrs Rowlings took her husband's arm and fell into step with him as the last of the mourners turned their backs on the grave. Amy nodded to Peter as he stepped out from behind the angel-topped plinth, before turning back towards the church gates as she heard her name called out.

'Amy!'

'Bodkin? You missed the service,' Amy said as the detective hurried along the path towards her, trying to hold his unbuttoned mac together. Two burly-looking, uniformed officers followed him up the path.

'I arrested Mrs de Vere on fraud charges a couple of hours ago. She's admitted filtering money into her own bank account from the charity, but then she couldn't really do anything else, not after I showed her the evidence that the bank sent me this morning.'

'Has she said anything about the murder?'

'She's denying having anything to do with that, but she is hinting that Daley might be implicated. She repeated the blackmail allegations too.'

'Do you believe her?'

'She might be just trying to get back at him because she believes he left her in the lurch. She's a very devious woman. We'll see if she changes her tune after a night in the cells. Meanwhile I'm going to enjoy interrogating our new vicar. I can't wait to wipe that smug look off his face.'

'What about Mavis?'

'She's sticking to her story. She claims she only ever fed the hemlock to Mr Villiers. She denies having given him the arsenic or indeed, the strychnine.'

'And do you believe her?'

'She's more convincing than Mrs de Vere, that's for sure. But there are still one or two things that don't stack up. Her husband came to see her this morning. He's not as senile as he's been painted. He was very quick to reply when I sat him down in my office and asked him a few questions.'

'We never really got to talk to him, did we?'

'He claims to know nothing about what his wife was up to. He could be telling the truth, but... well, time will tell. He's coming in again tomorrow for a longer chat. The cells are filling up fast, so I hope he is just as convincing then.'

'Are you here to arrest Reverend Daley?' Amy asked.

'Let's just say we're going to invite him to come to the station for a chat,' Bodkin replied. 'A long chat.'

Bodkin looked towards the church as Daley's terrified face

appeared around the corner of the building. He jerked his head back as he saw the detective beckon towards him.

'Go get him, lads,' Bodkin said, motioning the two policemen to come forward. 'Don't get too rough. He's not been charged with anything yet.'

As the two uniformed officers marched up the stone path towards the church, Amy pushed away a stray strand of hair from her face, then lowered her umbrella and pressed the button on the handle to collapse it.

'Bodkin? Did Doctor Fuller give you a contact number yesterday?'

Bodkin fished into his pocket for his wallet, then pulled a white card out of it.

'She did, why do you ask?'

'I thought I'd go to see Violet tomorrow. I promised I'd walk in her garden with her and I'd like to ask Doctor Fuller if that would be all right. I mean, the poor girl won't be getting a visit from her mother any time soon.'

'Her father didn't mention paying her a visit either.' Bodkin handed the card to Amy and flashed her a quick smile. 'I think that's a very kind and thoughtful thing to do. She obviously liked you. I'm sure it will do her the world of good.' He patted Amy's hand. 'It's very Christian of you.'

'Oh, it's nothing to do with Christianity, Bodkin. I just feel so sorry for the poor girl. I might make it a regular thing. It wouldn't hurt me to nip over to see her after church every other Sunday.'

'Just be careful she doesn't become too reliant on you, Amy. She's a very complicated young lady. Doctor Fuller told me her mood can flip from almost beatific calmness to a raging storm within a few seconds. Just don't let her get near anything sharp while you're in the gardens tomorrow.'

'Tomorrow will be the last chance I get to do anything this week. I'm back at the Mill on Thursday. The maintenance work is almost finished.'

Their conversation was cut short as they saw the two policemen march around the corner of the church with Mr Daley propped up between them.

'You're making a big mistake, Bodkin,' he said as he was marched past the detective and on to the waiting police car.

'I'd better go,' Bodkin said, pulling up his collar as the rain began to fall again. 'What have you got planned for the rest of the day?'

'I'm going with Mum and Dad to the reading of Mr Villiers' will. I don't think Godfrey Wilson will allow me to sit in, but I'd like to be there all he same.'

'Are we still on for a drink at the Old Bull tomorrow night?'

'That sounds nice. It will be a pleasant end to my week off. I'll have to be careful with how much I drink though. I'm getting used to having an extra hour in bed in the mornings.'

Godfrey Wilson was a late thirties gentleman with old fashioned good looks. He stood a little under six feet, with neatly parted, brown hair and a thin moustache. His keen, bright blue eyes wrinkled in the corners as he treated the Rowlings to a welcoming smile. He was wearing what Alice always called his 'Gangster outfit' – a navy pin-striped, double-breasted suit and tan coloured shoes.

'Hello, Amy, it's lovely to see you again,' he said. 'Alice said you might come along today.'

Amy took his hand and shook it.

'Hello, Godfrey. I hope you've got some good news for my dad.'

'AMY!' Mr Rowlings gave her a horrified look.

Godfrey laughed. 'He'll find out in a moment or two... sadly, you'll have to wait a little longer, Amy. You're not allowed in to hear the formal reading.' He offered his hand toward his office door. 'Mr Rowlings, if you'll come with me.'

Amy and her mother sat in the office while a bored-looking secretary filed away at her nails at the reception desk. Whatever Villiers had written into his will didn't take long to read because Mr Rowlings was shown back through the door only five minutes later.

'Well, that didn't take long, did it?' Godfrey said as he flashed Amy a smile.

'Was it good news, Dad?' Amy asked impatiently.

'I'll tell you outside,' Mr Rowlings replied, taking hold of his wife's hand.

'Oh, before you go, Amy, could I have a quick word?' Godfrey said as Amy turned to follow her parents out of the door.

The solicitor led her into his book lined office and offered her a seat at his highly polished, antique desk.

'Amy, this is a little delicate, but... we are having trouble locating someone mentioned in the Reverend Villiers' will. She's a young lady who goes by the name of Sadie Crabtree. She has been left quite a large sum, but as yet, I haven't been able to find her.' Godfrey hesitated, then went on. 'She's a... ahem... a prostitute by all accounts, but that's all I know about her. I did approach a couple of the ladies who patrol the streets after dark, but I think they thought I was with the police because I couldn't get anything out of them. I was reluctant to mention the money as I couldn't be sure who they'd pass the information on to, there are some rather shady characters involved in that industry.'

'How can I help?'

'Oh, I wasn't asking you to get involved, I just wondered if you knew anything about her or her family. It's a long shot, I know. I've already asked Alice.'

'I've never heard that name before,' Amy replied. 'I can ask around though, make a few low-key enquiries.'

'Oh, don't put yourself out, Amy. I just wondered if you knew anything about her, that's all.'

Amy pulled a card out of her bag and handed it to Godfrey.

'ARIA Investigations. Agent. Amy Rowlings. I love the pink card, Amy. Alice did mention that you had a new side-line.'

'Police accredited,' Amy said proudly as she pointed out the line on the card.

'So I see,' Godfrey lifted the lid of a card index and slipped Amy's card inside. 'I know where to come if I ever need a private investigator. We do use them now and again. I may have to use one to find Sadie, but I wouldn't ask you to get involved in anything murky like this.'

'Oh, I don't mind a bit of murk,' Amy replied.

'I wouldn't want you to be placed in harm's way, my dear. Believe me, there's murky and there's another level of murky. I would hate to think of you mixing with people like that. It could be quite dangerous, some of the men... Well, I'll leave it there. Thanks for listening and, if I am ever in need of your services, I'll be in touch. Was that Alice's number I saw on the back of the card?'

'Two hundred and fifty pounds! Wow, Dad. That's wonderful news. What are you going to spend it on?'

'I'm not going to spend it, Amy. I was going to donate it to charity, but your mother has dissuaded me from taking that course.'

Amy looked up the Gillingham Road as a green bus turned the corner about a hundred yards along. She stuck her hand out to alert the driver.

'So, does this mean you might think about getting a telephone?'

'It does not, young lady. I'm going to put it away for our retirement. It's a year and a half's wages. It will top up our old aged pensions. We won't have to worry about penury now.'

'But, Dad...'

Rowling stood back to allow the women to get on the bus before climbing onboard himself.

'Aren't you even going to have a holiday out of it?' Amy asked when they were all seated.

'We'll have our summer holiday at Margate, as usual,' Mr Rowlings replied.

Amy shook her head, sadly. 'I was hoping for Blackpool at least.'

Amy sat back in her seat and was silent for the rest of the journey as she thought about what Godfrey had just told her.

What a wonderful opportunity to prove myself. It would be the perfect, first, solo case for ARIA, she thought.

By the time they got off the bus at the Old Bull she had formulated a plan.

CHAPTER
FORTY-THREE

'I'M JUST GOING TO MAKE A QUICK PHONE CALL; I'LL SEE YOU BACK AT home.'

'Amy, Alice lives just along the lane. Have a walk down for a chat and save your money. You're obsessed with those infernal machines,' Mr Rowlings replied, shaking his head.

Amy opened the eight-pane door of the red telephone kiosk and stuck her head around the side of it.

'I'm not calling Alice as it happens. I'll tell you all about it at home.'

She pulled Doctor Fuller's card from her bag, then fished around in her purse for two brass pennies.

'Hello, Hanover House, Doctor Fuller speaking.'

'Hello, Doctor, this is Amy Rowlings, we met yesterday. I came to see Violet Brown with Inspector Bodkin.'

'Yes, I remember.'

'Ah, good... the thing is, Violet invited me to visit her, to take a walk around the gardens and I was wondering if you thought it would be all right if I called around tomorrow.'

'I think that's a great idea. Violet gets so few visitors and she seemed to really like you.'

'I really liked her too. What time would be convenient?'

'Make it around eleven. I hope the weather is better than it's been so far today though, or you'll have to bring your wellington boots with you.'

'Thank you, Doctor Fuller. I'm usually at work in the week but I'm off tomorrow. If it goes well, do you think I could make it a regular thing. Like every other Sunday or something?'

'You really are a very kind young lady, Miss Rowlings. I'm sure Violet will be delighted to see you.'

'Hanover House? Why on earth are you visiting Hanover House again?' Mrs Rowlings asked.

'I'm going to see young Violet. She's only a child and now that her mother's been arrested she won't get any visitors at all.'

'Oh dear, the poor girl, that is sad,' her mother replied.

'Well, I'm proud of you, Amy. I think it's a very charitable and Christian thing you're doing,' Mr Rowlings added.

'Of course, if we had our own telephone, you'd have known all about it without me having to explain,' Amy said with a sly smile.

'Will we never hear the last of this? You know my answer, Amy. My mind hasn't changed since you mentioned it last. However, I am prepared to share my good fortune with you. How would you like a ten-pound donation towards this radi-ogram thing you've got your heart set on?'

'REALLY!'

'Yes, really. Would that mean you have enough money to purchase the equipment?'

'No, I'd still be six or seven pounds short, but ten pounds would mean I'm much closer to my target.' She threw her arms around her father's neck. 'Thank you so much, Dad.'

'I'm a little disappointed now, I thought that might give you enough to buy one. You're only looking at second hand machines, aren't you?'

'Yes, but the model I want is thirty-three to thirty-five pounds. I can get a cheaper one for about thirty but I've got my heart set on the HMV 540. Uncle Maurice said it sounds really fantastic and they're all electric so I won't have to wind up the handle to play my records like I do now... oh, there's a radio built into it as well.'

'This... fantastic sound... will it be louder than the one you have now?' Mrs Rowlings asked.

'Oh yes! Much louder,' Amy replied.

'Oh dear,' said her mother.

At eight o'clock, Amy got herself dressed, ready to embark on her mission. Not wanting to be too obtrusive, she wore a grey, calf length pleated skirt, a navy knitted jumper and a pair of black, flat shoes. Pulling on her navy raincoat with the tie up belt, she studied herself in the mirror. Not quite happy with what she saw, she added a dark grey beret.

'I'm just nipping out, I won't be long,' she called as she hurried along the hallway.

By the time her mother opened the living room door to ask her where she was going at this time of night, she was gone.

Amy had timed her run perfectly and the long, green, single decker bus had already turned around at the terminus and was waiting at the bus stop as she approached. Thirty seconds after she climbed aboard, it pulled away.

Spinton station was built in 1868 by the South Eastern Railway company, its facia was re-covered using a sandstone veneer cladding in 1910. It boasted a fast line to London with only one stop at Gillingham.

The street outside the station was dimly lit with only one, working street light. Amy got off the bus at the stop outside the station entrance and stood for a moment in the main arch as she looked out into the damp night.

Underneath the single street light was a group of three woman. As a pair of men walked by on the opposite side of the road heading for the Dragon public house, they began to shout to attract their attention. One of the women opened her coat, then lifted up her skirt to reveal a stocking top to show the men what they were missing.

'Maybe on the way home, Ruby,' one of the men called back.

Amy waited until the men had gone into the pub before summoning up every bit of courage she could muster, and approached the women.

They were all in their mid-thirties and heavily made up. The woman called Ruby was the first to notice her.

'If you think you're going to make any money dressed like that, love, you'd better think again,' she said.

'Oh... I'm not here to... I mean I'm not a pr... I'm looking for someone,' Amy replied.

'Aren't we all, love,' said the taller of the women. The other two laughed at her remark.

'Good one, Fran,' said Ruby.

'I'm looking for a particular person,' Amy tried again. 'A young girl called Sadie. Do you know her?'

'Who wants to know, that's my first question,' said Fran,

giving Amy the once over. 'Are you another one of those Corporation do-gooders?'

'She's dressed like a do-gooder,' the third woman agreed.

'I'm not a do-gooder, I just want to find Sadie,' Amy said.

'What do you want her for? That's the second question, and I notice you still haven't answered my first one,' Fran said, as she narrowed her eyes at Amy.

'Maybe she wants a bit of company,' said the shorter woman, again getting a laugh.

Fran leaned forward and peered into Amy's face.

'Is it like Jen said, are you looking for company? It's still five bob, woman or man, it makes no difference.'

Amy fished about in her bag and brought out one of her pink cards.

'I'm Amy Rowlings, I'm with ARIA Investigations,' she said, holding out her card to Ruby.

'ARIA Investigations, eh? Well, Amy Rowlings, what do you want with our Sadie?'

'I'm afraid I can't tell you that, it's a personal matter,' Amy replied.

'She does want a bit of company then,' said Jen.

'All I can say, is that it's to her benefit,' Amy said, carefully.

'Has she come into some money then?' Ruby asked.

'I honestly can't say,' Amy replied. 'I'd love to tell you, honestly, but I promised I wouldn't. The person I'm working for said that I'm not allowed to.'

'Well, Amy. If you can't tell us what you want her for, we can't tell you where you might find her,' said Fran, turning her eyes back to the street where a man on a bicycle had slowed right down.

'Hello, handsome,' Fran said. 'Are you looking for business?'

'I'm not paying for an old boiler like you,' the man said. His eyes settled on Amy. 'I'd fork out a few bob for that one though.'

Fran threw him a scowl. 'You can't afford that one.'

The man propped his bike up against the wall and gave Amy the once over. 'I'd go to seven and six for a go at that.'

Amy stepped back with a look of abject terror on her face. 'I'm not a p... I'm just looking for someone.'

The man reached into his pocket and pulled out a handful of change. 'And you've found him, darlin. Come on, where do you ply your trade? Do you have a place or are we using the alley?'

He pointed to a narrow gap between the wall at the end of the station and a row of old terraced houses.

Amy shook her head and tried to hide behind Ruby as the man stepped towards her with a leer on his face.

'Please,' Amy said. 'Please don't.'

'Leave her alone,' Fran suddenly said.

'Bugger off you,' the man replied, reaching out a hand towards Amy. 'Come on, darlin, stop playing hard to get.'

'She said, leave her alone.' Ruby produced a sharp kitchen knife from inside her coat and pointed it at the man.

'All right, all right. No need to get like that. I was only asking.' He turned away from Ruby's baleful stare and swung his leg over his bike. 'What's she doing out here if she doesn't want business, anyway?'

'Thank you so much,' Amy said when the man had ridden away. She looked up and down the street nervously in case any more men were in the vicinity.

'You'd better get yourself back home or back to your church hall or wherever it is you've come from,' Fran said. 'It's not safe for the likes of you around here.'

Amy bit her lip, then stepped out from behind Ruby. 'I can't go home. Not until I've found Sadie.'

'She's got some guts, I'll give her that,' Jen said, tipping her head to the side as she looked at Amy. 'She's got some guts.'

'Listen, sweetheart,' Ruby said. 'I could tell you where Sadie is, but I don't do anything for nothing you see?'

'How much do you want?' Amy asked quietly.

'I'm out of ciggies. Nip over to the kiosk and buy us a packet of Craven A and I might just remember where I last saw her.'

Amy hurried across to the station kiosk and asked the vendor for a packet of Craven A cigarettes, handing over the shilling he requested in payment. When she returned to the street. She passed the packet of twenty to Ruby who tore it open, stuck one in her mouth and lit it with silver coloured Ronson lighter.

'Ah, that's better. I've been gagging for that for over an hour,' she said, offering the cigarettes around.

'I don't, thank you,' said Amy as the packet was offered to her.

'She's a right goody two shoes, isn't she?' said Jen.

'She's all right is Amy,' said Ruby, blowing a thick stream of smoke into the air. 'Now, fair's fair. If you go down Shunters Row here...' she pointed along the narrow alley that ran alongside the first terraced house, '... last door on the right, number twelve.'

'Thank you, Ruby,' Amy said, taking a step towards the alley. She came to a sudden halt when Ruby grabbed hold of the collar of her coat.

'You'll have to wait for a few minutes, yet. She's... entertaining someone. If you know what I mean.' Ruby winked and let go of Amy's coat.

'Oh... I see,' Amy said as she felt herself blush.

Just two minutes later, a man walked calmly out of the alleyway fastening his thick coat.

'Evenin', he said, nodding to the women.

'Off you go then,' said Ruby giving Amy a push. 'Don't knock, just walk straight in.'

Amy walked slowly down the alley, looking nervously at the doors on the right-hand side as she passed them. When she reached the last door, she ignored Ruby's advice and knocked gently on it.

When there was no reply, she knocked again, this time a little bit harder. When there was no response to that, Amy twisted the brass knob, pushed open the door and stepped inside.

She found herself in a dingy room with damp patches showing through the dirty wallpaper.

On the right-hand side sat a gas cooker and a sink, beyond that was a cupboard with a missing door. A couple of tins of soup sat on its only shelf. On the left was a single, unmade bed and at the side of that, a young girl stood, fastening up the buttons of her blouse.

The girl was no more than fifteen. Her fair hair hung loose around her shoulders, her pretty face was red around the eyes as though she had been crying. She looked up as she heard Amy cough.

'I don't do women,' she said as she fastened the top button of her blouse.

'I'm not... I don't want anything like that, Sadie,' Amy replied, pulling the card out of her pocket and holding it towards the girl.

'I'm Amy Rowlings and I'm working on behalf of Godfrey Wilson. He's a solicitor and—'

'Are you with the police?' Sadie reached towards a small

table on which sat two plates, some cutlery and a short, sharp knife.

'I'm not with the police. I'm here because of the Reverend Villiers.'

'The vicar? What about him?'

'He's dead, Sadie, and—'

'I know he's dead. I heard the news.' A sad look came over her face. 'He was a nice man. He looked after Ginny and me.'

'He still wants to look after you, Sadie. He left you some money in his will. Quite a lot of money.'

'He did what? Are you sure you've got the right person?'

Amy smiled. 'I'm sure. He wanted to look after you when he'd gone.'

'You're not messing me about?'

'No, I wouldn't do that, Sadie. I'm trying to help. The solicitor got nowhere when he was trying to find you.'

'The girls out there look after me. I bet they thought he was the police.'

'Don't let them send him away the next time he comes. There's money waiting for you.'

'How much?'

'I honestly don't know, Sadie, but my dad got two hundred and fifty pounds and he was the only other person mentioned in the will. He didn't have any relatives you see. All I know is, you are the main beneficiary, so it's going to be a lot more than two hundred and fifty.'

'Really? You're honestly not making this up?'

'I wouldn't. It's true, Sadie. It's the only reason I risked coming over here tonight.'

'You've got some guts; I'll give you that.'

'I've never been so scared in my life. There was a man, he...'

Sadie pulled a face. 'They're swine, the lot of them.'

She walked across to the cooker, picked up the kettle and shook it. 'Cuppa?' she said. 'About time I had a tea break.'

Amy nodded.

'Sit down on the bed, I'll make us a brew, the milk should be all right, I only bought it yesterday.'

As Amy sat down, she heard a door open behind her, she turned to find herself facing a fair-haired girl of about ten years of age.

'Ginny,' Sadie said as she put two tea bags into a pot. 'This is Amy Rowlings and she's come to help us get out of this dump.'

CHAPTER
FORTY-FOUR

SADIE RINSED AND DRIED TWO MUGS, THEN POURED TEA INTO THEM from an off-white pot. After eyeing up the contents of a half-full milk bottle she poured a splash of milk into Amy's cup but put none in her own.

'I have to save some for Ginny's breakfast,' she said.

'I could have done without,' Amy said, feeling guilty.

'You're a guest, so you get to have milk,' Sadie replied with a grin.

Amy looked around the dirty room almost expecting to see a rat or a cockroach under the table.

'How long have you lived here? Where are you parents?'

'Mum died two years ago. Dad cleared off when I was eight,' she said, matter-of-factly.

'So you've been on your own since then? Didn't the authorities step in to help?'

'We didn't tell them. They'd have farmed us out to some orphanage or other. They might even have split us up. I wasn't having that.'

'But how have you managed?' Amy asked.

Sadie pointed to the bed. 'I had no choice. I was still thirteen, I couldn't get a job anywhere that paid anything more than a pittance.'

'But what about school?'

'I left at Christmas. Ginny still goes. It's a struggle, but we manage. She's been really good, not letting on about our circumstances at school. They know I've been looking after her since Mum got ill, we just didn't tell them she'd died.' She looked across and smiled at her sister. 'Ginny's really clever. She'll pass her National Certificate easily when she takes it.'

Amy's face dropped. 'So you've been doing... this since you were thirteen? Oh, Sadie.'

'Someone has to look after Ginny. It's been my job since Mum died.'

Amy shook her head sadly. 'I'm so sorry, Sadie.'

'Why? It's not your fault is it? Look, I'll be honest, it's not something I enjoy doing and I only do it when we are desperate for the money. Men like young girls, they pay a bit extra, especially if you pull a school uniform on for them.'

'That man who just left was he...?'

'Jake? No, he's not one of the strange ones, he just wants straightforward sex.'

'What about the vicar? Did he want...? Amy tailed off, unable to ask the question.

'Oh, he didn't come around here for that? Is that what you thought?'

'There were rumours about him,' Amy said.

'He used to give me money towards the rent and food, but he never asked for anything back in return. We used to pray, the three of us. Didn't we, Ginny?'

'Pray, he gave you money then you'd pray?' Amy laughed. 'Oh that's so wonderful. He's been getting such a bad name.'

'He should be sainted,' Sadie said. 'We'd have been thrown out of here by now if it hadn't been for him. He really did his best for us. We always mention him in our prayers, don't we, Ginny?'

Amy looked heavenwards. 'I'll say a special prayer for him tonight.'

'So, what were you saying about this Godfrey chap?'

'Oh yes. I'm going to give him your address. He'll be over to see you very soon, hopefully tomorrow. You won't be in this place much longer, Sadie. You've got more than enough money to buy a little house somewhere nice now. He'll help you do that. He looks after my friend Alice's business interests. She's got a farm over on Long Lane. That's where I live too... Long Lane, not on her farm, though my dad says I might as well move in, the amount of time I spend down there.'

'How will I know it's him when he calls?' Sadie asked. 'There's some rum so and so's around here. The girls have protected me from them so far, but they can't do that forever. Before long one of them will get their claws into me.'

'You don't have to do this anymore. Not after tonight.' Amy reached for her bag. 'Have you got money for food? I haven't got much but I can let you have half a crown or so.'

'Jake just paid me three bob, so I've got enough for food until the weekend.'

'That's good. Right, Godfrey is a tall man, he dresses like a gangster, you know, a pin striped suit and black hat? He drives a gangster type car too, like Jimmy Cagney does in the movies. Mostly though, you'll know it's him when he speaks. He's very posh.'

'He's definitely not going to put Ginny in an orphanage?'

'No, he's a lovely man. He'll help you as much as he can. I'll help too if you need me. I'll leave you my card so you can get in touch. To be honest,' Amy looked around in disgust, 'I wouldn't mind betting this is the last night you'll spend in this place. Tomorrow night you might find yourselves in a nice little hotel.'

Tears suddenly filled Sadie's eyes. 'Did you hear that, Ginny, a hotel. Mr Villiers always did say he'd get us out of here.'

Amy finished her tea and put the empty mug on the rickety table.

'You have no idea how relieved I am to hear about Mr Villiers,' she said. 'My father will be overjoyed when he finds out. Mind you, he'll be less pleased when he finds out I've been over here.'

'You're so lucky to have parents who love you,' Ginny said quietly. 'I miss Mum.'

'Oh, Ginny.' Amy hurried across the room and took the child in her arms.

'She's looking down on you, don't worry. She'll always be looking out for you wherever you go.'

'I wish she could have stopped those men,' she said.

'Which men, Ginny?' Amy asked.

Ginny shook her head and went silent. Sadie put her cup on the table and stepped across to her sister.

'There are a lot of nasty men out there, Amy, but there are two that are particularly vile. They have been coming here for about three months, mostly on a Friday night but sometimes on a Saturday. Posh sounding men, they like me to dress up in my old school clothes and have me together. They're very rough. I always end up battered and bruised by the end of it. They do pay a bit more for their fun but... well, what could I do? They got more and more demanding as the weeks went on. They wanted me to find them another young girl to join us. I wasn't going to put anyone else though that, so I just kept saying I couldn't find anyone.'

She put her hand on her sister's head and gently stroked her hair. 'Anyway, this one night, the last time they were here, Ginny had a bad dream and walked in from the back room while they were still at it. Blimey! You've seen nothing like it. Their eyes lit up like all their Christmases had come at once. They told me that they wanted Ginny to join in. I told them, I wasn't going to allow that to happen, then one of them... the fat one with the moustache, slapped me around a bit, trying to get me to agree. When I still wouldn't the other one made a grab for her.'

'Oh my goodness. That must have been terrifying.'

'The vicar saved us both that night. I went for my little knife but the fat one pulled me back onto the bed and held me there while the other one went for Ginny. She tried to get back into the little room but he was quick for an old bloke and he got her. We were both screaming but we weren't expecting anyone to come to help. Then the vicar walked in.'

'Did that stop them?'

'Oh yes, he put the fear of God into them. He told them they were heading straight for the gates of hell. He got hold of their clothes and threw them towards the door and told them to get out. Thankfully, they did.'

'What happened then?'

'They got dressed by the door, they'd got a bit more confidence back by then. One of them said, "wait until the congregation find out where you go at the weekend." The vicar didn't care. He said, "it will be your reputations that suffer, not mine." Then he ordered them out. We tidied up as best we could, then we prayed for a while. He left about half an hour afterwards after giving me a ten-shilling note.'

'You see,' Amy said, taking Ginny's hand. 'Your mum was looking out for you. She sent the vicar to help.'

Ginny nodded silently and gave Amy a weak smile.

'Have you any idea who these men were?' Amy asked.

'No idea. They called each other Your Highness when they were here. "After you, your Highness", they'd say.'

Amy scowled.

'I wonder if the vicar knew who they were?'

'I don't know, he didn't follow them to the Dragon, not that night at least.'

'The Dragon?'

'Yes, it's a pub over the road from the station. Some nights when they were getting dressed, they'd talk about going in there for a nightcap.'

Amy checked her watch then got to her feet.

'I've got to go now, but I'll see you again before long. You've got my card if you need to talk to me.' She picked up her bag and headed for the door. 'Lock the door behind me and don't open it to anyone else tonight. You don't need to do this any longer. Just watch out for Godfrey tomorrow. I'll call him in the morning and ask him to get over here as soon as he can. Meanwhile, if you've got a suitcase. Pack it.'

Only Ruby and Jen were left standing under the lamp post as Amy walked out of the alleyway.

'You took your time,' Ruby said with a grin.

'Can you watch out for her, please, just for tonight?' Amy said. 'Don't let anyone else go in. She's having a night off.'

'Nice if you can afford to,' Jen said.

'Tomorrow, there'll be a posh sounding man looking for her. His name is Godfrey Wilson. He's going to be looking after her from now on. He'll probably take her and Ginny away tomorrow but don't be alarmed, they'll be well looked after until he can find them somewhere nice to live.'

'She has fallen on her feet then?' Ruby said with a smile. 'Good, if anyone deserves a bit of luck it's that girl.' She patted Amy on the shoulder. 'Don't you worry about her tonight. We'll look after her. There will always be at least one of us on watch.'

Amy leaned forward and gave her a peck on the cheek.

'Thank you so much. I'll sleep tonight, now.'

The Dragon was an old pub, one of the oldest in the town, it was also one of the busiest, even on a Tuesday night. When Amy pushed the door open and stepped inside, the thick smoke hit the back of her throat immediately. A group of four men were just finishing a game of darts, the final thrower having just hit a sixteen followed by a double eight. A bearded man sent a cloud of pale-yellow chalk dust into the air as he wiped the scores away with a board rubber.

Amy turned towards the bar as two of the darts players spotted her.

Wolf whistles suddenly echoed around the pub as thirty or more male faces turned towards her.

'OUT!' A man wearing a dirty, damp looking apron, yelled from behind the bar.

Amy stood her ground.

'I'm looking for someone,' she said.

'That'll be me then,' said a swarthy looking man as he blew a kiss towards her.

'I said, OUT!' the barman said. 'You'll lose me my licence. Women aren't allowed in pubs unaccompanied.'

'Never mind your licence, Judd,' a tall, skinny man said as he threw Amy a lecherous look. 'We can always find another landlord; we'll not find anything as nice as her in here any time soon. Anyway, she's not unaccompanied, she's with me, aren't you, darlin?'

By now the darts throwers had moved across from the board and were standing between Amy and the door.

'I saw her first,' the bearded man said.

'I'm looking for Joe Proudfoot. Is he here?' Amy said, panic beginning to well up inside her.

As if he had heard his name called, Joe walked into the bar, drying his hands on his shirt.

'Amy? What the hell are you doing here?'

'I came to see you, Joe,' she replied to a chorus of shouts.

'You lucky old swine, Joe.'

'Let me know when you've done, I'm next in line.'

Joe walked between the tables, easing men out of his way as he went. When he reached Amy, he put his arm around her shoulder and led her out of the pub to a round of loud boos. When they were safely on the pavement, Joe took his arm from around her, then pulled a hand rolled cigarette from his pocket and lit it with a match.

'Amy, what on earth are you doing? Apart from it being illegal for a woman to be in a pub on her own, you couldn't have picked a worse bar to have done it in.'

'That's a stupid law. Men go in on their own. Why is it illegal anyway? I go in the Old Bull with Alice, there are lots of women there.'

'That's because it's the snug and you're not on your own. It's not allowed in the main bar, Amy. Honestly, ask that Bodkin of yours.'

'I'm sorry, I didn't know, I just needed to ask you something,' Amy said.

'What question is so urgent that you have to come all the way across town to ask it?' Joe asked.

'You're in here most nights, aren't you, Joe? Every Friday and Saturday anyway.'

Joe nodded.

'Can you remember seeing a couple of old men in here? They were posh sounding; one was fat and had a moustache. It would have definitely been a Friday or a Saturday.'

Joe thought as he took a pull on his cigarette.

'The Major started drinking in here a while back. Do you mean him? Why do you want to know?'

'The Major, who's the Major?' Amy asked urgently.

'The chap who's always boasting about his Victoria Cross, though I'm not convinced he ever won one. He came in with that pharmacist chap, Hales, is it?'

Amy took hold of Joe's head with both hands and planted a kiss on his forehead.

The gardener laughed.

'You look like you just lost a penny and found a florin.'

Amy pushed away a strand of loose hair and grinned at her father's friend.

'Joe, I think I might have just cracked a murder case, wide open.'

CHAPTER
FORTY-FIVE

'Where are you going now that you've solved your murder?' Joe asked.

'Home, no, wait. I've got to tell Bodkin.'

'So, you're going to the police station?'

Amy checked her watch.

'No, he'll be home by now. He lives near the police station though.'

'Right, I'll walk you to the bus stop then, Amy. It really isn't safe for you around here.'

Amy fell in step with Joe and they walked up Station Road towards the bus terminus.

'Are you all right, Amy?' a woman's voice shouted from across the road. 'Is he bothering you?'

Joe looked at Amy, then at Ruby, who was standing on the edge of the pavement on the opposite side of the road.

'I'm fine thank you, Ruby, this is my father's friend, Joe, he's just walking me to the bus stop.'

'Make sure that's all you do too,' Fran shouted.

'Night, Amy, thanks for the ciggies,' yelled Jen.

Joe raised his eyebrows in puzzlement.

'What... how do...?'

'They're friends of mine,' said Amy as she waved goodnight to the girls.

The bus was already at the stop with its engine running, when they arrived.

'Joe, do me a big favour. Please don't tell Dad anything about tonight.'

Joe blew out his cheeks, then let the air escape, slowly.

'Mum's the word,' he said.

'Bodkin! Bodkin!' Amy screamed as she repeatedly pressed the buzzer. When there was no sign of the detective after thirty seconds, she began to hammer on the door. 'Bodkin!'

A few seconds later the door to flat two opened and a bare-footed Trixie, holding her dressing gown together at the front, stepped into the hall. She glared at Amy from the other side of the glass.

Amy waited for her to open the door, when she didn't, she began to hammer on it, before hitting the buzzer again.

'BODKIN!'

Shaking her head, a clearly exasperated Trixie opened the front door. Amy tried to barge past but the blonde was too quick and half closed the door, propping it open with her foot.

'I need to speak to Bodkin, it's urgent,' Amy said, angrily.

'Everything is urgent to you, isn't it?' Trixie jeered. 'It's not very ladylike is it ranting away the way you do? No wonder Bodkin steers clear. Don't think I didn't hear you yelling at him the other night.'

Amy tried to remain calm, but failed.

'Just let me...IN!' she screamed as she launched herself at the door.

Trixie pushed her shoulder against the other side of the glass and easily repelled her attack.

'Ask nicely,' she said, grinning at Amy.

Amy took a deep breath, then opening her mouth as if she was going to speak, she suddenly stamped her foot down on Trixie's bare foot. As the blonde hopped backwards, holding her foot, Amy stepped neatly through the gap before the door could close.

'What the...?'

Bodkin appeared at the top of his stairs. Thin swirls of steam followed him out of the bathroom door. His hair was dripping, water trickled down his chest and onto his blue trousers. His wet, bare feet slipped on the tiles as he tried to walk to the banister rail.

'Amy?'

Trixie hopped to the bottom of the stairs and lifted her foot.

'She attacked me, she's mad. I told you she was mad.'

Amy brushed past Trixie and climbed the first two steps.

'Bodkin. I've cracked it. It was FEAR!'

'Fear?' a puzzled look came across Bodkin's face.

'I told you she was crackers,' said Trixie, doubling over and trying to blow cool air onto her reddening foot.

'Amy. Come up. I have no idea what you're talking about.'

Bodkin lifted his towel and began to rub at his wet hair, he walked to his flat, leaving the door open for her.

'Now then,' he said as he grabbed a creased shirt and pulled it on.

'Fear,' Amy said again. 'Poirot's fourth motive in End House.'

'Okay,' Bodkin said. 'Who fears who?'

'Whom.'

Bodkin sighed. 'All right, who fears whom?'

'The killers. They were scared of what the vicar knew.'

'This looks like being a long story,' Bodkin said. 'Please, sit down, Amy, I'll put the kettle on while you tell me all about it.'

'So, you see, it must be Eugene Hales and Doctor Frasier, Bodkin. We didn't have the motive before but now we do. They were scared of Villiers spilling the beans about what they'd been up to. They had the means... well, Hales did; he was surrounded by arsenic and strychnine in his shop. What if he tampered with Villiers' paper wraps? What if he opened the stapled-up bag and doctored the powders? When that didn't kill him, what if he then sprinkled strychnine onto the vicar's sweets when he found them in the church hall?'

'It's a good theory, probably the best we've got yet.' He crashed his right fist into his left palm. 'Damn. If only we had those fingerprint samples.'

'It all makes sense, Bodkin, if we were at Wimbledon, the umpire would be shouting, game, set and match. There were two of them in on it which would have made it easy to move him to the lychgate seat.'

'Yes, it would, but why would they do that? And what about the bible reference that was chalked onto the floor? You'd have to really know something about the good book to be able to quote those particular two verses. Your father knows the bible backwards but even he had to look them up. I'm not sure either of them has ever picked a bible up in their lives.'

'Maybe that wasn't them. What if Mrs Rosegarden did that

when she found the body. She never really liked Villiers. She was always quoting the bible at him with regards to his drinking.'

'Again, it's possible, Amy.'

Bodkin rubbed his stubble covered chin. 'I was about to shave when you arrived,' he said.

'Never mind your chin, what about that pair? Are you going to arrest them tonight?'

'Tonight? No, not tonight, Amy, I need to give this a bit of thought and we know where they'll be in the morning anyway. Hales will be opening his shop and Frazier will be in bed until at least ten. They have no idea we're on to them. They've got no reason to run.'

He put up a hand to stop Amy's protest.

'Besides which. We don't have an empty cell to put them in.'

Twenty minutes later, Bodkin and Amy walked down the stairs, side by side. On hearing their footsteps, Trixie rushed out of her flat to confront them.

'Bodkin. I want you to arrest this... this... MANIAC, for assault.' She lifted her foot again and pointed to it.

'This is grievous bodily harm at bare minimum.'

'I don't think you want to pursue that, Trixie. You were obstructing a murder inquiry... and for the second time. Miss Rowlings has just delivered evidence that could lead to the arrest of Reverend Villiers' murderer.'

'I don't care if she's just brought evidence about an attack on the king,' Trixie said. 'First thing tomorrow, I'm putting in a complaint and I demand that you act on it.'

'Trixie, Trixie,' Bodkin said, soothingly. 'If I have to charge Miss Rowlings with assault, I'd have to charge you with theft.'

'Theft?'

'The typewriter you practice on every night, went missing from the typing pool a week or so after you arrived here. You wouldn't want me to bring that up, would you? It wouldn't only be a court appearance; you'd also lose your job.'

'That's my own typewriter, I brought it with me, just because it's the same model as the ones they use at work it doesn't mean—'

'It has a stamp on the back that says, PROPERTY OF SPINTON POLICE, Trixie,' Bodkin said quietly.

Trixie's mouth opened and closed a few times, then, turning away, she stormed back to her flat. As she reached the open door, she spun around and pointed a warning finger at Amy.

'You haven't won yet,' she spat.

'Maybe not,' Amy muttered to herself. 'But the score is two-nil to me, as things stand, and you just scored a spectacular own goal.'

Mr Rowlings appeared at the front door as Bodkin's car pulled up outside the house.

'Amy, where have you been? We've been worried sick about you. What on earth made you run off like that?' he asked.

'I asked her to go through a couple of boxes of old records with me, Mr Rowlings,' Bodkin said quickly. 'I was offered a job lot this morning and I haven't got a clue what's what. Amy is the expert, so she told me which ones to choose.'

'Ah, well, that's all right, then. I just wish you'd told us where you were going, Amy. We thought you might have got yourself into a spot of bother.'

'Me, Dad?' Amy said innocently. 'When have I ever been found in a spot of bother?'

CHAPTER FORTY-SIX

At ten-fifteen on Wednesday morning, Amy stood in front of the reception desk at the Wilson, Kendall and Beanney solicitor's office while Miss Johnston, Godfrey Wilson's secretary, finished filing a client's details in her desk index file.

'I'll only be a couple of minutes,' Amy said. 'He's been searching for someone and I—'

'He's busy all morning,' the secretary said.

'As I said, it will only take two minutes and the news will save him hours, later.'

'I'm sorry, but...'

'Amy, what a pleasant surprise. What are you doing here?' Godfrey Wilson smiled at Amy from the open door of his office.

Miss Johnstone pricked up her ears behind the desk.

'It's confidential, Godfrey. I'd better tell you in private.'

Amy gave the secretary her sweetest smile, then walked through into the solicitor's office.

. . .

'Amy, that's incredible,' the lawyer said after Amy had told him where to find Sadie. 'I wasted a whole day on the search. I couldn't get anywhere.'

'It's who you know,' Amy said with a smile. She suddenly became serious. 'Godfrey, I know it's asking a lot but could you get them out of there today. I'm really worried about them. Ginny is only eleven.'

'I'll go and see them straight away,' Godfrey said. 'And as for the authorities. They may have to become involved because of their ages. But I know a nice family who will foster the pair of them until Sadie reaches sixteen. They'll be well provided for and none of the seedier side of their story need ever be made public. Sadie is very comfortably off now. She received over two thousand pounds from Reverend Villiers.' He winked at Amy. 'That didn't come from me though.'

'I hope she settles in... I'm sure you can persuade her if anyone can, Godfrey. They need to be as far away from that place as it's possible to get.'

Godfrey nodded.

'I'll see to it. They'll be out of there today and the police will never know anything about her. I'll represent her if necessary.' The solicitor got to his feet. 'Now, I suppose you'll want to be paid for your efforts.'

'Oh, no, I wasn't expecting anything. It was my first solo ARIA investigation. It got a bit hairy at times but I loved it.'

'Wilson, Kendall and Beanney always pay our way, Amy. You have saved us a great deal of work. How does, five pounds commission sound?'

'Five pounds! That's over two week's wages,' Amy said. 'Are you sure?'

Godfrey led her back out into reception, opened a filing cabinet and took out a black metal tin.

'I'm taking five pounds out of petty cash, Miss Johnston, please write out a receipt for it. Miss Rowlings will sign.'

Back out on the Gillingham Road, Amy walked the four hundred yards until she came to the turn off that led to Hanover House. Delighted to have earned her first commission as an investigator, she turned towards the gatehouse, her head filled with the picture of the HMV radiogram she had seen in Uncle Maurice's catalogue.

At the gatehouse, Amy gave her name to the security guard who checked it against a list before handing over a paper chitty, then he opened the double gates and Amy stepped into the leafy grounds.

Violet spotted Amy long before she reached the front of the house and ran excitedly across the lawns to get to her. Connie, who was supervising Violet, ambled across the grass behind her.

'You came!' Violet screamed into Amy's ear as she threw her arms around her neck.

'Of course, I came, Violet, a promise is a promise and anyway, I so wanted to see your garden.'

'Come see what Toby has been doing,' Violet said, grabbing Amy's hand.

She led her across the lawns to the far side of the grounds where a line of tall horse chestnut trees lined the inside of the high wall. New beds had been dug and rows of shrubs interspersed with bedding plants had been planted. Behind the newly dug beds was a narrow path leading to three, brick sheds. At the side of the path was a long, slatted bench.

'Shall we sit here for a while,' Amy said. 'It's a beautiful spot.'

All three sat down and Violet immediately slipped her arm through Amy's and rested her head on her shoulder.

'Toby planted some forget-me-nots in there, they'll come into flower in May, so they'll be out in time for my birthday. Do you like forget-me-nots?'

'I love forget-me-nots,' Amy said. 'We have some blue ones in our garden at home.'

'Is you garden as big as mine?' Violet asked.

'No,' Amy said, shaking her head. 'I think you must have the biggest garden in the world, Violet. Mine is tiny in comparison.'

Violet smiled happily and snuggled up against Amy. 'It will be lunchtime soon. Toby will be coming to eat his sandwiches in his house.'

'His house?' Amy looked at her quizzically.

Violet pointed at the row of brick sheds behind her. 'That's his house, the one in the middle.'

'Ah, I see,' Amy replied with a smile. 'That's a very nice house.'

'We're going to live in it when we're married,' Violet said, happily.

Amy suddenly felt a nervous twitch in her stomach. As Violet got off the bench to explore some of the new cuttings that had been planted, she turned to Connie and whispered.

'Toby? Tell me about Toby.'

'He's one of the gardening staff. He's only young, probably nineteen or twenty. He's a friendly young man. He took a real shine to Violet right from the off.'

'Does Violet spend a lot of time with him when she's out here?'

'Not really, he has his work to do. The foreman gardener won't allow any shirking.'

'Is she always supervised when she's in the garden, Connie?'

'No, she's given free rein, pretty much. Whoever is on supervising duty usually sits reading on the bench in front of the main office. Doctor Fuller encouraged us to give her as much independence as possible.'

'You can't see these sheds from the house, can you?'

Connie shook her head.

'What are you getting at, Amy?'

'I'm hoping what I'm going to ask her next, doesn't get the answer I expect it to,' Amy replied. She turned to Violet who was humming a song to herself as she scanned the horizon with her hand over her eyes to shield them from the sun.

'Violet,' Amy began. 'Are you and Toby very good friends?'

Violet nodded.

'Did you used to come and see him in the winter? When it was cold and wet?'

Violet nodded again. 'We used to go into his house to keep warm.'

Amy hesitated, unsure of how to approach the subject.

'What... erm, what did you do inside?'

'We used to pretend to be mummy and daddy,' she said. 'He said we can be married properly when I get better.'

Connie's mouth dropped open.

'Violet. I don't want you to get upset, but can you tell me where Reverend Villiers touched you, when he hurt you?'

'Here,' Violet said, holding her hands to her head.

'He held your head?'

'Tight and it hurt when I tried to get away.'

'Did he touch you anywhere else?'

Violet grabbled the top of each arm.

'He got me here, and he used to shake me and shake me.'

Violet's eyes narrowed. 'He wanted my friends to go, but they didn't want to go, so they didn't.'

'One last question about the vicar, Violet, then I won't ask anything else and you can forget all about him, forever.'

'Okay then,' Violet said, brightly.

'Did he ever touch you anywhere else?' She touched her own breasts lightly. 'Here, for instance?'

Violet shook her head.

'What about here?' Amy put her hand on her lap.

'No, only Toby touches me in those places. But that's all right because we're going to be married.'

CHAPTER FORTY-SEVEN

Amy put the palm of her hand on her brow. 'Oh dear, poor Reverend Villiers. He was innocent all along.'

Connie was still dumbfounded by the revelations. 'My God, Amy, We have to tell Doctor Fuller...'

'Let's get Violet back to the house, Connie. I'll sit with her while you get the doctor.'

They walked slowly back to the house, Violet holding on to Amy's arm. 'Toby hasn't had his lunch yet.'

'He'll be over, soon, Violet. We just need to talk to the doctor for a moment.' She turned to Connie. 'Will you get into trouble for this?'

'I can't see how. I was only following her orders, she said she could have the run of the gardens.'

'I'd better let her father know,' Amy said. 'Though he's not always in the best of health mentally either.'

'Her father?'

'Mr Brown,' Amy said.

'Oh he's not her father. He's her step-father. I read her file when I first started looking after her. Mrs Brown only married... Gerald is it, about seven years ago. He's twice her age near enough but I bet she was glad of the security. Not many men would take a woman on with a seven-year-old child, especially one like Violet.'

'So who was her real dad?' Amy asked.

Connie shrugged. 'No Idea. I assume he cleared off when Violet began to get difficult to manage. Men tend to do that sort of thing. They like the simple life.'

Amy looked at her watch as they approached the house. She fished about in her bag and came up with Bodkin's card. 'Connie, can you do me a favour? Ring Bodkin, if he's not there, leave a message with a policeman called Ferris. Tell him all about Toby. He's going to want to talk to him shortly.'

'You can ring yourself if you like, Amy. Use the office phone.'

'I have to go, Connie. There's something I need to do.'

The Register Office was on Main Street, right next to the library. Amy walked into the reception area and found a young, suited man sitting behind a dark oak desk. His eyes lit up when he saw her walk in.

'Hello, madam. What can I do for you?'

'I'd like a look at the marriage records for the year nineteen-thirty-two, please?'

'Any reason in particular?'

Amy pulled a card out of her bag and handed it to the young man. 'ARIA Investigations. I'm Amy Rowlings,' she said.

'I'm not sure if—'

'Police accredited,' Amy pointed out.

'Well in that case... What year was it again?'

He led Amy to a private booth, then disappeared for a few minutes. When he returned he was carrying a thick, leather bound volume.

'Here it is,' he said, passing the book to Amy. He looked at her for a few moments with a furrowed brow, then his eyes lit up again. Didn't you used to go to St John's school?' he asked.

Amy opened the volume cover and nodded. 'I did, mind you, most of the other kids in town went there.'

'I was there too,' he said with a grin, thrusting his hand towards her. 'I'm Francis Smee. We moved away when I was thirteen but we came back about two years ago.'

'I do remember you, Francis,' Amy said with a wide smile. 'You were in Miss Doncaster's class.'

'I was, for my sins. How's that friend of yours from the farm... Alice, is it? You were always thick as thieves.'

'She's as good as ever,' Amy replied as she began to flip through the certificates in the book.

'Do you ever go to the pictures?'

Amy felt the offer of a date coming on. 'I do, I go with Alice and a couple of male friends every Saturday. We always end the night at the Old Bull.'

'I know the Old Bull. It was my dad's local before we left, he used to sit us out the back and bring us bottles of fizzy pop while he had a couple of pints.'

Amy smiled up at his memories as she continued to flick through the pages. When she got to July 1932, she suddenly stopped and placed a finger on the name at the top of the certificate. Brown. Gerald. Occupation. Miner. Address 43 Marigold Street. Spinton. DOB 29th November 1869.

Amy read the information directly below, then suddenly leapt to her feet.

'Oh my goodness. I might have got it all wrong!' She looked towards Francis and made a dialling motion with her fingers. 'Francis, I really need to use your telephone, it's an emergency.'

CHAPTER
FORTY-EIGHT

'Spinton Police, Constable Ferris sp—'

'Ferris, it's Amy, is Bodkin there? It's urgent.'

'He's in the building but he's interrogating Eugene Hales at the moment.'

'How's that going?' Amy asked.

'He's admitting to nothing, but then they all do at the beginning. Bodkin will crack him in the end. He always does.'

'That's what I'm calling about, Ferris. We... I might have got it wrong. Can you get a message to him?'

Ferris laughed. 'He's got a sign on the door that reads, DO NO DISTURB in huge letters.'

'Please, Ferris. I know he'll be angry, but I need to talk to him urgently. Tell him I've discovered something really important.'

'If it's about that Toby fellow at the mental home, then he knows. He sent Bradley out to arrest him for having se... for assaulting a minor.'

'It's not that, Ferris, this is new information, please, can you get him?'

'He's not long gone back in to the interview room, Amy. I daren't...'

'Ferris, PLEASE!' Amy begged. 'Tell him I think I got it wrong, but now I'm sure I know who did it... Look, I can't hang around here much longer. I'm going to get the bus to the church. Tell Bodkin to meet me at the lychgate in twenty minutes.'

'Amy, I can't—' Ferris said as the line went dead.

CHAPTER FORTY-NINE

Amy got off the bus at the stop opposite the church and walked smartly across the road to the main gates. Looking back up the road towards Middle Street, she watched the traffic for a few moments to see if Bodkin's car was on the way. When the stream of traffic dried up, she turned away from the road and made her way around the side of the church to the lychgate. When she reached it there was no sign of Bodkin.

Amy glanced down at her watch and looked up at the old Norman church tower to double check the time, then she began to pace backwards and forwards as she waited for the detective to arrive. After fifteen, long minutes, she sighed and stepped beneath the grey, lichen-covered, roof and followed the path that the townsfolk had used for centuries to bring their dead to the church.

On the far side of the ancient gate, Amy stopped and checked her watch again.

'Come on, Bodkin,' she whispered to herself.

Feeling increasingly nervous, Amy walked slowly to the

Belvedere crypt and craned her neck to look between the graves to see if Bodkin had somehow misread her message and was walking up to the church via the main path. Reverend Villiers newly covered grave was in her direct line of sight and she stepped forward to look at the four, floral tributes that had been laid on it.

'Not much to shout about, is it?' said a voice behind her. 'You'd think he'd have got a few more wreaths than that, wouldn't you? I mean, he's been here a long time.'

Amy turned to see the figure of Peter Kissman standing on the gravel and broken slate path that led to the vicarage gate. He was swaying slightly, holding a bottle of dark rum in his hand.

'A lot of people can't afford to give flowers,' Amy replied. 'You should know that, working here.'

'There weren't many people at his funeral though, and most of those that did turn up, only came because it was their civic duty.'

'He was my dad's friend,' Amy said. 'He might not have been universally adored but he was a good man.'

Kissman lifted the bottle of rum towards his mouth, then lowered it as he muttered a few words that Amy couldn't quite hear.

'A good man, eh?'

Amy stepped towards the groundsman.

'Peter. You don't need that stuff. You've been off the drink a long time now. Don't go letting yourself down now.'

'What do you know about anything?' Kissman spat, raising the bottle again and taking a long swig.

'Peter, think of Caroline. She wouldn't want to see you fall off the wagon again. It took you a long time to woo her. Don't spoil it now.'

Kissman looked hard at the bottle, then murmured something unintelligible. Tears began to run down his cheek.

'It's been so hard,' he said.

'I know, Peter, but drink isn't the answer to your problems, is it?'

Kissman suddenly hurled the bottle against the side of the stone crypt, spraying the surrounding area with rum.

'Cost me a day's pay did that.'

'You're better off without it, Peter,' Amy said carefully taking a quick glance towards the still empty lychgate.

'Are you expecting someone?' Peter asked.

'No, no one... I just came to say a few words over Mr Villiers grave.'

'Don't waste your words on him,' Kissman said with a snarl. 'He's not worth it.' He spat into the pool of glistening rum, then turned away from Amy. 'I've a good mind to dig him up again and put him back on display.'

'PETER!' Amy cried.

'It's no more than he deserves,' Kissman said. 'Do you know, I think I will do it. I'll get my shovel.'

'Don't, Peter,' Amy said, beginning to panic. 'What would Violet think?'

Kissman stopped dead and half turned towards Amy.

'How do you know about Violet?'

'I saw her this morning, Peter. I went to visit her at Hano—'

'STAY AWAY FROM HER!' the gardener shouted, pointing a finger at Amy.

Amy took a step back and looked over her shoulder towards the path again, it was still empty.

'Violet isn't very well, Peter.'

'I bloody well know she isn't very well,' Kissman said. 'I'm her father, I remember when she first got ill. She was only a child. It just wasn't fair.' His face crumpled and the tears began to fall. 'I wasn't there for her. I might have helped but... I was weak.'

'You couldn't have helped, Peter, not with her condition at least. Even the doctors are struggling to help her and they are experts.'

'God judged me and found me wanting,' Peter said amidst more tears.

Amy felt a sudden surge of pity. Stepping forwards she put her arm around the hunched over figure.

'Peter...' She stopped speaking as the wailing of a police siren got closer.

'Have you brought the police? You know, don't you?'

Amy nodded. 'I worked it out in the end, though it took a while.'

Kissman shot a glance towards the lychgate path as the siren wound down.

'I'm not going to hang,' he said. 'I'll do it myself. You can come with me. I'm sure God will welcome you.'

'Peter, no...'

Kissman grabbed Amy around the shoulders and spinning her around, began to drag her along the path. Amy tried to dig the heels of her sling back shoes into the gravel to slow down their progress but her right shoe came off and she was left dragging her bare heel into the sharp, broken slates.

When he reached his brick shed, Kissman threw the door open one handed, pushed Amy inside, then slammed it behind him before turning a rusty key in the lock.

'How do you want to go?' he asked. 'The quick way or the painful way?'

The wild-eyed groundsman pointed to his shelf where the bottles of cyanide and arsenic based insecticides were perched.

'Don't do this, Peter,' Amy begged. 'Think of Violet, think of Mavis.'

'Mavis doesn't belong to me anymore,' Kissman said. 'I ruined that too.' He reached up and grabbed a bottle of cyanide laced water. 'You'll have to go first, I'm sorry.'

Amy made a rush for the door but Kissman caught her as she tried to turn the key.

'BODKIN!' she screamed. 'BODKIN!'

Suddenly the door shook as someone on the other side aimed a kick at it. Seconds later it flew open and Amy saw Bodkin framed in the opening. He took in the scene with one quick glance, then reached out his hand towards Amy.

'Let her go, Peter. She's got nothing to do with any of this.'

Kissman pulled the stopper from the bottle and lifted it towards his mouth.

'Take her then. I'll go on my own.'

Amy crawled across the floor and pulled herself up using Bodkin's legs for support. When she was finally upright, she dropped her face onto the detective's chest.

'Thank you, Bodkin,' she panted.

'Put that down, Peter. It won't solve anything,' Bodkin said, reaching a hand out towards him.

'She knows!' Peter yelled, pointing a finger at Amy. 'She knows.'

'She's a clever girl is Amy,' Bodkin said as she pulled away from him and turned to face her attacker.

'Peter. Let's sit down and talk about it for a few minutes. Don't do anything silly,' she said, softly.

'Cyanide isn't an easy way out,' Bodkin added.

Kissman slumped down onto a rickety stool and held the bottle between his knees.

Bodkin pulled out a chair from underneath Kissman's work

bench and eased himself onto it. Amy stood at his side, looking sympathetically at the gardener.

'How did you find out about Villiers?' Bodkin asked.

'Mavis told me. I used to bump into her at the market place most Saturday afternoons. She wouldn't even acknowledge me for years, but a few months ago, she began to speak to me again. She'd heard I'd given up the bottle you see.' Kissman paused. 'Oh, I knew there was no way back for me. She'd remarried and seemed to have found a decent man. I asked her about visiting Violet, but she wouldn't have it. She said she was very ill and seeing me again might make her a lot worse.'

'What did you think about that?' Bodkin asked.

'I could understand her reasoning. I mean, I hadn't been a father to her anyway. What right did I have to worm my way back into her life? I'd made it a misery. It might even have been me that caused her to be ill in the first place. Daughters should have a loving father not a drunken, violent, abusive waste of good clean air, like the one she had.'

'So, Peter. Did Mavis tell you she was thinking about asking Villiers to try to help Violet?'

Kissman nodded.

'I was against it, but then she explained about the operation they were determined to put her through, so I agreed. Not that I had any say in the matter really.'

'Then what?'

'I didn't see her for a few weeks. When I did, she tried to avoid me. I chased after her and caught her up outside Woolworths and I pulled her into the alley that runs alongside. It took me a while, but I got it out of her.'

'How did you feel, knowing what he'd done to your daughter, Peter?'

'I was beyond furious. Any father would have been. I was

intent on killing him there and then. I told her I was going to go back to the church and throttle him.'

'But she dissuaded you?'

Kissman nodded. 'She said that she was going to deal with it. I thought that meant her going to the police, but she said that wasn't the way she was going to do it. She was ashamed, Inspector. Ashamed of what the ignorant people around here would say about Violet.'

Kissman closed his eyes, then hung his head.

'I meekly agreed, not knowing what she had planned. I assumed she would go to the church hierarchy or something, so I left her there and went home. I couldn't let it rest though. He deserved a lot more than a private dressing down from the bishop, so I hatched a plan to poison his wine. I had access to it every day. I just had to make up my mind which poison to use. I obviously didn't want to leave a clue pointing directly at myself. If I could do it and get away with it, that would be ideal.'

'But you didn't poison the wine in the end?'

'No, something else came up. About a week later, I was having my breakfast in the kitchen when Caroline got a bag of stomach powders out of the drawer, mixed one in a glass of water and took it through to the study for him. It was perfect. The next time I was on my own in the kitchen I stuck the whole bag in my pocket, brought it over here and tipped a knife's points worth of arsenic into the powder. It was easy, I only had to undo one end of the wrap. Once I'd shaken it up a bit and folded the end over again, you couldn't tell it had been touched.'

'But the arsenic didn't kill him?' Bodkin said. 'Didn't you use enough?'

'I only gave him enough to kill a big rat every day. I wanted him to suffer for a while before giving him the big dose.'

'Again, Peter, the arsenic didn't kill him. Strychnine did.'

'Yes. I decided to change tack when I bumped into Mavis on the market again. That's when she told me violet was pregnant. I honestly can't tell you what my reaction was, Inspector. I was just numb, devoid of any sort of feeling. When I got home, I decided his time was up. He had to go, but I wasn't going to give him an easy death. I'd seen the way the rats and moles thrashed about when they'd had a dose of strychnine and I thought, that was the way he deserved to go too.'

'But you didn't have any strychnine and you knew you would have to register if you wanted to get it legally,' Amy put in. 'You did know where you could find some though, so you broke into Mrs de Vere's shed.'

'I knew Joe had a stock. I'd given the councillor advice about strychnine, and Joe had said it worked a treat.'

'So, you have your strychnine, what happens now?'

'I just had to wait for an opportunity,' Kissman said, quietly. 'It wasn't long before one showed up.'

'That would be the night of the committee meeting?'

Kissman nodded slowly.

'That's right. I'd gone around to see Caroline; I'd finally built up the courage to ask her out. When I arrived, there was a part drunk bottle of wine on the counter. I knew there and then that I had my perfect opportunity.'

'Go on,' Bodkin said, leaning forward in his chair.

'All I needed was a few seconds on my own with the bottle, but that committee was due to break up so I had to be careful. Then I had a moment of inspiration. If it was later found out that both Caroline and I had taken a drink from the bottle, it would prove that it hadn't been tampered with while we were in the kitchen alone. So, I had a swig and got her to take one too. I was just thinking up a reason to get her to leave the kitchen for a couple of minutes when the bloody committee turned up. That put the kibosh on it.'

'And your ex-wife was on the committee, were you aware of that?'

'No, it was such a shock seeing her there, especially with what I was about to do.'

'She didn't let on she recognised you. Was she involved, Peter?'

'No, she knew nothing about it. When she looked at me I just shook my head quickly to let her know she wasn't to acknowledge me.'

'Is that when you decided to poison the sweets instead of the wine?' Bodkin asked.

'Yes, I worked out it would be far easier to sprinkle the strychnine crystals onto some sugary sweets than trying to get it to dissolve in a bottle of wine. It would be quicker too. I knew he had the sweets in his pocket because he'd popped one into his mouth just before he took his jacket off. It was a pineapple chunk if I remember rightly, sparkling with a coat of lovely sugar crystals.'

Kissman was silent for a while as he remembered the evening.

'I was so excited when I saw him take his jacket off and hang it on the back of the chair. It was all I could do to stop myself sitting down right there and then. Fortunately, I was able to control my emotions and it wasn't too long before someone suggested they pick a date for the next meeting, and they all went through to the study.'

'Everyone except Caroline,' Amy said.

'Indeed. I was scuppered again, so I tried to get her out to the rubbish bins. I intended to drop something that she would have to clean up, but as it was, she came out with some potato peelings while I was there and I didn't have the opportunity to spill anything on the floor.'

'Then what?' Bodkin asked.

'We went back in. I was getting a bit fretful by then; I can tell you. I thought the opportunity was gone. Then the party started to break up and everyone headed for the front door. Caroline joined them. It was perfect. I almost ran to get to the jacket, I opened up his side pocket and there were the beautiful sugar-covered sweets twinkling up at me. The top of the bag was open, all I had to do was sprinkle the strychnine on top. It took seconds.'

'You were almost caught though. Mrs de Vere came back to get a glass of water,' Amy said.

'Was it her? I didn't know who it was. I heard the sound of heels on the tiled floor in the hall and I was out of the back door in the blink of an eye.'

'So, you went to the pub for a few celebratory drinks,' Bodkin said.

'I wouldn't say, celebratory. I knew what I'd done was wrong, but he deserved it, didn't he? Even you have to admit that.'

'He didn't do—' Amy was cut off when Bodkin grabbed her wrist.

'We'll come to that later,' he said quietly.

'Okay, Peter, time has been called in the pub, what happened then?'

Kissman studied the ceiling before he spoke.

'I left at last orders as usual. There was hardly anyone about as I began walking home. Certainly no one around the church as I passed it. If he hadn't been making such a racket, I'd probably have missed his final moments, but as it was, I could hear him howling like one of those werewolves you see at the pictures. I thought I had to do something before anyone else heard, so I nipped in through the back gate and made my way past the Belvedere tomb... Villiers was thrashing about on the floor, screaming... it was awful. I know I wanted him gone, but not like that... his back was arched, his face was like one of those creatures in a horror film... All screwed up, grimacing, you know... Anyway, I thought I had better put him out of his misery. I wasn't feeling particularly guilty but... well, it wasn't something you'd want to witness, so I ran back to the grave I'd spent all morning digging and grabbed the broken shovel, but by the time I got back, he'd gone. He was just lying there, staring up at me.'

'Why didn't you just leave him where he was, Peter?' Bodkin asked.

'I don't know why, but all of a sudden, my mind was crystal clear and I knew what I had to do. The lychgate is the place where people have brought their dead for centuries. I thought it was only fitting that he should spend his last night there too. Not that I was going to set up a vigil or anything.'

'So, you drag him to the bench and get him into position, what then?'

'I took the sweets out of his pocket and dropped them into my own. No evidence left behind. I thought that might throw you off the scent, for a while at least. I was planning to go down to see my old mum in Leysdown the following week so I thought I might get away without being questioned until I'd had a chance to work out a perfect alibi.'

'What was with the bible quotation?' Bodkin asked.

Peter smiled and pulled a tattered envelope out of his pocket. From inside, he pulled a creased, yellowing sheet of paper. He read it himself then passed it to Bodkin.

'The Sally Ann gave me this at one of their meetings. They said I should either memorise it or carry it around with me at all times to remind me of what I had once been.'

Bodkin squinted at the old sheet of paper as he read aloud.

Romans 13.13-14

Let us walk honestly, as in the day; not in rioting and drunkenness, not in chambering and wantonness, not in strife and envying.'

But put ye on the Lord Jesus Christ, and make not provision for the flesh, to fulfil the lusts thereof.

'Those lines have kept me on the straight and narrow for years, Inspector. I recite them to myself every time I buy a drink. I have never been drunk since the day that piece of paper was given to me.' Kissman held out his hand for Bodkin to return the sheet. 'I thought it was more than fitting for the way Villiers had lived his life too and I left the message with him so he could take it on his final journey. Hopefully he'll be reciting it over and over in Hell.'

'And the broken bottle? Why get rid of that if it wasn't relevant to the investigation?'

'I saw it lying on the floor in front of the Belvedere tomb, and as I said, my mind was crystal clear. I decided that I might use it as a red herring. I thought you'd focus on the wine and it seems I was right. Besides which, pieces of the bottle would have had my fingerprints on them and I wanted to keep a very low profile. Everyone in the town knows about the broken lock on the Belvedere crypt, so I just prised it open with the blade of the shovel and scraped it all inside. I really didn't expect it to be found for months, years, if ever.'

'And the sweets? What did you do with those, Peter?' Bodkin asked.

'Oh, I dropped them into the bottom of the grave I'd dug for Mrs Constadine when I put the broken shovel back on the way out of the churchyard,' Peter replied. 'I hope she's got a sweet tooth.'

'You did send us on a wild goose chase over the wine bottle, Peter. Our investigation was focussed on that for a long time. Then there was the hemlock of course. We couldn't see how that fitted in with the other poisons.'

'The hemlock?' Kissman looked puzzled.

'Didn't Mavis tell you that she'd already poisoned the vicar with it? That was the reason he had the stomach trouble in the first place. The stomach trouble that gave you the chance to use the arsenic.'

'Mavis? But...'

'She didn't tell you because she knew you'd try to talk her out of it,' said Amy.

'She's in our cells, Peter, she's been charged with attempted murder.'

'No... Nooo, it wasn't her. It was me. I did it. I...'

'Peter, she's confessed,' Bodkin said quietly.'

'But what's going to happen to Violet? Who'll go to see her? She'll have no one. That Gerald isn't in his right mind most of the time.'

'I'll go to see her, Peter,' Amy said, softly. 'I'll make sure she's all right.'

Kissman lowered his head into his hands.

'How did you know it was me anyway?' he asked.

Amy put her hand on Bodkin's shoulder before she spoke.

'You were a suspect all the time, Peter, but we got so many other leads that you were dropped down the list of probables for a while. But when I found out that Violet was your daughter this lunchtime, I knew that you should be much higher up the list. I wasn't sure if you were in cahoots with Mavis but the more I thought about it, the more I found faults in my earlier thinking. The night before, I had been convinced that Eugene Hales was our killer, but it was the little things that didn't add up. You see, Mr Villiers had something on them, something big, something they couldn't allow to get out, but surely they'd have tried to talk him out of revealing their sordid secrets before resorting to murder. They'd have tried to bribe him maybe, or threaten him with a revelation of their own to humiliate him in public, and they had their chance to do that at the committee meeting. I think they were hanging around the church hall, hoping to get a private word with him after the meeting broke up. They wouldn't have just put the poison into his sweets before trying every other avenue. So, I think they were going to try to talk him out of exposing them in the days that followed, but they didn't have to in the end.'

'But apart from finding out I was Violet's dad? There must have been something else that pointed in my direction.'

'Yellow chalk,' said Amy. 'No one else had yellow chalk, but that's the only colour they used in the Dragon when they were playing darts the other night. You score for their darts team, don't you?'

Kissman sighed. 'I found half a stick of it in my pocket when I put the bag of sweets in there. That's what gave me the idea of writing the bible reference on the floor.'

Bodkin got to his feet and asked Peter to stand up.

'Peter Kissman. I am arresting you for the murder of Harold Villiers. You do not have to say anything unless you wish to do so, but what you do say may be given in evidence. Do you understand?'

Bodkin stood aside as two, burly officers took hold of Peter Kissman.

'Tell Violet and Mavis, I'm sorry,' he said as they walked him past Amy. 'But he deserved it. I don't regret doing it.'

Amy put her hand on his chest as the policemen came to a halt at the door. She gazed up at him with a look of pity on her face.

'Reverend Villiers did nothing to hurt your daughter, Peter. It isn't his baby. The father is a groundsman at Hanover House. All Mr Villiers ever did, was try to help Violet. You killed an innocent man.'

CHAPTER FIFTY

'It's Violet who I feel most sorry for,' Amy said as they stood by Kissman's shed, watching as he was led away along the broken slate and gravel path. 'She's alone for ever now.'

Bodkin sighed. 'There's always more than one innocent victim when a murder happens.' He pulled Amy's shoe from his pocket and passed it to her. 'I found this on the path. It looks like you're going to have to get it repaired again.'

Amy looked at the shoe with its swinging heel, then lifted her foot and slipped off the other one. Taking a tentative step forward, she screamed, 'ouch' as her foot hit the sharp pieces of broken slate.

Bodkin turned towards her and in one quick movement, swept her up in his arms.

'You'll cut your feet to pieces walking on that stuff,' he said, as he pushed his arm behind her knees.

Amy wrapped one arm around his neck and with her broken shoes dangling in her other hand, he carried her out of the churchyard.

When they reached the lychgate, Bodkin loosened his hold and prepared to put her back onto her feet, but before he could do so, Amy's arm tightened around his neck and she looked him in the eyes for a few seconds before kissing him softly on the lips.

'Sir Bodkin. My knight in shining armour rescues me once again,' she said.

'So, what happened to all the people you arrested?' Amy asked as she took a sip from her port and lemon. It was Saturday evening and they were standing with Alice and Ferris in the Old Bull.

'Mrs de Vere has been taken down to Maidstone. She'll appear on fraud and embezzlement charges at the assizes next month. Eugene Hales and Doctor Frazier were let go. We can't find any witnesses to what they were up to when they were prowling around the town looking for young women. There's not a hope in hell of getting Sadie or her sister into a witness box, and I wouldn't ask them to if there was. Hales and Frazier will have to keep a low profile now though. Once word gets out that they were arrested during a murder investigation, the mud will stick. From what I've heard, he's selling the pharmacy to Agatha.'

'What about Mavis?'

'I'm trying to get the charge reduced from attempted murder to a lesser charge and I think I might be successful in that. The poor woman was driven to near madness by what was happening to her daughter. Which of us wouldn't think about doing something similar if Violet had been our child? I got her to retract the bit about intending to kill him. I can't ever remember her saying that, can you?'

'Oh, Bodkin you're such a sweetheart,' Amy said, reaching up to stroke his cheek. She took another sip of her drink, then tipped her head to the side. 'What about Daley?'

'I think you'll find you have a stand-in vicar at the Sunday service tomorrow. He wasn't involved in a murder plot, nor indeed was Councillor de Vere, but he did get involved in the blackmail plot. Unfortunately, that is just her word against his, all he's admitting to is blackening Villiers' name so he could get his hands on the parish, but I reminded him that Mrs de Vere had yet to give evidence in court and his offer to hand over the money from the church fund will certainly be brought up in her fraud trial. So, I advised him that it was probably better to go now than hang around and wait for the inevitable. He's going back to university to finish his chemistry degree. I was told the bishop insisted on it. He doesn't want him anywhere near a church in future.'

'I suppose Peter will hang?'

Bodkin grimaced.

'I think it's inevitable, Amy, but then, you can't go around murdering people just because you think you have just cause. The law decides how people are punished. That's what it's there for.'

At last orders, Bodkin went to the bar and Amy stood alone near the fireplace, watching him. She was just thinking what a fine pair of shoulders he possessed when she felt a tug on her arm. She turned to find Francis Smee smiling at her.

'Remember me?' he said.

'Of course I do, I never thanked you for letting me use your telephone the other day; it was very kind of you.'

'Think nothing of it,' Francis said, smiling again and

showing off a perfect set of teeth. 'What, erm, what we were talking about the other day... the pictures, I wondered if... well, I wondered if you'd like to go with me one night. If your big brother doesn't mind, that is.'

Amy's eyes opened wide.

'He's not my brother, Francis, he's... he's... Bodkin,' she said.

At a quarter to eleven. Alice, Ferris, Amy and Bodkin crossed the road by the telephone box and began to walk along Long Lane. Ferris and Alice were in front, chatting about a musical that Ferris was hoping would come to the theatre in Gillingham soon.

Amy and Bodkin walked side by side, Amy deliberately walking slowly to leave a bigger gap between her and the couple in front.

'That young man in the pub? The one in the suit?' Bodkin said suddenly.

'Oh yes, what about him?'

'I saw you smiling and chatting to him, I just wondered... I just wondered what he wanted. I hung back until he left, I didn't want to interrupt anything.'

'He was asking me out on a date, actually. The pictures, next Saturday. He said he hoped my big brother wouldn't mind.' Amy tittered to herself behind the back of her hand.

'And what did you say to that?' Bodkin asked, carefully.

'What do you think I said, Bodkin? What should I have said?'

Bodkin looked straight ahead as the figures of Alice and Ferris disappeared into the night.

'I honestly don't know, he's your age, he's a good-looking lad, he's smart, he obviously has a decent job and I could tell he holds you in high esteem. You could do a lot worse.'

Amy tutted to herself, then put her arm through Bodkin's

and rested her head on his shoulder as they walked slowly along the lane.

'Bodkin,' she said softly. 'You don't understand women at all, do you?'

The detective shook his head solemnly. 'Not the slightest clue,' he replied.

'Well, I think it's time you learned a few things, Bodkin. I mean, if you and I are going to be seen out and about as a proper couple...'

'A proper couple?' Bodkin stopped dead, and taking hold of Amy's arm, he gently pulled her towards him. 'Do you mean that me and... you and I are... are going out... officially?'

Amy smiled softly, then on her tiptoes, she leaned forward and kissed him on the lips.

'You're the detective, Bodkin. Follow the clues.'

The End

Printed in Great Britain
by Amazon

61252186R00238